THE DIARY OF
A GOOD NEIGHBOUR

The
Diary of a
Good Neighbour

JANE SOMERS

Alfred A. Knopf   New York   1983

main

Library of Congress Cataloging in Publication Data

Somers, Jane.   The diary of a good neighbour.
1. Title.
PR6069.O42D5   1983   823'.914   82-48739
ISBN 0-394-52970-7

Manufactured in the United States of America

FIRST AMERICAN EDITION

THE DIARY OF
A GOOD NEIGHBOUR

The first part is a summing-up of about four years. I was not keeping a diary. I wish I had. All I know is that I see everything differently now from how I did while I was living through it.

My life until Freddie started to die was one thing, afterwards another. Until then I thought of myself as a nice person. Like everyone, just about, that I know. The people I work with, mainly. I know now that I did not ask myself what I was really like, but thought only about how other people judged me.

When Freddie began to be so ill my first idea was: this is unfair. Unfair to me, I thought secretly. I partly knew he was dying, but went on as if he wasn't. That was not kind. He must have been lonely. I was proud of myself because I went on working through it all, "kept the money coming in"—well, I had to do that, with him not working. But I was thankful I was working because I had an excuse not to be with him in that *awfulness*. We did not have the sort of marriage where we talked about real things. I see that now. We were not really married. It was the marriage most people have these days, both sides trying for advantage. I always saw Freddie as one up.

The word cancer was mentioned once. The doctors said to me, cancer, and *now* I see my reaction meant they would not go on to talk about whether to tell him or not. I don't know if they told him. Whether he knew. I think he did. When they took him into hospital I went every day, but I sat there with a smile, how are you feeling? He looked dreadful. Yellow. Sharp bones under yellow skin. Like a boiling fowl. He was protecting me. *Now*, I can see it. Because I could not take it. Child-wife.

When at last he died, and it was over, I saw how badly he

had been treated. His sister was around sometimes. I suppose they talked. Her manner to me was like his. Kindly. Poor Janna, too much must not be expected.

Since he died I have not seen her, nor any of that family. Good riddance. I mean, that is what *they* think of me. I would not have minded talking to his sister about Freddie, for I did not know much about him, not really. But it is a bit late for that.

When he died, and I found I was missing him so much, I wanted to know about times in his life he hardly ever mentioned. Like being a soldier in the war. He said he hated it. Five years. Nineteen to twenty-four. They were wonderful years for me. I was nineteen in 1949, beginning to forget the war, and making my career.

And yet we were close. We had all that good sex. We were perfectly adjusted in that, if nothing else. Yet we could not talk to each other. Correction. Did not talk to each other. Correction. He could not talk to me because when he started to try I shied away. I think the truth is he was a serious inward sort of person. Just the kind of man I would give anything for now.

When he was dead and I was going mad for sex, because for ten years I had always had anything I wanted there for the asking, I was sleeping about, I don't like to think how many. Or who. Once at an office party I looked around and saw I had had sex with half the men there. That gave me a shock. And always I had hated it: being a bit tight and after a good meal I am in a hurry, sex. It was not their fault.

That came to an end when Sister Georgie came to see me and said it was my turn for Mother. I felt very sorry for myself again. *Now* I think she might well have said something before! Husband, four children, small house—and she had had Mother since Daddy died, eight years. I had no children, and with Freddie and I both working there was no shortage of money. Yet there had never been a suggestion Mother should live with us. *Or one that I can remember.* But I was not the kind of person who looked after a widowed mother. Mother used to say what I spent on my face and my clothes would feed a family. True. It is no good pretending I regret that. It sometimes seems to me now it was the best thing in my life that—going into the office in the morning, knowing how I looked. Everyone took notice, what I was wearing, how. I looked forward to the moment when I opened the door and went through the typing pool and the girls smiled enviously. And then the executive offices, the girls admiring and wishing they had my taste. Well, I've that, if nothing else. I used to buy three, four dresses a week. I used to wear them once or twice, then into jumble. My sister took them for her good causes. So they weren't wasted. Of course that was before Joyce took me in hand and taught me really how to dress—style, not just fashion.

It was when Mother came to live with me I knew I was a widow.

It wasn't too bad at first. She wasn't very well but she amused herself. I couldn't bring a man home if I fancied him, but I secretly was quite glad. I can't ask you in, you see I have my aged mother, poor Janna!

It was a year after she came she got sick. I said to myself, Now, this time you aren't going to pretend it isn't happening. I went with her to the hospital. They told her it was cancer. They talked a long time about what would happen. They were kind and sensible. The doctors could not talk to me about what was happening to my husband, but they could talk straight to my mother about what was happening to her. *Because of what she was*. It was the first time in my life I wanted to be like her. Before that I had always found her embarrassing, her clothes, her hair. When I was out with her I used to think, no one would believe I could be her daughter, two worlds, heavy suburban respectable—and me. As I sat there beside her and she talked about her forthcoming death with the doctors, so dignified and nice, I felt awful. But I was scared witless, because Uncle Jim died of cancer, and now her—both sides. I thought: will it be my turn next? What I felt was, *it isn't fair*.

While Mother was dying I was doing my best, not like Freddie where I simply didn't want to know. But I couldn't do it. That is the point. I used to feel sick and panicky all the time. She went to pieces so fast. *Went to pieces*—that was it. I hate physical awfulness. I can't stand it. I used to go in, before leaving for work. She was in the kitchen pottering about in her dressing gown. Her face yellow, with a sick glisten on it. The bones showing. At least I didn't say, Are you feeling a bit better, that's good! I sat down with her and drank coffee. I said, Can I drop into the chemist's—because there were so many pills and medicines. And she said, Yes, pick up this or that. But I could not kiss her. Well, we aren't exactly a physically affectionate family! I can't remember ever giving my sister a good hug. A peck on the cheek, that's about it. I wanted to hold Mother and perhaps rock her a little. When it got towards the end and she was being so brave and she was so awfully ill, I thought I should simply take her into my arms and hold her. I couldn't touch her, not really. Not with kindness. The smell . . . and they can say it isn't infectious, but what do they know? Not much. She used to look at me so straight and open. And I could hardly make myself meet her eyes. It wasn't that her look asked anything. But I was so ashamed of what I was feeling, in a panic for myself. No, I wasn't awful, as I was with Freddie. But it must have seemed to her that there was nothing much there—I mean, as if *I* was nothing much. A few minutes in the morning, as I rushed off to the office. I was always latish back, after supper with someone from work, Joyce usually, and by then Mother was in bed. She was not asleep, I wished she was! I went in and sat with her. She was in pain, often. I used to get her medicines ready for her. She liked that, I could see. Support. Of a kind. We talked. Then Sister Georgie took to coming up two or three afternoons in a week and being with her. Well, I couldn't, I was working; and her children were at school. I used to come in and see them sitting together. I used to feel sick with envy because they were close. Mother and daughter.

Then when Mother went into hospital, Georgie and I took it in turns to visit. Georgie used to have to come up from Oxford. I don't see how I could have gone more often. Every other day, two or three hours in the hospital. I hated every second. I couldn't think of anything to say. But Georgie and Mother used to talk all the time. What about!—I used to listen, absolutely incredulous. They would talk about Georgie's neighbours, Georgie's neighbours' children, their husbands, their friends' friends. They never stopped. It was interesting. Because they were so involved with it all.

When Mother died I was pleased, of course. And so was Georgie. But I knew that it was very different, Georgie saying it, and my saying it. *She had a right to say it.* Because of what she was. Georgie was with Mother every minute of the day and night for a month before Mother went. I had learned by then not to hate the physical side so much, Mother almost a skeleton with yellow skin over it. But her eyes were the same. She was in pain. She did not pretend she wasn't. She held Georgie's hand.

The point was, Georgie's was the right kind of hand.

Then I was alone in our flat. Once or twice one of the men came home. It wasn't anything much. I don't blame them at all, how could I? I had already begun to understand that I had changed. *I couldn't be bothered!* How about that! Not that I didn't need sex. Sometimes I thought I'd go mad. But there was something dreary and repetitive. And the place was full of Freddie. I could see myself becoming a monument to Freddie, *having* to remember him. What was the use of it? I decided to sell the flat and get something of my own. I thought that out for a long time, months. I saw even then it was a new way of thinking for me. Working on the magazine, I think differently, quick decisions, like being kept on the top of a jet of water. I am good at all that. That was why I was offered the job in the first place. Funny thing, I hadn't expected it. Other people knew I was going to be offered assistant editor, not me. Partly, I was so involved with my image, how I projected myself. My image first was light-hearted, funny Janna with her crazy clothes, ever so clever and Girl Friday. Then, after Joyce, very expensive and perfect and smart and dependable, the person who had been there longest, with her smart trendy husband off-stage. Not that Freddie would have recognized himself in that. Then, suddenly (so it seemed) a middle-aged woman. Smart. *Handsome.* It was hard to take. It is still hard.

A handsome, middle-aged widow with a very good job in the magazine world.

Meanwhile I was *thinking* about how I ought to live. In Freddie's and my flat I felt I was being blown about like a bit of fluff or a feather. When I went in after work, it was as if I had expected to find some sort of weight or anchor and it wasn't there. I realized how flimsy I was, how dependent. That was painful, seeing myself as dependent. Not financially, of course, but as a person. Child-daughter, child-wife.

I wasn't in the way of thinking I should get married again. I couldn't see myself. Yet I was saying to myself, you must marry, you must, before it is too late. And it is what even now, sometimes, I want to do. Particularly now that I think I am not quite so awful as I was. But when I *think*, I know I shouldn't get married. Anyway, no one has asked me!

I sold the flat and got this one. A room to sleep in, a room to live in, a study. A large expensive block of flats. But I am hardly ever here. When I am, I think a lot.

This way of thinking . . . it is not so much thinking as holding things in your mind and letting them sort themselves out. If you really do that, slowly, surprising results emerge. For instance, that your ideas are different from what you had believed they were.

There are things I need to *think* out, which I haven't got around to yet.

Joyce, for one. That office of ours, top floor, sunlight and weather all around it. Her long table with her behind it, my long table with me behind it, facing each other. We've sat there for years now, opposite, making the magazine work. Then the long trestle down one side, with all the things we need on it, the machines, the drawing boards, the photographs. And the small table on the other where the secretaries sit when they come in to take notes, or anyone we want to talk to. It gives me pleasure to think of it, because it is so right, so apt, fits so exactly with what goes on. But I must think, must *think* . . . there is a feeling of discomfort, as if there is something *not* quite right.

After I moved into the new flat I soon saw that my life was entirely in the office. I had no life at home. *Home*. What a word! It was the place I prepared myself for the office, or rested after work.

One of the things I am *thinking* is that if I lost my job, there wouldn't be much left of me. I look at the clever girls, fighting their way up. I find myself looking at one, Phyllis, for instance, and reflecting. Yes, she's the right material, she can fit words together, interview anyone, edit, she has a mind like scissors, she never panics.

Does she understand how things *really* work? What do I mean by that? A great deal. Everything. She's pushy and impatient, you've got to know how to let things happen.

What I was thinking most of all was that I had let Freddie down and had let my mother down *and that was what I was like.* If something else should turn up, something I had to cope with, like illness or death, if I had to say to myself, Now, you will behave like a human being and not a little girl—then I couldn't do it. It is not a question of will, but of what you are.

That is why I decided to learn something else.

I saw in the paper the advertisement, Would you like to befriend an old person? The picture of a dear old lady. A dear, sweet old thing. Everybody's favourite granny. Ha! I rang up and went to see them. Miss Snow. Philanthropist. I went with her to visit Mrs York. We all three had tea together in a little flat in Kensington. It seemed to me false and awful. I thought Miss Snow was condescending but didn't know it. Mrs York, a large slow invalid, pale and with a puffy doughy face. Little complaining eyes. I could see she didn't like Miss Snow. I sat there and thought, what the hell am I doing here? What good does this do Mrs York? Am I to visit her once a week on Sundays and bring her cake and ask how her rheumatism is? Miss Snow knew I felt like this, and when we said goodbye on the pavement she was perfunctory. Yes, give me a ring, Mrs Somers, if you feel you want to do this work, and she got into her Mini and was off. A failure. Well, all in the day's work, she was thinking.

Someone else would have to be found for Mrs York. But I did not feel lacking this time. Mrs York was simply not for me. I used to look at the advertisement with the dear sweet old lady and think of awful Mrs York and feel a sort of jeer.

Meanwhile, opposite me, on the landing, Mrs Penny. She is seventy, she is alone, and she is longing for me to befriend her. I know this. I don't want to. She knows it. She would take over my life. I feel smothered and panicky at the idea of being at her beck and call.

But then I was in the chemist's and this happened.

I saw an old witch. I was staring at this old creature and thought, a witch. It was because I had spent all day on a feature, Stereotypes of Women, Then and Now. *Then* not exactly specified, late Victorian, the gracious lady, the mother of many, the invalid maiden aunt, the New Woman, missionary wife, and so on. I had about forty photographs and sketches to choose from. Among them, a witch, but I had discarded her. But here she was, beside me, in the chemist's. A tiny bent-over woman, with a nose nearly meeting her chin, in black heavy dusty clothes, and something not far off a bonnet. She saw me looking at her and thrust at me a prescription and said, "What is this? You get it for me." Fierce blue eyes, under grey craggy brows, but there was something wonderfully sweet in them.

I liked her, for some reason, from that moment. I took the paper and knew I was taking much more than that. "I will," I said. "But why? Isn't he being nice to you?" Joking: and she at once responded, shaking her old head vigorously.

"No, oh *he*'s no good, I never know what *he*'s saying."

He was the young chemist, and he stood, hands on the counter, alert, smiling: he knew her well, I could see.

"The prescription is for a sedative," I said.

She said, "I know *that*," and jabbed her fingers down on to the paper where I had spread it against my handbag. "But it's not aspirin, is it?"

I said, "It's something called Valium."

"That's what I thought. It's not a pain-killer, it's a stupefier," she said.

He laughed. "But it's not as bad as that," he said.

I said, "I've been taking it myself."

She said, "I said to the doctor, aspirin—that's what I asked for. But *they're* no good either, doctors."

All this fierce and trembling, with a sort of gaiety. Standing there, the three of us, we were laughing, and yet she was so very angry.

"Do you want me to sell you some aspirin, Mrs Fowler?"

"Yes, yes. I'm not going to take this stuff that stupefies you."

He handed her the aspirin, and took her money, which she

counted out slowly, coin by coin, from the depths of a great rusty bag. Then he took the money for my things—nail varnish, blusher, eye liner, eye shadow, lipstick, lip gloss, powder, mascara. The lot: I had run low of everything. She stood by watching, with a look I know now is so characteristic, a fierce pondering look that really wants to understand. Trying to grasp it all.

I adjusted my pace to hers and went out of the shop with her. On the pavement she did not look at me, but there was an appeal there. I walked beside her. It was hard to walk so slowly. Usually I fly along, but did not know it till then. She took one step, then paused, examined the pavement, then another step. I thought how I rushed along the pavements every day and had never seen Mrs Fowler, but she lived near me, and suddenly I looked up and down the streets and saw—old women. Old men too, but mostly old women. They walked slowly along. They stood in pairs or groups, talking. Or sat on the bench at the corner under the plane tree. I had not seen them. That was because I was afraid of being like them. I was afraid, walking along there beside her. It was the smell of her, a sweet, sour, dusty sort of smell. I saw the grime on her thin old neck, and on her hands.

The house had a broken parapet, broken and chipped steps. Without looking at me, because she wasn't going to ask, she went carefully down the old steps and stopped outside a door that did not fit and had been mended with a rough slat of wood nailed across it. Although this door wouldn't keep out a determined cat, she fumbled for a key, and at last found it, and peered for the keyhole, and opened the door. And I went in with her, my heart quite sick, and my stomach sick too because of the smell. Which was, that day, of over-boiled fish. It was a long dark passage we were in.

We walked along it to the "kitchen". I have never seen anything like it outside our Distress File, condemned houses and that sort of thing. It was an extension of the passage, with an old gas cooker, greasy and black, an old white china sink, cracked and yellow with grease, a cold-water tap wrapped around with old rags and dripping steadily. A rather nice old wood table that had crockery standing on it, all "washed" but grimy. The walls stained and damp. The whole place smelled, it smelled awful. . . . She did not look at me while she set down bread, biscuits and cat food. The clean lively colours of the grocery packages and the tins in that awful place. She was ashamed, but wasn't going to apologize. She said in an offhand but appealing way, "You go into my room, and find yourself a seat."

The room I went into had in it an old black iron stove that was showing a gleam of flames. Two unbelievably ancient ragged armchairs. Another nice old wood table with newspaper spread over it. A divan heaped with clothes and bundles. And a yellow cat on the floor. It was all so dirty and dingy and grim and awful. I thought of how all of us wrote about decor and furniture and colours—how taste changed, how we all threw things out and got bored with everything. And here was this kitchen, which if we printed a photograph of it would get us donations by return from readers.

Mrs Fowler brought in an old brown teapot, and two rather pretty old china cups and saucers. It was the hardest thing I ever did, to drink out of the dirty cup. We did not speak much because I did not want to ask direct questions, and she was trembling with pride and dignity. She kept stroking the cat— "My lovely, my pretty," in a hard but appealing sort of way—and she said without looking at me, "When I was young my father owned his own shop, and later we had a house in St John's Wood, and I know how things should be."

And when I left she said, in her way of not looking at me, "I suppose I won't be seeing you again?" And I said, "Yes, if you'll ask me." Then she did look at me, and there was a small smile, and I said, "I'll come on Saturday afternoon for tea, if you like."

"Oh I would like, yes I would." And there was a moment between us of intimacy: that is the word. And yet she was so full of pride and did not want to ask, and she turned away from me and began petting the cat: Oh, my little pet, my little pretty.

When I got home that evening I was in a panic. I had committed myself. I was full of revulsion. The sour, dirty smell was in my clothes and hair. I bathed and washed my hair and did myself up and rang Joyce and said, "Let's go out to dinner." We had a good dinner at Alfredo's and talked. I said nothing about Mrs Fowler, of course, yet I was thinking of her all the time: I sat looking around at the people in the restaurant, everyone well dressed and clean, and I thought, if she came into this restaurant . . . well, she couldn't. Not even as a cleaner, or a washer-up.

On the Saturday I took her some roses and carnations, and a cake with real cream. I was pleased with myself, and this carried me over her reaction—she was pleased, but I had overdone it. There was no vase for the flowers. I put them in a white enamel jug. She put the cake on a big old cracked plate. She was being rather distant. We sat on either side of the iron stove, and the brown teapot was on it to warm, and the flames were too hot. She was wearing a silk blouse, black dots on white. Real silk. Everything is like this with her. A beautiful flowered Worcester teapot, but it is cracked. Her skirt is of good heavy wool, but it is stained and frayed. She did not want me to see in her "bedroom", but I took a peep when she was in the "kitchen". The furniture was part very good: bookcases, a chest of drawers, then a shoddy dressing table and a wardrobe like a varnished packing case. The bed had on it an old-fashioned quilt, plump, of chintz. She did not sleep in the bed, I realized, but on the divan next door, where we sat. Everywhere in the room were piles of rubbish, what looked like rags, bundles of newspapers, everything you can think of: this was what she did not want me to see.

When we ate the cake, she said, "Oh, this is real cream," and told me about how, in the summers, she and her sisters were sent to an old woman in Essex.

"Every day of the summer we were out of doors. Lovely hot summers, not like the ones we have now. We got as brown as toffee. The old woman had a little cottage but no kitchen. She built a tripod under a cock of thatch in the yard, and she had a great iron pot on chains and she cooked everything for our dinners in the pot. First she put in the piece of beef, and around it the carrots and potatoes, and she had the pudding rolled in a floured cloth and that went in to boil at the same time. I used to wonder how it was the pudding tasted of jam and fruit and not the meat, but of course it was the flour the cloth had on it. And then she gave us great soup plates, and sat us on the steps, and we ate the meat and the vegetables, and then she peeled the cloth off the pudding, and it came out all crusty and rich, and gave us slices in the same plate we ate the meat off—but we had licked that clean as washed. And then she said, Off with you—and she boiled up water in the iron pot to wash our plates, and to wash herself, after, and we went off into the fields to pick flowers. Oh, I like to sit here and think of all that."

"And how old were you then?"

"Children. We were children. We went every summer—several summers. That was before my poor mother died, you see."

She talked about the old woman, who was so kind, and the little cottage, that had no running water, and only an outside lavatory in a little brick shed, and those hot summers, all afternoon. She talked and I listened. I did not leave till nearly seven. I came home, and switched on the fire, and thought it was time I did some cleaning. I sat by myself and thought of Mrs Fowler, by herself, the flames showing in the open front of her grate. I opened a tin of soup, and I watched television.

Next Saturday I took her a little pot of African violets and another cake.

Everything the same: the fire burning, the yellow cat, and her dirty white silk spotted blouse.

There was a reticence in her, and I thought it was because she had talked last Saturday for three hours, hardly stopping.

But it wasn't that. It came out almost when I was leaving.

"Are you a good neighbour?" she said.

"I hope perhaps I may become one," I said, laughing.

"Why, have they put you on probation, then?"

I did not understand, and she saw I didn't. It turns out that the Council employ women, usually elderly, who run into old people for a cup of tea, or to see if they are all right: they don't do much, but keep an eye on them. They are called Good Neighbours and they are paid so little they can't be doing it for the money. I made it my business to find out all this through the office. On the third Saturday I took her some fruit, and saw it was the wrong thing. She said nothing, again, till later, when she remarked that her teeth made it impossible for her to eat fruit.

"Can't you eat grapes? Bananas?"

She said, with humour, that the pension did not run to grapes.

And she was off, on the subject of the pension, and what coal cost, and what food cost, and "that Council woman who doesn't know what she is talking about". I listened, again. I have not pieced it all together yet. I see that it will be a long time before my ignorance, my lack of experience, and her reticence, and her rages—for now I see how they simmer there, making her eyes light up with what you'd think, at first, must be gaiety or even a sense of comedy—a long time before how she is, her nature, and how I am, my rawness, can make it possible for me to form a whole picture of her.

The "Council woman", a Mrs Rogers, wanted her, Mrs Fowler, to have a Home Help. But the Home Help cheated her and didn't do any work, and wouldn't wash her floors. The Home Help was just the way all these young women are now, lazy, too good for work. She, Mrs Fowler, was not too good to wash floors, she carries her own coal all along the passage, she sweeps her own chimney once a week as far up as she could reach with her brushes, because she is afraid of fire. And so she went on, about the social workers, and Home Helps, and—a Good Neighbour, she was kind enough to come once, and she said it was time I was in a Home, so I said to her, You know your way out.

"But, Mrs Fowler, you and I met in the chemist's, how could I be a Good Neighbour—I mean, an official?"

"They get up to anything," she said, bitter but distressed, for she was afraid I would be offended and not come back.

She went with me to the outside door when I left, and she was doing something I have seen on the stage or written in novels. She wore an old striped apron, because she had put it on to make the tea, and she stood pleating it with both hands, and letting it go smooth, then pleating it again.

"Shall I drop in during the week?" I asked.

"If you have time," she said. And could not resist, "And it

will make a bit extra for you." Yet she almost gasped as she
said this: she did not want to say it, because she wanted to
believe I was not an official, paid person, but just a human
being who likes her.

When I went in after work on Wednesday, I took in a copy of
our magazine. I was ashamed of it, so glossy and sleek and
slick, so *clever*—that is how it is presented, its image. But she
took it from me with a girl's mischievous smile, and a sort of
prance of her head—what remained of a girl's tossed hair—
and said, "Oh, I love these, I love looking at these things they
think up."

Because it was seven, I did not know how to fit myself in to
her. When did she eat her supper? Or go to bed? On the
newspapers on the table was a bottle of milk stout and a glass.

"I've drunk it or I'd offer you some," said she.

I sat down in the chair opposite hers and saw that the room,
with the curtains drawn and the electric light, seemed quite
cosy, not so dreadfully dirty and grim. But why do I go on
about dirt like this? Why do we judge people like this? *She* was
no worse off for the grime and the dust, and even the smells. I
decided not to notice, if I could help it, not to keep judging her,
which I was doing, by the sordidness. I saw that the electric
switches were broken, and made an excuse to go out to the
"kitchen": frayed cords trailing over the walls, only one switch
for the whole room, up on the light itself, which she could
hardly reach.

She was looking at the magazine, with a smile that was all
pleasure.

"I work for that magazine," I said, and she let the thing fall
shut and sat looking at me in that way of hers, as if she is trying
to make things fit, make sense.

"Do you? And what do you . . ." But she did not know what
questions to ask. I could not bring myself to say I was the
assistant editor. I said, "I do typing and all sorts." Which is
true enough.

"That's the main thing," she said, "training. It stands
between you and nothing. That, and a place of your own."

That evening she talked about how she had fought to get
into this flat, for at first she had been on the top floor back, in

one room, but she had her eye on the basement flat, and wanted it, and waited for it, and schemed for it, and at last, got it. *And they aren't going to get me out, and they needn't think it.* She spoke as if all this happened yesterday, but it was about the time of the First World War.

She talked about how she had not had the money for the rent of these rooms, and how she had saved it up, penny by penny, and then it was stolen, two years' scrimping and saving, by the wicked woman on the first floor, and she saved again, and at last she went to the landlord and said, You let me in down there. I've got the money for it. He said to me, And how are you going to keep the rent paid? You are a milliner's girl, aren't you? I said, You leave that to me. When I stop paying, then you can throw me out. "And I have never not paid, not once. Though, I've gone without food. No, I learned that early. With your own place, you've got everything. Without it, you are a dog. You are nothing. Have you got your own place?"—and when I said yes, she said, nodding fiercely, angrily, "That's right, and you hold on to it, then nothing can touch you."

Mrs Fowler's "flat" is rent-controlled, twenty-two shillings a week. About a pound in new money, but of course she doesn't think in terms of the new currency, she can't cope with it. She says the house was bought by "that Greek" after the war—the new war, you know, not the old one—for four hundred pounds. And now it's worth sixty thousand. "And he wants me out, so he can get his blood money for this flat. But I know a trick or two. I always have it here, always. And if he doesn't come I go to the telephone box and I ring his office and I say, Why haven't you come for your rent?"

I knew so little that I said to her, "But, Mrs Fowler, twenty-two shillings is not worth the trouble of his collecting it," and her eyes blazed up, and her face was white and dreadful and she said, "Is that how you see it, is that it? Has he sent you here, then? But it is what the rent is, by law, and I am going to pay it. Worth nothing, is it? It is worth the roof over my head."

The three floors above all have Irish families, children, people coming and going, feet tramping about: Mrs Fowler says that "she" makes the refrigerator door rattle to keep her awake at night because "she" wants this flat . . . Mrs Fowler lives in a nightmare of imagined persecutions. She told me of the ten-years-long campaign, after the first war, not the new one, when "that bitch from Nottingham" was trying to get her rooms, and she . . . She, it seems, did everything, there was nothing she did not do, and it all sounds true. But now upstairs there is an Irish couple, four children, and I saw the woman on the steps. "How is the old lady?" she asked, her periwinkle Irish eyes tired and lonely, for her husband is leaving her, apparently for another woman. "I keep meaning to go down, but she doesn't seem all that pleased when I do, and so I don't go."

I showed Mrs Fowler the issue of *Lilith* that has Female Images. She took it politely, and let it lie on her lap. It was only when it was ready to go to press that it occurred to me there was no old woman among the Images. I said this to Joyce, and I watched a series of reactions in her: first, surprise. Then shock, small movements of head and eyes said she was alerting herself to danger. Then she, as it were, switched herself off, became vague, and her eyes turned away from me. She sighed: "Oh, but why? It's not our age group." I said, watching myself in her, "They all have mothers or grandmothers." How afraid we are of age: how we avert our eyes! "No," she said, still rather vague, with an abstracted air, as if she were doing justice to an immensely difficult subject to which she had given infinite thought. "No, on the whole not, but perhaps we'll do a feature on Elderly Relations later. I'll make a note." And then she flashed me a smile, a most complex smile it was: guilt, relief, and—it was there still—surprise. Somewhere she was wondering, what has got into Janna? And there was in it a plea: don't threaten me, don't! And, though she had been meaning to sit down and join me in a cup of tea while we discussed the issue after next, she said, Must fly. And flew.

Something interesting has just occurred to me.

Joyce is the innovator, the iconoclast, the one who will throw an issue we've just got set up into the wastepaper basket, and start again, working all night, to get it down just *so*; Joyce presents herself—she *is*—this impulsive, dashing, daring soul, nothing sacred.

I, Janna, am classical and cautious, conservative and careful—this is my appearance, and how I think of myself.

Yet there are so often these moments between us, there always have been. Joyce says, "We can't do that, our readers won't like it."

Me, I have always believed our readers—and everybody else's readers for that matter—would take much more than they are offered.

I say, "Joyce, can we try it?"

But more often than not, whatever it is lands in the file I have labelled Too Difficult and which I leave out on my desk so that Joyce will see it and—so I hope, but most often in vain—be prompted to have another think.

The Images. (a) A girl of twelve or thirteen, and she gave us the most trouble. We discarded a hundred photographs, and finally got Michael to photograph Joyce's niece, aged fifteen actually but rather childish. We got a frank healthy sensuality, not Lolita at all, we were careful to avoid that. Miss Promise. (b) A girl about seventeen, emphasizing independence and confidence. Still at home but you are ready to leave the nest. (c) Leading your own life. Mid-twenties. Since in our experience women living their own lives, sharing flats, keeping down jobs, feel as if they are walking a tightrope, we chose something pretty and vulnerable. Needing Mr Right but able to do without. (d) Young married woman, with a child. Emphasizing the child. (e) Married woman with part-time job, two children, running home and husband.

And that was that.

Before a few weeks ago, I did not see old people at all. My eyes were pulled towards, and I *saw*, the young, the attractive, the well-dressed and handsome. And now it is as if a transparency has been drawn across that former picture and there, all at once, are the old, the infirm.

I nearly said to Joyce, "But one day we will be old," but it is a cliché so obvious, so boring! I can hear her say, "Oh, Janna, do we have to be so boring, so obvious, they don't buy us for that kind of thing." She always says, They buy *us*, we must make them want to buy *us*. One day I went into a filling station and I was tired after a long drive and I said, "Please fill me up." And the garage man said, "I'll be only too happy to fill your car up, madam."

When Mrs Fowler went into the kitchen to get some biscuits, I went with her and watched her pull up a stool to stand on so she could put on the ceiling light. I examined the frayed flexes, the damp walls.

Later I said to her, "I'm going to ask my electrician to come in here, otherwise you are going to kill yourself."

She sat quite still for a few minutes, then she raised her eyes, looked at me, and sighed. I knew this was a moment of importance. I had said something she had dreamed of someone saying: but now this was a burden on her, and she wished the moment, and me, away.

She said, "I've managed well enough." This was timid, and an appeal, and sullen.

I said, "It's a disgrace that you should have to be in these conditions. Your electricity, it's a death-trap."

She gave a snort of laughter at this. "A death-trap, is it?" And we laughed. But I was full of panic, inside me something struggled to run, to flee, out of the situation.

I felt trapped. I am trapped. Because I have made a promise to her. Silently. But it is a promise.

I went home and, as I opened my door, the door opposite crept open: Mrs Penny, on the watch. "Excuse me," she cried, "but I have been waiting for you to come home. I simply must ask a favour of you."

I said ungraciously, "What is it?"

"I forgot to buy butter when I went out and . . ."

"I'll bring it," I said, and in a surge of energy went into my flat, got half a pound of butter, thrust it into her hands, said, "Don't mention it," and ran back into my own place with a bang of the door. The bang was deliberate. She had butter, I knew that. What I was thinking was, she has a son and daughter, and if they don't look after her, *tant pis.* It's not my responsibility.

I was in a frenzy of irritation, a need to shake something off—Mrs Fowler. I filled the bath. I put every stitch of clothing I had worn that day ready for the launderette. I could feel the smelly air of Mrs Fowler's place on my skin and hair.

My bathroom, I realized that evening, is where I live. Probably even my home. When I moved here I copied the bathroom I had made in the old flat, to the last detail. But I did not do anything particular with the living room and bedroom, the study. Freddie joked that his rival was my bathroom.

I had the paint mixed especially, ivory with a tone of pink. I had Spanish tiles, very delicate and light, coral, turquoise, and ochre, and the blinds were painted to match the tiles. The bath is a grey-blue. Sometimes a room is perfect—nothing can be added and nothing changed. When Joyce saw it she wanted it photographed for the mag. I said no: it would be like being photographed nude. I bath every morning, every night. I lie in the bath and soak for hours. I read in the bath, with my head and knees floating on waterproof pillows. I have two shelves full of salts and bath bubbles. That evening I lay in the bath, adding hot water as it chilled, and I looked at my body. It is a solid firm white body. No fat on it. God forbid! But solid. It doesn't sag or droop yet. Well, no children. There was never time for children, and when I said to Freddie, Yes, I'll fit one in now, I did not get pregnant. He was cheerful and nice about it. I don't know how deeply he felt it. I know he wanted children, but not how much. I was careful not to find out, I suppose.

I came out of the bath and stood in the doorway wrapped in my bath sheet and looked at the bathroom and thought about Mrs Fowler. She has never had hot water. Has lived in that filthy hole, with cold water, since before the First World War.

I wished I had not responded to her, and I was wondering all evening how to escape.

In the morning I woke up and it was as if I was facing some terrible fate. Because I knew I was going to look after Mrs Fowler. To an extent, anyway.

I rang up the electrician. I explained everything to him. I went to work depressed and even frightened.

That night the electrician rang: Mrs Fowler had screamed at him, *What do you want?* And he had gone away.

I said I would meet him there next evening.

He was there at six, and I saw his face as she opened the door and the smell and the squalor hit him. Then he said to her, in a nice cheeky sort of way, "Well, you got at me good and proper last night, didn't you?"

She examined him slowly, then looked at me as if I were a stranger, stood aside, and went into her "living room" while I told him what to do. I should have stayed with her, but I had brought work home and I told her this.

"I didn't ask you to put yourself out," she said.

I struggled with myself, and then gave her a hug. "Oh, go on, don't be a cross-patch," I said, and left. She had tears in her eyes. As for me, I was fighting disgust, the stale smell of her. And the other smell, a sharp sweet smell which I didn't know.

Jim rang me yesterday and said he had done what he could to the place, put in new cable and switches at a height she could reach, and got her a bed lamp.

He told me the cost—as bad as I thought. I said I would send him a cheque. A silence. He wanted cash: thinking I might need him again for Mrs Fowler—and this thought was quite horrifying, as if I was acknowledging some awful burden for ever—I said, "If you come around now I'll give you cash." "Can do," said he. He arrived an hour later. He took the money, and stood waiting, and then, "Why isn't she in a Home? She shouldn't be living like that." I said, "She doesn't want to go into a Home. She likes it where she is."

Jim is a nice boy, not stupid. He was ashamed of what he was thinking, just as I am. He hesitated, and then said, "I didn't know there were people still living like that."

I said, worldly wise, the older experienced one, "Then you don't know much."

Still he lingered, troubled, ashamed, but insistent. "What's the good of people that old?" he said. And then, quickly, to cancel out what he had said, cancel what he was thinking, "Well, we'll be old one of these days, I suppose. Cheers then!"

And went. It was delicacy that made him say, *we'll* be old, not *I'll* be old: because for him I am old, already.

And then I sat down and thought. What he said was what people do say: *Why aren't they in a Home? Get them out of the*

*way, out of sight, where young healthy people can't see them,
can't have them on their minds!*

They are thinking—I have been thinking— I *did* think, what
is the point of their being alive still?

And I thought, then, how do we value ourselves? By what?
Work? Jim the electrician is all right, electricians are obviously
category one—if you can get them to come at all. What about
assistant editors of women's magazines? *Childless* assistant
editors? How about Joyce, editor, one daughter, who won't
speak to her, she says Joyce is beneath contempt for some
reason or another, I forget; a son, difficult. I get so bored with
these spoiled prima donnas, the teenagers.

How about Sister Georgie? Well, she's all right, children,
husband, good works. But how about Sister Georgie in fifteen
years' time? Statistically she'll be a widow, children gone,
she'll be in a flat, no use to anyone. How will she be judged
then?

How about my Freddie, if he had lived? A saint, no less,
putting up with spoiled child-wife. But in fifteen years? I see the
old men, lean and shadowy and dusty-looking, or fat and
sagging and grey, going about the streets with their shopping,
or standing at street corners, looking lost.

We are to judge people by their beautiful thoughts?

If my thoughts are not beautiful now, what are they likely to
be in fifteen, twenty years' time?

What is the *use* of Maudie Fowler? By the yardsticks and
measurements I've been taught, none.

How about Mrs Penny, a nuisance to her children, to
everyone in this building, and particularly to me—something I
simply cannot face? Silly woman with her plummy I-was-in-
India-in-the-old-days vowels, her secret drinking, her "refinement", her dishonesty.

Well, how about Mrs Penny? There's not a soul in the world
who'd shed a tear if she died.

When I had paid off Jim I had another of my long baths. It is
as if, in such a bath, my old self floats away, is drowned, a new
one emerges from the Pine-Needle Foam, the Satin-Self Gel,
the Sea-Breeze Ions.

I went to bed that night saying I had made a contribution to

Mrs Fowler's welfare that was more than she could possibly expect. And that it was enough. I simply would not go near her again.

In the morning I woke feeling ill, because of being so trapped, and I thought about how I was brought up. Very interesting: you'd say it was a moral household. Religion, of a mild kind. But the atmosphere was certainly one of self-approbation: *we* did the right things, were good. But what, in practice, did it amount to? I wasn't taught anything in the way of self-discipline, self-control. Except for the war, but that was from outside. I wasn't taught how to control my eating, I had to do that for myself. Or how to get up in the morning, and that was the hardest thing I ever had to do, when I started work. I've never known how to say no to myself, when I want something. We were never denied anything, if it was there. The war! Was it because of that, because so little was available, that children were allowed anything they wanted? But there is one thing I can thank Mother for, just one: and I lay in bed saying to her that morning, "Thank you for that. At least you taught me that if I make promises, I must keep them. That if I say I will do a thing, then I must do it. It isn't much to build on, but it's something."

Thank you.

And I went back to Mrs Fowler after work.

I had been thinking all day about my marvellous bathroom, my baths, my dependence on all that. I was thinking that what I spent on hot water in a month would change her life.

But when I went in, taking six milk stouts and some new glasses, and I cried out from the door, "Hello, I'm here, let me in, look what I've got!" and I strode in down that awful passage while she stood to one side, her face was a spiteful little fist. She wanted to punish me for her new electricity and her new comfort, but I wasn't going to let her. I went striding and slamming about, and poured out stout and showed her the glasses, and by the time I sat down, she did too, and she was lively and smiling.

"Have you seen my new boots?" I asked her, thrusting them forward. She bent to peer at them, her mouth trembling with laughter, with mischief.

"Oh," she half whispered, "I do like the things you wear, I do think they are lovely."

So we spent the evening, me showing her every stitch I had. I took off my sweater and stood still so she could walk round me, laughing. I had on my new camisole, *crêpe de Chine*. I pulled up my skirts so she could see the lace in it. I took off my boots so she could handle them.

She laughed and enjoyed herself.

She told me about clothes she had worn when she was young.

There was a dress that was a favourite, of grey poplin with pink flowers on it. She wore it to visit her auntie. It had been the dress of her father's fancy-woman, and it was too big for her, but she took it in.

"Before my poor mother died, nothing was too good for me, but then, I got the cast-offs. But this was so lovely, so lovely, and I did love myself in it."

We talked about the dresses and knickers and petticoats and camisoles and slippers and boas and corsets of fifty, sixty, seventy years ago. Mrs Fowler is over ninety.

And she talked most about her father's woman, who owned her own pub. When Mrs Fowler's mother died . . . "She was poisoned, dear! *She* poisoned her—oh yes, I know what you are thinking, I can see your face, but *she* poisoned her, just as she nearly did for me. She came to live in our house. That was in St John's Wood. I was a skivvy for the whole house, I slaved day and night, and before *they* went to bed I'd take up some thin porridge with some whisky and cream stirred in. She would be on one side of the fire, in her fancy red feathered bed jacket, and my father on the other side, in his silk dressing jacket. She'd say to me, Maudie, you feeling strong tonight? And she'd throw off all that feathered stuff and stand there in her corsets. They don't make corsets like that now. She was a big handsome woman, full of flesh, and my father was sitting there in his armchair smiling and pulling at his whiskers. I had to loosen those corset strings. What a job! But it was better than hauling and tugging her into her corsets when she was dressing to go out. And they never said to me, Maudie, would you fancy a spoonful of porridge yourself? No, they ate and drank like kings, they wanted for nothing. If she felt like a crab or a sole or a lobster, he'd send out for it. But it was never Maudie, would you like a bit? But she got fatter and fatter and then it was: Do you want my old blue silk, Maudie? I wanted it right enough! One of her dresses'd make a dress and a blouse for me, and sometimes a scarf. But I never liked wearing her things, not really. I felt as if they had been stolen from my poor mother."

I did not get home till late, and I lay in the bath wondering if we could do a feature on those old clothes. I mentioned it to Joyce and she seemed quite interested.

She was looking at me curiously. She did not like to ask questions, because something about me at the moment warns her off. But she did say, "Where did you hear about these clothes?" while I was describing the pink silk afternoon dress of a female bar owner before the First World War—who, according to Mrs Fowler, poisoned her lover's wife and tried to poison her lover's daughter. And the plum-coloured satin peignoir with black ostrich feathers.

"Oh, I have a secret life," I said to her, and she said, "So it seems," in a careless, absent way that I am beginning to recognize.

I went back to Maudie last night. I said to her, "Can I call you Maudie?" But she didn't like that. She hates familiarity, disrespect. So I slid away from it. When I left I said, "Then at least call me Janna, please." So now she will call me Janna, but it must be Mrs Fowler, showing respect.

I asked her to describe to me all those old clothes, for the magazine: I said we would pay for her expertise. But this was a mistake, she cried out, really shocked and hurt, "Oh no, how can you . . . I love thinking about those old days."

And so that slid away too. How many mistakes I do make, trying to do the right thing.

Nearly all my first impulses are quite wrong, like being ashamed of my bathroom, and of the mag.

I spent an hour last night describing my bathroom to her in the tiniest detail, while she sat smiling, delighted, asking questions. She is not envious. No. But sometimes there is a dark angry look, and I know I'll hear more, obliquely, later.

She talked more about that house in St John's Wood. I can see it! The heavy dark furniture, the comfort, the good food and the drink.

Her father owned a little house where "they" wanted to put the Paddington railway line. Or something to do with it. And he got a fortune for it. Her father had had a corner shop in Bell Street, and sold hardware and kept free coal and bread for the poor people, and in the cold weather there was a cauldron of soup for the poor. "I used to love standing there, so proud of him, helping those poor people . . ." And then came the good luck, and all at once, the big house and warmth and her father going out nearly every night, for he loved going where the toffs were, he went to supper and the theatre, and the music hall and there he met *her*, and Maudie's mother broke her heart, and was poisoned.

Maudie says that she had a lovely childhood, she couldn't wish a better to anyone, not the Queen herself. She keeps talking of a swing in a garden under apple trees, and long uncut grass. "I used to sit and swing myself, for hours at a time, and swing, and swing, and I sang all the songs I knew, and then poor Mother came out and called to me, and I ran in to her and she gave me fruit cake and milk and kissed me, and I ran back to the swing. Or she would dress me and my sister Polly up and we went out into the street. We had a penny and we bought a leaf of chocolate each. And I used to lick it up crumb by crumb, and I hoped I wouldn't run into anyone so I must share it. But my sister always ate hers all at once, and then nagged at me to get some of mine."

"How old were you, on the swing, Mrs Fowler?"

"Oh, I must have been five, six . . ."

None of it adds up. There couldn't, surely, have been a deep grassy garden behind the hardware in Bell Street? And in St John's Wood she would have been too old for swings and playing by herself in the grasses while the birds sang? And when her father went off to his smart suppers and the theatre, when was that? I ask, but she doesn't like to have a progression made, her mind has bright pictures in it that she has painted for herself and has been dwelling on for all those decades.

In what house was it her father came in and said to her

mother, "You whey-faced slop, don't you ever do anything but snivel?" And hit her. But never did it again, because Maudie ran at him and beat him across the legs until he began to laugh and held her up in the air, and said to his wife, "If you had some of her fire, you'd be something," and went off to his fancy-woman. And then Maudie would be sent up by her mother with a jug to the pub, to stand in the middle of the public asking for draught Guinness. "Yes, I had to stand there for everyone to see, so that *she* would be ashamed. But she wasn't ashamed, not she, she would have me over the bar counter and into her own little back room, which was so hot our faces were beef. That was before she poisoned my mother and began to hate me, out of remorse."

All that I have written up to now was a recapitulation, summing-up. Now I am going to write day by day, if I can. Today was Saturday, I did my shopping, and went home to work for a couple of hours, and then dropped in to Mrs F. No answer when I knocked, and I went back up her old steps to the street and saw her creeping along, pushing her shopping basket. Saw her as I did the first day: an old crooked witch. Quite terrifying, nose and chin nearly meeting, heavy grey brows, straggly bits of white hair under the black splodge of hat. She was breathing heavily as she came up to me. She gave her impatient shake of the head when I said hello, and went down the steps without speaking to me. Opened the door, still without speaking, went in. I nearly walked away. But followed her, and without being asked took myself into the room where the fire was. She came in after a long time, perhaps half an hour, while I heard her potter about. Her old yellow cat came and sat near my feet. She brought in a tray with her brown teapot and biscuits, quite nice and smiling. And she pulled the dirty curtains over, and put on the light and put the coal on the fire. No coal left in the bucket. I took the bucket from her and went along the passage to the coal cellar. A dark that had no light in it. A smell of cat. I scraped coal into the bucket and took it back, and she held out her hand for the bucket without saying thank you.

The trouble with a summing-up afterwards, a recap, is that you leave out the grit and grind of a meeting. I could say, She was cross to begin with, then got her temper back, and we had a nice time drinking tea, and she told me about . . . But what about all the shifts of liking, anger, irritation—oh, so much anger, in both of us?

I was angry while I stood there on the steps and she went down past me without speaking, and she was angry, probably, thinking, this is getting too much! And sitting in that room, with the cat, I was furious, thinking, well if that is all the thanks I get! And then all the annoyances melting into pleasure with the glow of the fire, and the rain outside. And there are always these bad moments for me, when I actually take up the greasy cup and have to put my lips to it; when I take in whiffs of that sweet sharp smell that comes from her, when I see how she looks at me, sometimes, the boiling up of some old rage . . . It is an up-and-down of emotion, each meeting.

She told me about a summer holiday.

"Of course, we could not afford summer holidays, not the way all you girls have them now. Take them for granted, you do! They had put me off work from the millinery. I did not know when they would want me again. I felt tired and run-down, because I wasn't eating right then, they paid us so bad. I answered an advertisement for a maid in a seaside hotel in Brighton. Select, it said. References needed. I had no references. I had never been in service. My mother would have died to think of it. I wrote a letter and I had a letter back asking me to come, my fares paid. I packed my little bag and I went. I knew it was all right, there was something about her letter. It was a big house, set back a bit from the road. I walked up the front path, thinking, well, I'm not in service here yet! And the housekeeper let me in, a real nice woman she was, and said Mrs Privett would see me at once. Well, let me say this now, she was one of the best people I have known in my life. The kindest. I often think of her. You know, when everything is as bad as it can be, and you think there's nowhere you can turn, then there's always that person, that one person . . . She looked me over, and said, Well, Maudie, you say you have no experience, and I value your honesty. But I want a good class of girl because we have a good class of people. When can you start? Now, I said, and we both laughed, and she said later she had had the same feeling about me, that when I arrived it would be all right. The housekeeper took me up to the top of the house. There was a cook, and a scullery maid, and a boy, and the housekeeper, and the two girls for waiting at the tables, and four housemaids. I was one of the housemaids. We were in one of the attics, two big beds up there, two to a bed. I wasn't to start till the morning, and so I ran down to the beach, and took off my shoes. There was the lovely sea. I had not seen the sea since my mother died, and I sat on the beach and watched the dark sea moving up and down and I was so happy, so happy . . . and I ran back through the dark, scared as anything because of the Strangler . . ."

"Because of the *what*?"

And here she told a long story about some newspaper scare of the time, a man who strangled girls when he found them alone . . . It was so out of key with the rest of what she was telling me, and yet this was, is, something in Maudie, a strain of horror-shivering masochism that comes out suddenly and then goes again. At any rate, she ran quaking up through the dark, through the dark garden, with the hot breath of the Strangler on her neck, and the door was opened by the housekeeper, who said, Oh there you are, Maudie, I was worrying about you, but the mistress said, Don't worry, I know where she'll be . . . "You know, I've often and often thought about this, when it is so easy to be nice, why are people nasty? Everything in that big house was nice, all the people in it, and even the guests too, no one unkind or quick or sharp. It was because of her, Mrs Privett. So why are people unkind to each other?

"She had kept my supper for me, and it was a lovely supper too, and she sat with me while I ate. And then up I went to bed. It was dark through the house, with the gas lights burning on the landings, but at the very top the sky was light, there were the three other girls, and oh, we did have such a good time. We lay half the night and told each other stories, ghost stories and all, and we frightened each other with the Strangler, and we ate sweets and laughed . . .

"And next morning, we had to get up at six. And by the time it was breakfast I was so hungry, but she, Mrs Privett, gave us the same food the hotel guests had, and better, and she came into the kitchen while we were all eating to make sure we had it. We ate great plates of porridge and real milk, and then kippers or haddock if we liked, or eggs any way we liked, and then all the toast and marmalade and butter we could eat, and sometimes she sat with us too, and said, I like to see young things eating. You must eat well, or you can't do your work. And that was what all the meals there were like. I've never eaten like that before or since. And then . . ."

"And what work did you do? Was it hard?"

"Yes, I suppose it was hard. But we knew how to work in those days. We got up by six and cleaned the grates through the house and started the fires, and we had the big dining room cleaned and shining before we took the guests their trays of tea and biscuits. And then we did the public rooms, everything just so and polished, and then we had our breakfast. And then we did all the bedrooms, right out, no skimping on the cleaning, Mrs Privett wouldn't have it. And we did the flowers with her, or the silver or the windows. And then we had our dinners, wonderful food, everything the guests had. And then we took the mending up to the attics and while we did that we had a bit of a skylark around. She didn't mind. She said she liked to hear us laughing, provided we got the work all done. And then we came down to do the tea, trays and trays of bread and butter and cakes and stuff, the four of us served all that while the waiting girls went off for the afternoon. And then we had some time off, and we went down to the beach for an hour or so. And then we four maids would sit with the babies and children while the parents went out to the theatre or somewhere. I loved that, I loved little children. We all loved that. And there was a big late supper, about ten at night, with cakes and ham and everything. And we all had either Sunday afternoon or Saturday afternoon off. Oh, it was wonderful. I was there three months and I got so fat and happy I couldn't get into my clothes."

"And then?"

"And then the autumn was coming, and the hotel closed.

Mrs Privett came to me and said, Maudie, I want you to stay with me. In the winters I open a place on the sea, in Nice that was. France. She wanted me to go with her. But I said no, I was a milliner, that was my trade, but it broke my heart not to go with her."

"Why did you *really* not go with her?" I asked.

"You are sharp," she said. "You are right. It was Laurie. I went away from London to Brighton and didn't say where I was, so he would value me, and he did. He was waiting for me when I got off the train, though how he found out I never did know. And he said, So you're back? As you can see, I said. Tomorrow you are coming for a walk, he said. Am I? I said.

"And so I married him. I married him instead of the German. I married the wrong man."

I gave a grimace at this, and she said, "And did you marry the wrong one too?"

"No," I said, "he married the wrong woman."

And this tickled her so much she lay back in her chair, her brown old wrinkled hands squeezing her knees, and she laughed and laughed. She has a young fresh laugh, not an old woman's laugh at all.

"Oh, oh, oh," she cried, "I had never thought of that. Well, Laurie thought he married the wrong woman, but then what woman would have been right? For he never stayed with any one of us."

That was this afternoon. I did not leave her until after six. She came with me to the outside door and said, "Thank you for getting the coal. You mustn't mind me, dear, mustn't mind my ways."

Sunday.

I saw *The White Raven*. I see that I am like Maudie, the housemaids—I like being frightened. After the film I came back here for my usual Sunday evening's occupation, making sure clothes are all prepared for the next week, grooming. I saw that I had spent all day alone and that is how I spend my weekends, usually. Solitary. I did not know I was until Freddie died. He liked us to have proper dinner parties every week or so, and we had his colleagues and their wives, and I asked girls from work, usually Joyce and her husband. My food was perfect, and Freddie did the wine. We were proud of how well we did it. And all that has been blown away, gone. I never saw his associates after the funeral. When I wondered if I would have the perfect little dinner parties, I couldn't be bothered. At work, I am seen by everybody as this self-sufficient competent woman, with a full life. Friends, weekends, entertainment. I go each week to three or four lunches, drinks parties, receptions for the mag. I don't like this, or dislike it, it is part of my job. I know nearly everyone, we all know each other. Then I come home after work, if I am not having supper with Joyce to discuss something, and I buy take-away, and then—my evening begins. I go into the bathroom and stay there two, three hours. Then watch a little television. At weekends I go about by myself. How do you describe such a person? And yet I am not lonely. If anyone had said to me, before Freddie died, that I could live like this, and not want anything different . . . And yet I must want something different? I shall spend a weekend with Georgie. *I shall try again.* I did not go in to Maudie today, thinking it all too much. I am sitting here writing this, in bed, wondering if she expected me. If she was disappointed.

Monday.
Dropped in after work, with some chocolates. She seemed stand-offish. Cross because I did not go in yesterday? She said she had not gone out because it was cold, and she felt bad. After I got home I wondered if she wanted me to go and shop for her. But after all, she got along before I blew into her life—*crashed* into it.

Tuesday.
Joyce said she didn't want to go to Munich for the Clothes Fair, trouble with husband, and her children playing up, would I go? I was reluctant, though I enjoy these trips: realized it was because of Maudie Fowler. This struck me as crazy, and I said I'd go.
Went in to Maudie after work. The flames were bursting out of the grate, and she was hot and angry. No, she didn't feel

well, and no, I wasn't to trouble myself. She was so rude, but I went into the kitchen, which stank of sour food and cat food that had gone off, and saw she had very little there. I said I was going out to shop for her. I now recognize these moments when she is pleased that I will do this or that, but her pride is hurting. She lowers her sharp little chin, her lips tremble a little, and she stares in silence at the fire.

I did not ask what to get, but as I left she shouted after me about fish for the cat. I got a lot of things, put them on her kitchen table, boiled up some milk, took it to her.

"You ought to be in bed," I said.

She said, "And the next thing, you'll be fetching the doctor."

"Well, is that so terrible?"

"He'll send me away," she said.

"Where to?"

"Hospital, where else?"

I said to her, "You talk as if hospital is a sort of prison."

She said, "I have my thoughts, and you keep yours."

Meanwhile, I could see she was really ill. I had to fight with her, to help her to bed. I was looking around for a nightdress, but I understood at last she did not use one. She goes to bed in vest and drawers, with an old cardigan pinned at the throat by a nice garnet brooch.

She was suffering because I saw that her bed was not clean, and that her underclothes were soiled. The sweet stench was very strong: I know now it is urine.

I put her in, made her tea, but she said, "No, no, I'll only be running."

I looked around, found that a chair in the corner of the room was a commode and dragged it close to the bed.

"Who's going to empty it?" she demanded, furious.

I went out of the kitchen to see what the lavatory was like: a little cement box, with a very old unlidded seat, and a metal chain that had broken and had string extending it. It was clean. But very cold. No wonder she has a cough. It is very cold at the moment, February—and I only *feel* how cold it really is when I think of her, Maudie, for everywhere I am is so well heated and protected. If she is going out to that lavatory from the hot fire . . .

I said to her, "I'll drop in on my way to work."

I am sitting here, in bed, having bathed and washed every scrap of me, hair too, writing this and wondering how it is I am in this position with Maudie.

Wednesday.
Booked for Munich. Went in to Maudie after work. The doctor was there. Dr Thring. An old man, fidgety and impatient, standing by the door, *I* knew because he was farther from the heat and smell of the place, and he was saying, to an angry, obstinate, tiny old woman, who stood in the middle of her floor as if she was in front of the firing squad, "I won't go into hospital, I won't, you can't make me," "Then I won't come in to look after you, you can't make me do that." He was shouting. When he saw me, he said, in a different voice, relieved, desperate, "Tell her, if you're a friend, she should be in hospital."

She was looking at me quite terrified.

"Mrs Fowler," I said, "why don't you want to go into hospital?"

She turned her back on us both, and picked up the poker, and jabbed the flames with it.

The doctor looked at me, scarlet with anger and the heat of the place, and then shrugged. "You ought to be in a Home," he said. "I keep telling you so."

"You can't force me."

He exclaimed angrily and went into the passage, summoning me to follow. "Tell her," he said.

"I think she should be in hospital," I said, "but why should she be in a Home?"

He was quite at the end of his tether with exasperation and—I could see—tiredness. "Look at it all," he said. "Look at it. Well, I'll ring up the Services." And off he went.

When I got back, she said, "I suppose you've been arranging with him."

I told her exactly what I said, and while I was speaking she was coughing, mouth closed, chest heaving, eyes watering, and was thumping her chest with the heel of her fist. I could see that she didn't want to listen to what I said.

*   *   *

Thursday.

Went in on my way to work. She was up, dressed, in front of the fire, face glittering with fever. Her cat was yowling, unfed.

I took out her commode, full of strong stinking urine, and emptied it. I gave the cat food on a clean dish. I made her tea and some toast. She sat with her face averted from me, ashamed and sick.

"You should have a telephone," I said. "It's ridiculous, having no telephone. I could ring you from the office."

She did not answer.

I went off to work. There was no social thing I had to do today, no luncheon, etc., and the photographers' session was cancelled—the trains are on strike. I said to Joyce I'd work at home, and she said she'd stay in the office, it was all right. She let me understand home is difficult for her at the moment: her husband wants a divorce, she does not know what to do, she is seeing lawyers. But she is pleased to be in the office, though in better times she does a lot of work at home too.

I went in to Maudie on my way home, and found there Hermione Whitfield, from what she refers to as "Geriatrics".

We understood each other at first glance: being alike, same style, same clothes, same *image*. She was sitting in the chair opposite Maudie, who was bundled up in all her black. She was leaning forward, smiling, charming, humorous.

" But, Mrs Fowler, there are so many things we could do for you, and you won't co- . . ." But she dropped "co-operate" in favour of " . . . let us."

"And who are you?" she asked me, in the same charming, almost playful style, but heard it herself, and said, in the chummy democratic mode of our kind (but I had not thought at all about these distinctions till today), "Are you a Good Neighbour? No one told *me* anything about *that.*"

"No," I said, "I am not a Good Neighbour, I am Mrs Fowler's friend."

This was quite outrageous, from about ten different viewpoints, but most of all because I was not saying it in inverted commas, and it was only then that I thought how one did not have *friends* with the working classes. I could be many things to Mrs Fowler, including a Good Neighbour, but not a friend.

She sat there, blinking up at me, the firelight on her hair. Masses of soft golden hair, all waves and little ringlets. I know what all that careful disorder costs. Her soft pink face, with wide blue eyes, done up with grey and blue paints and powders. Her white fluffy sweater, her grey suede trousers, her dark blue suede boots, her ... I was thinking, either "the welfare" get paid more than I had believed or she has a private income. It occurred to me, standing there, in that long moment of pure discordance, for what I had said did not fit, could not be taken easily, that I was examining her like a fashion editress, and for all I knew she might be quite different from her "image".

Meanwhile, she had been thinking. "Mrs Fowler," said she, getting up, smiling prettily, radiating helpfulness and light, "very well, you won't go into hospital. I don't like hospital myself. But I can get a nurse in to you every morning, and I can send in a Home Help and ..."

"I don't want any of those," said Maudie, her face averted, poking savagely at the flames.

"Well, remember what there is available for you," she said, and gave me a look which meant I should follow her.

I was then in a position where I had to talk about Maudie behind her back, or say to Hermione, "No, we will talk here." I was weak, and followed Hermione.

"My name is ..." etc., and so forth, giving me all her credentials, and she waited for mine.

"My name is Janna Somers," I said.

"You are perhaps a neighbour?" she said, annoyed.

"I have become fond of Mrs Fowler," I said; and at last this was right, it enabled her to let out an involuntary sigh of relief, because the categories were back in place.

"Oh yes," she cried, "I do so agree, some of these old things, they are so lovable, so ..." But her face was saying that Maudie is far from lovable, rather a cantankerous old nuisance.

We were standing in that awful passage, with its greasy yellow walls where coal dust lay in films, the smell of cat from the coal cellar, the cracked and shaky door to the outer world. She already had her hand on the doorknob.

"I drop in sometimes to Mrs Fowler," I said, "and I do what I can." I said it like this so she would understand I would not be relied upon to do her work for her.

She sighed again. "Well, luckily, she has to be rehoused soon."

"What! She doesn't know that!" I recognized my voice had the panic in it Maudie would feel, if she had heard.

"Of course she knows. This place has been scheduled for years."

"But it belongs to some Greek or other."

"Oh no, it can't do!" she began decisively, and then I saw her rethink. Under her arm she had a file stuffed full. She hung her handbag on the doorknob, pulled out the file, opened it. A list of houses for demolition or reconstruction.

I already knew that she had made a mistake, and I wondered if she was going to admit it, or cover up. If she admitted it, I would give her full marks—for this was a contest between two professionals. We were in competition, not for Mrs Fowler—poor Maudie—but for who had authority. Although I had specifically repudiated authority.

A biro between her pretty lips, she frowned over the papers spread on her lifted knee while she stood on one leg.

'Well, I'll have to look into it," she said. And I knew that it would all be allowed to slide away. Oh, how well I know that look of hers, when someone has inwardly decided not to do anything while presenting an appearance of confident competence!

She was about to go out.

I said, "If I could persuade her, what Services is she entitled to?"

"Home Help, of course. But we tried that before, and it didn't work. A Good Neighbour, but she didn't want one . . ." She gave me a quick doubtful look, and went on. "She's not entitled to Meals on Wheels, because she can manage and we are so pressed . . ."

"She's over ninety," I said.

"So are many others!"

"But you'll arrange for the nurse to come in?"

"But she says she doesn't want one. We can't force ourselves on them. They have to co-operate!" This triumphantly, she had scored a point.

She bounded up the steps and into a red Escort, and waved to me as she went off. Pleased to be rid of me. A bright smile, and her body was saying, These amateurs, what a nuisance!

I went remorsefully back to Maudie, because she had been discussed behind her back. She sat with her face averted and was silent.

At last: "What have you decided, then?"

"Mrs Fowler, I do think you ought to have some of the Services, why not?"

Her head was trembling, and her face would have done for The Wicked Witch.

"What I want is Meals on Wheels, but they won't give me that."

"No Home Help?"

"No. They sent me one. She said, Where's your Hoover! Too good for a carpet sweeper. And sat here drinking my tea and eating my biscuits. And when I sent her shopping, she couldn't be bothered to take an extra step to save a penny, she'd pay anything, I could shop cheaper than she, so I told her not to come back."

"Well, anyway . . ." And I heard there was a different note in my voice. For I had been quite ashamed, watching Hermione, seeing myself, all that pretty flattering charm, as if she had—I had!—an eye directed at the performance: how well I am doing it! How attractive and kind I am. . . . I was fighting to keep that note out of my voice, to be direct and simple. "Anyway, I think you should think about taking what is available. And to start with, there's the nurse every morning, while you don't feel well."

"Why should I need a nurse?" she inquired, her face averted.

This meant, Why, when you are coming in to me twice a day? And, too, But why should you come in, it's not your job. And, most strongly, *Please, please.*

If I were with someone like Hermione, my husband, Joyce, Sister Georgie, I would say, "What an emotional blackmailer, you aren't going to get away with *that.*" The fine nose of our kind for advantage, taken or given.

By the time I left I had promised I would continue to go in morning and evening. And that I would ring up "them" saying she did not want a nurse. And when we said goodbye she was cold and angry, frantic because of her helplessness, because she knew she should not expect so much of me, and because . . .

And now I am sitting here, feeling quite wild myself, trapped is what I'm feeling. And I have been all evening in the bath, thinking.

About what I really care about. My life, my real life, is in the office, is at work. Because I have been working since I was nineteen, and always for the same magazine, I've taken it for granted, have not seen that this *is* my life. I was with the magazine in its old format, have been part of three changes, and the second of these I could say was partly because of me. Joyce and I made it all happen. I have been there longer than she has: for she came in as Production Manager, mid-sixties, when I had already been there fifteen or twenty years, working my way through all the departments. If there is one person in that magazine who can be said to *be Lilith*, it's me.

And yet I take it all for granted. And I am not going to jeopardize what I really care about for the sake of Maudie Fowler. I shall go to Munich, not for two days, as I said today, but for the usual four, and I shall tell her she must say yes to the nurse.

Friday—in Munich.

Went in to Maudie this morning. She in her chair, staring at a cold grate, inside a carapace of black rags. I fetched her coal, made her tea, fed the cat. She seemed to be cold, yet with the glitter of fever. She was coughing and coughing.

I said to her, "Mrs Fowler, I am going to Munich and I shall be away four days." No response at all. I said, "Mrs Fowler, I have to go. But I am going to ring up Hermione Whitfield and say you must have a nurse. Just till I come back." She went on staring into the cold grate. So I began to lay the fire—but did not know how, and she forced herself up out of her warm nest and slowly, slowly put in bits of paper, bits of wood, a fire-lighter, built up the fire. I looked around—no newspaper, no more fire-lighters, nothing.

I went out to the shop, and on the way back saw that there was a skip in the road outside her door, and there were plenty of little slats of wood, old laths from the demolished walls—she had been collecting these to start her fire. Conscious of how I must look, in all my smart gear, I filled a carrier bag with these bits of wood. While I was doing this, I chanced to glance up and saw that I was being observed from various windows. Old faces, old ladies. But I did not have time to take anything in, but rushed down with the wood and the groceries. She was again in her listless pose in front of the now roaring fire.

I did not know whether a nurse would build a fire.

I asked, "Will a nurse make up a fire for you?"

She did not answer. I was getting angry. And was as distressed as she. The whole situation was absurd. And yet it could not be any other way.

When I stood up to leave I said, "I am going to ring up and ask for a nurse and *please* don't send the nurse away."

"I don't want any nurse."

I stood there, worried because I was late, and it was Conference day and I've never ever been late. And worried about her. And angry. And resentful. And yet she tugged at me, I wanted to take that dirty old bundle into my arms and hug her. I wanted to slap her and shake her.

"What is all this about hospital," I asked, "what? You'd think you were being threatened with . . . what is so terrible about it? Have you ever been there?"

"Yes, two winters ago. Christmas."

"And?"

She was sitting straight up now, her sharp chin lifted in a combative way, her eyes frightened and angry.

"No, they were kind enough. But I don't like it. They fill you with pills and pills and pills, you feel as if your mind has been taken from you, they treat you like a child. I don't want it . . ." And then she added, in the tone of one trying to be fair, and at this attempt leading her into more, more than she had intended. " . . . There was one little nurse. She rubbed my back for me when I coughed . . ." And she looked at me quickly, and away, and I knew she had wanted me to rub her back for her. It had not occurred to me! I do not know how!

"Well," I said, "no one is going to force you to hospital."

She said, "If they'd take me in after last time." And suddenly she was laughing and alert, her enjoying self.

"What did you do?" I said, pleased to be able to laugh with her.

"I walked out!" And she chuckled. "Yes, I had had enough. And I was constipated with all that good eating, because I am not saying they don't feed you, and I was feeling farther and farther from myself every minute with the pills. I said, Where are my clothes? They said, You can't go home in this weather, Mrs Fowler, you'll die of it. For there was snow. I said, You bring me my clothes or I'll walk out in your hospital nightdress. And so they brought them. They would not look at me or speak to me, they were so angry. I walked down into the hall and said to the porter, Call me a taxi. My bits of money had been stolen in the hospital ward. But I was going to tell the driver and ask him to bring me home for the love of God. If God is anyone they know these days. But there was a woman there in reception and she said, I'll take you, love. And brought me home. I think of her. I think of them who do me good, I do." And she gave me the most marvellous merry smile, her girl's smile.

"For all that, I have to go to Munich. I'll be away for four days, and you know very well you can't manage. I want to hear you say, in so many words, you don't want a nurse. I'm treating you seriously, not treating you like a child! If you say no nurse, I'll do no more. But I think you should let me. A nurse isn't going to be the end of the world."

"And how about all the pills then?"

"All right. But say it, you don't want me to ring a nurse." And I added, really desperate, "For God's sake, Maudie, have some sense." I realized I had called her by her Christian name, but she was not put out.

She shrugged. "I have no choice, I suppose."

I went over to her, bent down to kiss her, and she put out her cheek, and I kissed it.

I went off, waving from the door, I hope not a "charming" wave.

*   *   *

I was late for the Conference.

First time. This Conference is in my view what gives the mag its life. It was my idea. Later I'll write down an analysis, it would help me clear my thoughts, for I see they need clearing, about the office, work, everything. This afternoon I was alone: Joyce at home because she's going to be in the office all the time I'm in Germany. I was trying to get information about the Services. I have all the leaflets as dished out to the consumers, *Your Pension Rights* and that kind of stuff. No, I want to find out how it all really works. After a while I knew what I had to do. I have to find That One Person. If this is a law for our kind of work, then it probably is everywhere. (Maudie talks about there always being *the one person*, though she means it in a different sense.) Joyce and I use it all the time. Long ago, we discovered that if you want to make things work, you have to look for *The One Person* in a department or an office who is in fact running it, or who knows about it, or is—in some way or another—real. Well, Hermione is certainly not that. No. You have to have people like Hermione, if only because there aren't enough of the others: it's not that they don't do any work, or are useless, but they are peripheral. To find out how to get Maudie what she really needs, and what could help her, I can't use Hermione. But I rang her this afternoon—she was out— and left a message that Mrs Fowler will need a nurse for five days. And then something warned me, and I told my secretary to ring Hermione, and then Joyce's secretary too. She can't be left with no one, for four days.

Wednesday.

First, my state of mind *before* I went in to Maudie. I flew back from Munich midday, went straight to the office recharged, all systems go. I adore these trips. What I adore is my efficiency. I like making things work, knowing how to do it. I like them knowing me, giving me *my* room, remembering my tastes. Saw friends through weekend. Rather, "friends", work contacts, then Monday and Tuesday, the Fair. What I like is *being in control*. I am so full of energy, I eat exactly what I should, don't drink a mouthful too much, hardly sleep, rush around all day. I know exactly how to present myself, and how to use it. I saw myself, coming into the Show, Monday morning, sitting down, people smiling and greeting: and at the same time I was back fifteen years, seeing myself through *those* eyes, the way I saw, at thirty, the established women who had been doing it for years. I admired them, wished to be one of them, and while I examined them, minutely, every little detail, I was looking for what *they* overlooked, signs of processes that would lead to their being replaced by others, me among them. Of those women whom I examined then, one remains, though some still are in the field in other ways. I have spent four days wondering what is at work in me which will lead me to be thrown out, or to remain in the office at some less taxing job, while—who?—goes off on these trips. I cannot see what it is. Simply ageing? Nothing to do with it! That I will get bored with it all? I cannot believe that, yet.

When I got into the office Joyce was waiting for me so she could go home: without ever formally arranging it, we make sure one of us is always there. She looked tired. She said she had had a dreadful time since I left, with her husband, she'd tell me, but not now, and off she went. There was a message from Hermione Whitfield that she had not got my message about the nurse till Monday, and that then Mrs Fowler refused to let the nurse in. This brought me back with a bump to my London self. I have worked all afternoon, mostly on the telephone, and then the photographers for tomorrow. But I was thinking at the same time about Joyce. I have understood that this business with her husband means the end of our working together, or at any rate, a change. I am sure of it. This made me depressed and anxious, before I even left the office. Another thing I have understood in a way I didn't before: Joyce is my only real friend. I mean, *friend*. I have a relationship with her I've had with no one, ever. Certainly not Freddie.

I was coming straight home, because I was suddenly tired. But made the taxi put me off at Maudie Fowler's. I stood there knocking and banging on the door. Freezing. Not a sound. I got into a panic—was she dead?—and noted, not without interest, that one of my reactions was relief. At last, an agitation of the curtains at the window of her "front room", which she seems never to use. I waited. Nothing happened. I banged and banged, absolutely furious by then. I was ready to strangle her. Then the door opened inwards, sticking and scraping, and there she was, a tiny little bundle of black, with her white face sticking up out of it. And the *smell*. It is no good my telling myself I shouldn't care about such details. I care terribly. The smell . . . awful, a sour, sweet-sharp reek. But I could see she was only just able to stand there.

There was nothing "charming" about me, I was so angry.

"Why do you keep me out in the cold?" I said, and went in, past her, making her move aside. She then went on ahead of me down the passage, a hand on a wall to steady her.

In the back room, a heap of dead cinders in the grate. There was an electric fire, though; one bar, and it was making noises which meant it was unsafe. The place was cold, dirty, smelly, and the cat came and wound itself around my legs miaowing. Maudie let herself slide into her chair and sat staring at the grate.

"Well, why didn't you let the nurse in?" I shouted at her.

"The nurse," she said bitterly. "What nurse?"

"I know she came."

"Not till Monday. All the weekend I was here by myself, no one."

I was about to scream at her, "Why didn't you let her in when she came on Monday?" but saw there was no point.

I was full of energy again—anger.

"Maudie," I said, "you are the limit, the end, you make things worse for yourself. Well, I'll put the kettle on."

I did. I fetched coal. I found the commode full of urine, but no worse, thank goodness. Thank goodness was what I thought then, but I see one gets used to anything. I then went out into the street with a carrier bag. A grey sleety rain. There I was, in all my smart things from Munich, scrabbling about in the skip for bits of wood. And again, faces at the windows, watching me.

Inside, I scraped out the grate, clouds of dust flying about, and laid the fire. With a fire-lighter. Wood and coal. Soon it was burning.

I made tea for both of us, having scalded the *filthy* cups. I must stop being so petty about it. Does it matter, dirty cups? Yes! Yes, yes, yes, *yes*.

She had not moved, but sat looking at the flames.

"The cat," she said.

"I've given her some food."

"Then let her out for a bit."

"There's sleet and rain."

"She won't mind."

I opened the back door. A wave of cold rain came straight in at me, and the fat yellow cat, who had been pressing to get to the door, miaowed and ran back again, to the coal cellar.

"She's gone to the coal cellar," I said.

"Then I suppose I'll have to put my hand in it," she said.

This made me so angry! I was a seethe of emotions. As usual, I wanted to hit her or shake her and, as usual, to put my arms around her.

But my mind luckily was in control, and I did everything I should, without, thank God, being "humorous" or charming or gracious.

"Have you been eating at all?"

No response.

I went out again to shop. Not a soul in the corner shop. The Indian sitting there at the cash desk looked grey and chilled, as well he might, poor soul.

I said I was buying food for Mrs Fowler, wanting to know if she had been in.

He said, "Oh, the old lady, I hope she is not ill?"

"She is," I said.

"Why doesn't she go into a Home?"

"She doesn't want to."

"Hasn't she a family?"

"I think so, but they don't care."

"It is a terrible thing," he said to me, meaning me to understand that his people would not neglect an old woman like this.

"Yes, it is a terrible thing, and you are right," I said.

When I got back, again I thought of death. She sat there, eyes closed, and so still, I thought not breathing.

But then, her blue eyes were open and she was looking at the fire.

"Drink your tea," I said. "And I'll grill you a bit of fish. Can you eat it?"

"Yes, I will."

In the kitchen I tried to find anything that wasn't greasy, and gave up. I put the fish on the grill, and opened the door briefly to get in some clean air. Sleet notwithstanding.

I took her the fish, and she sat herself up and ate it all, slowly, and her hands trembled, but she finished it and I saw she had been hungry.

I said, "I've been in Munich. To see all the clothes for the autumn. I've been seeing all the new styles."

"I've never been out of England."

"Well, I'll tell you all about it when you are a bit better."

To this she did not respond. But at last, just when I thought I would go, she remarked, "I've a need for some clean clothes."

I did not know how to interpret this. I did see—I have become sensitive enough for that—at least that this was not at all a simple request.

She wanted me to buy her clothes?

I looked at her. She made herself look at me, and said, "Next door, you'll find things."

"What?"

She gave a trembling, discouraged sort of shrug.

"Vest. Knickers. Petticoat. Don't you wear underclothes, that you are asking?"

Again, the automatic anger, as if a button had been pushed. I went next door into the room I knew she didn't like me in.

The bed that has the good eiderdown, the wardrobe, the dressing table with little china trinkets, the good bookcases. But everywhere piles and heaps of—rubbish. I could not believe it. Newspapers dating back fifty years, crumbling away; awful scraps of material, stained and yellow, bits of lace, dirty handkerchiefs, shreds of ribbon—I've never seen anything like it. She had never thrown anything away, I think. In the drawers, disorder, and they were crammed with—but it would take pages to describe. I wished I had the photographer there—reflex thought! Petticoats, camisoles, knickers, stays, vests, old dresses or bits of them, blouses . . . and nothing less than twenty years old, and some of them going back to World War One. The difference between clothes now and then: these were all "real" materials, cottons, silks, woollens. Not a man-made fibre there. But everything torn, or stained, or dirty. I pulled out bundles of things, and every one I examined, first for interest, and then to see if there was anything wearable, or clean. I found at last a wool vest, and long wool drawers, and a rather nice pink silk petticoat, and then a woollen dress, blue, and a cardigan. They were clean, or nearly. I worked away in there, shivering with cold, and thinking of how I had loved myself all these last days, how much I do love myself, for being in control, on top; and thought that the nearest I could get to poor Maudie's helplessness was remembering what it had been like to be a child, hoping that you won't wet your pants before you get to the lavatory.

I took the clothes into the other room, which was very hot now, the flames roaring up. I said to her, "Do you want me to help you change?" The sideways, irritable movement of the head, which I knew now meant I was being stupid.

But I did not know why.

So I sat down opposite her, and said, "I'll finish my tea before it's freezing." I noted that I was drinking it without feeling sick: I have become used to drinking out of grimy cups, I noted that with interest. Once Maudie had been like me, perpetually washing herself, washing cups, plates, dusting, washing her hair.

She was talking, at random I thought, about when she had been in hospital. I half listened, wishing that doctors and nurses could hear how their hospitals are experienced by someone like Maudie. Prisons. Reformatories. But then I realized she was telling me about how, because she had not been well enough to be put in the bath, two nurses had washed her in her bed, and I understood.

"I'll put on the kettles," I said. "And you must tell me what to do."

I put on two kettles, found an enamel basin, which I examined with interest, for I have not seen any but plastic ones for a long time, and searched for soap and a flannel. They were in a hole in the wall above the sink: a brick taken out and the cavity painted.

I took the basin, kettles, soap, flannel, a jug of cold water, next door. Maudie was struggling out of her top layer of clothes. I helped her, and realized I had not co-ordinated this at all. I rushed about, found newspapers, cleared the table, spread thick papers all over it, arranged basin, kettles, jug, washing things. No towel. I rushed into the kitchen, found a damp dirty towel, rushed into the front room and scrabbled about, seeming to myself to be taking all day. But it was really only a few moments. I was bothered about Maudie standing there, half naked, and ill, and coughing. At last I found a cleanish towel. She was standing by the basin, her top half nude. There is nothing of her. A fragile rib cage under creased yellow skin, her shoulder bones like a skeleton's, and at the end of thin stick arms, strong working hands. Long thin breasts hanging down.

She was clumsily rubbing soap on to the flannel, which, needless to say, was slimy. I should have washed it out first. I ran next door again, tore a bit off an old clean towel and took it back. I knew she wanted to tick me off for tearing the towel; she would have done if she had not been saving her breath.

I slowly washed her top half, in plenty of soap and hot water, but the grime on her neck was thick, and to get that off would have meant rubbing at it, and it was too much. She was trembling with weakness. I was comparing this frail old body with my mother's: but I had only caught glimpses of her sick body. She had washed herself—and only now was I wondering at what cost—till she went into hospital. And when Georgie came, she gave her a wash. But not her child-daughter, not me. Now I washed Maudie Fowler, and thought of Freddie, how his bones had seemed to sort of flatten and go thin under flesh that clung to them. Maudie might be only skin and bones but her body doesn't have that beaten-down look, as if the flesh is sinking into the bones. She was chilly, she was sick, she was weak—but I could feel the vitality beating there: life. How strong it is, life. I had never thought that before, never felt life in that way, as I did then, washing Maudie Fowler, a fierce angry old woman. Oh, how angry: it occurred to me that all her vitality is in her anger, I must not, must *not* resent it or want to hit back.

Then there was the problem of her lower half, and I was waiting for guidance.

I slipped the "clean" vest on over her head, and wrapped the "clean" cardigan round her, and then saw she was sliding down the thick bunches of skirt. And then it hit me, the stench. Oh, it is no good, I *can't* not care. Because she had been too weak or too tired to move, she had shat her pants, shat everything.

Knickers, filthy . . . Well, I am not going on, not even to let off steam, it makes me feel sick. But I was looking at the vest and petticoats she had taken off, and they were brown and yellow with shit. Anyway. She stood there, her bottom half naked. I slid newspapers under her, so she was standing on thick wads of them. I washed and washed her, all her lower half. She had her big hands down on the table for support. When it came to her bottom she thrust it out, as a child might, and I washed all of it, creases too. Then I threw away all that water, refilled the basin, quickly put the kettles on again. I washed her private parts, and thought about that phrase for the first time: for she was suffering most terribly because this stranger was invading her privateness. And I did all her legs again, again, since the dirt had run down her legs. And I made her stand in the basin and washed her feet, yellow gnarled old feet. The water was hot again over the flaring gas, and I helped her pull on the "clean" bloomers. By then, having seen what was possible, they were clean to me, being just a bit dusty. And then the nice pink petticoat.

"Your face," I said. For we had not done that. "How about your hair?" The white wisps and strands lay over the yellow dirty scalp.

"It will wait," she said.

So I washed her face, carefully, on a clean bit torn off the old towel.

Then I asked her to sit down, found some scissors, cut the toenails, which was just like cutting through horn, got clean stockings on, her dress, her jersey. And as she was about to put on the outside clothes of black again, I said involuntarily,

"Oh, don't—" and was sorry, for she was hurt, she trembled even more, and sat silent, like a bad child. She was worn out.

I threw out the dirty water and scalded the basin, and filled a kettle to make fresh tea. I took a look out of the back: streams of sleet, with crumbs of greyish snow, the wind blowing hard—water was coming in under the kitchen door; and as for thinking of her going out into that to reach the lavatory, that freezing box—yet she *had* been going out, and presumably would again.

I kept saying to myself, She is over ninety and she has been living like this for years: she has survived it!

I took her more tea, and some biscuits, and left her drinking them by her big fire.

I put all the filthy outer clothes I had taken off in newspaper and folded them up and dumped them in the rubbish bin, without asking her.

And then I made a selection among the clothes from the drawers, and stripped the filthy sheets from her bed, and the pillowcases, and went out into the rain to the launderette, leaving them with the girl there to be done.

I made the place as neat as I could, put down food for the cat, who sat against Maudie's leg, being stroked. I cleared everything up. All this time Maudie sat staring into the flames, not looking at me when I looked at her, but watching me as I moved around, and when she thought I didn't know.

"Don't think I don't appreciate it," she said as I laboured on, and on. I was sweeping the floor by then, with a hand brush and pan. I couldn't find anything else. The way she said this, I couldn't interpret it. It was flat. I thought, even hopeless: she was feeling perhaps, as I had had a glimpse of, remembering myself as a child, helpless in a new way. For, very clearly, no one had ever done this kind of thing for her before.

I went back to the launderette. The Irish girl, a large competent girl with whom I had exchanged the brisk comradeship of equals when leaving the stuff, gave me the great bag of clean things and looked into my face and said, "Filth. I've never seen anything like it. Filth." She hated me.

I said, "Thanks," did not bother to explain, and left. But I was flaming with—embarrassment! Oh, how dependent I am on being admired, liked, appreciated.

I took the things back, through the sleet. I was cold and tired by then. I wanted to get home . . .

But I cleared out the drawers of a large chest, put the clean things in, and told Maudie where I had put them.

Then I said, "I'll drop in tomorrow evening."

I was curious to hear what she'd say.

"I'll see you then" was what she said.

And now I am alone, and have bathed, but it was a brisk businesslike bath, I didn't soak for hours. I should have tidied everything, but I haven't. I am, simply, tired. I cannot believe that this time yesterday I was in the hotel, pampered guest, eating supper with Karl, cherished colleague. Flowers, venison, wine, cream—the lot.

It seems to me impossible that there should be *that*—there; and then Maudie Fowler, *here*. Or is it *I* who am impossible? I certainly am disoriented.

I have to think all this out. What am I to do? Who can I discuss it with? Joyce is my friend, she is my friend. She *is* my friend?

Thursday.

Joyce came in to collect work to take home. She looks awful. I said to her, "How goes it?" She said, "He wants me to go with him to the States." I asked, "For good?" She said, "For good." She looked at me, I looked at her. This is how we converse: in shorthand. She said, "I've got to fly. Tell John I've got the cover finished. I've done the Notes. I'll be in all tomorrow, Janna." And off she went. This means: her husband has been offered a professorship, he wants to take it, he wants her to give up her job here and go with him, she doesn't want to go, they quarrelled to the point of divorce, the children don't want to go to the States—and this afternoon I had the feeling that Joyce would probably go to the States. And that's the end of that.

I went in to Maudie on the way home: her door was on the latch. Fire blazing. Cat on bed asleep. Maudie, asleep. An empty teacup on the arm of her chair. I took the cup to safety, left a note: See you tomorrow, and fled hoping she wouldn't wake before I left.

I am sitting here in my dressing gown by the electric fire. I should clean out this flat. I should really wash my hair.

I am thinking of how Maudie Fowler one day could not trouble herself to clean out her front room, because there was so much junk in it, and then she left it and left it; going in sometimes, thinking, well, it's not so bad. Meanwhile she was keeping the back room and the kitchen spotless. Even now she does her own chimney once a week, and then scrubs the grate, brushes up the dust and cinders—though less and less thoroughly. She wasn't feeling well, and didn't bother, once, twice—and then her room was not really cleaned, only the floor in the middle of the room sometimes, and she learned not to look around the edges or under the bed. Her kitchen was last. She scrubbed it and washed shelves, but then things began to slide. But through it all she washed herself, standing at the kitchen table, heating water in the kettles. And she kept her hair clean. She went sometimes to the public bath-houses, for she had told me she liked going there. Then she left longer and longer between washing her hair . . . and then she did not wash her clothes, only took out the cleanest ones there were, putting them back grubby, till they were the cleanest; and so it went on. And at last, she was upright in her thick shell of black, her knickers not entirely clean, but not so bad, her neck dirty, but she did not think about it, her scalp unwashed. When they took her to hospital, they washed her all over and washed her hair too. She sometimes thought humorously, when they cart me off back to hospital, I'll get another proper wash! But she, Maudie Fowler, was still there, alert, very much all there, on guard inside that old witch's appearance. *She* is still there, and everything has collapsed around her, it's too difficult, too much.

And I, Janna, am sitting here, in my clean, scented dressing gown, just out of my bath. I should do my nails again, though. I should clean my flat, or ask someone in to clean it. I was in my bath for only a few minutes tonight.

By this time next year my whole life will have changed. I know it, though I don't know how.

I shall go down and visit Georgie next weekend. *If I dare leave Maudie.* It is ridiculous. *Where is that one person?*

Friday.
I went in on my way to work. She was better. Had been out to shop for herself. She looked quite nice and fresh—so I see her now, I no longer *see* the old witch. I said I was going to visit my sister Georgie. She laughed at the name. She said, "One of these days I'll visit my sister, I expect." I already knew what that meant, and I said, "I'll take you, Maudie." "Janna and Georgie," she said. "My sister and I, we were Maudie and Polly, and when we went out dressed up in our white coats and little hats, we were a picture." I said, "Georgie and I were a picture too, I expect. I remember pink dresses and berets. I'll see you Sunday night when I come back." "If you have the time," she said. I noted that I could have given her a nice sharp slap, but laughed and said, "I'll see you."

Sunday Night.
The train was very late. Did not go in to Maudie. Now it is midnight. I have done the usual Sunday-night things, seeing my clothes are ready for the week, hair, make-up, nails.

Well, it has been a painful weekend. When I got there Georgie was alone, because Tom and the children had gone off on some visit. Was very pleased, can't stand those brats of hers. Tom is all right, but a married couple is a married couple. I wanted to talk to Georgie. My thought was, specifically: now I am grown up, perhaps she will take me seriously? For years I used to go down, when I *did* go down, rather princessing it. Good old Georgie and good old Tom. She has never bothered about her clothes and things much. I used to wear my most outrageous clothes and take copies of the mag and enjoyed telling her about my life and times. She listened in her way of no-comment. Clever little sister Janna. Correction, Jane. She wasn't going to call me Janna, Jane it was and Jane it will be, to the end. How many times I have said to her, Georgie, no one calls me Jane, no one, I want to be Janna. I can't remember to, says she, making a point, and that's that. She thinks Janna is a smart little name to go with a smart little job. I used to sit through those weekends, when I did go, wondering how she stuck it, but of course she was thinking the same of me. It is not that she despises me, exactly, though she certainly thinks what I do pretty peripheral, it is that she cannot imagine any sane person doing it.

When I went into the house I was very alert to everything, the way I am at the moment—contrasts. Because of Maudie Fowler. Georgie's house is exactly the house my parents lived in always. I call it country-suburban, comfortable, conventional, conservative, all of a piece from the landscapes on the walls to the books on the bed table. My flat is, Freddie's and mine was, both international-contemporary. On the rare occasions Georgie has stayed a night, she has made a point of saying she has *enjoyed* my things. They are such fun, says she.

Georgie had a cold supper for us and seemed at a loss what to do after it. We were in her living room, curtains drawn, some snow outside, not enough for my taste but more than she wanted. She says it makes work. She works hard, Georgie does, the house, the cooking, looks after husband, four children, chairwoman of this, patron of that, secretary of the local reading circle, good works. I sat one side of the fire, she on the other. I tried to talk about Mother. I need to know about her. I never talked to her, a bit more to Father. But Georgie has put me into the category of the irresponsible one who doesn't care about family. And that's that. I kept giving her openings, even asked once, I wonder what Mother would have thought?

At last I talked about my trip to Munich. She liked that. Your glamorous goings-on, she calls all that. She wanted to know how the hotel was, my friends, how the fashion shows are organized, how this is done and that is done. I recognize myself in all this. Not a word about the styles and the fashions, but *how it all works*. So we are like each other after all. Suddenly, when I was in bed, I had a thought that made me sit up again and turn on the light. It was this. Before Granny died, she was ill for about two or three years, can't remember (which is a point in itself), and she was at home with Mother, who was looking after her. I was working like a demon then, it was the first rebirth of the mag, and I simply behaved as if Granny being ill had nothing to do with me. Not my affair! I can remember switching off from the moment I heard the news. But Mother had her at home there, and Father wasn't too well either. Granny had diabetes, heart trouble, bad eyes with operations for cataract, kidney trouble. I used to hear news of all this, relayed in Mother's brisk letters: and I haven't kept the letters, and I remember not wanting to read them. *Now* I know what it costs, looking after the very old, the helpless. I find myself exhausted after an hour or two, and want only to run away somewhere out of it. But where did Mother run to? Who helped her? Not me! Not once, I never went near her.

Sunday morning, Georgie and I had breakfast alone together. Some snow outside. Pretty. Trees and bushes full of snow and birds feeding off stuff Georgie hangs in the branches. She said Tom was coming back with the kids, because the weather was frightful where they were. I said to her, quite desperate because I knew once they had got back, that was that, "Georgie, were you around much when Granny was dying?"

She gave me a surprised look at this. She said, "No, I didn't get home much. I was pregnant twice while that was going on, and Kate was a baby." She was now looking at me in an impatient sort of way.

"I want to know about it," I said. "I have been thinking that I did nothing to help."

She said finally, "No, you didn't," and she wouldn't have said another word. I had to digest that she and Tom had attitudes about me, *my* behaviour, that were established and set, Jane was this and that and the other; and probably these were Mother's attitudes too, and Father's.

I said, "It has only recently occurred to me that I never lifted a finger all the time Granny was dying."

"No, you didn't," she said, in that same shutting-you-out way.

"Well," I said, "recently I've had a little to do with an old person, and I know now what Mother had to cope with."

"I suppose better late than never," said Sister Georgie.

This was much worse than I had expected. I mean, what she thought of me was so much worse that I was burning with—

no, alas, not shame, but it was embarrassment. Not wanting to be so badly thought of. I said to her, "Can you tell me anything about it?"

"Well, what on earth do you want to know?" She was exasperated. Exactly as if some small child had said to her, she having hit her thumb with a hammer, Does it hurt?

"Look, Georgie," I said, "all right, I've seen recently that . . . I could have done more than I did. All right? Do you want me to grovel? It *is* better late than never. I want to know more about Mother."

"She was in *your* flat for two years before she died," said Sister Georgie, making a great amazed incredulous astonishment out of it.

"Yes, I know. But it was since then that I . . ."

Georgie said, "Look, Jane, I'm sorry but . . . you just turn up here after all that, and say, I'd like a nice little chat about Mother. Jane, it simply isn't *on*," she said. She was literally inarticulate with anger. And I, with surprise. I realized that there were years of resentment here, criticism of little sister Jane.

I made a last try. "Georgie," I said, "I am sorry. I am sorry I didn't help Mother with Granny, and I want very much to discuss it all."

"I suppose one of these weekends I'll get a telephone call, when you've got nothing better to do, and you'll turn up, all fine and fancy free, not a hair out of place, and you'll say, Oh, Georgie, I was wondering what was it like having Mother here for ten years, with four kids, no help, and she becoming an invalid . . ."

At which point the telephone rang outside and she went to answer it. I sat there, I was numb. That was the word. Not that I hadn't felt bad about Mother living with Georgie all that time, for after all I was working, and we did only have a small flat, Freddie and I, and . . . and . . . and. But it had never occurred to me that Georgie was not going to talk to me this weekend. If ever. She was too angry. She was, and she is, so angry and bitter about me.

When she came back, she said, "I'm going down to the station to get Tom and the kids." She said to me, "I'm sorry

Jane, but if you are beginning to get some sort of sense of responsibility into you at last, it might perhaps occur to you that it isn't easy to have you just turning up with a light question or two: *How about Granny dying? How was it? Did it hurt?* It was all awful, Jane. *Do you understand?* It was dreadful. I went down there when I could, pregnant as hell or with the baby, and found Mother coping. Granny was bed-ridden at the end. For *months.* Can you imagine? No, I bet you can't. Doctors all the time. In and out of hospital. Mother was doing it all. Father couldn't help much, he was an invalid himself . . . Anyway, I've got to go to the station."

And off she went.

I nearly ran after her, to ask to be put on a train home, but stuck it out. Tom and the kids filled the house with clatter and clang, the record players went on at once of course, a radio, the house vibrating with din. Tom came in and said, How are you?—and went. The kids banged into the kitchen, where I was, Jilly, Bob, Jasper, Kate. Hi, hi, hi, hi, all round. It is established that I think Georgie's kids are awful and spoiled brats, but they might be all right when they grow up. I am the glamorous Aunt from London and the High Life. I send them presents of money at Christmas. When we meet I tell them I think they are awful and good for nothing. They tell me it is because I don't understand them. It is a cheerful game of mutual insult. But I *do* think they are awful. I cannot under-stand how they are allowed to do as they like, have what they like, go where they like. I have never heard either Georgie or Tom say once, No, you can't have that. Never. The whole house is *crammed* with their possessions, clothes, toys, gear, mostly unused or used once or twice. I keep thinking of growing up during the war and having nothing. And recently I have been thinking about the Third World having nothing. Of course, Georgie would say it is *trendy* to have such thoughts, but, as she would say, Better late than never.

Anyway, I sat in the kitchen and listened to the sheer din of those kids all over the house, and Georgie came back and I could see she was ready to talk, if I wanted, but suddenly I found myself saying, "Georgie, you are ready enough with criticism of me, but look at those children of yours."

"Yes, I know what you think," she said, her back turned to me. And I knew at once that this was a sore point.

"Tell me," I said to her, "when have they ever done anything they didn't want to do? Have you and Tom ever tried to teach them that the world isn't a celestial milk bar with milk shakes and cream topping for ever there at the touch of a button?"

"You may well be right. I'm not saying you are not," said she, making it humorous, "and now I have to get the lunch. If you want to help, stay, and if not, go and talk to Tom."

I took her at her word, went to find Tom, but he did not want to talk to me, being busy at something. I found the decibel level in the house intolerable, pulled on my big boots and went for a walk in the snow, came back for lunch. As usual, the parents were like appendages to the scene of the four children, who did not let them finish a conversation if they had the temerity to start one, or talked across them at each other, and behaved exactly as if Georgie and Tom were useful servants they could treat as they liked.

How has it come about that this is what families are like now? In the living room, afternoon, this was the scene. Jilly, seventeen, nagging because she had wanted to visit a friend and couldn't for some reason, so she was sulking and making the whole family pay for it. Bob, sixteen, an over-fat good-looking boy, practising the guitar as if no one else existed. Jasper, fifteen, whining and nagging at his father to go with him to some local football match. Kate, thirteen, cheeks flaming, hair wild, tarting around the room in one of Georgie's dresses, in a sort of locked hysteria, the way teenage girls get. This was for my benefit, because she wants to come to London and "be a model". Poor girl! Tom was sitting in a corner trying to read, and answering questions from his offspring in an abstracted irritable voice, and Georgie was waiting on all of them, in perfect good humour and patience; shouting to make herself heard from time to time, Yes, all right, Kate. Yes, Jilly, I'll do it tomorrow. Yes, Jasper, it's under the spare-room bed. And so on.

I said at last, "Well, this wicked Aunt is about to leave. No, don't bother, I shall go to the station by myself."

With what relief did I turn my back on this scene of happy

contemporary family life and went out to the front door, followed by Georgie.

"Well," I said, "don't say it, I don't understand what children are, and I am not entitled to say a word, because of my selfish childishness, but all I can say is . . ."

"And you are probably right," she said, in exactly the same humorous self-denying voice she uses for the children.

I walked through the already slushy snow to the station, waited a little. I like stations, the anonymity, the freedom of being alone in a crowd. I like being alone. Period.

And here I am alone. I should go to Maudie.

I should, very soon, think all this out.

But what I do know is this. When people die, what we regret is, not having talked to them enough. I didn't talk to Granny, I don't know what she was like. I can hardly remember Grandpa. Ditto Mother. I don't know what she thought about anything, except that I am selfish and silly. (Which is what I think about Georgie's brats.) What did she think about Tom? Georgina? The grandchildren? What did it mean to her, having to nurse Granny, and her own husband, for—I am afraid it was probably four years. What was she like when she was young? I don't know. I shall never know now. And of course, there is Freddie: I lie awake sometimes, and what I want is, not that he should be there to make love to me, though I miss that dreadfully, I want to talk to him. Why didn't I talk to him while he was there?

I didn't want to, that is the answer. *I didn't want to know.*

Monday Night.

I woke this morning in a panic, heart pounding, eyes prickling, mouth dry. I said to myself, a bad dream, that's all; but it stayed. On the way to work, I realized it was because of Joyce probably going to the States. Apart from missing her, everything at work will change. I shall be offered the editorship, but that isn't the point.

As I walked through the secretaries' room, Phyllis looked sharply at me, then came after me and asked, Are you all right? Full marks for noticing. I knew of course that she knew I am anxious about Joyce leaving. But when I sat in a heap at my table, and Phyllis brought me black coffee and said if I liked she would do the photographers' session, I saw that she had thought it all out. She took a heap of files from my table, and I saw her look, long and cool, at Joyce's table, Joyce's place, and she was thinking, that will be mine.

And why not?

Because she isn't Joyce. I mean, specifically, that she is thirty years old, a hard, clever, noticing girl, but that she isn't—cooked. I know perfectly well I don't like her because she makes me think of how I was. But there's more than that. I ask myself, trying to be fair, never mind about what you need, has she got what *Lilith* needs?

I sat there in that office of ours, Joyce's and mine, and decided not to think about Phyllis, I can't cope with that yet. I was thinking about Joyce: what was it I had not seen in her that only a month ago I would have taken it for granted that she wouldn't go to America! But I've been judging her marriage by mine. Of course, she has children; but no, that isn't it. He's a nice enough man. I don't know him. Have never talked to him: we have a joking relationship.

I was wanting Joyce to come in early, but it was nearly lunchtime. She looked dreadful, ill, unkempt. She sat down, got up again to fetch herself coffee, came back with it, sat in a sprawl, lit cigarettes and let them go out, messed with her work, watered the plants on her windowsill, did everything but let herself look at me.

Then she buzzed, in came Phyllis, Joyce said, "I'm not happy about Wine, I've made the notes, please go and see our wine expert, what's-his-name. What *is* his name—and his address, where is it?"

"Don't worry," says Phyllis, "I know where it is."

She takes Joyce's notes, smiles nicely, and out she goes.

And now Joyce allows me a brief smile, a grimace really, and actually looks at me. We laugh.

We look together at Phyllis, through the door into the filing room. We are taking in her clothes, her hair, her make-up, her shoes. Habit. Then Joyce loses interest in her, goes back into her thoughts.

Phyllis hasn't got a style yet. Not as Joyce and I have. I sat there wondering if I could help Phyllis to a style, as Joyce helped me. It is only now as I sit writing this, I think how odd that I was analysing Phyllis and how she could look, when I was wild with misery about Joyce, wanting to say, For God's sake, *talk*. I knew she had made up her mind to leave, and she felt bad about me: I needed for us to *talk*.

Joyce is the only person I have talked to in my life. And yet for the most part we talk in smiles, silences, signals, music without words, 'nuff said.

At last I couldn't stand it, and said, "Joyce, I want to know why, you must see that."

She was half turned from me, her cheek on her hand. She made a leave-me-alone irritable gesture.

I sit here, one in the morning, writing it down. My mind is so clear and sharp, whirling with thoughts. I've just had a new thought, it is this: writing is my trade, I write all the time, notes to myself, memos, articles, and everything is to *present* ideas, etc., if not to myself, then to others. I do not let thoughts fly away, I note them down, I *present them*, I postulate the outside eye. And that is what I am doing now. I see that as I write this diary, I have in mind that observing eye. Does that mean I really intend to publish this? It certainly wasn't in my mind when I began writing it. It's a funny thing, this need to write things down, as if they have no existence until they are recorded. Presented. When I listen to Maudie talk, I have this feeling, quick, catch it, don't let it all vanish, record it. As if it is not valid until in print.

Oh, my thoughts are whirling through me, catch them . . .

I was sitting there with Joyce, both of us cold and sick, miserable, and I was examining us both, out of habit, as I had Phyllis. Two women editors, first-class women's magazine (read by a lot of men), late nineteen-seventies going on to the eighties.

When I read diaries from the past, what fascinates me is what they wore, what they ate, all the details. It isn't difficult to work out what people were likely to be thinking—not so different from us, *I* believe—but how did a woman make up her bed, or lay her table, or wash her underclothes; what did she have for breakfast, in 1780, in a middle-class household, in a provincial English town? What was a day in the life of a farmer's wife, north of England, on the date Waterloo was fought?

When Joyce came to work here she made us all conscious we were tatty! The mid-sixties—tat! And yet her style was, as she said, high-class gipsy, which looks messy easily. She is tall, thin, with a mass of black curls and waves, careful disorder, and a thin pale face. Or that is how her face looks, emerging from all that hair. Black eyes that are really small, but made up huge and dramatic. Her clothes cost the earth. Today she wore a black and rust striped skirt and waistcoat and a black silk sweater and her thick silver chain with amber lumps. Her jewellery is very good, never any oriental semi-rubbish of the kind I can afford to wear, because of *my* style. She is beautiful: but it is a young woman's style. She has kept her hair black. Soon she will have to change her style, to fit being not young.

I was still in mini-dresses, beads and gauds and frips, when Joyce took me in hand. Ever since, my style has been classical-expensive. I wear silk shirts and silk stockings, not nylon, and dresses that look at first glance as if I am not trying. I found a real dressmaker, who cares about every stitch, and I look for special buttons in markets, and handmade lace, and I get jerseys and jackets knitted for me. My style is that at first people don't notice, and then their eyes come back and they examine detail, detail, the stitching on a collar, a row of pearl buttons. I am not thin, but solid. My hair is straight, and always perfect, a silvery gold. Grey eyes, large by nature and made larger.

We couldn't be more different, Joyce and I, except in the trouble we take. But Joyce takes less than me because of her family.

Phyllis is a slight, strong girl, attractive. Fairish. She is always in the new fashion, and therefore there's nothing to remark. I've seen her watching Joyce and, rightly, discarding that style for herself. I've seen her observing me: *how does she do it?* I'll show her if she asks, take her to the dressmaker and the knitting woman, choose her hairdresser . . . that is what I was thinking as I sat there with Joyce, in all that misery: I was mentally abdicating, and expressing it through clothes, through a style!

Yet I have no conscious intention of giving up.

At lunchtime we drank coffee and smoked. Then she said, "I must go home," and I cried out, "*Joyce!*" She said, "Don't you see, I can't do it, I can't!" And I said, "Joyce, you cannot just go off home like that, I have to know."

She sighed, and sat down, made herself come together, and actually looked at me.

"Know?"

"Understand. I don't understand how you can give all this up . . . what for?"

She said, "Have you had the experience, suddenly finding out that you didn't know yourself?"

"Indeed I have!"

"I thought I would agree to a divorce easily."

"Has he got a girl?"

"Yes, the same one, you know. He would take her instead of me."

"All this time he has really been married to the two of you, then?"

"It amounts to that. He said to me at one stage, You have your job, I'm going to have Felicity."

I was sitting there being careful, because I didn't want her to fly off home, and I knew she could easily do that.

I was thinking what I call women's lib thoughts. *He* has a job as a matter of course, but when *she* does, he has to bolster himself up with a girl on the side. But I have got so bored with these thoughts, they aren't the point; they never were the point, not for me, not for Joyce. Phyllis is into women's lib, consciousness-raising, and she makes it clear that Joyce and I are unliberated. Joyce and I have discussed this, but not often—because it isn't the point! Once Joyce said to Phyllis, curious rather than combative, Phyllis, I hold down a very good, well-paid job. I have a husband and two children and I run my home and my family. Would you not say I am a liberated woman, then? *Isn't that enough?* And Phyllis smiled the smile of one who knows better and allowed: A step in the right direction. And afterwards Joyce and I laughed. We had one of those sudden fits of laughing, music without words, that are among the best things in this friendship of ours.

"If you don't go to the States, he'll take Felicity?"

"He will marry her."

"Is that what you mind?"

She shook her head. Again she was not looking at me. I was confused, didn't know what it was she feared, in facing me. At last she said, "You are such a self-sufficient one."

This was the last thing I expected—the child-wife, child-daughter—and I said, "*I*, self-sufficient?"

And she just shook her head, oh, it's all too much for me, and crouched holding on to the desk with both hands, looking in front of her, cigarette hanging from her lips. I saw her as an old crone, Mrs Fowler: fine sharp little face, nose and chin almost meeting. She looked ancient. Then she sighed again, pulled herself out, turned to me.

"I can't face being alone," she said, flat. "And that's all there is to it."

If I say my mind was in a whirl, that is how it was.

I wanted to say, But, *Joyce*—my husband died, it seems now overnight—what is it you are counting on? I could have said, Joyce, if you throw up this work and go with him, you might find yourself with nothing. I could have said . . . and I said nothing, because I was crying with a sort of amazed anger, at the impossibility of it, and worse than that, for I was thinking that I had not known Joyce at all! I would not have believed that she could say that, think it. More: I knew that I could not say to Joyce, Your attitude to death is stupid, wrong, you are like a child! It's not like that, what are you afraid of? Being alone—what's that!

For I had discovered that I had made a long journey away from Joyce, and in a short time. My husband had died, my mother had died: I had believed that I had not taken in these events, had armoured myself. And yet something had changed in me, quite profoundly. And there was Maudie Fowler, too.

It seemed to me, as I sat there, crying and trying to stop, biting on my (best-quality linen monogrammed) handkerchief, that Joyce was a child. Yes, she was a child, after all, and

I could say nothing to her of what I had learned and of what I now was. That was why I was crying.

"Don't," said Joyce. "I didn't mean to—open old wounds."

"You haven't. That's not it." But that was as near as I could come to *talking*. I mean by that, saying what was in my mind. For then we did talk, in a sensible dry sort of way, about all kinds of things, and it is not that I don't value that. For we had not, or not for a long time, talked in this way. The way women communicate—in becks and nods and hints and smiles—it is very good, it is pleasurable and enjoyable and one of the best things I've had. But when the chips are down, I couldn't say to Joyce why I had to cry.

She said, "You are different from me. I've been watching you and I can see that. But if he goes to the States, I'll be alone. I'll not marry again, I know that. And anyway, if you have been married to a man, you can't just throw him aside and take up another—*they* can do that . . ."

"Or think they can."

"Yes, or think they can, without penalties, I mean. And so I don't see myself marrying someone else. The kids, they don't want to go to the States, but if he went and I stayed, they'd commute and I know that pretty soon they'd be there rather than here, more opportunities, probably better for the young. I'd be alone. I don't know how to be alone, Jan."

And I could not say to her, Joyce, your husband is fifty-five, he's a workaholic . . .

"You are prepared to be a faculty wife?"

She grimaced at this. "I shan't get anything like this job, of course not. But I expect there'd be something."

As she left, she said, "No, and I haven't even finally made up my mind. I know how I'm going to miss all this—and you, Jan. But I have no choice." And with that she went out, *not* looking at me.

And that is what I was left with, the *I have no choice*. For I do not know what it is, in that marriage of hers—I would never have suspected—the existence of anything that would make it inevitable she would say, *I have no choice*.

Joyce has been the best editor this magazine has ever had. She has never put her home and family first . . . and yet . . . I see how, when she came in, the flexibility began that everyone welcomed: working at home from the telephone, working late or early when necessary. We all said, It's a woman's way of dealing with things, not office hours, but going along with what was necessary. And now I am thinking that what was *necessary* was Joyce's marriage, her home.

She would easily stay after work to eat supper with me, in the office, in a restaurant: working meals. And yet there were times when she had to be at home. I was what made all this possible: *I* have never said, No, I can't stay in the office late as usual, I have to get home. Or only when Freddie and I did our dinner parties. I've never ever said, This afternoon, I have to go early, Freddie will be in early. But it seems to me that something like that has been going on with Joyce: her marriage, her children, her work. She incorporated all of it, in a marvellous flexible way. "Can you hold the fort this afternoon, Jan?" In a sense, I've been part of her marriage, like that girl Felicity! These wholes we are part of, what *really* happens, how things really work . . . it is what has always fascinated me, what interests me most. And yet I have only just had the thought: that I have been, in a sense, part of Joyce's marriage.

Joyce *is* going to America. She will give up a wonderful job. Very few women ever get a job like this one. She will give up family, friends, home. Her children are nearly grown up. She will be in a country that she will have to learn to like, alone with a man who would have been happy to go with another, younger girl. *She has no choice.*

Well, women's lib, well, Phyllis, what do you have to say to that?

What, in your little manifestoes, your slamming of doors in men's faces, your rhetoric, have you *ever* said that touches this? As far as I am concerned, nothing. And, believe me, Phyllis makes sure that all the propaganda is always available to me, spread on my desk.

The reason why girls these days get themselves together in flocks and herds and shoals and shut out men altogether, or as much as they can, is because they are afraid of—whatever the power men have that makes Joyce say, I have no choice.

I can live alone and like it. But then, I was never really married.

After I reached home, the telephone: Joyce, her voice breathless and small. Because she had cried herself dry, I knew that.
She said, "Jan, we make our choices a long time before we
think we do! My God, but it's terrifying! Do you know what I
mean?"

"Yes," I said. "I know what you mean."

And I do. And it *is* terrifying. What choices have I already
made that I am not yet conscious of?

I have not been in to Maudie Fowler since Friday evening.

Tuesday.

Joyce not at work. Phyllis and I held the fort. After work I
went in to Maudie. She took a long time to answer the door,
stood looking at me for a long time, not smiling, not pleased; at
last stood aside so that I could come in, went ahead of me along
the passage, without a word. She sat down on her side of the
fire, which was blazing, and waited for me to speak.

I was already angry, thinking, well, and so she doesn't have a
telephone, is that my fault?

I said, "I did not get back on Sunday night until very late,
and last night I was tired."

"Tired, were you?" And then, "On Sunday evening I waited
for you. I had a bit of supper for us both."

I noted in myself the usual succession of emotions: the
trapped feeling, then a need to escape, then—of course—guilt.

"I am sorry, Maudie," I said.

She turned her head and stared at the fire, her mouth a little
open, and gasping.

"Have you been well?"

"Well enough."

I was thinking, look, I've washed you head to foot, of your
stinking shit, and now you . . . but I had to think, too, that I
made a promise and hadn't kept it. I must never do that again.

It took nearly an hour before she softened, got up to make us
tea. I had to stay another two hours. Before I left she was
talking freely again. A long story about her father's fancy-
woman, who, her mother "properly and safely" dead, had not
only made a skivvy of her, Maudie—"though I've told you all

about that, I know"—but then set about poisoning her.

"She poisoned my mother, I know she did, if no one else knew, and my Aunt Mary believed me. She said there was no point going to the police, they'd never take my word against my father, he was in with the police, he was always in with anyone who would do him good, he'd have the inspector in at Christmas for whisky and cake, and he and his fancy-woman'd send a cask of ale up to the boys at the station with a ham and pudding. If I went to them, just a girl, and terrified I was, and ill with it, and said, My father's woman poisoned my mother and now she's doing for me, it's arsenic—well, would they listen? My Aunt Mary said, Look, you leave home and come to me when you can do it without making trouble. I'm not facing that brother of mine in a fight, he's not one to cross, he's one to get his own back. But when it's the right time, you'll find a bed and a bite with me. Well, I got sicker and weaker. Months it went on. I tried not to eat at home, I'd go running to my sister, the one that died—no, I've not mentioned her, she makes me feel too bad. She was always the weakly one, she got on their nerves. She married at fifteen. She married against my father, and he said, Never darken my doors. Her man was no good and couldn't keep her. She had three little children, and my mother would send me with a pie or some bread, anything that wouldn't be missed, and I'd see her, so pale and weak, the children hungry. She'd take a little nibble, to keep her strength up, and then make her children eat the rest. My mother died, and then there was no food in that house at all. I went to my father and said, My sister's dying of lack of food and warmth. Said he, I told her not to marry him, and that was all he ever said. She died, and he didn't go to the funeral. The husband took the one child still alive, and I never heard more. Before she died, I'd be sitting with her, I'd be faint with hunger because I was afraid to eat at home, and she dying of hunger because there was no food, and we were company. It was an awful time, awful—I don't know why people say 'the good old days', they were bad days. Except for people like my father . . ." And Maudie went on and on about her father.

When I asked, "How about your other sister?" she said, "She'd married and gone, we did not hear of her much, she was keeping out of the way of Father, he didn't like her man either. Once I went to her and said, Polly, our sister Muriel is starving, and her children with her, and all she said was, Well, I've got nothing to spare for her. Yet her food safe was stuffed with joints and pies and custards.

"After Muriel died, I did not even have anywhere to go and sit, and I ate as little as I could because I knew there was poison in it. *She* would come up to my room—they'd put me up in the attic, just as if I was a servant—with milk and broth and say, Drink it, drink it, and I'd pour it into the slop pail and then creep down to empty the slop pail so she couldn't know. I could taste the poison in it, I knew there was poison. Sometimes I went to pick up the bread that people threw to the birds, but I was afraid of being seen. We were known, you see, we were well thought of, Father with his goings and comings and his carriage and his free ways, and *she* with her pub. I was the daughter at home, the people envied me for my easy time. Yet I was on a thin bed at the top of the house in an attic, not a whisper of heat, never a new dress, or anything of my own, only her old clothes to cut down, and afraid to eat. Well, one evening it all came to a head, for I was in bed, too weak and sick to get up, and she had a glass full of sugared milk, and she said, I'm going to stay here till you drink it. I don't want it, I said. I don't want it. But she said, I'm going to sit here.

"She had on a pink silk dressing gown with feathers that had grey velvet ruches around the neck, and high-heeled pink slippers. She had put on plenty of weight with all her liking for food and drink, and she was red in the face, and she was sighing and saying, Oh my God, the stairs, and Oh my God, it's cold up here. Yet she never thought that I had to climb up and down the stairs, nor that I had to live in that cold. And yet there were two empty bedrooms on the same floor they had theirs. Later my Aunt Mary said to me, Of course they didn't want you on that floor with them, they didn't want you to hear their goings-on. What goings-on? I said, for I didn't care about all that, I hated all that, I'm like my mother. I shut my mind to it. And besides, they weren't married: she had a husband in a hospital somewhere, so she couldn't marry my father. Now I look back and wonder at it all: people were strict in those days, and yet I don't remember her suffering for her living out of the marriage bond with my father. But I wouldn't have noticed: all I thought of was how not to eat in that house. That night, I had to drink the milk at last, though the taste in it sickened me. Then I pretended to sleep. And she went lumbering downstairs at last. I put my finger down my throat and brought up the milk. Then I put my other dress into my mother's little bag and I crept out of the house.

"I had no money, he never gave me any, ever, though I kept the house for him, cleaned it, did it all. I walked out to the village my auntie was in. It's part of London now, you'd not know it was a village so recently, it was beyond Neasden. I got there as the streets filled with carts and horses and noise. I was nearly falling as I walked. I got to her house and rang and rang and when she came she caught me as I fell. She said I could stay with her, and pay her back when I was well enough to earn. She wrote to my father that Maudie had come to stay with her for a little, that was how she put it. And my father said nothing at all, though I waited and waited for a sign. Not for years did he acknowledge my existence. And my aunt fed me up and made me eat. She was poor herself. She couldn't give me what she said I should have, cream and wine and stuff, but she did what she could. I was so thin and small I used to start shaking if I walked a few steps, but I got better, and then Auntie apprenticed me to a milliner in the West End. She got the money from my father. I don't know what she said, but she got it."

It was nearly ten before I got home. I was full of the strong black tea Maudie drinks and feeling a bit sick myself, and so I couldn't eat. Sympathy, no doubt with anorexia, for I suppose that was what poor Maudie was suffering from after her mother died. I have had a brief and efficient bath, and have finished writing this, and now I must go to bed. But I really wanted to write down the thoughts I have been having about the office.

I told Maudie that I would not be in tomorrow night, but that I would definitely come and have tea with her Thursday.

*   *   *

Wednesday.

Joyce was not in the office and there was no message. That has never happened. The atmosphere in the office restless, a bit giggly, like school when there's uncertainty. Phyllis and I worked together all day, and without a word being said how to behave so as to calm things down. We were brisk and efficient and kept at it. We will work easily together. But oh, she is so *young*, so young, so black and white and either/or and take it or leave it. Her cool crisp little mouth. Her crisp competent little smile. Phyllis has bought her own flat, we—the firm—helped her. She lives for her work, who should know better how than I? She sees herself editing the mag. Why not?

I write that, and wonder at it.

Now I shall write about *my* career, for I am very clear in my mind about it all because of the shocks and strains of the last few days, with Joyce, and then having to be alert and awake all the time with Phyllis.

I came straight into the office from school. No university, there wasn't the money; and I wasn't good enough for university! It just didn't present itself as a possibility.

When I started work for *Little Women*—Joyce and I so christened that phase of the mag, a shorthand—I was so pleased and relieved at getting this glamorous job, in journalism, I wasn't looking for anything higher. 1947, still a war atmosphere. It was a graceless production, bad paper, because of the war: full of how to use cheap cuts of meat and egg powder. How to make anything into something else—Joyce's description of it. I, like everyone else, was sick sick sick of it all. How we all longed to throw off the aftermath of war, the rationing, the dreariness. There was a woman editor then too. I wasn't into criticizing my superiors then, my sights went no higher than being secretary to the production manager. I just didn't think about Nancy Westringham. They were all gods and goddesses up there. Now I see she was just right for that phase of the mag. Old-style, like my mother and my sister, competent, dutiful, nice—but I mean it, nice, kind, and my guess is never an original thought in her life. My *guess* it has to be: if there is one thing I regret, it is that I wasn't awake enough during that phase to see what was going on. But of course then

I hadn't learned *how* to see what was going on: what is developing inside a structure, what to look for, *how things work*.

They were changing the mag all right, better paper, brighter features, but it wasn't enough. There had to be a new editor, and I should have seen it, should have been watching. It wasn't only that I didn't know how to observe: I was too drunk on being young, attractive and successful. At school no one had ever even suggested I might have capacities, and certainly my parents never did. But in the office, I was able to turn my hand to anything. I was soon just the one person who was able to take over from anyone sick or incapable. I cannot remember any pleasure in my life to match that: the relief of it, the buoyancy, tackling a new job and knowing that I did it well. I was in love with cleverness, with myself. And this business of being good at clothes. Of course, the fifties were not exactly an exciting time for clothes, but even so I was able to interest everyone in what I wore. My style then was sexy, but cool and sexy, just a little bit over the edge into parody: in that I anticipated the sixties and the way we all slightly mocked the styles we wore.

I would give a lot now to know *how* it happened that Boris became editor. But it is too late now. When I ask the oldies who are still with us, they don't know what I am asking because they don't think like that.

At any rate, Boris became editor in 1957, and he represented "the new wave". But he didn't have it in him. I was by then in the position Phyllis is now: the bright girl everyone expects great things of. The difference is, I didn't know it. I liked being good at everything, and I didn't mind working all hours. I adored everything I had to do. I was already doing all kinds of work well beyond what I was paid for, beyond what I was described as being. I was a secretary in Production. By then I had begun to watch what was really happening. The immediately obvious fact was that Boris was not very effective. Amiable, affable, trendy—all that, yes. He had been appointed by the Board when Nancy resigned; was asked to leave. He had the large room that is used now by the photographers, a large desk, a secretary who had a secretary, and a PR girl. He was

always in conference, on the telephone, at lunch, giving inter-
views on the role and function of women's magazines.
"Women's Lib" hadn't been born, though not till I came to
write this did I remember that.

What was really happening was that other people were
doing his work for him, me among them. *The formal structure
of the office did not correspond at all with what was happening.* The mag had brightened up a little, but not much, and Mr
Right was implicit in everything. We did not think clearly
about it, but carried on much as before, with better paper and
some decent photographs.

The moment Joyce arrived, we all became conscious of
exactly what we were doing, and for whom. Market Analysis,
reports from experts; we certainly took notice of all that, but
we had our own ideas. The backbone and foundation of the
mag, what interests us most, is *information*. Birth control, sex,
health, social problems generally. Nearly all the articles we
have on these topics would have been impossible in *Little
Women*, everything had to be wrapped up. This is the part of
the mag I do. As for clothes, food, wine, decor, what has
changed is the level of the photography. Not what is said,
fashion is fashion is fashion, and food is food, but how it is
presented. When I first began working, there were a lot of
articles like "I Am a Widow: How I Brought Up Two Girls", or
"I Am Married to a Paraplegic", or "Alice Is Blind But She
Runs a Business School". All those have gone: too down-
market! *Lilith* deliberately set out to take a step up in the
world, and we made that happen.

I've said that when Joyce came in, mid-sixties, she changed
me: she changed everything else. What interests me now is that
the change took place *against* the apparent structure. She was
Production Manager and I was her assistant. We were together
in the office we have now. It was we two who ran the mag. It
was obvious to us that we ran it, but Boris didn't notice. Joyce
used to say that in her last job she did all the work for her boss,
who had to be allowed to think he was doing it. So nothing had
changed for her. Far from resenting it all, we were worried that
people would notice. And of course they did. Now we wonder
why we thought that they wouldn't. The point was, we loved

the work, we loved transforming the mag. We used to go to the Board Meetings, once a fortnight, sit quietly there, on one side, with Boris at the top of the table, and the Board Reps at the other end, and we hardly opened our mouths. I used to brief Boris before meetings, about what he should say.

The actual structure during that time was Joyce and me running everything, with the photographers coming into prominence, because it was really in the sixties that they did. All the decisions were made in our office, it was always full of people. Suddenly—and Joyce had been there only a couple of years—she was made editor and given complete freedom. New format, new everything. She was clever: several mags that were too Swinging Sixties bit the dust, but the format Joyce created—that we created—survives.

Almost at once the real structure became the same as the formal, the official structure. When Boris left, his great awful *dead* office was turned over to the photographers, and it came to life at once; and the room Joyce and I had been using became the Editors' Room. Then I realized how much effort and nervous strain had gone into everything when what was really happening didn't match with the formal organization. Now, looking around at other offices, other businesses, I see how often there is a discordance.

And what has been growing up inside *this* structure, what is the future? Now I know it is not Joyce and me! But I wonder if it is really me and Phyllis? What is it I am not seeing because I am too involved with what is *now*? It seems to me that things change suddenly, overnight, or seem to: but the change has been growing up inside. I cannot see any change inside: and yet I think about it a good deal.

All I can see is that there is so much less money around for spending, and so our glossy lively even impudent format, or formula, may have to go, and something sterner and more dedicated supplant it.

Dedicated to *what*? Well, if I could foresee that! I do not get any feeling of pleasure or wanting to be part of it when I think that perhaps we will be into "making everything into something else". Clothes to last—well, that has already begun—beef as a luxury instead of a staple, buying jewellery as an investment . . . the last issue but one, we printed recipes from wartime, as a joke, but to those of us who were young during the war and just after it, it wasn't a joke. I heard the girls in the typists' pool laughing, Phyllis making fun of stretching meat with forcemeat balls. I could do a feature on the food Maudie remembers. I expect the typists' pool would fall about if they could hear Maudie on how, when she was a child, the mother of a family made a big batter pudding to "fill them up" before the meat course, so they were satisfied with a little bit of meat, and then after the meat, batter pudding again, with jam. When I think of the war, of that contriving and making-do, the dreary dreary dreary boredom of it, oh I can't face it all again, I can't, I can't . . . but so far no one has said that we must.

I married in 1963. It was shortly before Joyce came. I have written all that history, and only now have thought to mention that I married.

A week since the last—no, ten days.

I went in to Maudie as promised, though I was frantic with work. Did not stay long, in and out. Then, into the office: Joyce not there, no message either again. Phyllis and I coped. Everyone coped. An elegiac mood, for lost lovely times. She made *Lilith*, but if she doesn't come in to work, for days at a time, the waters close over her. She is hardly mentioned. But certainly thought of, by me at least. By me, by me! I have been raging with sorrow. I was uneasy, ashamed, thinking Freddie dies, my mother dies, hardly a tear, just a frozen emptiness, but Joyce slides out of my life and I grieve. At first I thought, look at me, what a wicked woman, but then I knew that since I could allow myself to mourn for Joyce, I have admitted—mourning, have admitted grief. I have been waking in the morning soaked in tears. For Freddie, my mother, for God knows what else.

But I haven't the time for it. I'm working like a demon. Meanwhile I rage with sorrow. I do not think this is necessarily a step forward into maturity. A good deal to be said for a frozen heart.

*   *   *

When I went in to Maudie next I found her angry and cold. With me? No, it came out that "the Irish woman" upstairs had again been turning on the refrigerator to "insult" her. Because I had just come from an atmosphere where things are dealt with, not muttered and nitpicked, I said, "I'm going upstairs to talk to her," and went, with Maudie shouting at me, "Why do you come here to interfere?" I knocked upstairs, ground floor. A lanky freckled boy let me in, I found the large beautiful Irish girl with the tired blue eyes, and three more lean golden freckled children watching TV. The refrigerator is a vast machine, bought probably at the second-hand shop down the street, and it came on while I was there, a trundling grinding that shook the whole flat. I could not say, Please sell the fridge. You could see that this was poverty. I mean poverty nineteen-seventies. I have a different criterion now, knowing Maudie. Everything cheap, but of course the kids properly fed and clean clothes.

I said, Mrs Fowler seemed to me to be ill, had they seen her?

On the girl's face came that look I seem to see everywhere now, a determined indifference, an evasion: "Oh well, but she's never been one for asking, or offering, and so I've given up."

All the time, she was listening—and in fact the husband came in, a thin dark explosive Irishman, and very drunk. The kids exchanged wide looks and faded away into the inner room. They were scared, and so was she. I saw that she had bruises on her forearms.

I thanked them and went off, and heard the angry voices before I had closed the door. Downstairs I sat down opposite that tiny angry old woman, with her white averted little face, and said, "I've seen the fridge. Have you never had one? It is very old and noisy."

"But why does she make it come on at one in the morning, or even three or four, when I'm trying to get my rest?"

Well, I sat there explaining. Reasonable. I had been thinking about Maudie. I like her. I respect her. And so I'm *not* going to insult her by babying her . . . so I had decided. But faced with her that night, as she sat in a sort of locked white tremble, I found myself softening things up.

"Very well then, if it's as you say, why does she have to put it just over where I sleep?"

"But probably it has to go where there's an electric point."

"And so much for my sleep, then, is that it?"

And as we sat there, the thing came on, just above us. The walls shook, the ceiling did, but it wasn't a really unbearable noise. At least, I could have slept through it.

She was sitting there looking at me in a way part triumphant: see, you can hear it now, I'm not exaggerating! and part curious—she's curious about me, can't make me out.

I had determined to tell her exactly what was going on in the office, but it was hard.

"You must be quite a queen bee there then," she remarked.

I said, "I am the assistant editor."

It was not that she didn't take it in, but that she had to repudiate it—me—the situation. She sat with her face averted, and then put her hand up to shield it from me.

"Oh well, so you won't be wanting to come in to me then, will you?" she said at last.

I said, "It's just that this week it's very difficult. But I'll drop in tomorrow if you'll have me."

She made a hard sorrowful sort of shrug. Before I left I took a look at the kitchen; supplies very low. I said, "I'll bring in stuff tomorrow, what you need.'

After a long, long silence which I thought she'd never break, she said, "The weather's bad, or I'd go myself. It's the usual—food for the cat, and I'd like a bit of fish . . ." That she didn't complete the list meant that she did accept me, did trust me, somehow. But as I left I saw the wide blank stare at me, something frantic in it, as if I had betrayed her.

In the office next day not a sign of Joyce, and I rang her at home. Her son answered. Measured. Careful. No, she's in the kitchen, I think she's busy.

Never has Joyce been "busy" before. I was *so* angry. I sat there thinking, I can go in to Maudie Fowler and help her, but not to Joyce, my friend. And meanwhile Phyllis was attending to the letters. Not from Joyce's table, but at a chair at the secretaries' table. Full marks for tact. I said to her, "This is crazy. I'm going to see Joyce now. Hold the fort." And went.

I've been in Joyce's home a hundred times, always, however, invited, expected. The door opened by the son, Philip. When he saw me he began to stammer, "She's—she's—she's . . ." "In the kitchen," I said for him. He had, as it were, gone in behind his eyes: absented himself. This look again! But is it that I didn't notice it before? A prepared surface, of one kind or another; the defences well manned.

I went into the kitchen. The son came behind me, like a jailer, or so I felt it (rightly). In the kitchen, a proper family kitchen, all pine and earthenware, the daughter, sitting at the table, drinking coffee, doing homework. Joyce standing over the sink. She looked far from an expensive gipsy, more a poor one. Her hair hadn't been brushed, was a dowdy tangle, careless make-up, nails chipped. She presented to me empty eyes and a dead face, and I said, "Joyce, it's not good enough," and she was startled back into herself. Tears sprang into her eyes, she gasped, turned quickly away and stood with her back to me, trembling, like Maudie. I sat at the table and said to the two children, "I want to talk to Joyce, please." They exchanged looks. You could say insolent, you could say scared. I saw that it would take very little to make me very sorry for them: for one thing, having to leave their schools and go off to the States, everything new. But I was angry, angry.

"Give me some coffee," I said, and she came with a cup, and sat down opposite me.

We looked at each other, straight and long and serious.

"I can't stand this business of nothing being said, nothing being said."

"Nothing is being *said* here either."

"Are they listening at the door?"

"Don't you see, Mother has been captured. Back from the office."

"Do you mean to say they have resented it, your being so successful and all that?"

"No, they are proud of me."

"But."

"Everything has fallen apart around them, and they haven't known for months if they are going to have Felicity for a mum or me. Now they know it is me, security, but they are terrified. Surely you can see that?" She sounded exactly like my dear sister Georgie, talking to the delinquent—me—and I wasn't going to take it.

"Yes, indeed," I said, "but we are talking of a young man and a young woman, they are not little children."

"Dorothy is seventeen and Philip is fifteen."

She looked hard and fierce at me, I looked angrily at her.

I said, "How did we get like this, so soft, so silly, so babyish? How?"

"Oh God," she said. "Oh God, oh God! Oh God—Janna!"

"Oh God, *Joyce*," I said to her. "But I mean it. And don't patronize me. Is nothing that I say to anyone worth anything?"

"What the hell are you talking about?"

Now we were both furious and liking each other the better for it. Our voices were raised, we both imagined "the children" listening.

"I'm talking about these ghastly *wet* spoiled brats we produce."

"You haven't produced any."

"Oh, thank you—and so that's the end of that then, the end of me! Thank God I haven't then. When I look at—"

"Listen, Janna . . ." Spelling it out, as to an idiot. "Is nothing really due to them, owed to them? They have a father who has had what amounts to a second home for years. Recently they have had to accept their parents are going to divorce. Now the family is going to stay together . . ."

"And what is due to us, your work, to me?"

She sat there, spoon in a coffee mug, and it tinkled against the side with her trembling.

"A crisis in the family, a choice, you wonder if perhaps you might actually have to live alone at some time, along with x billion other women—and all you are in your work counts for nothing, falls to pieces."

By then we were both shaking, and very ashamed. We could see ourselves, two women shouting at each other in a silent house.

"Wait, Janna," she said. "Wait." And she made a business of getting up to put on the kettle again, and took her time about sitting down. And then, "Do you imagine I don't feel bad about you, our friendship? I'm in pain." She was shouting again. "Do you understand? I am in pain. I've never in my life felt like this. I'm being split in half, torn apart. I want to howl and scream and roll about . . . and so I am cooking family meals and helping with the homework. Strangely enough."

"And I, strangely enough, am in pain too."

And suddenly we began to laugh, in the old way; we put our heads down on the kitchen table and laughed. The "kids" came in, hearing us: with scared smiles. I, Janna Somers, "the office", had proved every bit as much of a threat as they had feared. Seeing those scared faces, I knew I was going to give in if I didn't watch it: but my mind was saying, I am right, I am right, I am right . . .

And perhaps I am not right, after all.

I said, "I'd better get back to work."

She said, "I know that you and Phyllis are doing quite well without me."

"Quite well."

"Well then."

And I went back as fast as I could to the office. To my real home. Leaving Joyce in her real home.

Later.

I took the things in to Maudie and sat with her. I was very tired, and she saw it.

She said in a timid old voice, "You mustn't think you have to come in here, if you're tired."

"Why not?" I said. "You need some help, you know that." And I added, "I like you. I like knowing you, Maudie."

She nodded, in a prim measuring way, and there was a small pleased smile. "I'm not saying I'm not the better for it, because I am."

I went out for the second time to the shop opposite because I had forgotten tea.

It was sleeting. I got the bits of kindling from the skip. All along these streets, the houses are being "done up". Four of them in Maudie's very short street. Four skips loaded with "rubbish". Including perfectly good chairs, mattresses, tables, and quantities of wood in good condition. People sneak out for the wood. There must still be quite a few fireplaces in these houses. But not for long, not when they are "done up".

I came out from the shop, and there on the pavement were two old women, wrapped up like parcels. I recognized a face: from the window opposite.

I was frozen. And wanted to get home.

But already I knew that these occasions cannot be rushed.

The conversation:

"Excuse me, I wanted to ask, how is Maudie Fowler?"

"She seems all right."

"Are you her daughter, dear? You do take good care of her."

"No. I am not her daughter."

"Are you a Good Neighbour?"

"No, I am not that either." I laughed, and they allowed me small polite smiles.

I say "old women", and that is a criticism of me, no individuality allowed them, just "old women". But they seemed so alike, little plump old women, their faces just visible behind thick scarves, coats, hats.

"Maudie Fowler has always kept herself so much to herself, and we were wondering."

"Well," I said, "she's over ninety, isn't she?"

A reproving silence. "I am ninety-two dear, and Mrs Bates here is ninety-one."

"Well, I'd say Maudie was feeling her age."

This was too direct and I knew it, but had started off like that and couldn't change course. Oh yes, I know very well by now that these conversations should be allowed to develop.

"You know Mrs Rogers, do you, dear?"

"Mrs Rogers?"

"She is one of The Welfare."

"No, I don't."

All this with the sleet blowing across us and our faces turning blue.

"She wants to see you, so she says."

"Well, what about?"

"Seeing as you are a Good Neighbour, then there's another that needs it."

"Well, I'm not one," I said.

"Then goodbye, dear. We mustn't keep you in the cold."
And they went together toddling along the pavement, arm in
arm, very slowly.

Joyce came back next day, and sat at her desk and went
through the motions of working, and did work, but *she* was
not there. She is simply not with us. She looked awful, badly
dressed, even dusty, her hair greying at the roots, and a greyish
edge to her black sweater.

Looking at her, I made an appointment with the hairdresser
at once. And determined to devote an evening to my own care.

This is that evening. I have had a real bath, hours of it. I've
done my fingernails, my toenails, my eyebrows, my ears, my
navel, the hard skin on my feet.

What has made me, for so many years, that perfectly
groomed person, whom everybody looks at and thinks, how
does she do it? has been my Sunday nights. Never did I allow
anything to interfere with that. Freddie used to joke about it
but I said, Make jokes, I don't care, I have to do it. On Sunday
nights, after supper, for years and years I've chosen my outfit
for every day of the week ahead, made sure there has been not a
wrinkle or a crease, attended to buttons and hems, cleaned
shoes, emptied out and polished handbags, brushed hats, and
put anything even slightly soiled for the cleaner's and the
launderette. Hours of it, every Sunday night, and when all those
pairs of skilled and knowledgeable eyes examined me at work,
there has never been, but literally, a hair out of place. Grooming. Well, if I can't keep it up, my style is in the wastepaper
basket, just as Joyce's style is now. A high-class gipsy, turned
slattern, is bizarre; if my style is neglected, there's nothing left
but a dowd.

And now I shall make myself do it: buttons, shoes, collars,
ironing, ironing, ironing, and not so much as a thread of
loosened lace on a petticoat.

*   *   *

The Diary of a Good Neighbour

Over three months have gone.
It has been a choice between proper baths and the diary. I've had to have something to hold on to.

Joyce came back to work, but she was a ghost, a zombie. Felicity announced she was pregnant, husband Jack asked Joyce to be "generous", Joyce said she wished he would make up his mind, he said, You are vindictive, she said, I must be crazy to want you at all. The poor children are both going crazy and punishing Joyce—she says.

It isn't that she doesn't do the work as usual, but she's not in it. As for what I used to rely on so much, the good atmosphere, the way we used to work together as if we were one person— no, gone. We—Phyllis and I— support her, all the time, tact, tact, tact, oh full marks to all of us, everyone in Editorial, and I watch all this, fascinated, because of *how it works*. The woman who made the mag, because she did, it was her *push*, is fading out. I saw a film on telly, elephants supporting with their trunks a dying friend. It reminded me. Because Joyce *is* fading out. It can't go on like this, is the *unspoken* thought. Unspoken, too, is that I will be the new editor. Meanwhile, Joyce says that she will stay in London, with the children, and she will be divorced. The children for the first time ring up here, making demands. Ridiculous, like, where is the jam, where did you put my sweater? Joyce patient, and *anguished*. For them. Very well, but there are limits to the people one can be sorry for. I'm learning my limits: small ones. Maudie Fowler is all I can manage.

It's been wet, cold, dismal. Nearly every evening after work I've been in to Maudie. I've given up even thinking that she ought to agree to be "rehoused"; I said it just once, and it took her three days to stop seeing me as an enemy, as one of "them". I *am* housed, says she, cough, cough, cough from having to go out at the back all weathers into the freezing lavatory, from standing to wash in the unheated kitchen. But why do I say that? Women of ninety who live in luxury cough and are frail.

It is a routine now. I go in about seven, eight, after work, and bring in what she has said she needs the night before. Usually she's forgotten something, and I go out again to the Indian shop. He, the Indian man, a large pale man, pale grey really, who suffers from this weather, always asks after her, and shakes his head, and gives me some little thing for her: some sweets or some biscuits. When I give these to Maudie, she looks fierce and angry: she's proud, but she's moved.

While I shop she makes us tea. She has had supper at six, when she eats cake and jam and biscuits. She says she can't be bothered to cook properly. She doesn't want me to waste time cooking for her, because "it would take away from our time". When she said this I realized she valued our time of sitting and talking: for some reason I was not able to see that, for I am defensive and guilty with her, as if *I* am responsible for all the awful things that have happened. We sit there, in that fug and smell—but nearly always I can switch off as I go in, so that I don't notice the smell, just as I refuse to notice the smeared cups. And she . . . entertains me. I did not realize it was that. Not until one day when she said, "You do so much for me, and all I can do for you is to tell you my little stories, because you like that, don't you? Yes, I know you do." And of course I do. I tell her about what I have been doing, and I don't have to explain much. When I've been at a reception for some VIP or cocktail party or something, I can make her see it all. Her experience has included the luxurious, and there was her father: "Sometimes, listening to you, it makes me remember how he used to come home and tell us he'd been to Romano's or the Café Royal or the music hall, and he'd tell us what all the nobs ate and drank." But I don't like reminding her of her father, for she sits with her face lowered, her eyes down and hidden, picking in distress at her skirt. I like it when her fierce alive blue eyes are sparkling and laughing; I like looking at her, for I forget the old crone and I can see her so easily as she was, young.

She is wearing these nights a cornflower-blue cotton with big white spots: an apron, made from a dress she had when she was young. I said I liked it so much, so she tore out the sleeves and cut down the back: an apron. The black thick clothes I threw into the dustbin were retrieved by her. I found them rolled into newspaper in the front room. Stinking. She had not worn them, though. There is a photograph of her, a young woman before she was married, a little wedge of a face, combative eyes, a great mass of shiny hair. She has a piece of her hair before it went grey. It was a rich bright yellow.

We sit on either side of the black stove, the flames forking up and around, a teapot on the top, with a filthy grey cosy that was once . . . why do I go on and on about the dirt? Our cups on the arms of our chairs, a plate of biscuits on a chair between us. The cat sits about washing herself, or sleeps on her divan. Cosy, oh yes. Outside, the cold rain, and upstairs, the Irish family, quarrelling, the feet of the kids banging on the uncarpeted floors, the fridge rumbling and shaking.

She tells me about all the times in her life she was happy. She says she is happy now, *because of me* (and that is hard to accept, it makes me feel angry, that so little can change a life), and therefore she likes to think of happy times.

A Happiness.

"My German boy, the one I should have married but I was silly, we used to spend Sundays. We took a penny bus ride up to where we are sitting now, or perhaps a stage further. Green fields and streams and trees. We'd sit on the edge of a little bridge and watch the water, or find a field without cows and eat our food. What did we eat? I'd cut cold meat from the joint, as much as I liked, because Mother wasn't dead then, and clap it between two bits of bread. But I liked his food best, because his parents were bakers. Did you know the bakers were often Germans then? Well, his parents could just read and write, but he was a real clever one, he was a scholar. He did well later, more fool me, I could have had my own house and a garden. But I didn't marry him, I didn't. I don't know why. Of course, my father wouldn't have liked a foreigner, but he didn't like what I did marry, he could never say yes to any choice of ours, so what would have been the difference? No, I don't want to think of that, I spent enough time when I was younger thinking, Oh what a fool—when I'd come to understand what men were. You see, I didn't know then. Hans was so kind, he was a gentleman, he treated me like a queen. He'd lift me down from the stiles so gently and nice, and we spread a little white cloth and put out the lovely white rolls and the cakes from the bakery. I used to say, No, I must eat mine, and you eat yours, and mine always ended up being given to the birds.

"I think of those days, those Sundays. And who would believe it now? Where we sit in these streets, running streams, and birds . . . What happened to the streams? you are thinking. I know, I know how to read your face now. Well, you might well wonder where all that water is. It is underneath the foundations of half the houses along here, that's where. When they built this all up, and covered the fields, I used to come by myself and watch the builders. By myself. My German boy had gone off by then because I wouldn't marry him. The builders scamped everything then, as they do now; some things never change. They were supposed to make the water run in proper conduits, away from the houses, but they didn't trouble themselves. Sometimes, even now, when I walk along, I stop at a house and I think, yes, if your basements are damp, it's because of the water from those old streams. There's a house, number seventy-seven it is, it changes hands, it can't keep an owner, it's because it's where two little streams met, and the builders put the bricks of the foundation straight into the mud and let the water find its way. They did make a real channel for the water lower down, it runs along the main road there, but the little baby streams we used to sit by and put our feet in, they were left to make their own way. And after those Sundays, when the dusk came, oh, how lovely it all was, he'd say, May I put my arm around your waist? And I'd say, No, I don't like it—what a fool. And he'd say, Put your arm in mine then, at least. So we'd walk arm in arm through the fields to the bus, and come home in the dark. He'd never come in, because of Father. He'd kiss my hand, and he'd say, Maudie, you are a flower, a little flower."

A Happiness.

Maudie was apprenticed to a milliner's and worked for them off and on for years. The apprenticeship was very hard. Living with her aunt, who was so poor, and gave her breakfast and supper, but not much more, Maudie had to do without a midday meal or walk most of the way to work. The workshop was near Marylebone High Street. She would calculate whether shoe leather would cost more than her fare. She said she could beg cast-off shoes from her cousin, who never got all the wear out of them, or pick up second-hand boots from a market. But she had to be neatly dressed for her work, and that was her biggest trouble. Her aunt did not have money for Maudie's clothes.

Her employer's wife gave her a skirt and a blouse once. "She valued me, you see. We had to have a decent appearance because the buyers would come into the workrooms. Oh, don't think it was from a good heart, she didn't have one. She didn't want to lose me. It was years before I could buy myself a nice brown cloth dress of my own, and my own shoes. And when I did, oh, I'll not forget that day. I went without so much for that dress. And I wore it on the Sunday first so Laurie could see it. And who gave you that? he said, for that was what he was like, tugging at my arm and hurting it. Who was it, tell me? It wasn't you, I said to him, and as I pulled my arm from him, it tore under the arm. Not much, but the dress was spoiled. Oh yes, a person has his stamp all through him. You know what I'm saying? But *I* didn't know that then. It wasn't long before I knew that in everything he did, it was the same: a new dress I'd saved and gone without for, but he tore it the first time I put it on. But it didn't matter, I mended it, it didn't show, and I went into the workroom and peacocked around, and the girls all clapped and sang 'A Little Bit of What You Fancy Does You Good'.

"That was just before I was promoted, and soon I got another dress, a blue foulard, but I never loved another dress as I loved that first one I paid for myself.

"Oh what times we did have in that workroom. There were fifteen of us, apprentices and milliners. We sat all around a long table, with the boxes of trimmings on trestles behind us, and the hats and bonnets we were working on on their forms in front of us. We used to sing and lark about. Sometimes when I got a bit carried away, *she* used to come up and say, Who's making all that noise? It's Maudie! The rule is, silence when you work. But I had to sing, I was so enjoying myself, and soon we were all singing, but she didn't want to lose me, you see.

"Did I tell you how I learned to know that I was a value to her? If I did, I'll tell you again, because I love to think of it. You see, *he* used to go off to Paris, and see the new season's hats in the shops, and sometimes in the workrooms of the Paris milliners, for he knew people who could snatch him a glimpse. He knew how to remember a hat or a bonnet that would do for us. He used to keep it all in his mind, and nip out quick and draw it. He couldn't draw really, but he'd have the main things, a shape or the set of a ribbon. And then he'd come back and say, You do this, see, it's this shape and that colour, made of velvet or satin, you do what you can. Well, it was as if I could see the real hat behind the scribble on the paper, and I'd work away there, and finish it, and I'd say to him, Is that anywhere near it, Mr Rolovsky? And he'd take it up and stare and say, Well, it's not too bad, Maudie. That pleased me. But then I saw how he'd come and stand behind me and watch while I worked, always me, not the others, and then the way he snatched up the hat when I'd done, for he was so greedy, you see, he couldn't hide it. I saw then I'd come near what he'd seen in Paris. And the girls all knew too, and we'd give each other winks. *She* saw us at it, and she said, That's enough, I don't see what there is to wink at. For she was clever, the missus was, but she wasn't clever at anything but her job, which was making the workroom pay. Have you noticed that at all? A person can be clever as can be, in one direction, and stupid in another. *She* thought we didn't know what she was trying to cover up, and yet it was all plain to us. I had a gift, you see, I had it in my fingers and in my mind's eye, and it was worth everything to them, because when the buyers came in, he always showed them my work first, and it was always my work that he charged the most for.

"I've stood outside the showrooms, just off Bond Street they were, and looked at the hats in the window, only two or three of course, not crammed the way the windows for cheap hats were done, and the hats were always mine. And snapped up as soon as I could do them.

"Yes, I can see from your face what you're wanting to say, and you're right. I never got paid extra for it. I got the top wages for the job, but that was never much, never enough to free my mind of worrying about the future. Yes, you are right again, don't think I haven't thought and thought about why I didn't go somewhere else, or say, Give me what I am worth to you or I'll leave. But for one thing, I loved that work so, I loved it all, the colours and the feel of the materials; and then the other girls, we had worked together so long by then, and we knew each other and all our troubles, and then . . . Well, of course there was more to it. For one thing, it was partly my fault. *He* wanted me to go to Paris. Oh no, if he had anything else in mind, he couldn't let it be that. He said, The wife'll come too, don't you worry, it will all be fair and right. What he wanted was for me to come with him into the workrooms when he could sneak himself in, and look at the hats for myself. He was really getting carried away by it all, he imagined my coming back to London and copying all those hats and bonnets, hundreds of them, I daresay, not just the few he could keep in his mind. And he said he would pay me properly for it. Well, being him, being *that* pair, I knew better than to think it would be much, but it would be a lot for me. And yet I couldn't bring myself, I said no.

"That was twice I was invited to France, when I was a girl, once with Mrs Privett and once with that pair of . . . One a real lady and then two nasty penny-pinchers, the good and the bad.

"Yes, I know what you are thinking. It was Laurie. He'd never have let me hear the end of it if I'd gone to Paris, even if I'd gone with a regiment of guards to look after me, he'd have taken it out of me. And it was bad enough as it was, before we even married, I had bruises on my arms, and it was always: Who was it? Who looked at you? Who gave you that handkerchief?—because I used to pinch and save for proper linen hankies with real lace, I loved them, I loved pretty things. But he never knew I could have gone to Paris then. And if I had, perhaps I might have stayed, I might have married a Frenchie. I could have married a German, couldn't I? Sometimes I look back and I see that my life had these chances, leading to something wonderful, who knows? And yet I never took them, I always said, No, no, to what was offered.

"And yet I had such happy times, I think except for Johnnie they were the best in my life, better even than Hans and our

Sundays. I like to sit here and think back to us girls, sitting around those lovely hats, oh they were so beautiful those hats, singing and larking and telling stories, and *she* always around, Maudie here and Maudie there, it's always you who are the ringleader, she'd say, but I was her best and she knew it, and though she'd like to have seen the last of me, because *he* had his eye on me, and everyone knew it, she had to put up with me, didn't she? And I didn't care. I'd sing away, I'd sing—shall I sing you one of my songs? Yes, I will . . ."

And Maudie sits singing the old music-hall songs, some I've never heard of. Her voice is off pitch now, keeps cracking, but you can hear what it was like in her laugh.

A Happiness.

"I must have got pregnant the night of our wedding. Nine months to the day, it was. And Laurie was so pleased once we knew. Would you believe it, I was so silly, I didn't know what was wrong with me! I crept off to the doctor and said, I am sickening, I'm dying, I feel so ill, and I feel this and that. And I lay down and he felt my stomach, and he sat down behind his table and he laughed. Oh, it was a nice laugh, it didn't make me feel bad, but I did feel silly. He said, Mrs Fowler, didn't it occur to you that you are pregnant? What's that? said I. You are going to have a baby, said he. Oh go on, I said, it can't be—for I hadn't got the expectation of it into my mind at all.

"And then I told Laurie and he cried, he was so pleased. We were in the front room of a house in the next street to this. He painted the room beautifully, for he was a good tradesman, no one could say otherwise, he painted it a lovely shining cream, and the garlands on the ceiling he painted gold and blue, and the skirting boards and the picture rail blue. And he bought a little chest and made that blue, and kept buying little coats and hats—oh, sizes too big, Johnnie didn't get into them for two or three years after Laurie left me. But I was so happy, I thought I was a queen for those few months. He treated me like I was a piece of crystal or a new cup. He kept buying me all sorts of fancies, for I was after pickles and chocolate and ginger and stuff, and they cost him.

"And then the baby was born, my Johnnie. And you'll never guess. From that moment on there was never a kind word for me. How is it a grown man behaves like a little boy? He was jealous, jealous of a baby! But I didn't know then that was how it was going to be. I used to tease him, and then he hit me. All the good times were over. I used to sit there in my nursing chair, which he had made for me, and nurse the baby, and look at the lovely painted ceiling, and think, oh I'm so hungry, so hungry, because Johnnie was such a feeding baby, he sucked and sucked. I'd say, Laurie, get me a bit of lamb for a stew, buy me some bacon, we'll have it with dumplings. And he'd say, What am I going to use for money? And he was in work. Well, I'll not fill your ears with the misery of it when I understood what the future was to be, because what I like is, to look back and think of me sitting like a queen in that lovely room, in my lovely chair, with Johnnie, and thinking how when Laurie got used to it we'd all be so happy."

A month later.

I've never worked as hard as this! If I keep a skeleton of this diary going, then perhaps later . . .

Joyce is just holding herself together, but she is not with us. I am doing all the interviewing, parties, running about, lunches, conferences. We keep her out of sight mostly. Her defences are well inside herself, not where mine are, outside in clothes, hair, etc. She looks awful, a mess. In addition, this series of articles on clothes as an expression of the mood of the seventies, sixties, fifties. They wanted more. I seem never to be able to lose it, undervaluing myself. I would not have thought of myself as able to write for a serious sociological mag, but here I am. So I get up at six to do the work for that.

And I see Maudie every evening, or if not I make sure she knows I'm not coming. I go in, exhausted, but then I shop and do a little bit of cleaning, and then I slump and listen, and listen. Sometimes she tells it well, and laughs, and knows she is pleasing me. Others, she mutters and is fierce and won't look at me, sitting there in my lovely clothes. I have bought a whole new outfit, madly expensive, I feel it as a bulwark against chaos. She leans over and feels the silk of my shirt, none of this cheap Chinese stuff, no. She strokes my skirt, and then looks up into my face, with a sigh, for she knows how good my things are, who better? And then she will turn away her little face and put her hand up to her cheek to shield it, and stare into the fire. Shuts me out. And then she starts again, forgiving me with a little laugh: So what have you been doing today? But she doesn't want to know, my world is too much for her, she wants to talk . . .

"And then one day he left me, he said, You don't care for me now you've got *him*, and he took up his tools and he left. I didn't believe it. I was waiting for him to come back, for years as it turned out. But there I was, with nothing to pay the rent with. I went to the Rolovskys and asked—oh, that was hard, I'd never begged of them before. I had said I was getting married, you see, and *she* had given me a hard time, making me work all hours, to get as much out of me as she could before she lost me. And here I was again, after not even two years. Well, she made a favour of it. And someone else was forewoman now. And it wasn't the same in the workroom. For one thing, I didn't have the heart to sing and dance. I put Johnnie with a baby-minder. She wasn't a bad woman, but it wasn't what I wanted for him. I'd be sick worrying, has she given him his medicine, or his milk? For he was delicate, he always had a cough. But I had enough to keep us. Then the people where I was said they wanted my room. They didn't want a baby, that was what they meant. And they did want all that lovely blue and gold for themselves. And so I came here. The woman who had the house didn't mind a baby, but I had to keep him quiet, she said. I was on the top floor then, the little room at the back. It was cheap, and we looked out at the trees there, lovely it was. But I found it hard to pay for everything. I went to my aunt, but she could only just manage for herself. She said, Go to your father. But he had said if I married Laurie I should never darken his door. And he was right, for once . . . Did I tell you about my wedding?"

And Maudie sat laughing, laughing, and pulled out a drawer and showed me a photograph. A tiny woman, under an enormous flowered hat, in a neat tight dress. "Yes," says she,

"I looked a proper mess. I had been saying yes and no, yes and no, because what would happen was, I'd say, No, and then he'd start his squeezing and wanting, and I'd say, Yes, and he'd say, I suppose Harry (there was another boy who fancied me) won't have you, so I'd say, No. But at last we got to say yes at the same time. I borrowed my cousin Flo's best hat and her church gloves. My dress was my own. I sent a message to Father and said I was getting married on Sunday. He came over to Auntie's and Laurie was there, and he stood in the doorway and said to me, If you marry *him* that is the last time you'll see me. Well, I hadn't seen him for nearly ten years as it was. I said, Will you come and see me married at least?

"On that morning Laurie was worse than I'd ever seen him, fit to burst with black looks and pinches and grumbles. We walked to church with my Auntie, and we were quarrelling all the way. There was Father, all in his best striped clothes and top hat, oh what a dresser he was! And *she* was there too, she had got so fat, and I couldn't help crowing secretly, she could hardly walk, all in purple and black feathers, and by then I'd come to know what was really good and what wasn't, and I could see she was nothing, we wouldn't have her in our workroom. But I was nothing too, that day, I could have got a hat from the workroom for the wedding to marry in, but I didn't want a favour from the Rolovskys. And so we were married, sulking and not looking at each other. After the wedding, there was a photographer who took this, and then when Father went off towards the carriage with *her*, I ran after them and said, Can I come with you? But you've just got married, said she, really astonished she was, and I don't blame her. And Father said, That's right, you come home and don't waste time on *him*. So I got into the carriage and left Laurie at the church . . ." And at this Maudie laughs and laughs, her strong, girl's laugh.

"After I'd enjoyed myself at home for a little, and eaten my fill of everything, I thought, Well, I have a husband, and I said to them, Thanks, but I'd better be off home, and I went, Father saying, Never darken my doors. And I didn't, for he died soon after of a stroke. And they didn't tell me about the funeral.

"But my sister was there, right enough. Suddenly she began

showing herself off and buying herself clothes, and then they moved to a better house. I knew Father had left something to us both, and I went to *her* and said, Where is what Father left me? And she couldn't look me in the face. What makes you think you had anything coming? she said. You never came to see us, did you? But who threw me out? I said. And we quarrelled and quarrelled and she shrieked at me. I went to my sister, willing myself to do it because she always treated me so bad, and I said, Polly, where's my share of the money? *She* has got it, my sister said. You'll have to go to a lawyer. Well, how could I do that? You need money for lawyers. I and Laurie were all lovey-dovey just then, and we both of us found it such a nice change, we didn't want to waste any of it.

"Much later, when I was so down and poor and in need of everything, I went to my sister, and she must have told *her*, for one day when I got back from work the landlady said a big woman in feathers and scarlet had been and left me a parcel. It was some of my mother's clothes, that's all, and her old purse with two gold guineas in it. And that's all I ever had from my father. For I never saw *her* again."

Maudie's very bad time.

"I worked so hard and so hard. I used to get up so early and take Johnnie to the minder's, and then to work, and work all day till six or seven. And then back to pick up Johnnie, and she'd be cross, often, because I was late and she wanted to be rid of him. And I'd get home and find not enough food for him and me. I was earning badly then. Mrs Rolovsky never forgave me for leaving when I married and then coming back. I wasn't the pet any longer, and she was always taking her chance to fine me, or give me a hat that would take twice as long as the others. We were paid by what we'd got done, you see. And I never was able to scamp my work. I had to do it properly even if I was to suffer. And then we were put off. We were put off most summers. Oh, no security then, no pensions, nothing. She'd say, Pick up your cards as you go out, and leave your address, and we'll contact you when there's work.

"That war was coming, it was nearly on us, and times were

bad. I didn't know what to do. I had a little saved, but not much. I had Johnnie home from the minder's, that was something because I hardly ever saw him awake when I was working, but how to feed him? The landlady said, No, no credit on the rent. I kept the rent paid, but often and often I went to bed on cold water so Johnnie could have a cup of milk. It went on and on, and that was such a wonderful summer. I was wild with hunger. I'd go into the gardens and see if there was bread lying there the birds hadn't eaten. But others had the same idea, and I'd be there first, hanging around, pretending I wasn't watching while the people spread out the bread for the birds. Once I said to an old woman, I need that more than the birds. Then earn it, said she. I never forgot that, and I'll never forget it. For there was no work. I tried to get a cleaning job, but they wouldn't have me cleaning with a child hanging around. I didn't know what I would do.

"Then suddenly Laurie turns up, and finds me in bed on a Sunday afternoon, with my arms around Johnnie. I felt so faint and sick, you see. Oh, what a commotion, what a to-do! First, of course, it was all shouts, Why did you move without telling me? And then it was, You know I'd never let you go without! Then prove it, I said, and off he went and came back with groceries. I could have done with biscuits and tea and dried peas and stuff I could have kept, but no, being Laurie, it was all fancy cakes and ham. Well, I ate and Johnnie ate, and after all that he took us out for some food. I'm your Daddy, says he to Johnnie, and of course the little boy is pleased. And then, he went off. Back tomorrow, says Laurie, but I didn't see him for months.

"Meanwhile I'd hit the bottom. I went to Relief. In those days there was a Board stuffed with snobby ladies and gentlemen, and you'd stand there, and they'd say, Why don't you sell your locket, if you're so poor—it was my mother's—have you got any personal belongings, we can't keep people who have their own resources. Their own resources! You say you have a little boy, and they say, Then you must force your husband to contribute. You couldn't explain to the likes of them about the likes of Laurie. Well, they said I could have two shillings a week. That was high summer still, and no end to it in sight.

They sent a man around. I'd pawned everything, except a blanket for Johnnie, for I was sleeping under my coat. He came into our room. Bed with a mattress but no bedclothes, a wooden table—this one here, that you like. Two wooden chairs. A shelf that had on it a bit of sugar and half a loaf of bread. He stood there, in his good clothes, and looked at me and Johnnie, and then he said, Have you sold everything you can? And I had, even my mother's locket. And he leaned forward and pointed to this . . ." Maudie showed me the long dark wood stick with which she pushes back and opens the curtains. "What about this? he said. How am I to open and close my curtains? I said. Are you expecting me to sell my curtains as well? Shall I sell the bed and sleep on the floor, then?

"He was a little ashamed then, not much, it wasn't his job to be ashamed of what he had to do. And that was how I got my two shillings a week."

"And could you live on it?"

"You would be surprised what you can live on. Johnnie and I, we ate bread, and he got some milk, and so we lived until the autumn and there was a note from the Rolovskys: they'd take me on but at less money. Because of the hard times. I would have worked for half what they gave. I slowly got back the blankets from the pawnshop, for the winter, and I got my pillows, and then . . . One day, when I got to the baby-minder's, no Johnnie. Laurie had come and taken him away. I begged and screamed and begged, but she said he was the child's father, she couldn't refuse a child to his father—and I went mad, running about the streets, and going everywhere. No one had heard anything. No one knew. I was very ill then. I lay in bed, I didn't care, I thought I would die and I would have welcomed it. I lost my job at the Rolovskys', and that was the end of them, for me. When I was up, I got myself a job cleaning, to tide me over, because without a child they'd employ me. And when I saved up enough I went to a lawyer. I said, How can I get my child back? But where is your husband? he said. I don't know, I said. Then how can I help you? he said. I don't know, I said. You must advertise for him, he said. But where? I said. Isn't there a way of finding out where people are? Yes, but it costs money, he said. And I haven't got any, I said.

"And then he came over to me and put his hands all over me, and he said, Very well, Maudie, you know what you can do if you want me to help you. And I ran, and I ran, out of that office, and I was scared to go near a lawyer again.

"All this time, Laurie had Johnnie down in the West Country with a woman he had then. Much later, when I met Johnnie again, he told me she was good to him. Not his father, for his father was off soon, to another woman, he could never stay with one woman. No, this woman brought him up. And he did not know he had a mother, he didn't know about me. Not till quite recently, but I'll tell you another time, another time, I'm all roiled up and upset with thinking about it all, and I meant to tell you something nice tonight, one of the times I like to think about, not a bad time . . ."

A nice time.

Maudie was walking down the High Street, and she saw some hats in a window. She was appalled at the way the hats were made. She went in and said to a woman who was making a hat, Don't you know how to put a hat together? And the woman said, No, she had been left a widow with a bit of money and thought she would make hats. Well, said Maudie, you have to learn how to make a hat, as you have to learn to scrub a floor or bake a loaf. I'll show you. She was a bit huffy at first, but she wanted to learn.

"I used to go in there, and she'd show me what she'd done, and I'd make her pick it to pieces again, or I'd make her whole hat, for the skill was in my fingers still, and it is now, I know. And yes, I can see from your face what you are thinking, and you're right. No, she didn't pay me. But I loved it, you see. Of course, it wasn't like the Rolovskys', not the West End, nothing in the way of real good silks and satins, just cheap stuff. But all the same, between us, we made some lovely hats and she got a name for it. And soon she sold the shop for the goodwill—but the goodwill was me, really, and that wasn't in any contract and so I don't know what happened afterwards . . ."

*   *   *

A nice time.

Maudie was working for an actress who was at the Lyric Theatre, Hammersmith. She was prepared to take an hour's journey there, and an hour back, because this woman was so gay and laughing and always had a joke. "She lived alone, no man, no children, and she worked. Oh, they work so, these poor actresses, and I used to make her supper ready for the oven, or a good big salad on a plate, and get her fire laid, and go home thinking how she'd be so happy to come in and see everything so nice. And sometimes after a matinée she'd say, Sit down, Maudie, share my supper, I don't know what I'd do without you. And she'd tell me all about the theatre. She wasn't a star, she was what they call a character actress. Well, she was a character all right. And then she died. What of? I was so upset I didn't want to know. It was a sudden death. I got a letter one day, and it was, she had died, sudden. So I didn't go back, though I was owed a fortnight's money."

"When was that?"

For all the time I am trying to get her life mapped, dated.

"When? Oh, it was after the war. No, the other war, the second war."

Maudie doesn't talk about the first war as a war. She was sick with worrying about Johnnie, for she thought that her husband would be in the army, and where was Johnnie? She went "to the Army" and asked, did they know anything about a Laurie Fowler, and they said, But what part of the country does he come from?

"I was so desperate, I went on my knees. I didn't know I was going to, but there I was, with all those officers around me. Please, please, I said. They were embarrassed, and I don't blame them. I was crying like a river. They said, We'll see what we can do. We'll let you know.

"And a long time afterwards, and I was waiting for every visit of the postman, a card: We have been unable to trace Laurence Fowler. And the reason was, he joined up from Scotland, not England, for there was a woman in Scotland he was living with he needed to get away from."

*   *   *

So that is what a month of visiting Maudie looks like, written down! But what of the evening when I said to myself, I am so tired, I am so tired, I *can't*, but I went? It was an hour later than usual. I stood outside that crumbling door, knock knock, then bang bang bang. Faces in the upper windows. Then at last she stood there, a little fury with blazing blue eyes.

"What do you want?"

"I am here to visit you."

She shrieked, "I haven't got time, and dragging down this passage, getting the coal, is bad enough."

I said to her, hearing myself with some surprise, "Then go to hell, Maudie," and went off without looking back. This was without real anger on my part, almost like reading lines in a play. Nor was I worried that evening, but made good use of my spare time having a real bath.

Next day, she opened the door on my second knock, and said, "Come in," standing aside with an averted unhappy face. Later she said, "You don't have to take any notice of my nonsense."

"Yes, I do, Maudie, of course I do. If you say a thing, I have to believe you mean it."

And, a few days later, she was stiff and silent. "What's wrong, Maudie?"

"I'm not going to, I'm not leaving here, they can't make me."

"Who's been this time?"

"*She* has."

"Who is *she*?"

"As if you don't know."

"Oh, so you're back at that, then. I'm plotting against you!"

"Of course you are, you all do."

We were shrieking at each other. I am not at all ashamed of this, yet I've never, or not since I was a child, quarrelled in this way: quarrelled without spite or passion, even with a certain enjoyment. Though I know it is not enjoyable to Maudie. She suffers afterwards.

"But was there someone else to see you, then?"

"Yes."

"What's her name?"

With a blazing blue look, she said, "Rogers, Bodgers, Plodgers, something like that." And, later, "They can't make me move, can they? This house is privately owned?"

I sent for the information. If the flat is condemned, then she'll have to move. By any current housing standard, it should be condemned. By any human standard, she should stay where she is. I want to contact this Mrs Rogers. I know I can ring up the "Welfare" and ask, but this isn't how things happen—oh, no! You have to let things work themselves out, you must catch something at the right time.

I found the two old women again waiting for me the other day. Mrs Boles and Mrs Bates. Bundles of coats and scarves, but their hats had flowers and bright ribbon. Spring.

"Oh, you do run about," says Mrs Bates. "And how is Maudie Fowler?"

"She is the same."

"Mrs Rogers was asking after you," she said.

"Do you know what about?"

"Oh, she's ever so good, Mrs Rogers, running about, just like you."

That is how things happen. Now I am waiting to run into Mrs Rogers somewhere.

Another five weeks have gone. Nothing has changed . . . and yet of course it must have. Same in the office, with Joyce, same with Maudie. But I've met Vera Rogers. On the pavement, she was talking to the old women. They called, she turned, an anxious friendly smile, she was across the street and with me. She is a smallish thin girl. I was actually going to write: *a size twelve.* When am I going to stop thinking of people first in terms of what they wear? Phyllis asked me recently, what was my sister like, and I said, She wears good jersey suits and good shoes and cashmere. Phyllis laughed exactly the sort of laugh I'd have meant her to, only a year ago.

Vera stood in front of me on the windy pavement, smiling an anxious, warm, apologetic smile. Brown friendly eyes. Pink nail varnish, but chipped. Yes, of course this says something about her: she's overworked. Clothes down-market Jaeger, pleasant, not exciting. I knew that here she was, "the one". There was not much need for all the opening moves. I said, "I was hoping to run into you." She said, "Yes, I would so much like to talk to you about Mrs Fowler." I said, "She's terrified she will be forcibly rehoused." She said, "Yes, but we can stave it off a bit." I said, "Meanwhile, what would help her most is Meals on Wheels." She said, "She's active, you see, she can get about, she's not really entitled . . . but if you think . . ." I said, "She can't make herself cook any more, you see, she lives on bits and pieces."

She began to laugh. She said, "I must tell you something really funny, it happened to me last week. I went to see one of my cases, she's ninety-four. Deaf, arthritic, but she does everything for herself, cooks, cleans, shops. There I was, watching her prepare her lunch. A meat pie, cabbage cooked in soda, and then cream cake. I said to her, Do you ever eat any fresh stuff, fruit or salad? What? she shouted at me."

Vera took such pleasure in telling me this, but she was anxious too, in case I wouldn't find it funny, and she touched my arm once or twice, as if to say, Oh, I hope you'll laugh.

"You must eat fruit and vegetables, I shouted at her. You need vitamins. Every time I come to see you, I never see a vestige of green, or an apple or an orange. And she said, What, what, what? though I knew she could hear, and then when I repeated it, she said, And how old did you say *you* were, dear? And then I thought about all my aches and pains, and I've been eating all the right things since I was a child."

And so we laughed, and she looked relieved.

"I've got to get home to the old man," said she. "I'll fix the Meals on Wheels. But if we could get a free moment at the same time we could have a real talk." And she went running along the street to a yellow VW and nipped off, smartly, into the traffic.

Maudie is so pleased about the meals coming in every midday, though they aren't very nice. Stodgy and badly cooked.

I have realized how *heavy* everything is for her. Yes, I knew this before, but not really, until I saw her delight when I said she was on the list for Meals. She thanked me over and over again.

"You see, *you* did it, but *she* wouldn't, oh no, not she!"

"Did you ask her?" I said.

"What's the use, I've asked often enough, but they say I need a Home Help."

"And so you do."

"Oh well, if that's it, then say it! I've looked after myself before and I can do without you."

"Oh, you are so difficult, Maudie. What's the matter with a Home Help?'

"Have you ever had one?"

At which I laughed, and then she laughed.

Now we are nearly into summer.

What has happened since I sat down last to this unfortunate diary of mine? But I don't want to give it up.

I've met Vera Rogers several times, and we talk—on the pavement, once for a snatched half-hour in a café. We talk in shorthand, because we neither of us have time.

Once she asked how I got involved with Maudie, and when she heard, said, with a sigh, "I had hoped you were really a Good Neighbour, because I know someone who I think might accept a Good Neighbour. She's difficult, but she's lonely."

This was a request, put delicately and with embarrassment, but I said that Maudie was enough.

"Yes, of course she is," she said at once.

I told her what work I do, and then she had to be told *why*. As if I understood it myself! Why am I bound to this Maudie Fowler as I am? I said, "I like her, I really do."

"Oh yes, she's wonderful, isn't she?" said Vera warmly. "And some of them, you'd like to strangle. I used to feel wicked when I started this work, I believed I had to like them all. And then, when I'd been with some difficult old cat for an hour, and I couldn't get anywhere, I'd find myself thinking, God, I'll hit her one of these days, I will."

"Well, I've felt that about Maudie often enough."

"Yes, but there's something else."

"Yes, there is."

I told Maudie how much Vera likes her, and she closed up in an angry pinched mask.

"But *why*, Maudie?"

"She didn't lift a finger to help."

"But how can she if you don't tell her what you want?"

"All I want is to be left alone."

"There you are, you see."

"Yes, here I am alone, except for you."

"Vera Rogers doesn't just have one person to visit, she has sometimes ten or more in a day, and she's on the telephone arranging and getting things done. I see you every day, so I know what you want."

"They'll have to carry me out screaming," said she.

"She's on your side, she's trying to prevent you from being moved."

"That's what she tells you. They were around here again today."

"Who?"

"Do you know what he said, that Greek? You can stay in one room, and we'll do up the other, he said. And then when we've finished that, you can move in. Me, here in all that dust and mess. And it's months they take to improve a place."

"Then that must have been the landlord, mustn't it?"

"Yes, that's what I said. They are all in it together."

At the Indian shop, I hung around until the owner, Mr Patel, said, "Mrs Fowler was out on the street yesterday, screaming and shouting."

"Oh yes, what did she say?"

"She was screaming, None of you were around trying to get me hot water and a bath when I had a baby, none of you cared when I didn't have food to give him. I've lived all my life without running hot water and a bath, and if you come back I'll get the police."

Mr Patel says all this slowly, his grave concerned eyes on my face, and I didn't dare smile. He keeps his eyes on my face, reproachful and grave, and says, "When I was in Kenya, before we had to leave, I thought everyone in this country was rich."

"You know better now, then."

But he wants to say something else, something different. I waited, picked up some biscuits, put them back, considered a tin of cat food.

At last he says, in a low voice, "Once, with us, we would not let one of our old people come to such a life. But now—things are changing with us."

I feel I personally should apologize. At last I say, "Mr Patel, there can't be very many like Mrs Fowler left."

"I have six, seven, every day in my shop. All like her, with no one to care for them. And I am only one shop."

He sounds as if he is accusing me. He is accusing my clothes, my style. I am out of place in this little corner shop. And then, feeling as if he has wronged me, he takes a cake from the shelves, one that Maudie likes, and says, "Give it to her."

Our eyes meet again, and this time differently: we are appalled, we are frightened, it is all too much for us.

That was eight days ago.

Joyce may go after all to the States. The girlfriend had an abortion. Husband Jack took this badly: he wanted her to have the baby. He has been having a sort of breakdown, and Joyce has been comforting him. This has been going on for weeks.

When she told me:

"It appears he has been longing for us to have another child."

"Did you know?"

"Well, I knew he wouldn't mind, but not that he cared so much."

"If you had known?"

"Yes, I think I would."

"So now you are both blaming the other?"

"Yes."

Joyce with a cigarette dangling, eyes screwed up, holding up photographs, one after another, Yes, to this one, No to that. Her hair dyed again, but with the dusty look. Her hands unkept. She *looks* fifty. There is something weird and witchlike about her. I've said to her, "Joyce, you must change your style, it's too young." And she said, "When I know if I'm going or not, I'll know which to choose, won't I?"

Joyce is always on the verge of tears. A word, a joke, a tone of voice—she'll turn her head sharply, screw up her eyes, peer at me, at Phyllis, at whomever, the tears welling up. But she shakes them away, pretends there's nothing. Phyllis and I have this unspoken thing: we watch every syllable, word, suggestion, so that Joyce will not suddenly betray herself, and start crying.

Later. How long? I forget. Some days.

Joyce said to me today that she said to Jack, Your trouble is, you want to take this situation with you to the States. Home, children, wife the sympathetic comforter—and girlfriend as well, in a separate place. You can't choose. That's why you are so ill.

And he said to her she was heartless and cold.

Four months before he leaves. He should have told them over there if a wife, or no wife, children or not.

"Perhaps he will go by himself in the end," I mused, forgetting about not upsetting her.

She turned her head in that quick startled way she has now, she leans forward frowning, peering at me. My old friend Joyce, she is a thousand miles away, in some sort of black place, and she peers out at me, thinking, who is this quacking idiot?

"Alone!" she said, in a brisk schoolmistress voice.

"Why not?"

"There's something missing in you, I've always said so," she says, coldly, filing me away.

"Or perhaps there is in you."

I told her about Maudie Fowler, who has lived alone now for something like sixty years. Joyce got up as I spoke, picked up her bag, her briefcase, collected things from her desk.

"How did you get to know her?"

I told her. Joyce listened.

"Guilt," she said at last. "Guilt. If you want to let it get to you, that's your affair."

She was on her way to the door. I said, "Joyce, I want to tell you about it, properly, I really do. I want to talk about it."
She said, "Well, not now."

It is summer. Not that I am seeing much of it.
When did Joyce get ill? It must be over a month now. The truth was, we were all relieved, because it made what really was the truth official. I have been running around from morning to night. In the hospital, this scene: Joyce's husband, the two children, husband's *ex*-mistress, her new boyfriend. Joyce lying back, looking at them all from inside this black place she is in, smiling when she remembers to. Now he wants her to go to America, but she says she doesn't have the energy to think about it. But of course she will go.
Because of all this, I don't stay so long at Maudie's, though I have not missed one day. She understands why, I have told her. But the way she *feels* it is, I'm letting her down. I sit there, trying not to look at my watch, and she is remembering only bad things. I say, "Tell me about the day you went to the Heath with Johnnie, and you found blackberries and made a pie with them?" But she sighs, and sits rubbing those old fingers up and down her (filthy) skirts. Then she tells me about . . .
Her sister, Polly, who has had seven children, always summoned Maudie to look after her, each childbed. Maudie was always delighted, even gave up whatever job she might have, and took herself to her sister's, and looked after everything for weeks, more than once months. Then, says Maudie, it was always the same, the sister got jealous, because Maudie loved the children and they loved her. She found an excuse to say, You are turning my children against me, you are after my husband. Is it likely, says Maudie, the nasty scrimping thing, he grudged me the food I ate while I was working as a slavey. He'd say, if I put a bit of meat on my plate, We'll have to buy an extra bit of beef on Sunday, while Maudie honours us with her presence. Meanwhile, I was working eighteen hours a day for them. Between births, Maudie heard nothing of her sister, but she wasn't worried: There'd be another baby, I knew that, because he had to have what he had to have.

Now Maudie talks a lot about sex, and I see that it has been enormous and awful to her, and she has never understood it or ceased to be tormented by it. She says her husband, while he was still treating her like a queen, would leap on her like a tiger, like a wild beast. She says she can't understand it, one moment all lovey-dovey, and the next they have their nails into you. Her husband has been with one woman after another, and she has been brooding about it all her life: *why?* For Maudie has slept with one man, her awful husband. She knows that there are women who like it, and she looks at me while she talks, with a certain modesty and diffidence, because I might be offended if I knew she was wondering if I was "like that".

Yet, she has had other experiences. Upstairs, for some years, there was a woman who became her friend, and this woman "liked it". She used to tell Maudie how she would wait all day until the night, because another life began at night, and it was her real life. Maudie said to me, "She told me that when they had finished all that, she had to sleep lying behind his back, so that she could hold his thing. That *thing* . . ." cries Maudie, almost weeping with disgust, wonder, and disbelief. "Yes, it was out of respect, she said to me." And Maudie sits there, amazed, after thirty or forty years of thinking about it. Suddenly: "I wouldn't give them that much satisfaction, it's the stick they beat you with!"

And then I laughed (and I wasn't comfortable at all, thinking my own thoughts, for that just about summed it up, never mind that we had such a wonderful sex life, Freddie and I), and she said, "I have been watching your face. I can see you think differently. But I can't help it. And now all the time the newspapers, the magazines, the telly, sex, sex, sex, and I think sometimes, am I mad, are *they* mad?"

I laugh and laugh. She laughs too. But it is a wild unhappy laugh, not at all her girl's laugh that I love to hear.

Such is the power of—?—that Maudie refers to that awful husband of hers, even now, as My man. She has seen him half a dozen times in half a century. One day, a knock at the door, and there stood her husband. But this young man said, "Mother? I'm your son Johnnie." "Well, come in then," said she. "I had put it out of mind, you see. I had made myself ill

with fretting. Once I had to go to the doctor, and he said, Mrs
Fowler, you must either find your child or put him out of your
mind. How could I find him? He might be in America or
Timbuctoo! And slowly I did forget him. And so when he was
there—I am your son Johnnie, he said—we became friends,
because we took to each other. And then there was the war. He
did well in the war, he was an engineer, and he married an
Italian girl, but it came to no good, for she went off with
another man, and do you know what I dreamed the other
night? Oh, it was a doleful dream, so bad and low. I dreamed
there was a wonderful cherry tree, like the cherry tree there
was out the back here before it fell down in a big storm. Big
black cherries, soft and lovely and shining. And I stood one
side of it, and poor Johnnie stood on the other, and we were
trying to lean up and reach the cherries, and we tried and tried,
but no matter how we pulled the boughs down, they sprang
back, and the cherries were out of reach . . . And we stood
there, Johnnie and I, and we were crying."

Long after Johnnie was a grown man and had gone to
America, where he vanished, and forty years after Laurie had
left her, stealing her child, Maudie wrote a letter to her
husband, asking him to meet her. They met on a bench in
Regent's Park.

"Well, what do you want?" he said.

"I was thinking, perhaps we could make a home for Johnnie," she said to him. She explained that they could find a
house—for she knew he always had money, wheeling and
dealing—and make it nice, and then an advertisement in the
paper in America.

"For Johnnie has never had a nice home," she explained to
her husband.

"And what did he say?"

"He bought me a fish supper, and I didn't see him for five
years."

A marvellous hot blue day.

I said to Phyllis, "Hold the fort," and I ran out of the office,
to hell with it. I went to Maudie, and when she answered the

door, slow, slow, and cross, I said, "I'm taking you to the park for a treat." She stared at me, *furious*. "Oh, don't," I said to her. "Oh, darling Maudie, don't, *please*, don't let yourself get angry, just come."

"But how can I?" she says. "Look at me!"

And she peers up at the sky past my head. It is so blue and nice, and she says, "But . . . but . . . but . . ."

Then suddenly she smiles. She puts on her thick black-beetle coat and her summer hat, black straw, and we go off to the Rose Garden Restaurant. I find her a table out of the way of people, with rose bushes beside her, and I pile a tray with cream cakes, and we sit there all afternoon. She ate and ate, in her slow, consuming way, which says, I'm going to get this inside me while it is here!—and then she sat, she simply sat and looked, and looked. She was smiling and delighted. Oh, the darlings, she kept crooning, the darlings . . . at the sparrows, at the roses, at a baby in a pram near her. I could see she was beside herself with a fierce, almost angry delight, this hot brightly coloured sunlit world was like a gorgeous present. For she had forgotten it, down in that ghastly basement, in those dreary streets.

I was worried that it would all be too much for her inside that thick black shell, and it was so hot and noisy. But she did not want to leave. She sat there until it closed.

And when I took her home she was singing dreamily to herself, and I took her to her door, and she said, "No, leave me, leave me, I want to sit here and think about it. Oh, what lovely things I have to think about."

What did strike me, when I saw her out there in the full sunlight: how yellow she is. Bright blue eyes in a face that looks as if it has been painted yellow.

Three days later.

Another gorgeous afternoon. Went to Maudie, said, "Come to the park."

She said irritably, "No, no, you go, I can't."

"Oh come on," I said, "you know you like it once you get there."

She stood holding to the door handle, distressed, angry, dishevelled. Then she said, "No, oh dreadful, dreadful, dreadful," and shut the door in my face.

I was *furious*. I had been thinking, as I drove to her, how she sat in the rose garden, crooning with delight. I went back to the office, furious. Worked till late. Did not go in to Maudie. Felt guilty, as I wallowed about with the hot water making me new again: kept seeing how she stood there, holding herself up, heard the mutter, Dreadful, dreadful . . .

A week has passed, it is dreary and chilly again. End of summer? Maudie seems to me, perhaps, really ill? . . . I know so little about old people! For all I know, all this is normal! I keep setting aside a time to think about her, but I am so busy, busy, busy. I rush in to her, at all hours, I say to her, I'm sorry, Maudie, I've got so much work. Last night I went in late and fell asleep in her chair. This morning I rang up the office and said I was not feeling well. In all my years there I think I've been ill twice, and I never take days off.

Phyllis said, "That's all right, I'll hold the fort!"

Maudie's day.

She wakes inside a black smothering weight, she can't breathe, can't move. They've buried me alive, she thinks, and struggles. The weight shifts. Oh, it's the cat, it's my pretty, she thinks, and heaves. The weight lifts, and she hears a thud as the cat arrives on the floor. Petty? she asks, for she is not sure, it is so dark and her limbs are so stiff. She hears the cat moving about and knows she is alive. And warm . . . and in bed . . . Oh, oh, she says aloud, I must get to the toilet or I'll wet the bed again. Panic! Have I wet the bed already? Her hand explores the bed. She mutters, Dreadful, dreadful, dreadful, dreadful, thinking how, a few days ago, she had wet the bed, and the trouble and difficulty of getting everything dry.

But it is as if her hand has disappeared, she can't feel it. She clenches and unclenches her left hand, to know she *has* hands, and waits for the tingling to begin in her right. It takes a long time, and then she pulls out the half-numb right hand from under the clothes and uses the left to massage it awake. She still does not know if she has wet the bed. Almost she sinks back into the black bed, black sleep, but her bowels are moving and she smells a bad smell. Oh no, no, no, she whimpers, sitting there in the dark, No, dreadful, for she believes she might have shat in the bed. At last, with such effort and trouble, she climbs out of the bed, and stands beside it, feeling in it to see what is there. She can't be sure. She turns, carefully, tries to find the light switch. She has a torch by the bed, but the batteries ran low, she meant to ask Janna to get new ones, and forgot. She thinks, surely Janna would think to look for herself, she knows how I need the torch! She finds the switch, and there is light . . . and anxiously she inspects the bed, which is dry. But she has to get to the toilet. She never uses the commode for more than a pee. She must get herself to the outside toilet. But there is a hot wet thrusting in her bowels and she gets herself to the commode, just in time. She sits there, rocking herself, keening. Dreadful, dreadful, for now she will have to take the pot out, and she feels so low and bad.

She sits there a long time, too tired to get up. She even sleeps a little. Her bottom is numb. She pulls herself up, looks for the paper. No lav paper, because she doesn't use it in here. She cannot find anything to use . . . At last she struggles to the cupboard, her bottom all wet and loathsome, finds an old petticoat, rips off a piece, uses it to clean herself, and shuts down the lid on the smell—and worse, for while she does allow herself a fearful peep, she refuses to let her mind acknowledge that there is something wrong with her stool. Dreadful, she mutters, meaning the stuff her bowels seem to produce these days, and shoves the curtains back off the windows.

It is light outside. But it is summer, it could be the middle of the night still. She cannot bear to think of the difficulties of getting back into bed, and then out of it again. Her little clock has its face turned away from her, she doesn't want to cross the room to it. She pulls around herself an old shawl, and huddles in the chair by the dead fire. No birds yet, she thinks: has the dawn chorus been and gone or am I waiting for it? She thinks of how, a child, she lay with her sisters in the bed in the cottage of the old woman in the summers, and woke to the shrill violence of the dawn chorus and slept again, thinking of the lovely hot day ahead, a day that had no end to it, all play and pleasure and plentiful tasty meals.

And so Maudie drifts off to sleep, but wakes, and sleeps and wakes for some hours, each time remembering to move her hands so that they don't stiffen up too much. At last she wakes to the cat rubbing and purring around her legs. Which are stiff. She tests her hands. The right one gone again. With the left she caresses the cat, Pretty, petty, pretty pet, and with the right she tries to flex and unflex fingers until she is whole again.

Morning . . . oh, the difficulties of morning, of facing the day . . . each task such a weight to it . . . She sits there, thinking, I have to feed the cat, I have to . . . I have to . . . At last, she drags herself up, anxious, because her bowels are threatening again, and, holding on to door handles, chair backs, she gets herself into the kitchen. There is a tin of cat food, half empty. She tries to turn it on to a saucer, it won't come out. It means she has to get a spoon. A long way off, in the sink, are her spoons and forks, she hasn't washed up for days. She winkles out the cat food with her forefinger, her face wrinkled up—is it smelling perhaps? She lets the saucer fall from a small height on to the floor, for bending forward makes her faint. The cat sniffs at it and walks away, with a small miaow. Maudie sees that under the table are saucers, bone dry and empty. The cat needs milk, she needs water. Slowly, slowly, Maudie gets herself to the sink, pulls out of it a dirty saucer which she has not got the energy to wash, runs water into it. Finds a half bottle of milk. Has it gone off? She sniffs. No. She somehow gets the saucer on to the floor, holding on to the table and nearly falling. The cat drinks all the milk, and Maudie knows she is hungry.

Under the table not only the saucers, one, two, three, four, five, but a cat mess. This reminds Maudie she has to let the cat out. She toils to the door, lets out the cat, and stands with her back to the door, thinking. A general planning a campaign could not use more cleverness than Maudie does, as she outwits her weakness and her terrible tiredness. She is already at the back door: the toilet is five steps away; if she goes now it will save a journey later . . . Maudie gets herself to the toilet, uses it, remembers there is the commode full of dirt and smell in her room, somehow gets herself along the passage to her room, somehow gets the pot out from under the round top, somehow gets herself and the pot to the toilet. She splashes a bit as she empties it, and, looking, smelling, her mind has to acknowledge that there is something very wrong. But she thinks, as long as *she* (meaning Janna) does not see what I am making, no one will know. *And they won't put me away* . . .

When all that is done it seems to her that a long time has passed, yet she knows that it is still early, for she cannot hear those noisy Irish brats. She needs a cup of tea very badly, all her energy has gone into the cat.

She stands by her kitchen table, holding on to it, thinking of how she will carry the cup of hot reviving tea next door. But hot tea makes you run, no, better cold milk. She gets the cold milk into the glass. That is the end of the milk. She needs: milk, toilet paper, cat food, matches, tea, and probably a lot else, if she could think of it.

Perhaps Janna will come soon and . . .

She looks sternly at the cat mess, which seems to her a long way down, measuring it in her mind with the need to stoop, and thinks, Janna will . . .

She gets herself and the milk next door. Sits down. But she is cold now, summer or not. She sits in that old chair of hers, by the cold grate, and feels the heat leaking out of her. She has to get the fire made. Should she plug in the heater? But it takes so much electricity, she is only *just* balancing her needs with her pension. She at last struggles up and plugs it in. The room has the warm red glow of the heater, her legs seem to loosen and become themselves. She sits there, sipping her milk, and muttering, Dreadful, dreadful, dreadful.

Then she drifts off into a dream that Janna has taken her into her own home and is looking after her. She is fiercely possessive of this dream, and cuddles and cossets it, taking it out and adding to it whenever she sits there by herself, but she knows it will not happen. *Cannot* happen. But why not? It was impossible that Janna should fly into her life the way she did, who would ever have thought of it? And then how she comes in and out, with her jokes and her flowers and cakes and stuff, all her stories about her office, she is probably making it up, after all, how can she, a poor old woman, know better, if Janna chooses to embellish it all a little? So why, then, should not another impossible thing happen, that she should be taken into a lovely warm flat and there she would be looked after, things done for her . . .

Or Janna would come and live here. There is that room next door . . . That is what Maudie really wants. She does not want to leave here. Get yourself your own place and never let go of it: Maudie repeats this whenever she is tempted—as now—to leave here and go and live with Janna. No, no, she mutters, she will have to come here. And she sits there, sometimes dozing, thinking of how Janna is living there, looking after her, and of how, when she wakes in the night, alone and frightened that she is in the grave, she can call out, and hear Janna's reply.

But soon her bowels force her to get up. Although she emptied the pot she did not wash it out, and it is disgusting to her. So she goes outside to the toilet, letting in the cat, who is waiting and who goes to the saucer with the smelly food in it, and disdains it, and patiently comes into the room with Maudie. Who, now she is up, decides to make a fire. It takes her over an hour, the crawling along the corridor to get the coal, the crawling back, the raking of the ashes, the lighting of the fire. She blows at it in small shallow puffs, because she gets dizzy, so it takes a long time to get going. Then she sits again, longing for a cup of tea, but refusing herself, because above all else she dreads the demands of her bladder, her bowels. She thinks, the Meals on Wheels will be here soon . . . it is only eleven, though. Perhaps they will be early today? She is hungry, she is so hungry she cannot now distinguish between her hunger pangs and the possibility that she must go again to the toilet. Before the cheerful young Meals on Wheels woman, who has a key, slams in and out, calling, Hello, Mrs Fowler, you all right—she has had to go out to the lavatory again.

It is early. Only half past twelve. Maudie at once takes the two small foil containers to the table and, hardly looking at what is in them, eats everything. She feels much better. She thinks, oh, if Janna would come now, and if she said, Come to the park, I'd not growl and grumble at her, I'd love to go. But she sees out of the window that it is raining. What a summer, she mutters. The cat is on the table sniffing at the empty containers, and Maudie is distressed at her greed, for she knows the cat is hungry and she should have shared.

Out she goes to the cold smelling kitchen and reaches about—yes, oh joy, there is a full unopened tin. So happy is Maudie that she even does a little dance there, clutching the tin to her chest. Oh, petty, petty, she cries, I can feed you. At last the tin is opened, though Maudie cuts her forefinger on the tin opener. The cat eats every bit. Maudie thinks, and now she should go out, to save me letting her out later . . . but the cat won't go out, she takes herself back into the room with the fire, sinks to sleep on Maudie's bed. Which has not been made. Maudie should make up her bed—she thinks, it's not nice for Janna. She does not, but sits in the chair by the fire, and leans forward to stack it up with coal, and then sleeps like the dead for three hours. Though she does not know what time it is, five in the afternoon, when she wakes, for her clock has stopped.

The cat is still asleep, the fire is out . . . she builds it up again. She could do with something. She *has* to have a cup of tea. She makes herself a full pot, brings the biscuits, and has a little feast at her table. She feels so much better for the tea that it is easy to disregard how she has to go out to the toilet once more, twice, three times. Her bowels are like an angry enemy down there, churning and demanding. What's wrong with you then? she cries, rubbing her hand round and round on the little mound of her belly. Why won't you leave me alone?

She ought to have a wash . . . she ought . . . she ought . . . but Janna will come, Janna will . . .

But Maudie sits there, waiting, and Janna does not come, and Maudie gets up to let out the insistent cat, and Maudie fetches the coal, and Maudie attends to the fire, and Maudie searches about to see if there is a little brandy, for suddenly she feels bad, she feels trembly, she could fall to the ground and lie there, she is so empty and tired . . . No brandy. Nothing.

She can go out to the off-licence? No, no, she could not possibly get herself up the steps. Janna has not come and it is getting dark. That means it must be getting on for ten. Janna is not coming . . . and there is no milk, no tea, no food for poor petty, nothing.

And Maudie sits by her roaring furious fire thinking bitterly of Janna, who does not care, wicked unkind cruel Janna . . . In the middle of all this, loud knocks at the door, and Maudie's relief explodes into a raucous shout: Oh, all right, I'm *coming*. And scrambles along the passage, crabwise, to the door, afraid Janna might fly off before she gets there. Terrible, terrible, she mutters, and her face, as she opens the door, is fierce and accusing.

"Oh my God, Maudie," cries Janna, "let me in, I'm dead. What a day."

Oh then, if she's tired I can't ask her . . . thinks Maudie, and stands aside as Janna comes crashing in, all energy and smiles.

In the room, Maudie sees Janna smile as she sees the wonderful fire, and sees, too, a wrinkling of her nose, which is at once suppressed.

Janna says, "I said to the Indian man, Don't close, because he was closing, wait, I must get Mrs Fowler some things."

"Oh, I don't need anything," says Maudie, at once reacting to the news that she has to be beholden to the Indian man, with whom she quarrels nearly every time she goes in . . . he overcharges, he is cheating her over her change . . .

Janna, thank goodness, has taken no notice, but is whirling around in the kitchen, to see what is missing, and out she rushes with a basket, before poor Maudie can remember the batteries. In such a hurry, she always is! And they are all like that, rushing in, rushing out, before I have time to turn myself round.

In no time Janna comes crashing back, slam the outside door, slam-bang this door, with a basket full of stuff which Maudie checks, with such relief and thankfulness. Everything is here, nice fresh fish for the cat and a tin of Ovaltine. Janna has thought of everything.

Has she noticed the cat mess, the unwashed stuff in the sink . . . ?

Maudie goes quietly to sit by the fire, on a smile from Janna which says, It is all right. Janna cleans up the cat mess, does the washing-up, puts away the crockery, and does not think, because she is young and so healthy, to leave out on the kitchen table some saucers and a spoon and the tin opener so that Maudie won't have to bend and peer and rummage about.

Maudie sits listening to Janna working away, *looking after me*—and thinks, oh, if she doesn't remember about the commode . . .

But when Janna comes in, she brings a small bottle of brandy and two glasses, and, having handed Maudie her brandy, she says, "I'll just . . ." and whisks out the dirty pot and takes it away.

I hope there is nothing left in it for her to notice, Maudie worries, but when Janna brings back the scoured pot, smelling nicely of pine forests, she says nothing.

Janna lets herself crash down into the chair near the fire, smiles at Maudie, picks up her glass of brandy, swallows it in a mouthful, says: "Oh, Maudie, what a day, let me tell you . . ." And she sighs, yawns—and is asleep. Maudie sees it, can't believe it, knows it is so, and is in a rage, in a fury. For she has been waiting to talk, to listen, to have a friend and some ordinary decent communication, perhaps a cup of tea in a minute, never mind about her bowels, and her bladder . . . And here is Janna, fast asleep.

It is so dark outside. Maudie pulls the curtains over. Maudie goes out to the back door and sees that all the dirty saucers are gone from under the table, and the cat mess gone, and there is a smell of disinfectant. She lets in the cat, and takes the opportunity for a quick visit to the lavatory. She comes back, and pokes up the fire, and sits down opposite Janna, who is sleeping like . . . the dead.

Maudie has not had this opportunity before, of being able to stare and look and examine openly, to pore over the evidence, and she sits leaning forward, looking as long as she needs into the face of Janna, which is so nicely available there.

It's an agreeable face, thinks Maudie, but there's something . . . Well, of course, she's young, that's the trouble, she doesn't understand yet. But look at her neck there, folded up, you can see the age there, and her hands, for all they are so clean and painted, they aren't young hands.

Her clothes, oh her lovely clothes, look at that silk there, peeping out, that's real silk, oh *I* know what it's worth, what it is. And her pretty shoes . . . No rubbish on her, ever. And she didn't get any change out of what she paid for that hat of hers! Look at it, she flings it down on the bed, that lovely hat, the cat is nearly on top of it.

Look at those little white quills there . . . the Rolovskys used to say that they never had anyone to touch me for making those little quills. I could do them now, it is all here still, the skill of it in my fingers . . . I wonder if . . .

Maudie carefully gets up, goes to the bed, picks up the lovely hat, goes back to her chair with it. She looks at the satin that lines the hat, the way the lining is stitched in—blown in, rather; oh yes, the one who did this hat knew her work all right! And the little white quills . . .

Maudie dozes off, and wakes. It is because the fridge upstairs is rumbling and crashing. But almost at once it stops—that means it has been on for a long time, because it runs for an hour or more. Janna is still asleep. She hasn't moved. She is breathing so lightly that Maudie is afraid, and peers to make sure . . .

Janna is smiling in her sleep? Or is it the way she is lying? Oh, she's going to have a stiff neck all right . . . is she going to stay here all night then? Well, what am *I* expected to do? Sit up here while the night goes? That's just like them, they think of nobody but themselves, they don't think of me . . .

Rage boils in Maudie Fowler, as she sits caressing the lovely hat, looking at sleeping Janna.

Maudie sees Janna's eyes are open. She thinks, oh my *Gawd*, has she died? No, she is blinking. She hasn't moved anything else, but she is lying there in the chair, eyes open, looking past Maudie at the window that has hours ago shut out the wet and blowy night with old greasy yellow curtains.

Maudie thinks, she is taking a long time to come to herself, surely? And then Janna's eyes move to her face, Maudie's: Janna looks, suddenly, terrified, as if she will get up and run—and for a moment all her limbs gather together in a spring, as if she will be off. And then the horrible moment is past, and Janna says, "Oh, Maudie, I have been asleep, why didn't you wake me?"

"I have been looking at this gorgeous hat," says Maudie, stroking it delicately with her thick clumsy fingers.

Janna laughs.

Maudie says, "You could stay the night next door, if you like."

Janna says, "But I have to be home to let in a man to do the electricity."

Maudie knows this is a lie, but does not care.

She thinks, Janna has been asleep here half the night, as if this is her place!

She says, "I have been thinking, this is the best time of my life."

Janna sits straight up in her chair, because, being young, her limbs don't stiffen up, and she leans forward and looks into Maudie's face, serious, even shocked.

"Maudie," she says, "you can't say that!"

"But it's true," says Maudie. "I mean, I'm not talking about the short joyful days, like carrying my Johnnie, or a picnic here and a picnic there, but now, I know you will always come and we can be together."

Janna has tears filling up her eyes, and she blinks them back and says, "For all that, Maudie . . ."

"Will you remember to bring me in some batteries for my torch?" says Maudie, in the humble but aggressive way she makes requests.

Janna says, "I tell you what, I'll bring in my torch from the car, and you can have that."

She goes out, in her usual striding way, but then comes back to say, "Maudie, it's morning, the sky is alight."

The two women stand in Maudie's entrance and see the grey light in the streets.

Maudie does not like to say that now she will probably lie on her bed, with the curtains drawn, and stay there for some hours. She suspects Janna of intending not to sleep again that night. Well, she's young, she can do it. She would so much like to have Janna's torch, because after all Janna might not come in tomorrow—no, today.

But Janna kisses her, laughs, and goes rushing off down the dingy wet pavements. She has forgotten her hat.

*   *   *

Janna's day.

The alarm makes me sit up in bed. Sometimes I switch it off, sink back, today not: I sit in the already bright morning, five o'clock, and look through the day ahead: I cannot believe that by the time I end it I shall have done so much. I make myself jump out of bed, I make myself coffee, I am at my typewriter ten minutes after I am awake. I should have put in: I emptied my bladder, but I am still "young" and do not count that among the things that have to be done! But today I shall write down the visits to the loo, otherwise how can I compare my day with Maudie's? The articles I wrote, so tentatively, and without confidence, last year, have become a book. It is nearly finished. I said it would be done by the end of this month. It will be. *Because I said it would be.* That I do what I say gives me such strength! And then, there is a project no one knows about: a historical novel. It was Maudie gave me the idea. I think of that time as quite recent, my grandmother's; but Vera Rogers speaks of it as I might speak of, I don't know, let's say Waterloo. I plan a historical novel, conceived and written as one, about a milliner in London. I long to begin it.

I work hard until eight. Then I drink coffee and eat an apple, shower, am into my clothes, am off, in half an hour. I like to be there by nine, and I always am. Today, Phyllis was late. No Joyce. I collected mail for the three of us and called the secretary and it was done and out of the way by ten and the Conference. Phyllis most apologetic: she is like me, never late, never away, never ill. The Conference is as usual, lively and *wonderful*. It was Joyce who said it would be like a Think Tank. Everyone, from the PRs and the photographers' assistants to Editorial, encouraged to have ideas, no matter how wild, how crazy, because you never know. As usual, Phyllis writes it all down. It was she who volunteered to do it, and both Joyce and I knew, when she did, that she was thinking, it is a key position. Phyllis does not let these ideas disappear, she lists them, she has them duplicated on all our desks through all the departments. An idea that drops out of sight might emerge again a year later. Today somebody revived one, that the "uniforms for women" series should include the types of clothes worn, for instance, by female television announcers or women going out to dinners with their husbands for career reasons. That is, a certain kind of dinner gown, or style, as uniform . . . that makes my style a uniform! But I knew that! I wear it all the time. Even, said Freddie, in bed. I never wear anything but real silk, fine cotton, lawn, in bed . . . he used to joke that if I were to wear a nylon nightie, it would be the same for me as if I committed a crime.

Thinking about Freddie in the office, I surprised myself in tears, and was glad that I had said I would interview Martina, and got to Brown's Hotel just in time. I am *never* late. She easy to interview, professional, competent, no time wasted, full marks. I got back at twelve thirty, asked Phyllis if she would do the Eminent Women Luncheon. She said firmly no, she could not, I must. I am a stand-in for Joyce, who is the eminent woman, but she is ill, and Phyllis is of course right, was right to look surprised: for it would not be appropriate for Phyllis to do it. Once I would not have made such a slip, but the truth is, my mind is more and more on my two books, the one nearly finished, my lovely historical novel soon to be started.

I look at myself in the washroom. I forgot this morning about the Luncheon, no marks for that, I am slipping! A button hanging on its thread, and my nails were not perfect. I did my nails in the taxi. The Luncheon agreeable, I made a speech on behalf of Joyce.

On the way back from the Luncheon I go into Debenham's and up to the top floor, and there I look for Maudie's kind of vests, real wool, modest high petticoats, and long close-fitting knickers. I buy ten knickers, and three vests, three petticoats— because she wets her knickers now, and sometimes worse. Rush, rush, rush, but I'm back by three thirty. I phone to make an appointment with the hairdresser, another for the car. Phyllis said she felt awful. She looked it. So apologetic, such a criminal! For God's sake, go to bed, I said, and swept all her work from her desk to mine. I did the recipes, summer food, I did Young Fashion, went off with the photographers to Kenwood for a session, came back and worked by myself in the office, no one else there, until nine. I love being by myself, no telephones, nothing, only the watchman. He went out for Indian take-away, I asked him to join me, we had a quick supper on the corner of my desk. He's nice, George, I encouraged him to talk about his problems, won't go into that, but we can help, he needs a loan.

I was tired by then and suddenly longing for bed. I did some more work, rang Joyce in Wales, heard from her voice that she was better, but she was noncommittal. I don't give a damn, she said, when I asked if she were going to the States. She is saying, too, I don't give a damn about you either. This made me think about the condition of not giving a damn. On my desk, in the "Too difficult" basket, an article about stress, how enough stress can cause indifference. It is seen in war, in hard times. Suffer, suffer, emote, emote, and then suddenly, you don't care. I wanted this published. Joyce said, No, not enough people would recognize it. Irony!

I said good night to George at nine thirty, and got a taxi to where I leave my car, and drove up towards home, thinking, no, no, I can't go in to Maudie, I simply cannot. When I banged, I was irritable, I was tired, I was thinking, I hope she is in the lavatory and doesn't hear. But when she opened, I could see by her face . . . I switched on everything I have, and made myself crash in, all gaiety and liveliness, because I am afraid of her black moods, for once she starts I can't shift her out of them. That is why I arrived, female Father Christmas, HM the Queen Mum, all radiant, I have to stop her muttering and raging.

When I reach her back room, it is hot and smelly, the smell hits me, but I make myself smile at the fire. I see from her face what is needful, and I go into the kitchen. I was nearly sick. I whirl around the kitchen, because I know the Indian grocer is about to close, and I run across the road, saying, "Please, just another minute, I need stuff for Mrs Fowler." He is patient and kind, but he is a grey-violet colour from tiredness. Sometimes he is in here from eight until eleven at night. Often by himself. He is educating three sons and two daughters . . . He asks, "How is she?" I say, "I think she isn't well." He says, as always, "It is time her people looked after her."

When I get back, I cut up fish for the cat. It is no good, I cannot make myself appreciate cats, though that makes me an insensitive boor. I clean up the cat's mess, I get the brandy and glasses. I realize I have forgotten the vests and knickers in the office. Well, tomorrow will do. I take out her commode, because she is *not* looking at it, with a trembling pride on her face I know only too well by now. As I wash it, I think, here's something very wrong. I shall have to tell Vera Rogers. I rinse the inside of the commode carefully and use a lot of disinfectant.

When I sit down opposite her, with brandy for her and me, I fully mean to tell her about the Luncheon, with all the famous women, she'd like that, but—that was the last I remember, until I came to myself, out of such a deep sleep I could not find myself when I woke. I was looking at a yellow little witch in a smelly hot cave, by her roaring fire, her yellow shanks showing, for she had no knickers on and her legs were apart, and on her lap she held my hat, and she was using it for some bad purpose . . . I was terrified, and then suddenly I remembered, I am Jane Somers, I am here, in Maudie's back room, and I fell asleep.

She did not want me to go. She made an excuse about batteries for her torch. I went to the door into the street, and it was morning. We stood there, looking up—oh, England, dismal and drear, a grey wet dawn. It was four thirty when I got home. I had a long, long proper bath, and then to my book again.

But I cannot concentrate on it. I am thinking about Maudie's "This is the best time of my life". What I cannot stand is, that I believe she means it. My running in at the end of the day, an hour, two hours, so little, is enough to make her say that. I want to howl when I think of it. And too, I feel so trapped. She might live for years and years, people live to be a hundred these days, and I am a prisoner of her "This is the best time of my life", lovely gracious Janna, running in and out, with smiles and prezzies.

I wrote Maudie's day because I want to understand. I *do* understand a lot more about her, but is it true? I can only write what I have experienced myself, heard her say, observed . . . I sometimes wake with one hand quite numb . . . But what else is there I cannot know about? I think that just as I could never have imagined she would say, "This is the best time of my life", and the deprivation and loneliness behind it, so I cannot know what is behind her muttered "It is dreadful, dreadful", and the rages that make her blue eyes blaze and glitter.

And I see that I did *not* write down, in Janna's day, about going to the loo, a quick pee here, a quick shit, washing one's hands . . . All day this animal has to empty itself, you have to brush your hair, wash your hands, bathe. I dash a cup under a tap and rinse out a pair of panties, it all takes a few minutes . . . But that is because I am "young", only forty-nine.

What makes poor Maudie labour and groan all through her day, the drudge and drag of *maintenance*. I was going to say, For me it is nothing; but the fact is, once I did have my real proper baths every night, once every Sunday night I maintained and polished my beautiful perfect clothes, maintained and polished *me*, and now I don't, I can't. It is too much for me.

Late summer, how I hate it, blowzy and damp, dowdy and dusty, dull green, dull skies; the sunlight, when there is any, a maggot-breeder; maggots under my dustbin, because I hadn't touched my own home for days.

Maudie has been ill again. Again I've been in, twice a day, before going to work and after work. Twice a day, she has stood by the table, leaning on it, weight on her palms, naked, while I've poured water over her till all the shit and smelly urine has gone. *The stench.* Her body, a cage of bones, yellow, wrinkled, her crotch like a little girl's, no hair, but long grey hairs in her armpits. I've been worn out with it. I said to her, "Maudie, they'd send you in a nurse to wash you," and she screamed at me, "Get out then, I didn't ask you."

We were both so tired and overwrought, we've been screeching at each other like . . . what? Out of literature, I say "fishwives", but she's no fishwife, a prim, respectable old body, or that's what she's been in disguise for three decades. I've seen a photograph, Maudie at sixty-five, the image of disapproving rectitude . . . I don't think I would have liked her then. She had said to herself, I like children, they like me, my sister won't let me near her now she's not breeding, she doesn't need my services. So Maudie put an advert in the Willesden paper, and a widower answered. He had three children, eight, nine, ten. Maudie was given the sofa in the kitchen, and her meals, in return for: cleaning the house, mending his clothes, the children's clothes, cooking three meals a day and baking, looking after the children. He was a fishmonger. When he came in at lunchtime, if he found Maudie sitting having a rest, he said to her, Haven't you got anything to do? He gave her two pounds a week to feed them all on, and when I said it was impossible, she said she managed. He brought home the fish for nothing, and you could buy bread and potatoes. No, he wasn't poor, but, said Maudie, he didn't know how to behave, that was his trouble. And Maudie stuck it, because of the children. Then he said to her, Will you come to the pictures with me? She went, and she saw the neighbours looking at them. She knew what they were thinking, and she couldn't have that. She cleaned the whole house, top to bottom, made sure everything was mended, baked bread, put out things for tea, and left a note: I am called to my sister's, who is ill, yours truly, Maude Fowler.

But then she took her pension, and sometimes did small jobs on the side.

The Maudie who wore herself "to a stick and a stone" was this judging, critical female, with a tight cold mouth.

Maudie and I shouted at each other, as if we were family, she saying, "Get out then, get out, but I'm not having those Welfare women in here," and I shouting, "Maudie, you're impossible, you're awful, I don't know what I'm going to do with you."

And then, once, I burst out laughing, it seemed so ridiculous, she there, stark naked, spitting anger at me, and I, rinsing off her shit and saying, "And what about your ears?"

She went silent and trembling. "*Why are you laughing at me?*"

"I'm not, I'm laughing at us. Look at us, screaming at each other!"

She stepped back out of the basin she had been standing in, gazing at me, in angry appeal.

I put the big towel around her, that I'd brought from my

bathroom, a pink cloud of a towel, and began gently drying her.

Tears finding their way through her wrinkles . . .

"Come on, Maudie, for God's sake, let's laugh, better than crying."

"It's terrible, terrible, terrible," she muttered, looking in front of her, eyes wide and bright. Trembling, shivering . . . "It's terrible, terrible."

These last three weeks I've thrown away all the new knickers I bought her, filthy and disgusting, bought two dozen more, and I've shown her how to fill them full of cotton wool as she puts them on.

So, she's back in napkins.

Terrible, terrible, terrible . . .

It is the end of August.

I am lying in bed writing this with the diary propped on my chest.

Just after writing the last *terrible*, I woke in the night, and it was as if my lower back had a metal bar driven into it. I could not move at all from my waist down, the pain was so awful.

It was dark, the window showed confused dull light, and when I tried to shift my back I screamed. After that I lay still.

I lay thinking. I knew what it was, lumbago: Freddie had it once, and I knew what to expect. I did not nurse him, of course, we employed someone, and while I shut it out, or tried to, I knew he was in awful pain, for he could not move at all for a week.

I have not been ill since the children's things, like measles. *I have never been really ill.* At the most a cold, a sore throat, and I never took any notice of those.

What I was coming to terms with is that I have no friends. No one I can ring up and say, Please help, I need help.

Once, it was Joyce: but a woman with children, a husband, a job, and a house . . . I am sure I would never have said, "Please come and nurse me." Of course not. I could not ring my sister—children, house, husband, good works, and anyway she doesn't like me. Phyllis: I kept coming back to Phyllis, wondering why I was so reluctant, and thinking there is something wrong with me that I don't want to ask her, she's quite decent and nice really . . . But when I thought of Vera Rogers, then I knew Vera Rogers is the one person I know who I could say to, "Please come and help." But she has a husband, children, and a job, and the last thing she wants is an extra "case".

I managed, after half an hour of agonized reaching and striving, to get the telephone off the bed table and on to my chest. The telephone book was out of reach, was on the floor, I could not get to it. I rang Inquiries, got the number of my doctors, got their night number, left a message. Meanwhile, I was working everything out. The one person who would be delighted—*at last*—to nurse me was Mrs Penny. Over my dead body. I am prepared to admit I am neurotic, anything you like, but I cannot admit her, *will not* . . .

I would have liked a private doctor, but Freddie was always a bit of a socialist, he wanted National Health. I didn't care since I don't get ill. I wasn't looking forward to the doctor's visit, but he wasn't bad. Young, rather anxious, tentative. His first job, probably.

He got the key from the downstairs flat, waking Mrs M., but she was nice about it. He let himself in, came into my room, "Well, and what is wrong?" I told him, lumbago; and what I wanted: he must organize a nurse, twice a day, I needed a bedpan, I needed a thermos—I told him exactly.

He sat on the bottom of my bed, looking at me, smiling a little. I was wondering if he was seeing: an old woman, an elderly woman, a middle-aged woman? I know now it depends entirely on the age of a person, what they see.

"For all that, I think I'd better examine you," he said, and bent over, pulled back the clothes which I was clutching to my chin, and after one or two prods and pushes, to which I could not help responding by groaning, he said, "It's lumbago all right, and as you know there's nothing for it, it will get better in its own good time. And do you want pain-killers?"

"Indeed I do," I said, "and soon, because I can't stand it."

He produced enough to go on with. He wrote out a prescription, and then said that it was unlikely he could get a nurse before evening, and what did I propose to do in the meantime? I said that if I didn't pee soon I would wet the bed. He thought this over, then offered to catheterize me. He did—quickly, painlessly. He had to find a kilner jar in the kitchen, no pot of course, and as there seemed no end to the stream of pee, he ran into the kitchen and searched frantically for anything, came back with a mixing bowl, into which the end of the rubber tube was transferred. Just in time. "Goodness," said he, admiring the quarts of pee.

"How are you going to manage," he asked, "if there's no nurse? Isn't there a neighbour? How about someone on this floor?"

"No," I said. I recognized on his face the look I've seen on, for instance, Vera's, and have felt on mine: toleration for unavoidable eccentricity, battiness.

"I could get you into hospital . . ."

"No, no, no," I moaned, sounding like Maudie.

"Oh, very well."

Off he went, cheerful, tired, professional. You'd not know he was a doctor at all, he could be an accountant or a technician. Once I would not have liked this, would have wanted bedside manner and authority—but now I see Freddie's point.

From the door, he said, "You were a nurse, weren't you?"

This made me laugh, and I said, "Oh, don't make me laugh, I shall die."

But if he can say *that*, then it is Maudie I have to thank for it. What would Freddie think of me now?

A nurse came in about ten, and a routine was established—around the animal's needs. The animal has to get rid of x pints of liquid and a half pound of shit; the animal has to ingest so much liquid and so much cellulose and calories. For two weeks, I was exactly like Maudie, exactly like all these old people, anxiously obsessively wondering, am I going to hold out, no, don't have a cup of tea, the nurse might not come, I might wet the bed . . . At the end of the two weeks, when at last I could dispense with bedpans (twice a day) and drag myself to the loo, I knew that for two weeks I had experienced, but absolutely, their helplessness. I was saying to myself, like

Maudie, Well, I never once wet the bed, that's something.

Visitors: Vera Rogers, on the first day, for I rang her saying she had to get someone to Maudie. She came in first before going to Maudie. I looked at her from where I lay absolutely flat, my back in spasm, her gentle, humorous pleasant little face, her rather tired clothes, her hands—a bit grubby, but she had been dealing with some old biddy who won't go into hospital, though she has flu.

I told her that I thought there is more wrong with Maudie than the runs, found myself telling her about her awful slimy smelly stools. And I said that it was no good expecting Maudie to go into hospital, she would die rather.

"Then," said Vera, "that is probably what she will do."

I saw she was anxious, because she had said that: sat watching my face. She made us some tea, though I didn't dare drink more than a mouthful, and we talked. *She* talked. I could see, being tactful. Soon I understood she was warning me about something. Talking about how many of the old people she looks after die of cancer. It is an epidemic of cancer, she said—or that is what it feels like to her.

At last I said to her, "Do you think Maudie has cancer?"

"I can't say that, I'm not a doctor. But she's so thin, she's just bones. And sometimes she looks so yellow. And I've got to call in her doctor. I must, to cover myself, you see. They are always jumping on us, for neglect or something. If I didn't have to consider that, I'd leave her alone. But I don't want to find myself in the newspapers all of a sudden, Social Worker Leaves 90-Year-Old Woman to Die Alone of Cancer."

"Perhaps you could try a nurse again, to give her a wash? You could try her with a Home Help?"

"If she'll let us in at all," says Vera. And laughs. She says, "You have to laugh, or you'd go mad. They are their own worst enemies."

"And you must tell her I am ill, and that is why I can't get in to her."

Vera says, "You do realize she won't believe it, she'll think it is a plot?"

"Oh no," I groan, for I couldn't stop groaning, the pain was so dreadful (*terrible, terrible, terrible!*), "please, Vera, do try and get it into her head . . ."

And there I lie, with my back knotted, my back like iron, and me sweating and groaning, while Vera tells me that "they" are all paranoid, in one way or another, always suspect plots, and always turn against their nearest and dearest. Since I am Maudie's nearest, it seems, I can expect it.

"You are very fond of her," announced Vera. "Well, I can understand it, she's got something. Some of them have, even at their worst you can see it in them. Others of course . . ." And she sighed, a real human, non-professional sigh. I've seen Vera Rogers, flying along the pavements between one "case" and another, her hands full of files and papers, worried, frowning, harassed, and then Vera Rogers *with* a "case", not a care in sight, smiling, listening, all the time in the world . . . and so she was with me, at least that first visit. But she has been in several times, and she stopped needing to cosset and reassure, we have been talking, really talking about her work, sometimes so funny I had to ask her to stop, I could not afford to laugh, laughing was so painful.

Phyllis visited, once. There she was (my successor?), a self-sufficient cool young woman, rather pretty, and I had only to compare her with Vera. I took the opportunity of doing what I know she's been wanting and needing. She has been attempting my "style", and I've told her, no, never never compromise, always the best, and if you have to pay the earth, then that's it. I looked carefully at her dress: a "little dress", flowered crêpe, skimpy, quite nice, and I said to her, "Phyllis, if that's the kind of dress you want, then at least have it made, use decent material, or go to . . ." I spent a couple of hours, gave her my addresses, dressmaker, hairdresser, knitters. She was thoughtful, concentrated, she very much wanted what I was offering. Oh, she'll do it all right, and with intelligence, no blind copying. But all the time she was there, I was in agony, and I could no more have said to her, "Phyllis, I'm in pain, please help, perhaps we could together shift me a centimetre, it might help . . ." than Freddie or my mother could have asked me for help.

And as for asking for a bedpan . . .

Mrs Penny saw my door open, and crept in, furtive with guilt, smiling, frowning, and sighing by turns. "Oh, you're ill, why didn't you tell me, you should ask, I'm always only too ready to . . ."

She sat in the chair Phyllis had just vacated, and began to talk. She talked. She talked. I had heard all of it before, word by word she repeats herself: India, how she and her husband braved it out when the Raj crumbled; her servants, the climate, the clothes, her dogs, her ayah. I could not keep my attention on it, and, watching her, knew that she had no idea whether I was listening or not. Her eyes stared, fixed, in front of her at nothing. She spilled out words, words, words. I understood suddenly that she was hypnotized. She had hypnotized herself. This thought interested me, and I was wondering how often we all hypnotize ourselves without knowing it, when I fell asleep. I woke, it must have been at least half an hour later, and she was still talking compulsively, eyes fixed. She had not noticed I had dropped off.

I was getting irritated, and tired. First Phyllis, now Mrs Penny, both energy-drainers. I tried to interrupt, once, twice, finally raised my voice: "Mrs Penny!" She went on talking, heard my voice retrospectively, stopped, looked scared.

"Oh dear," she murmured.

"Mrs Penny, I must rest now."

"Oh dear, oh dear, oh dear . . ." Her eyes wandered off from me, she looked around the room, from which she feels excluded because of my coldness, she sighed. A silence. Then, like a wind rising in the distance, she murmured, "And then when we came to England . . ."

"Mrs Penny," I said firmly.

She stood up, looking as if she had stolen something. Well, she had.

"Oh dear," she said. "Oh dear. But you must let me know any time you need anything . . ." And she crept out again, leaving the door open.

I made sure after that, that whoever went out, shut it; and I took no notice when the handle turned, timid but insistent, and I heard her call, Mrs Somers, Mrs Somers, can I get you anything?

Supposing I were to write *Mrs Penny's day?* Oh no, no, no, I really can't face that, I can't.

I have been on the telephone for hours with Joyce in Wales. We have not been able to talk at all, not for months. But now she rings me, I ring her, and we talk. Sometimes we are quiet, for minutes, thinking of all the fields, the hedges, the mountains, *the time* between us. We talk about her marriage, her children, my marriage, my mother, our work. We do not talk about Maudie. She makes it absolutely clear, *no.* She has said that she is going to the States. Not, now, because she is afraid of being alone when she is old, because she *knows* she *is* alone and does not care. But it is the children, after all the insecurity, the misery, they want two parents in one house. Even though they are nearly grown up? I cannot help insisting, and Joyce laughs at me.

I said to her, "Joyce, I want to tell you about Maudie, you know, the old woman."

And Joyce said, "Look, I don't want to know, do you understand?"

I said to her, "You don't want to talk about the one real thing that has happened to me?"

"It didn't *happen* to you"—fierce and insistent—"for some reason or other you made it happen."

"But it is important to me, it is."

"It must be to *her*, that's for certain," said she, with that dry resentment you hear in people's voices when sensing imposition.

I said to her, "Don't you think it is odd, Joyce, how all of us, we take it absolutely for granted that old people are something to be *outwitted*, like an enemy, or a trap? Not that we owe them anything?"

"I don't expect my kids to look after me."

And I felt despair, because now I feel it is an old gramophone record. "That's what you say now, not what you will say then."

"I'm going to bow out, when I get helpless, I'm going to take my leave."

"That's what you say now."

"How do you know, why are you sure about me?"

"Because I know now that everyone says the same things, at stages in their lives."

"And so I'm going to end up, some crabby old witch, an incontinent old witch—is that what you are saying?"

"Yes."

"I can tell you this, I am pleased about one thing, I'm putting thousands of miles between myself and my father. He's an old pet, but enough's enough."

"Who's going to look after him?"

"He'll go into a Home, I expect. That is what *I* shall expect."

"Perhaps."

And so we talk, Joyce and I, for hours, I lying flat on my back in London, trying to outwit the next spasm that will knot my back up, she in an old chintz chair in a cottage on a mountainside, "on leave" from *Lilith*. But she has sent in her resignation.

I do not ring up my sister. I do not ring up my sister's children. When I think about them I feel angry. I don't know why. I feel about these infantile teenagers as Joyce does about me and Maudie: Yes, all right, all right, but not now, I'll think about it later, I simply haven't the energy.

Four weeks of doing nothing . . .

But I have been thinking. *Thinking*. Not the snap, snap, intuitions-and-sudden-judgements kind, but long slow thoughts. About Maudie. About *Lilith*. About Joyce. About Freddie. About those brats of Georgie's.

Before I went back into the office, I visited Maudie. Her hostile little face, but it was a white face, not a yellow one, and that made me feel better about her at once. "Hello," I said, and she gave me a startled look because I have lost so much weight.

"So you really have been ill, then, have you?" said she, in a soft troubled voice, as we sat opposite each other beside that marvellous fire. When I think of her, I see the fire: that sordid horrible room, but the fire makes it glow and welcome you.

"Yes, of course I have, Maudie. Otherwise I'd have been in."

Her face turned aside, her hand up to shield it from me.

"That doctor came in," she said at last, in a small lost voice. "*She* called him in."

"I know, she told me."

"Well, if she is a friend of yours!"

"You are looking better than you were, so it might have something to do with the doctor!"

"I put the pills in the toilet!"

"All of them?"

A laugh broke through her anger. "You're sharp!"

"But you *are* looking better."

"So you say."

"Well," I said, taking the risk, "it could be a question of your dying before you have to."

She stiffened all over, sat staring away from me into the fire. It seemed a long time. Then she sighed and looked straight at me. A wonderful look, frightened but brave, sweet, pleading, grateful, and with a shrewd humour there as well.

"You think that might be it?"

"For the sake of a few pills," I said.

"They deaden my mind so."

"Make yourself take what you can of them."

And that was a year ago. If I had had time to keep this diary properly, it would have seemed a builder's yard, bits and odds stacked up, lying about, nothing in place, one thing not more important than another. You wander through (I visited one for an article last week) and see a heap of sand there, a pile of glass here, some random steel girders, sacks of cement, crowbars. That is the point of a diary, the bits and pieces of events, all muddled together. But now I look back through the year and begin to know what was important.

And the most important of all was something I hardly noticed. Niece Kate turned up one night, looking twenty and not fifteen, the way they can these days, but seemed crazy, stammering and posing and rolling her eyes. She had run away from home to live with me, she said; and she was going to be a model. Firm but kind (I thought and think), I said she was going right back home, and if she ever came to spend so much as an afternoon with me, she could be sure I wasn't going to be like her mother, I wouldn't wash a cup up after her. Off she went, sulking. Telephone call from Sister Georgie: How can you be so lacking in ordinary human sympathies? Rubbish, I said. Telephone call from niece Jill. She said, "I'm ringing you to tell you that I'm not at all like Kate."

"I'm glad to hear it," I said.

"If I lived with you, you wouldn't have to baby me. Mother makes me tired, I'm on your side."

"Not as tired as she must permanently be."

"Aunt Jane, I want to come and spend the weekend."

I could easily hear, from her tone, how *she* saw glamorous Aunt Jane, in Trendy London, with her smart goings-on.

She came. I like her, I admit. A tall, slim, rather lovely girl. Willowy is the word, I think. Will droop if she's not careful. Dark straight hair: could look lank and dull. Vast grey eyes: mine.

I watched her eyes at work on everything in my flat: to copy in her own home, I wondered?—teenage rebellion, perhaps; but no, it was to plan how she would fit in here, with me.

"I want to come and live here with you, Aunt Jane."

"You want to work in *Lilith*, become part of my smart and elegant and amazing life?"

"I'm eighteen. I don't want to go to university, you didn't, did you?"

"You mean, with me as your passport to better things, you don't need a degree?"

"Well, yes."

"You've done well in your exams?"

"I will do well, I promise. I'm taking them in the summer."

"Well, let's think about it then."

I didn't think about it. It was all too bizarre: Sister Georgie ensconced in my life, that was how I saw it.

But Jill came again, and I made a point of taking her with me to visit Maudie, saying only that she was an old friend. Maudie has been in better health recently. Her main misery, the incontinence, is checked, she is doing her own shopping, she is eating well. I have been enjoying flying in and out to gossip over a cup of tea. But I am so used to her, have forgotten how she must strike others. Because of this stranger, the beautiful clean girl, Maudie was stiff, reproachful for exposing her. A cold aloof little person, she said yes and no, did not offer us tea, tried to hide the stains down the front of her dress where she has spilled food.

Niece Jill was polite, and secretly appalled. Not at old age; Sister Georgie's good works will have seen to it that her children will not find that a surprise; but because she had to associate old age and good works with glamorous Aunt Jane.

That evening, eating supper together, she studied me with long covert shrewd looks, while she offered prattle about her siblings and their merry ways.

"How often do you go in to see her?" she inquired delicately enough; and I knew how important a moment this was.

"Every day and sometimes twice," I said at once, with firmness.

"Do you have a lot of friends in, do you go out for parties, dinner parties?"

"Hardly ever. I work too hard."

"But not too hard to visit that old . . . to visit . . ."

"Mrs Fowler. No."

I took her shopping to buy some decent clothes. She wanted to impress me with her taste, and she did.

But at the time Sister Georgie and her offspring were a very long way down on my agenda.

I have worked, oh how I have worked this year, how I have enjoyed it all. They made me editor. I did not say I would only take it for a year or so, was accepting it only for the perks, the better pension, had other plans. Have finally understood that I am not ambitious, would have been happy to work for ever, just as things were, with Joyce.

Joyce left to live in America. Before she went, a dry, indifferent telephone call.

I said to Phyllis, You'd better have Joyce's desk, you have done her work long enough. She was installed in half an hour. Her looks of triumph. I watched her, had my face shielded with my hand. (Like Maudie.) Hiding my thoughts.

Cut your losses, Janna, cut your losses, Jane!

I said, When you are settled, we should discuss possible changes. Her sharp alert lift of the head: danger. She does not want changes. Her dreams have been of inheriting what she was wanting so long and envying.

Envy. Jealousy and envy, I've always used them interchangeably. A funny thing: once a child would have been taught all this, the seven deadly sins, but in our charming times a middle-aged woman has to look up envy in a dictionary. Well, Phyllis is not jealous, and I don't believe she ever was. It was not the closeness and friendship of Joyce and me she wanted, but the position of power. Phyllis is envious. All day, her sharp cold criticisms, cutting everyone, everything, down. She started on Joyce. I found myself blazing up into anger, Shut up, I said, you can be catty about Joyce to other people, not me.

Discussions for months, enjoyable for us all, about whether to change *Lilith* for *Martha*. Is *Lilith* the girl for the difficult, anxious eighties?

Arguments for *Martha*. We need something more workaday, less of an incitement to envy, an image of willing, adaptable, intelligent service.

Arguments for *Lilith*. People are conditioned to need glamour. In hard times we need our fun. People read fashion in fashion magazines as they read romantic novels, for escape. They don't intend to follow fashion, they enjoy the idea of it.

I did not have strong opinions one way or the other. Our circulation is only slightly falling. *Lilith* it will remain.

The contents won't change.

I brought home the last twelve issues of *Lilith* to analyse them.

It is a funny thing, while Joyce and I *were Lilith*, making everything happen, our will behind it, I did not have uneasy moments, asking, Is the life going out of it, is the impetus still there, is it still on a rising current? I know that the impetus is not there now, *Lilith* is like a boat being taken on a wave, but what made the wave is far behind.

Two thirds of *Lilith* is useful, informative, performs a service.

In this month's issue: One. An article about alcoholism.

* * *

Nearly all our ideas are filched from *New Society* and *New Scientist*. (But then this is true of most of the serious mags and papers.) I once fought a battle with Joyce for us to acknowledge our sources, but failed: Joyce said it would put off our readers. Phyllis rewrote the article, and called it: The Hidden Danger to You and Your Family. Two. An article about abortion laws in various countries. Three. My article about the Seventeeth-Century Kitchen. All garlic and spices! Fruit and meat mixed. Salads with everything in the garden in them. And then the usual features, fashion, food, drink, books, theatre.

I have started my historical novel. Oh, I know only too well why we need our history prettied up. It would be intolerable to have the long heavy *weight* of the truth there, all grim and painful. No, my story about the milliners of London will be romantic. (After all, when Maudie comes to die she won't be thinking of trailing out to that freezing smelly lavatory, but of the joyous green fields of Kilburn, and of her German boy, and of the larks the apprentices got up to as they made their lovely hats, good enough for Paris. She will, too, I suppose, be thinking of "her man". But that is an intolerable idea, I can't stand for that.)

Yesterday, as I drove home, I saw Maudie in the street, an ancient crone, all in black, nose and chin meeting, fierce grey brows, muttering and cursing as she pushed her basket along, and some small boys baiting her.

The thing that at the time I thought was going to be worst turned out not bad at all. Even useful. Even, I believe, pleasurable.

I was standing at the counter of the radio and TV shop down the road, buying a decent radio for Maudie. Beside me, waiting patiently, was an old woman, her bag held open while she muddled inside it, looking for money.

The Indian assistant watched her, and so did I. I was at once matching what I saw with my first meeting with Maudie.

"I don't think I've got it here, I haven't got what it costs," she said in a frightened hopeless way, and she pushed a minute radio towards him. She meant him to take it to pay for repairs he had done on it. She turned, slowly and clumsily, to leave the shop.

I thought it all out fast, as I stood there. This time I was not helpless in front of an enormous demand because of inexperience, I had known at first look about the old thing. The dusty grey grimy look. The sour reek. The slow carefulness.

I paid for her radio, hastened after her, and caught her up as she was standing waiting to be helped across the street. I went home with her.

For the pleasure of the thing, I rang Puss-in-Boots when I got home.

"You are the person I saw with Mrs Fowler?"

"Yes, I am," I said.

A silence.

"Do you mind if I say something?" said she, efficient, but not without human sympathy. "So often we find well-meaning people making things so much worse without intending to."

"Worse for whom?"

I was hoping she might laugh, but she is not Vera Rogers.

"What I mean is, specifically, that often well-meaning people take an interest in some geria— . . . some old person, but really it is a hang-up of their own, you see they are working out their own problems, really."

"I would say that that is almost bound to be true, in one way or another," said I, enjoying every minute of this. "But while it might or might not be bad for me, the poor old geriatric in question is likely to be pleased, since she is obviously friendless and alone."

Another silence. Evidently she felt obliged to think out my remarks to their conclusions, in the light of her training. At length she said, "I wonder if you'd find an Encounter Group helpful?"

"Miss Whitfield," I said, "there's this old woman, don't you think you should drop in and visit her?"

"If she's so bad, why hasn't her doctor referred her?"

"As you know, most of these doctors never go near the old people on their lists, and the old people don't go near the doctors, because they are afraid of them. Rightly or wrongly. Afraid of being *sent away*."

"That is really a very old-fashioned concept."

"The fact is, at some point they do get sent away."

"Only when there is no other alternative."

"Well, in the meantime, there's poor Annie Reeves."

"I'll look into it," said she. "Thank you so much for involving yourself when you must be so busy."

I then rang Vera.

Vera said, What was her name, her address, her age, her condition. Yes, she knew about Mrs Bates, who lived downstairs, but Annie Reeves had always refused any of the Services.

"She won't refuse them now," I said.

Vera and I met at the house. I took a morning off work. The door was opened by Mrs Bates, in her fluffy blue dressing gown, and her hair in a blue net.

She looked severely at me, and at Vera. "They took Mrs Reeves to hospital last night," she said. "She fell down. Upstairs. It's not for the first time. But she hurt her knees. So it would seem."

Between Vera and me and Mrs Bates vibrated all kinds of comprehension, and Mrs Bates's disapproving looks were meant to be seen by us.

"Well, perhaps it's a good thing, we can get her rooms cleaned."

"If you think you can do thirty years' cleaning in a morning," she stated, standing aside to let us in.

The house was built about 1870. Nothing cramped or stinted. A good staircase, with decent landings. Annie Reeves's place at the top full of light and air. Nice rooms, well proportioned, large windows.

The front room, overlooking the street, larger than the other. Fireplace, blocked up. A brownish wallpaper, which, examined, showed a nice pattern of brown and pink leaves and flowers, very faded and stained. Above the picture rail the paper was ripping off and flapping loose because water had run in from the roof. There was an old hard chair, with torn blue cushions where the stuffing showed, near the fire. Some dressing tables and a chest of drawers. Linoleum, cracked and discoloured. And the bed—but I feel I cannot really do justice to that bed. Double bed, with brown wood headboard and footboard—how *can* I describe it? The mattress had been worn by a body lying on it always in one place so that the ticking had gone, and the coarse hair inside was a mass of rough lumps and hollows. The pillows had no covers, and were like the mattress, lumps of feathers protruding. There was a tangle of filthy dirty blankets. It was *dirty*, it was disgusting. And yet we could see no lice in it. It was like a very old bird's nest, that had been in use for many years. It was like—I cannot imagine how anyone could sleep in it, or on it.

We opened the drawers. Well, that I had seen before, with Maudie, though these were worse. And I wondered, and I wonder now, how are these hoards of rubbish seen by those who let them accumulate?

One of Annie Reeves's drawers contained—and I make this list for the record: half an old green satinet curtain, with cigarette holes in it; two broken brass curtain rings; a skirt, stained, ripped across the front, of white cotton; two pairs of men's socks, full of holes; a bra, size 32, of a style I should judge was about 1937, in pink cotton; an unopened packet of sanitary towels, in towelling—never having seen these, I was fascinated, of course; three white cotton handkerchiefs spotted with blood, the memory of a decades-old nosebleed; two pairs of pink celanese knickers that had been put away unwashed, medium size; three cubes of Oxo; a tortoise-shell shoehorn; a tin of dried and cracked whiting for ladies' summer shoes; three chiffon scarves, pink, blue, and green; a packet of letters postmarked 1910; a cutting from the *Daily Mirror* announcing World War Two; some bead necklaces, all broken; a blue satin petticoat which had been slit up both sides to the waist to accommodate increasing girth; some cigarette ends.

This had been stirred around and around, it seemed, so that the mess would have to be picked apart, strand by strand. Well, we didn't have time to deal with that: first things first.

Vera and I went into action. I drove to the first furniture shop and bought a good single bed and a mattress. I had luck, they were delivering that morning. I came back behind the van with two young men to make sure they did deliver, and they carried it upstairs. When they saw what was there, they looked incredulous. As well they might. I bribed them to take the old bed down, with the mattress, to the dustbins. Meanwhile, Vera had bought blankets, sheets, pillows, towels. There was exactly half of one old towel in the place, and it was black. Looking out of the filthy windows, we could see neighbours in their gardens speculating over the mattress, with shakes of the head and tight lips. Vera and I wrestled the mattress to the top of my car, and we took it to the municipal rubbish heap.

When we got back the Special Cleaning Team were on the doorstep. Since the place was far beyond the scope of ordinary Home Helps, this flying squad of intrepid experts had been called in by Vera. They were two weedy young men, amiable and lackadaisical, probably from too much take-away junk. They stood about upstairs in the front room, smiling and grimacing at the filth, and saying, "But what can we do?"

"You can start with buckets of hot water and soda," I said. Vera was already looking humorous.

I have not yet mentioned the kitchen. When you went into it, it seemed normal. A good square wooden table in the middle, an adequate gas stove, two very good wooden chairs, each worth at present prices what I would pay for a month's food, ripped and faded curtains, now black, once green. But the floor, the floor! As you walked over it, it gave tackily, and on examination there was a thick layer of hardened grease and dirt.

The two heroes winced about on the sticky lino, and said, How could they use hot water when there wasn't any?

"You heat it on the stove," said Vera, mildly.

"Look," I said, "aren't you for the rough work the Home Helps can't do?"

"Yes, but there are limits, aren't there?" said one of them reproachfully.

"Someone has got to do it," I said.

They did sweep the front room, and pushed a mop hastily over the floor. But over the kitchen floor, they went on strike. "Sorry," said they, and went off, good-natured to the end.

Vera and I pushed the big table out, with the dresser and the chairs, though they were stuck to the lino with decades of grease. We prized up the lino: it would not come up easily. Under this layer was another, and between them was a half-inch layer of grease and dirt. In all we prized up three layers of lino.

Then Vera had to go home to her family problems.

That weekend I scrubbed the floors, washed down walls and ceilings, emptied drawers, scrubbed them, cleaned a stove encrusted with thirty years of dirt. Finally, I filled plastic bags with this silent story, the detritus of half a lifetime, and took them to the municipal dump.

Mrs Bates marked my comings and goings up and down the stairs, sitting in her little parlour, drinking tea, and from time to time offering me a cup.

"No, I haven't been up there, not for ten years," she said. "If you give her an inch, it's make me a cup of tea, fetch me this and that. I'm nearly ten years older than she is. Are you going to be her Good Neighbour, may I ask? No?"

Her rosy old face was distressed, reproachful. "You had her old mattress out there for everyone to see. Outside *my* place— they'll think . . . And your hands, all in that dirt and muck . . ."

What was upsetting her as much as anything was that it was not for me, such a lady and all, to do this filthy work.

She gave me a key. I took it knowing she was offering me more than I was ready to take. Oh, I'm under no illusions now! Every street has in it several, perhaps a dozen, old women, old men, who can only just cope, or suddenly can't cope; who dream of absent daughters and sons and granddaughters, and anyone coming near them must beware, beware! For into that terrible vacuum you can be sucked before you know it. No, I shall not put myself, again, into the situation I am with Maudie, who has only one friend in the world.

I drop in, for a few minutes, in the character they assigned me, because I am not in any of their categories, am unexplainable, of wayward impulsive benevolence. My main problem is that Maudie should never know I am visiting anyone else, for it would be a betrayal. Eliza Bates, Annie Reeves, live around the corner from Maudie.

If I take Annie a present, I have to take Eliza one, for Eliza watches me as I go up past her to the top floor. Eliza was in service, and knows what is good, and gets it, thus exemplifying, I suppose, To those who have will be given. I take her bread from the good bakery, a new romantic novel, a certain brand of Swiss chocolate, chaste white roses with green fern. Annie knows what she likes and that British is best, and I take her chocolate like sweet mud, a sickening wine that is made specially for old ladies, and small pretty flowers tied with satin ribbon.

Annie Reeves was in hospital for six weeks. She bruised a leg, but although they tell her she could walk again properly, she is on a walking frame and refuses. She is now a prisoner at the top of that house, with a commode that must be emptied, and Meals on Wheels, Home Help, a nurse.

Eliza Bates disapproves utterly of Annie Reeves, who let herself go, who was drinking up there by herself—oh yes, Eliza Bates knew what went on!—who let the dirt accumulate until Eliza sat imagining she could hear the bugs crawling in the walls and the mice scuttling. "I'm not like *her*," says Eliza, firmly, to me, with a little churchy sniff.

"I'm not like *her*," says Annie, meaning that Eliza is a hypocrite, she never was interested in church until her husband died, and now look at her.

Annie yearns for the friendship of Eliza. Eliza has spent years isolating herself from the woman upstairs who has so rapidly gone to pieces, and who is not ashamed now of stumping about on a frame when there's no need, and of getting an army of social workers in to her every day. They call each other Mrs Bates, Mrs Reeves. They have lived in this house forty years.

The Welfare are trying to "rehabilitate" Annie. I would have reacted, only a few weeks ago, to the invitation to this campaign, with derision, even with cries of But it is cruelty! Since then, I've seen Eliza's life, and understand why these experts with the old will fight the lethargy of age even in a man or woman of ninety or more.

I have become fond of Eliza; this quite apart from admiring

her. If I am like that at ninety! we all exclaim; and feel the threats of the enemy ahead weakened.

Eliza Bates's day.

She wakes at about eight, in the large front that was where she slept in the big double bed with her husband. But she has a nice single bed now, with a bedside table, and a little electric fire. She likes to read in bed, romantic novels mostly. The room has old-fashioned furniture: again this mixture of "antiques" and stuff that wouldn't fetch fifty pence. It is very cold, but she is used to it, and goes to bed with a shawl around her and hot bottles.

She makes herself a real breakfast, for she learned long ago, she says, never to let yourself get sloppy with meals. Then she does out one of her three rooms, but not as thoroughly as she once did. About eleven she makes herself coffee. Perhaps one of her many friends comes in. She has a special friend, a much younger woman, of about seventy, from opposite, who is "very young for her age", wears fancy hats and clothes, and is a tonic for Eliza, always running over with something she has cooked, or making Eliza go out to the pictures. Every day Eliza goes to a lunch club, run by the Welfare for old people, and may afterwards detail everything, such as that the meat was boiled to rags, the sprouts too hard, or the rice pudding had just the right amount of nutmeg. For she was once a cook in a family. Until recently she stayed for a couple of hours to "work": old people make calendars, paint Christmas cards, do all kinds of small jobs, some very well, for they may use skills of a lifetime. But now, says Eliza, she feels she must begin to cut down a little, she is not as strong as she was. After the lunch, and a cup of tea and a chat, she and one, or two, or three friends will go shopping. These are the old ladies I once did not see at all but, since Maudie, have watched creeping about the streets with their bags and their baskets—and I could never have guessed the companionableness, the interest of their lives, the gaiety. They love shopping, it is clear; and what shop they will patronize and what not on a given day is the result of the most intricate and ever-shifting tides of feeling. That Indian doesn't keep a clean shop, but he was observed sweeping out yesterday, so they'll give him a second chance. They'll go to the supermarket this week, because there's a new girl with a lovely smile who puts things into their baskets for them. The man at the hardware spoke roughly to one of them last week, and so he will lose the custom of five or six people for weeks, if not for ever. All this is much more to their point than cheap lines of biscuits or a reduction in the price of butter for old-age pensioners. After shopping, Eliza brings one of them home with her to tea, or goes to them. When she gets home she sits down for a little at the kitchen window, where she can see all the washing lines that dance about the sky when there's a wind, and she looks down into the jungle of the garden, and remembers how the lilac there was planted on that afternoon thirty-five years ago, and that corner now so overgrown that used to be such a picture.

She is rather afraid of early evening, so I have discovered. Once, going past to Annie, I saw her, her cheek on her hand. She turned her face away as I said, Oh, Eliza, good evening!— and then, when I went in, concerned, she gestured at the other wooden chair and I sat down.

"You see," said she, "you should keep busy, because if you don't, the grumps lie in wait for you . . ." And she wiped her eyes and made herself laugh.

And then, amazingly, she put on her hat again.

"Eliza, you aren't going out? Shouldn't you rest?"

"No. I should not. I must keep moving if I feel low . . ." And she went off again, creeping around the block, a dumpy brave little figure in the dusk.

She does not bother with supper, perhaps a piece of cake, or a salad. She is often visited by her friend from opposite after supper, or she listens to the radio. She doesn't like the telly. And so she spends her evening, until she goes off to bed, very late, often after midnight.

And, two or three times a week, from spring to late autumn, she is off on coach trips to famous places, or beauty spots, organized by the Welfare or one of the two churches she uses. For Eliza is very religious. She is a Baptist, and she also goes to the Church of England church. She goes to church on Sundays twice, mornings and evenings, and to church teas and bazaars and jumble sales, to lectures on Missionary Endeavour in India and in Africa. She is continually attending weddings and christenings.

When she asked me what I did and I told her, toning it down a little, she understood everything, for she has worked for people in positions of responsibility, and asked me all kinds of questions that had never occurred to me, such as: Did I think it right, having no children, taking the job of a man who might have a family to keep? And loves to talk about—not the clothes she wore half a century ago—but the fashions she sees on the streets on the young girls, which make her laugh, she says, they seem so crazy, they seem as if the girls are having such a good time. She likes to see them, but she wonders if they know what it is like not ever to have a new dress, only what could be got in their sizes at the pawnshop.

For her poor mother had been left by her husband one day. He went off and was never heard of again. She had three small children, two girls and a boy. The boy, says Eliza, was not up to anything, he was born lazy, and would never work to help out, and he too went off when he was fourteen, and never sent back so much as a card at Christmas. Eliza's mother had worked for the two of them. The pawnshop at the corner had their sheets, and often their clothes, from the Mondays to the Fridays, when they were redeemed again. And the woman who kept it used to put aside a good coat for the girls, or a pair of shoes she knew would fit. And she would say, "Well, if that poor soul can't get in in time to redeem it, you'll have first chance."

Eliza brought out one evening an old postcard, *circa* World War One, of a ragged orphan girl with bare feet. When I had examined it, thinking how romantic, for that was how the poor girl was presented, all the harshness taken away from the truth, Eliza said, "That girl was me—no, I mean, I was like that. When I was twelve I was out scrubbing steps for the gentry for a penny. And I had no shoes, and my feet were sick with the cold and blue, too . . . They were wicked times," says Eliza, "wicked. And yet I seem to remember we were happy. I can remember laughing and singing with my sister, though we were often enough hungry. And my poor little mother crying because she could not keep up with herself . . ."

Eliza, disliking televison, will go across the road to watch *Upstairs, Downstairs.* This makes me cross; but then I ask myself, Why then am I into writing romantic novels? The truth is intolerable, and that is all there is to it!

Gracious Lady!

It occurred to me that Hermione Whitfield and the rest of them (male and female) and Vera and myself are in fact the legitimate descendants of the Victorian philanthropist lady, and have taken her place.

Here is my new romantic novel:

My heroine is no titled lady, but the wife of a well-off man in the City. She lives in Bayswater, one of the big houses near Queensway. She has five children, to whom she is a devoted mother. Her husband is not a cruel man, but insensitive. I described him using language frankly stolen from a letter in one of the virulent Women's Movement newspapers Phyllis used to leave on my desk. He is incapable of understanding her finer points. He has a mistress, whom he keeps in Maida Vale, much to our heroine's relief. As for her, she occupies herself in visiting the poor, of whom there are very many. Her husband does not resent these activities, because it takes her mind off his. Every day she is out and about, dressed in her simple but beautiful clothes, accompanied by a sweet little maid who helps her carry containers of soup and nourishing puddings.

Of course, I do not allow that these invalids and old people she sustains are in any way difficult (though one, an ancient who carries wounds from the Crimean War, she describes with a small deprecating smile as *difficile*). None of them screams and rages, like Maudie, or repeats the same ten or twelve sentences for an hour or two hours of a visit, as if you haven't heard them before hundreds of times, or gets sulky and sullen. No, they may be living in dreadful poverty, never knowing where their next crust is coming from, living on tea and marge and bread and potatoes (except for the offerings of the

Gracious Lady), they may have not enough coal, and have vile or brutal husbands or wives dying of tuberculosis or childbed fever, but they are always fine and gallant human beings, and they and Margaret Anstruther enjoy friendships based on real appreciation of each other's qualities. Margaret A. certainly does *not* have the vapours, the languors, the faints; I do not permit a suggestion of the dreadful psychosomatic illnesses those poor women actually suffered from. For she does not allow herself to be bored, which was the real cause of lying for years on a sofa with a bad back or the migraine. (I have been brooding about writing a critical book called *The Contribution of Boredom to Art*. Using Hedda Gabler, whose peculiar behaviour was because she was crazy with boredom, as exemplar.) No, Margaret suffers nothing but unspoken love for the young doctor whom she meets often in those poor homes, and who loves her. But he has a *difficile* invalid wife, and of course these fine souls would never dream of transgressing. They meet over deathbeds, and sickbeds, and alleviate the human condition together, their eyes occasionally meeting, songs without words, and even glistening, very rarely, with the unshed tear.

What a load of old rubbish! Rather like *Upstairs, Downstairs*, and I adored that and so did everyone else.

But the research I've done (extensive) has led me to a real respect for those unsung heroines, the Victorian philanthropist ladies, who were patronized then, probably (how do we know, really?) by their husbands, and despised now. A pity they were so often silent about what they did, are so often written about rather than speaking for themselves. For they must have been a really tough breed, knowing by every-day, year-in-year-out slog and effort what Jack London and Dickens and Mayhew got by brief excursions into poverty and then retreating again, enough facts garnered. When I think of what it must have been like for them, going into those homes, late nineteenth century, early twentieth, the sheer, threadbare, cold, grim, grimy *dreadfulness* of it, worn-out women, rickety children, brutalized men—no, no, I won't go on. But I know one thing very well, and that is that Maudie and Annie and Eliza are rich and happy compared with those people.

Annie will say, as the helpers go flying in and out, "I think of my poor old mum, she had none of this."

"What happened to her, then, who looked after her?"

"She looked after herself."

"Did she have her health?"

"She had shaky hands, she dropped cups and plates a lot. She used to push a chair around as a support when she fell and broke her hip. And we took her in some food and a bit of stout sometimes."

"Was she alone then?"

"She was alone—years. She lived to seventy. I've done better than her, haven't I? By ten years and more!"

I know very well that what I hear from Eliza about her life is not all the truth, probably nothing like it; and I commend her, as I would the writer of a tale well-told. Those long hot summers, with never a cloud! Those outings with her husband! Those picnics in the park! Those Christmases! That group of loving chums, always meeting, never a cross word!

Occasionally there are moments when the veil is lifted, oh only for a moment. She is very condemning, poor Eliza, full of morality, cannot understand how this woman can do that, or that this. She was angry for days over a newspaper story about an elderly woman who left her husband for a young man. It's filthy, she said, filthy. And, a few moments later, in another voice, a hurrying light dream-voice: If it'd been now I could have left, I could have left him, and been rid of . . .

I am very much afraid that, yet again, what it was she wanted to be rid of was sex . . .

Eliza has not had children. She wanted them.

Did she ever go to the doctor and ask?

"Oh yes, I did, and he said there was nothing wrong with me, I should ask my husband to come."

"I suppose he wouldn't?"

"Oh, you couldn't ask him a thing like that, he wouldn't have heard of it," she cried. "Oh no, Mr Bates knew his rights, you see . . ."

Downstairs, Eliza, an example to us all . . .

Upstairs, the deplorable Annie Reeves.

Vera Rogers and I have lunch, half an hour as we fly past each other.

I say to Vera, "What interests me is this: *when* did Annie make that decision to become as she is now? For we make decisions before we know it."

"Oh no, it's not like that at all. Eliza has always been like that, Annie has always been like that!"

"What a pessimist. We don't change, then?"

"No! Look at Maudie Fowler! She was always like that, I expect. Recently I met a cousin after twenty years—nothing changed, not a syllable or a habit."

"Good God, Vera, you're enough to make one want to jump off a cliff!"

"I don't see that at all. No, people are what they are all through them."

"Then why are you trying so hard with Annie?"

"You've got me there. I don't think she'll change. I've seen it before, she's decided to give up. But let's try a bit longer, if you don't mind, and then we'll know we've done our best."

Our campaign for Annie is everything that is humane and intelligent. There she is, a derelict old woman, without friends, some family somewhere but they find her condition a burden and a scandal and won't answer her pleas; her memory going, though not for the distant past, only for what she said five minutes ago; all the habits and supports of a lifetime fraying away around her, shifting as she sets a foot down where she expected firm ground to be . . . and she, sitting in her chair, suddenly surrounded by well-wishing smiling faces who know exactly how to set everything to rights.

Look at Eliza Bates—everyone cries. See how she has so many friends, goes on so many trips, is always out and about . . . But Annie will not try to walk properly, go out, start a real life again. "Perhaps when summer comes," she says.

Because of Eliza Bates I have understood how many trips, jaunts, bazaars, parties, meetings Maudie could be enjoying, but does not. I thought it all over. I rang Vera, whose voice at once, when she knew what I was asking, became professionally tactful.

"What are you saying?" I asked at last. "You mean, there's no point in Maudie Fowler starting anything new because she's not likely to stay as well as she is for long?"

"Well, it is a bit of a miracle, isn't it? It must be getting on for a year now, she's holding her own, but . . ."

I went off to Maudie one Saturday, with some cherry liqueur I brought back from Amsterdam, where I was for the spring show. Like Eliza, Maudie knows, and enjoys, the best. We sat opposite each other drinking, and the room smelled of cherry. Outside drawn curtains a thin spring rain trickled noisily from a broken gutter. She had refused to let the Greek's workmen in to mend it.

"Maudie, I want to ask you something without your getting cross with me."

"Then I suppose it's something bad?"

"I want to know why you didn't ever go on these trips to country places the Council organizes? Did you ever go on one of their holidays? What about the Lunch Centre? There are all these things . . ."

She sat shading her little face with a hand grimed with coal dust. She had swept out her chimney that morning. Fire: she tells me she has nightmares about it. "I could die in my bed here," says she, "from smoke, not knowing."

She said, "I've kept myself to myself and I see no reason to change."

"I can't help wondering about all the good times you could have had."

"Did I tell you about the Christmas party, it was before I met you? The Police have a party. I got up on the stage and did a knees-up. I suppose they didn't like me showing my petti-coats."

I imagined Maudie, lifting her thick black skirts to show her stained knickers, a bit tipsy, enjoying herself.

"I don't think it would be that," I said.

"Then why haven't they asked me again? Oh, don't bother, I wouldn't go now, anyway."

"And all these church things. You used to go to church, didn't you?"

"I've been. I went once to a tea, and then I went again

because that Vicar said I wasn't fair to them. I sat there, drinking my tea in a corner, and all of them, not so much as saying welcome, chatter chatter among themselves, I might as well have not been there."

"Do you know Eliza Bates?"

"Mrs Bates? Yes, I know her."

"Well then?"

"If I know her why do I have to like her? You mean, we are of an age, and that's a reason for sitting gossiping together. I wouldn't have liked her young, I'm sure of that, I didn't like her married, she gave her poor man a hard time of it she did, couldn't call his home his own, I don't like what I've seen of her since, she's never her own woman, she's always with ten or more of them, chitter-chatter, gibble-gabble, so why should I like her now enough to spend my dinners and teatimes with her? I've always liked to be with one friend, not a mess of people got together because they've got nowhere else to go."

"I was only thinking you might have had an easier time of it."

"I'm not good enough for Eliza Bates. And I haven't been these last twenty years. Oh, I'm not saying I wouldn't have enjoyed a bit of an outing here or there, I sometimes go up to the church when they've got a bazaar on, I look out for a scarf or a good pair of boots, but I might not be there at all for all the notice those church women take of me."

"Why don't you come out again to the park? Or I could take you for a trip on the river. Why not, it's going to be summer soon?"

"I'm happy as I am, with you coming in to sit with me. I think of that afternoon in the Rose Garden, and that's enough."

"You're stubborn, Maudie."

"I'll think my own thoughts, thank you!"

Some weeks after she had left, a telephone call from Joyce, at five in the morning.

"Are you ill?" was what came out of me; as if I'd written her off somewhere inside me.

"No, should I be?"

"Ringing so early."

"I'm just off to bed. Oh, of course, the time difference."

"It's all right, I'm just getting up to start work."

"Good old Janna," says Joyce, in a new vague way, and it is derisive.

"Oh, Joyce, are you drunk?"

"You certainly are not!"

"Did you ring me up actually to tell me how it is all going? Flat? Husband? Children? Job?"

"Certainly not. I thought to myself, how is Janna, how is my old mate, Janna? So how are you? And how is that old woman?"

I said, "As far as I can make out, she is suspected of having cancer."

"Congratulations," says Joyce.

"What is that supposed to mean?"

"Cancer. It's all over the place. Well, I don't see that it's worse than anything else. Do you? I mean, TB, meningitis, multiple sclerosis . . ." And Joyce went on, a long list of diseases, and I sat there thinking, she can't be all that drunk. No, she's pretending to be for some reason. Soon she was talking about how diseases fall out of *use*. Her very odd phrase. "If you read Victorian novels, they died like flies of diseases we don't have now at all. Like diphtheria. Like scarlet fever. Like, for that matter, TB."

And so we went on, for half an hour or more. At last I said, "Joyce, this is costing you a fortune."

"So it is. Good old Janna. Everything has to be paid for?"

"Well, yes, it has been my experience."

"Because you have *made* it your experience." And she rang off.

Soon she rang again. Five in the morning.

"I like to think of you working away there, me old pal, while I fiddle at parties . . ."

"I've done a romantic novel," I told her. "You're the first I've told. And they like it."

"Romance . . . quite right. I, for one, have never had enough of it. I look back and what I see is, me always working too hard for any fun. And that's what *you* see when you look back, Janna. Obviously."

"I'm having fun now."

A long, long silence.

"Don't tell me, because I won't believe it."

"I enjoy writing these romantic novels. I've started another. *Gracious Lady*, do you like it?"

"Gracious. That's a word I've understood. I've come on an important clue to the American female character. Graciousness. It comes from *Snow White*. Generations of American girls see *Snow White*, model themselves on her . . . bestow themselves graciously on this one and on that one thereafter . . ."

"And I enjoy writing serious articles."

"You must be working too hard to enjoy yourself."

"Nonsense. It's because I am working so hard. And I enjoy the old ladies. I enjoy that world, what goes on, I never suspected it even existed before."

"Good for you."

Joyce again: "Another party?" I asked.

And she said, "That's what one *does*, here."

I always ask her what she is wearing, so as to get a picture of her, and she always says, Exactly what everyone else is.

For she says the Americans are the most conforming people on earth, and even when they rebel they do it in droves, and always wear the same as the other non-conformers. She was taken to task several times for her style. She thought it was because she was really too old for it, but no, she was asked severely why the British "always look like gipsies". It is our wild romantic nature, said she, but abandoned her style, cut her hair, and now has a wardrobe full of well-cut trousers, shirts, sweaters, and variations on the little dress. When you enter a room, she says, the eyes of everyone present give you the once-over to make sure you are inside the prescribed limits.

She is enjoying herself, because that is what one *does*. Her husband is enjoying himself: he has a new girlfriend, who happens to be Joyce's colleague. Good God! cries Joyce, at one, two, three in the morning (there) before she goes to bed, to me surrounded by early-morning cups of coffee (here), when I think of all that ridiculous anguish before I left! Here no one dreams of staying married for one second after one of them has stopped enjoying it.

The children too are enjoying themselves, and look on their native land as backward and barbarous, because we are poor and do not have such well-stocked refrigerators.

There has been a new development in the office: politics.

I don't know whether to count it as serious, or not. I think, probably, serious. There is something in the air, something new, I don't like it, but then, I am getting on, and I don't like change . . . because of this was tolerant, to start with. Patronizing? But I saw *them* as patronizing. Revolutions are hardly my line, but they have after all not been absent in my lifetime, and it seems to me that I do not deserve to be tolerated as I am being. As I *was* being. For I have put my foot down. Suddenly, as I moved about the office, it seemed that I was met by groups or couples who fell silent, as if their exchanges were too deep for understanding by this outsider. Yet what they say we have all heard a thousand times; the political clichés scattered about, I could not take them seriously. Most of all I could not take it seriously when these young ones, all middle-class, go on about middle-class values, the destruction of, the replacement by, the rottenness of, the necessity to expose of. There is, actually, one really working-class young man in the place, a photographer, and his father is a printer: which remark could lead me into a long analysis of what is and isn't working class in this our so middle-class land. But I am not going to follow these schoolmen into hair-splitting. What is real about them is not the infinite variety of their religious stances, their dogmatism, but the passions they bring to their arguments. There is a spirit in the office that was never there before, a snarling, envious nasty atmosphere, which makes it inevitable that everyone has to criticize, to diminish anyone not aligned in precisely the same way as themselves; and, as well, to criticize and condemn most of the time everyone in the same group who temporarily or otherwise disagrees with them. What gets me about all this is that we have learned about all this from a thousand sources, books, TV, radio, and yet these youngsters go on as if they are doing something for the first time, as if they have invented all these stale phrases.

It was about the time I was becoming really perturbed by all this that I understood what Vera had been telling me.

Vera and I enjoy our lunches, baked beans or an omelette and a cup of coffee, as we fly around. We enjoy what we do, or rather, to be accurate, we enjoy being able to do it, and do it well.

"Gawd," says Vera, sitting down with a flop, letting a pile of files two feet thick drop to the floor as she reaches for a cigarette, "Gawd, Janna, I tell you, if I had only known when I applied, no you sit there and let me blow off steam, you'll never believe it . . ."

"I wouldn't have," I say, "if I hadn't been watching it in my own office."

What I would never believe is that it is now Thursday, and there have been seven meetings already that week which she ought to have attended.

"These meetings are about nothing, *nothing*, Janna, please believe me, any sensible person could fix whatever it is up in five minutes with a few words. There are so many meetings because they adore meetings, meetings are their social life, honestly, Janna, it is the truth. It took me a long time to cotton on, but once I saw it . . . What is the matter with them? To begin with, when I started, I asked myself if there was something wrong with me. You know how it is when you are new? They'd say, Aren't you going to come to this meeting, that meeting? I'd go. Do you know, they actually set up meetings where they act out each other's roles, can you beat it? They say, Now you be an old woman, you be her husband. Or they discuss this and that. Do you know, there are some part-time workers who are never out of the office at all actually working with the clients? My assistant, so-called, she's part-time, and she hasn't been out of the office since Monday morning, she's been at meetings. I believe she thinks that is what her job is. And it's every evening after work, every blasted night. And then they go off to the pub together, exactly the same lot of people. They can't bear to separate. And if you think that's the end of it, no, the birthdays, the anniversaries, I tell you, if they could hire a bed of Ware large enough, they'd spend all their lives together in it, having a meeting. Well, I did go to some, I did my best, and then I said, Count me out. So they think I'm very odd now. They are always saying to me, as if I were peculiar, and perhaps I am, though I doubt it, There's this meeting tonight, aren't you going to come? I say, Tell me all about it in the morning. You can explain it all to me, I'm stupid, you see, I don't seem to be able to understand politics."

I went back to the office armed by this new insight. It was all true. They call meetings every day, to discuss work hours, lunch hours, work loads, management, the policy of the mag, me, the political bias of the mag, the state of the nation. Many of them in working time. I called Ted Williams, the Trade Union representative, and said as far as I was concerned he was the only sensible person among the lot and I was going to forbid all meetings except for those which he called. He laughed. He thinks these middle-class revolutionaries a joke. (Let's hope they don't have the last laugh.)

I called a meeting of the entire staff, nearly a hundred present, and I said this was the last meeting permitted in working hours except for those convened by the Trade Union representative. And from now on, they could conduct their social lives outside the office. Shock. Horror. But of course they were thoroughly enjoying this confrontation with the Enemy, namely me, namely the Force of Reaction.

I had lunch with Vera, and I said to her, as she moaned about that week's ten meetings, "Hold your horses. You seem to think this is a disease peculiar to your Welfare Workers. No, it's a national disease. It's everywhere, like a plague. Meetings, talking, it's a way of *not* getting anything done. It's their social life. They are lonely people, most of them, without adequate social outlets. Therefore, meetings. Anyway, I've forbidden them in *Lilith*."

"You haven't!"

"I've instituted one meeting a week. Everyone has to come. No one can speak at all for more than a minute unless it is extremely urgent. I mean urgent. And so they go to the pub to have meetings about me."

"The thing is, poor creatures, they don't know it's their social lives, they really believe it's politics."

I sit here, conscientiously looking back over my year . . . I look at that word, conscientiously. I am not going to repudiate it! As I look I think of Joyce's lazy, affectionate: *Good old Janna*. Well, all right. As I sit here, conscientiously looking over the year, I note again how hard I have worked, how hard. And yet, as I said to my dear niece Jill when she rang to inquire, "I hope you aren't working too hard, Aunt Jane?" meaning, Oh, don't work too hard, don't be boring, don't do difficult and dutiful things, what will happen to my dream of glamour and easy fun?—"I've never in my life worked as hard as your mother, and that would be true if I worked twenty hours a day."

"Can I come and stay the weekend?"

"Please do. You can help me with something."

She came. That was only a month ago.

I told her to write an article about the influence of two world wars on fashion. I watched her face. I had already tried the idea out in the think session. I said that, in the First World War, everyone in the world became used to pictures of masses of people in uniform. For the first time on that scale. Conditioned to the idea of uniforms, you are more amenable to following fashion; following fashion, you are more amenable to uniforms. In the Second World War, everyone in the world *saw* millions of people in uniform. The boss nation wore tight sexually provocative trousers, buttocks emphasized. Since the Second World War, everyone over the world wears tight sexually emphatic uniforms. A *world* fashion. Because of a world war.

I made this dry and factual, no excitement in it. I wanted to see how she would react. She listened. I watched her. Strained she was, but trying.

"I don't think I can write an article like that."

"Yet, or not at all?"

"Yet."

"When are you sitting your exams?"

"In a few weeks. Are you still seeing Mrs . . . ?"

"Mrs Fowler? Yes, I am."

Suddenly her passionately rejecting face, her real distress, which told me how threatened she felt.

Just as I would have done—alas, so recently—she cried out: "Why doesn't her family look after her? Why doesn't the Welfare put her into a Home? Why does she have to impose on you?"

I've just taken three weeks' leave. I have a lot owed to me. I've never taken all that I could, even when Freddie was alive. Nor did Freddie. It has occurred to me: was Freddie's office *his* home? If so, it was only because of what he had to put up with from me. We went for short motoring holidays, usually in France, and ate and slept well. We were pleased to get home.

Phyllis was, of course, delighted to be left in charge. She has a look of satisfaction, which she has to keep hidden. Why? Everything has always been given to her so freely and easily. Take her clothes. Her style, mine adapted, couldn't be better for her. Soft silky clothes, everything sleek and subtle, golden brown hair. Sometimes little frills at wrists and throat—I could never wear those, alas, I'm too solid. Slim good gold jewellery showing in the opening of a plain coffee shirt that has the gentlest shine to it, a fine chain visible under a cuff whose thin stripes echo it. She goes to my dressmaker, my hairdresser, my knitter, she uses the shops I told her about. And yet it is as if she has had to steal all this expertise from me: because I unfairly kept it from her. Thus, when she sees me observing her new outfit, thinking, oh well done, Phyllis!, she has the need to hide the small superior smile that goes with: That's right, I've got one over on you! Amazing girl.

It is not only I who am wondering if Phyllis's new lusciousness mirrors something inward. I watch her in the photographers' rooms. They, their working areas, have always been the pole, the balance, to our office, Joyce's and mine—Phyllis's and mine. Two power centres. Michael, who never took any notice of the girl, is now interested. And she in him. Quite different from me and Freddie: slapdash, casual, *equal*. At any rate, neither of them ever concedes an inch. I watch them in a characteristic scene. He is slanted back against a trestle table, legs crossed at the ankle, thus exposing the full length of his front in soft corduroy, the promising bulge on show. His head is slightly averted, so that he smiles at her across the curve of his cheek. He is good-looking, this Michael, but until just recently I haven't been faced with it. And Phyllis has one buttock on a desk, the other leg a long angled curve. In something pretty and soft, like black suede, or an unexpected bright colour, she presents the length of herself to him, and her hair slips about her face as they discuss—and oh how competently—their work. He lets his eyes travel up her body in a sober appreciation that mocks itself, and she opens her eyes in sardonic appraisal of the soft bulge presented to her. Then they go off to lunch, where, more often than not, they discuss layout or advertising.

I enjoy watching this game, but could not let my enjoyment be evident, for Phyllis would feel something was being stolen from her. Oh, *Joyce*, I have no one with whom to share these moments.

How I have enjoyed my three weeks. I did not go away, because I could not bear to leave Maudie for so long: if that is crazy, then let it be.

Joyce rang up. She is drinking far too much.

"Why do you never ring me, Janna?"

"It is your place to ring me. It was you who went away."

"God, you're relentless."

"Very well, I am."

"I see you sitting there, writing—what is it? *Gracious Lady?*"

"I've nearly finished another serious sociological-type book called *Real and Apparent Structures.*"

"I suppose you have all this energy because you have no emotional life?"

"Emotional life being defined as husband, children, or even a lover?"

"Even a lover. Don't you want one, Janna?"

"I'm afraid of one."

"Well, that's frank at least."

"More than you are, these days, Joyce."

"Frank? I reek of emotional sincerity. I'm in an Encounter Group, did I tell you? Ten of us. We scream abuse at each other and relive our ghastly childhoods."

"I didn't know you had a ghastly childhood."

"Neither did I. But it seems I must have had."

"The truth at last, is that it? Emotional truth?"

"You wouldn't know about that, Janna."

"Love is what I know nothing about. Yes, I know that."

"*Well?*"

"Well, do you know something? Those years we sat working together, never a cross word, understanding each other, that was love, as far as I am concerned. *You* think now that love is all this screaming and shouting and *relating*."

"Of course, I'm now an American. As good as."

"I'll think my own thoughts then, thank you."

And again:

"What are you doing, Janna?"

"I finished *Real and Apparent Structures* ten minutes ago."

"That's going very fast, isn't it?"

"I've had three weeks' leave."

"No temptation for a little trip to Paris, Amsterdam, Helsinki?"

"I've been very much enjoying my own city, believe it or not."

"Talking to dreary old women?"

How I do adore the feast of possibilities this city always is. But I didn't know how much until I had three long lovely weeks, all by myself, long spring days, to please myself in. Suddenly I was surrounded by oceans of time. I understood I was experiencing time as the old do, or the very young. I would sit on a wall along a garden and watch birds busy in a shrub. I don't know a blackbird from a starling. I'd sit in a café and, with all the afternoon in front of me, listen and look while two girls giggled about their boyfriends. Their intense enjoyment. Enjoyment, it's what I've missed in my life, what I've scarcely known the name of, I've been so busy, oh I've always worked so hard.

I could learn real slow full enjoyment from the very old, who sit on a bench and watch people passing, watch a leaf balancing on the kerb's edge. A small wind lifts it: will it fall over, be blown under wheels, be crushed? No, it rests, a thick juicy green leaf, shining and full of sap, probably plucked off some branch by a pigeon. The wheels of a shopping basket spin past, just missing the leaf. The shopping basket belongs to a girl who has a child in it. She is in love with the child, smiling and bending to it, as it looks confidingly up at her, the two isolated by love together on the pavement, watched by old people who smile with them.

I love sitting on a bench by some old person, for now I no longer fear the old, but wait for when they trust me enough to tell me their tales, so full of history. I ask, Tell me, what did you wear on your wedding day? And for some reason there's always a laugh, a smile. "You want to know that then, do you, well, it was white, you see, with . . ." Or I ask, Did you fight in the old war, you know, the 1914–18 war. "You could say I did . . ." And I sit and listen, listen.

I love—all of it, all of it. And the more because I know how very precarious it is. My back has only to say, No, stop! I have only to break a bone the size of a chicken's rib, I have only to slip once on my bathroom floor, whose tiles are dense with oils and essences—at any moment, fate may strike me with one of a hundred illnesses, or accidents, all of them unforeseen, but implicit in my physical make-up or my character, and there you are, I shall be grounded. Like Maudie, like all these old things whom I smile at now as I go about among them, because I know them now, can tell from how they bend so carefully to jerk the wheels of a shopping basket on to a pavement, from how they pause to steady themselves against a lamp-post, how precarious their being upright at all is to them—for they have already been felled several times, and picked themselves up, put themselves back together, each time with more and more difficulty, and their being on the pavement with their hands full of handbag, carrier bag, walking stick, is a miracle . . . Solitude, that great gift, is dependent on health, or an approximation to health. When I wake in the morning, I know that I can shop, cook, clean my flat, brush my hair, fill my bath and soak in it . . . and now I greet each day with—*what a privilege, what a marvellous, precious thing, that I don't need anyone to assist me through this day, I can do it all myself.*

I blow in to Maudie, who these days, because she is feeling better, is pleased to see me, does not shout and slam doors.

She can't get enough of anecdotes about my glamorous life. I search my memory for things to tell her.

"Can I have some tea, Maudie? Listen, I want to tell you something that happened . . ."

"Sit down, darling. Have a rest."

"It was in Munich."

"Munich, was it? Is that a nice place, then?"

"Lovely. Perhaps one day you'll see it."

"Yes, perhaps I will. Well, what happened?"

"You know how quickly these models have to change their clothes at the shows? Well, there was this girl, she came on in a green evening dress, and her black hair fell down . . ." I watch Maudie's face to see if she has seen what I am seeing, but not yet. "A gorgeous green glittering evening dress, and her hair piled up, black and gorgeous, then suddenly, down it slides . . ." Maudie has seen it, she tosses up her hands, she sits laughing. "And all of us, the buyers, the presenters, everybody, we laughed and laughed. And the girl, the model, she stood there, sheets of black hair all down her back and shoulders, tossing her head and making a theatre out of it."

"And you all sat there laughing . . ."

"Yes, we laughed and laughed . . . you see, it never happens. It's impossible. That's why we all laughed."

"Oh, Janna, I do love hearing about what you do."

I have had time to listen to Annie Reeves, to Eliza Bates.

Annie sits in a hard little chair by a blocked-in fire, wearing an old flowered wrap. Down the front of it rivers of food, cigarette droppings.

"Don't think I don't appreciate what you did for me, Mrs Bates said you did all this cleaning."

"I and Vera Rogers."

"You are a Good Neighbour, I suppose."

"No, I'm not."

A long, thoughtful inspection.

"Vera Rogers is not so much a Good Neighbour as she's a social worker?"

"That's right."

"Well, it's all too much for me." She says this giving due allowance to every word. Annie Reeves talks almost entirely in clichés, but for her they aren't clichés, they are words shining with evident truth. Listening to her is like hearing an earlier stage of our language. She says, "You are not old if you are young in heart. And I am young in heart." She has heard these words, thought about them, knows they apply to her, uses them with respect. She says, "I don't like being with old people, I like the company of young people like you." She says, "If they had told me when I was young I could end up like this, then I wouldn't have believed them." She says, "Time doesn't wait for any of us, whether we like it or not."

Annie has been a waitress all her life. From fourteen till seventy, when she was retired against her will, Annie has tripped from a serving hatch to a table with eggs, chips, spam, baked beans, fried steak, and fried fish. She has worked in cafés and dining rooms and in canteens for the staff in big stores, and in two world wars fed soldiers and airmen from Canada and Australia and America, some of whom wanted to marry her. But she is a Londoner, says she, she knows where she belongs. Annie achieved the summit of her ambitions when she was sixty. She got a job in a real posh coffee shop. She cut sandwiches and filled rolls with amazing foreign cheeses (which she would not taste herself) and served espressos and cappuccinos and rich cakes. She worked ten years under a man who was clearly a nasty piece of work and exploited her, but she loved the work so much she didn't care. When she was seventy, she was told to leave. As she had only worked ten years there, she did not get a pension, but a clock which she had to pawn when bad times began, which they did at once, for she went to pieces. Her life had always been in her work, since her husband died, as a result of getting a shell splinter in his lung in the First War. She went to pieces very fast, drinking, and thinking about the good times and how in the last place, the coffee bar, she knew all the customers and they knew her, and sometimes they took her to pubs and bought her a nice port, and the barrow boys in the streets used to call out, There's our Annie, and gave her peaches and grapes. She was, for fifty-five years, one of those smiling, maternal waitresses who make a restaurant, a café, bringing people back to it.

In her bad time she sat drinking in the Private Bars till they closed. Then she wandered about the streets by herself, having no friends in her own area, since she had hardly ever been in it, except at night or on Sundays, when she washed her hair and prepared her uniforms for the week ahead. Meeting impecc-able Eliza Bates in the streets, herself a dirty half-drunk old woman, she would turn aside and look into a shop window and pretend she hadn't seen her.

Annie talks of food a lot. Again I listen to details of meals eaten sixty, seventy years ago. The family lived in Holborn, in a now demolished tenement that had stone stairs and two lavatories, one for one side of the building, one for the other. Everyone was supposed to clean the lavatories and the stairs, but only two or three women actually did this work, the others shirked. The father was a labourer. He drank. He was con-tinually losing his job. Three children, Annie the oldest. In hard times, which were frequent, the children would run down to the shops for six eggs, sixpence; for yesterday's stale bread, kept for the poor by the German bakers. For the liquid from boiling sheep's heads, given away free to the poor; they brought back a jug of this, the mother made dumplings, and that is what they ate for supper. They got sixpennyworth of scraps from the butcher and made stew. Enormous boiled puddings full of fruit, with sugar sprinkled on, were used to stay appetites—just as Maudie remembered. When they were flush, the family had the best of everything in the food line, for the father went up to the butchers' auctions on a Saturday night, when the meat was sold that would spoil, and came back with a large sirloin for half a crown, or a leg of mutton. They ate eels and potatoes and parsley sauce, brought from the eel shop in a basin, or thick pea soup with potatoes in it. They got their milk from an old woman who had a cow. The cow had its head sticking out over the door in a shed in the back yard, and went moo when the children came in. The old woman sold buttermilk and butter and cream.

The family bought "specks" from the greengrocer: apples that had a brown spot on them; or yesterday's greens. Just as good as new, they were, and sometimes no money asked at all, just given away.

At the baker's, if they bought that day's bread, the German woman would always give the children a makeweight, cakes from yesterday. And in the market a man made sweets standing at a stall under a canopy, boiling toffee over a flame, and then spread it with coconut or walnuts or hazelnuts, and he always gave the children the little crushed splinters from when he broke up the toffee with his little hammer.

And then, the clothes. Annie, as she says herself, was a good-time girl and did not marry until she was over thirty. Her money went on clothes. She was slim, she had her hair marcelled for half a crown every week, she would buy clothes on the never-never from the shops in Soho. She had a black lace dance dress with a red rose on it, and wore it at the policemen's ball. She had a navy-blue costume with white piping that fitted her like a glove. She wore little hats with veils, because the boys liked them. A brown skirt wrapover, buttoned all down one side with buttons the size of spoons. A coat-dress, in blue velour with revers. Each time she summons the ghost of yet another garment from sixty, fifty, forty years ago, she says, They don't make the clothes like that now, just as she says about the yellow fat on the beef, There's no food like that now, and she is right.

I asked her what she did with all her old clothes: this always interests me, for very few garments actually wear out. "I wore them until I got fed up with them," she says, not knowing what it is I want to know.

"And then what?"

"What do you do with yours, then?"—examining my clothes, but not as Maudie did, with such skilled knowledge. "You've nice clothes, do you wear them out, then?"

"No, I give them to Oxfam."

"What's that?"

I explain. She simply cannot take it in. But this is not all she can't take in: Annie's mind froze, or stopped, or reached saturation at some point probably about ten years ago. Sometimes, as I sit up there, listening to the same stories, I try something new.

I've told her that I work for a women's magazine. She knows the name, though she has never read it. She is incurious. No, that's wrong: the machine that is her mind cannot admit anything outside an existing pattern. Thus, I will say, Today I went to see a new young dress designer, she's making clothes for . . . But almost at once I must retreat from the general to the specific, for I see from her eyes that she has *not taken it in.* "I saw a lovely dress," I say, "it was blue with . . ."

Annie often sits at her window two floors up, watching the street, waiting for something interesting to happen. She is alone except for when the Home Help, the nurse, the Meals on Wheels are rushing in and out. All her life, until ten years ago, was spent in company, and she was never alone, she says. But people are indoors these days, with their tellies, not milling about the streets having adventures, as she and her sister did, two bright pretty young things, the West End their oyster, using it, knowing how to evade dangers. They would allow themselves to be picked up by a pair of calculating salesmen, were taken to Romano's, had a real slap-up dinner, and then, when some kind of reward was due from them, said, We'll slip into the Ladies, if you don't mind, just for a moment—but they knew ways out and about and around, and remained in debt to their salesmen. Or they got themselves taken to the music hall or the theatre, and faded away into a crowd, or into a police station with a false story, or the Underground. For they were good girls, they were, as Annie tells me every other day. That part of her life, the five years before her sister married (more fool her) and the two young girls were not yet twenty, Annie in her first job, these years were the best of her life, she sits thinking of them—those and the coffee bar. That is what she would like to see now, looking down out of her window, a lively quick-witted noisy crowd, and if there were barrows and street trading, so much the better. But no, nothing like that these days. And as for those young people she sees down there, she doesn't have a good word for them. The young people, the descendants, in fact, of her young self and her sister, ten or twelve boys and girls from the flats at the corner, lively, black, brown, and white, unscrupulous and thieving, sometimes go strolling through this street, part of their territory. But what they see is old faces looking from windows, these houses are all full of the old and elderly, and the area is too dull for them, as it is for Annie.

How Annie grumbles and complains, she is so dull, it is so dreary . . .

Poor Eliza Bates's tales are all of the very far past, when her husband was alive, her sister.

Now she has no one. There is a niece somewhere, she believes, but she's lost her address. A brother-in-law has just died. She sighs and looks distressed when she mentions him. "He was the last, the last, you see," she murmurs. Then makes herself smile.

And her "young" friend, the woman of seventy, married a man she met at the Lunch Centre and has gone off to live in Scotland. This has shocked Eliza Bates. She is often scandalized. I never appreciated that word until I knew Eliza Bates. Hearing something that shocks her, which is often, she lifts both hands, fingers spread, to the level of her shoulders, her eyes widen, she gasps, she cries, Oh, oh, oh! I never would have thought it!

About her lost "young" friend, she expostulated, I wouldn't ever have believed *she* was like that!

Meaning, believe it or not, she suspects the poor woman of marrying her raddled stick-like old swain for the pleasures of the bed.

Not so Annie upstairs, who at moments may look like that worldly-wise, world-loving female who turned the handle of the barrel-organ while Irene was being raped in *The Forsyte Saga*, her ravaged face a grinning triumph. Our Annie has created—to suit what she thinks we expect from her—a timorous, refined, refraining persona, one from whom all unpleasant facts must be kept. For instance, she delights in telling us how often her father, her mother, her husband, kept from her the sight of a dog run over in the street, news of a dead relative, even a passing funeral. For she was such a sensitive, delicate soul. (Child-daughter! Child-wife!) Oh yes, Annie, the pretty raider of the West End streets, fashioned for herself at the same time a pouting, coy, simpering style which, I think, was all her swains saw of her. Probably the Canadian airman, the Australian soldier, the American sailor, fighting men of two world wars, all of whom "took her out" and bought her presents, the salesmen and the Burlington Berties, never ever saw this exulting unscrupulous, exploiting female who now, when forgetting about her simper and her refinement, may wink and say, Oh, *I* knew how to take care of myself, *I* knew my way about, *I* never gave anything I didn't mean to!

But almost at once this female will vanish, as Annie remembers the needs of respectability, and she will again become a coy little girl; even sitting—this eighty-five-year-old woman—in the simpering pose of a three-year-old, which says silently, Oh I'm such a delicate little thing, so sweet . . .

I have a feeling that Annie has done a lot of thinking about what she may and may not tell us, and that her tales will always be heavily edited.

But sometimes there are flashes: a phrase from an advertisement, or from a popular song, and she'll light up—Little night nurse, he called me, she crooned the other day; and then, remembering I was there, she shot me a half-scared, half-triumphant smile. Yes, night nurse—well, I like to sit here and remember I've had a good life.

Driving home, I saw a company of old ladies on the pavement, all hatted and scarved in the chill spring evening. They had all been to Hatfield, by coach, on a church outing. Among them, Eliza Bates. Little old ladies, chirping and chirruping away. The company that is too good for Maudie. The Vicar was there with his lady aides. Eliza was being supported by her friends. I realized that she is seen by them as frail, getting frailer. I rang up Vera; she said, "She's lost her last relative, her best friend's married and gone, you've got to expect . . ."

I also saw Maudie again, out in the harsh spring light, toiling along, gasping. The bright yellow of her face, that painted look. I don't have to ring Vera to ask.

At the end of the three weeks, I decided, simply, to work less. They like my *Milliners*. They like my *Fashion Changes*.

I shall work part-time, and they must get a new editor. I want to enjoy myself, to slow down . . .

My sister Georgie rang, in the way she does now, in a cautious noncommittal way, checking up on her irresponsible sister. I, without thinking, said that I will work part-time and inside two minutes Jill was on the telephone.

"Aunt *Jane*," she was gasping. "It can't be true. It can't."

I was silent, for far too long.

She was weeping. "Aunt Jane, you *promised*."

I did? I made a promise?

After thought, I wrote to her, encouraged her to do well in her imminent exams, and told her to come and see me when she knew how she had done. I can almost hear the cold and censorious breaths from the Arctic of my Sister Georgie: Really, Janna, do you never think of anyone but yourself?

Joyce again:

She says, "I've been working away at fixing up our new apartment, and I've just finished scrubbing the kitchen, and I thought of *you*."

"And how is the new apartment, how is America, how is university life, how is the campus wife?"

"I think I am about to get a job as counsellor."

"What council?"

"No, counselling, I am going to counsel."

"Whom?"

"Those who need counselling."

"On behalf of whom?"

"Those who know the answers."

"And you are of course going to be properly paid for it?"

"Adequately. Money for jam. But it really ought to be you, Janna. Advice has been less my forte than yours."

"I have never given advice."

"What are long erudite articles of a sociological bent if not advice?"

"And how is your husband liking America?"

"He is adjusting."

"And how are your sprightly children?"

"They are adjusting and relating to peer groups."

"And how are *you*, Joyce?"

"It is possible that I am too old or too stiff-necked to adjust."

"Oh, does that mean you are coming home?"

"I didn't say that, Janna."

"I see."

"I thought you would."

"Well, I miss you."

"I miss you."

"Goodbye."

"Goodbye."

Well, so that was the year. As Virginia Woolf said, It is the present moment. It is Now.

I have told them they must get an editor, I want to come in perhaps two, three days a week, or mornings. Phyllis's reproach. She is good as assistant editor, working with me. Am I to stay full-time because of Phyllis, because of Jill? That is what their demands amount to. Silent demands—Phyllis. Most voluble and exclamatory—Jill.

But the waters will close over me as easily and thoroughly as they have over Joyce.

The young ones in the office treat me with charming casualness, the new house style—certainly not mine, and where did it come from? Everything is much more inefficient, slapdash. They have started meetings again, lunch hours, coffee breaks. "Oh, excuse me, Janna, we are having a meeting."

"Enjoy yourselves," I say, having given this battle up. Revolutionaries to a man they are, these well-educated, well-paid, well-fed young people who, like me, spend as much on their clothes as would feed families. Well, the house of revolution has many mansions, I say to them, and they agree to find it amusing.

Michael and his mates are "into" a serious study of brainwashing techniques, propaganda, the use of slogans, conversion—all that kind of thing. From the point of view, of course, of combating them when used on them and their comrades.

I say, "But it doesn't seem to have occurred to you that *you*

and your employees will be using them on your opponents—
probably me?"

"Oh, Janna, don't be like that."

"No, I'd find it all rather endearing than not," I say, "if
there's not a quite serious prospect of you and your lot getting
into power. Not, of course, that any of you would survive ten
minutes. You'd be eliminated in the first wave!"

"We're realists, we are."

"Romantics every one. Romanticism is not the best quality
in a new ruling class."

"Well, you should know about romance," says Michael,
brandishing the proof copy of *The Milliners of Marylebone*,
which is being avidly read in the office by everyone. "But why
not a *serious* novel about them? They were shamefully exploited," he cries.

"I shall leave that to you," I say. "In my opinion the truth is
intolerable, it is more than we can stand, it has to be prettied
up."

"Escapist."

But when I gave him the proofs of my serious book, *Fashion
Changes*, he didn't read it. This is because, I know, he wants
me in a certain category: elderly reactionary who cannot face
reality.

Maudie is ill. She looks dreadful. She sits opposite me, and
draws the curtains in full daylight so that I can't see her face,
but I hear her breathing come short as she shifts position in her
chair, see her hands go protectively over her stomach. She
drinks little sips of tea, as if they might be poison, then drinks,
suddenly, cup after cup as if it might wash something away.

All this last year I've been going to the doctor to get her
prescriptions, and getting them made up, because she won't
see the doctor. She won't.

I said to her today, "Maudie, you ought to let the doctor see
you."

"If you've all decided it, then I shall have to do as I'm told."
Sullen.

"No, it's up to you."

"That's what you say."

I realized in fact she wants me to call the doctor, but won't say so. Is he going to prescribe new pills? If a dictator wished to subjugate a population, all he would have to do would be to come on the telly screen and say, And now, all of you, it is time to take your little white pill. Just take your little white pill for me, dear . . .

For if you ask Annie, you ask Eliza, What is that pill you are taking? they never think of replying, I am taking Mogadon, Valium, Dioxin, Frusemide, they say, It is a big yellow pill, it is a little white pill, it is a pink pill with a blue band . . .

The doctor came today. I wasn't there. Maudie: "He says I've got to go for another examination."

"I'll go with you."

"Please yourself."

Today I took Maudie to hospital. I filled in the form for her and said she was not prepared to be examined in front of students. When our turn came, I was called in first. Large many-windowed room, the table of Authority, the big doctor, and many students. Their *young* unknowing faces . . .

"How am I going to teach my students if I can't show them any patients?" he asked me.

I said, "It's too much for her."

He said, "Why is it? It's not too much for me, and I am sure it is not too much for you when you're sick."

This was so *stupid* I decided not to bother. "She's very old and very frightened," I said, and left it at that.

"Hmmmmmmmmm!" And then, to the students, "So I suppose I'll have to order you to take yourselves off."

This was my cue to give in, but I wasn't going to.

Off went the students. There remained the consultant, myself, a young Indian man.

"You'll have to put up with my assistant."

Maudie comes slowly in, not looking at us, supported by the nurse. She is put in the chair next to me.

"And what is your name?" asks the big doctor.

Maudie does not look up, but she is muttering. I know she is saying that she watched me fill in the form with her name.

"How do you feel?" asks the big doctor in a loud clear voice.

Now Maudie lifts her head and stares at him, incredulously.
"Have you got a pain?" asks the doctor.
"My doctor said I had to come up here," says Maudie,
trembling with fear and with rage.
"I see. Well, Dr Raoul will examine you for me, and then
you'll come back here."
Maudie and I are taken to a cubicle.
"I'm not going to, I won't," says she to me, fiercely.
I simply begin taking off her coat, a bully just like the doctor,
and then the smell hits me. Oh, if only I could get used to it.
"Why should I?" she complains. "It's not what I want, it's
what you all want."
"Why don't you let them examine you while you are here?"
I take off her dress, and see that her underclothes are all
dirtied, though I know she put out clean ones for today. She is
shaking. I take off everything but her knickers and hide her in
the enormous hospital dressing gown.
We have to wait a long time. Maudie is sitting upright on the
examination table, staring at the wall.
At last in comes the Indian doctor. Charming. I like him and
so does Maudie, who patiently lies down for him and allows
him to examine her very thoroughly. (Please lie down for me,
Mrs Fowler, please turn over for me, please cough for me,
please hold your breath for me; it's the formula, insulting, used
in all hospitals and Homes, by everyone working with the old,
who have to be treated like small children.) He listens to her
heart, he listens for a long time to her lungs, and he then, very
gently, uses his brown hands to feel her stomach. A tiny little
belly, you wonder what happens to all the food she eats.
"What's there? What's in there?" she demands, fierce.
"So far, nothing, as far as I can see," smiling, delightful.
And suddenly, in strides the big doctor. He shouts, "What
do you mean by sending the X-rays for the oesophagus to the
Records? I need them now."
The Indian doctor straightens, stands looking at his boss
over the body of Maudie, his brown hands on her yellow
stomach.
"I must have misunderstood you," he said.
"That's no excuse for incompetence."

Suddenly, Maudie: "Why are you cross with him? He's very nice."

"He may be nice, but he's a very bad doctor," says the tyrant, and withdraws.

We three do not look at each other.

The Indian doctor is pulling up Maudie's knickers and helping her sit up. He is angry, we can see.

"Well, I suppose he feels better after that," says Maudie, bitterly.

Back in the big doctor's room, Maudie, the Indian, and I, in three chairs facing him.

I know that things are bad, because of the bland competence of the man and because of something about the Indian doctor's attitude towards Maudie. But Maudie is leaning forward, her bright blue eyes on the big man's face: she is waiting for the word from Olympus. It comes: oh, very nicely done, I admired that, full marks.

"Well now, Mrs Fowler, we've examined you thoroughly, and there's nothing that we can't get under control. You must be sure to eat . . ." And so he goes on, looking from his notes, to her, smiling, looking back as if to check up his facts, a beautiful performance. And I was thinking, I won't know till the report has gone to Maudie's doctor, and Vera has rung him up, and I have rung Vera, and then I can know: meanwhile, because I'm not real next of kin, but only the person who's nearest to Maudie, I'll have to lump it.

In the taxi, Maudie is an upright tense suffering trembling bundle of thick black, and she says, "What about the pains in my stomach, what about those?"

She has not said anything to me about pains before, and I did not know what to say, except that her doctor would come.

"Why? You take me up there, all that performance, that consultant, whatever he calls himself, Lord Muck, but after all that, back home I go, and I can't even be told."

It has taken ten days, while Maudie has been ill with worry. She knows she has something badly wrong. The big doctor wrote to the little doctor. Vera rang him. Vera rang me: Maudie has cancer of the stomach.

Vera says to me, "It's bad, it's awful—but you know, they can control pain now, they know exactly how to do it. So when she has to go into hospital . . ."

Vera is worried that I am worried—and I am. Very. Meanwhile, Maudie is told she has a stomach ulcer and is given mild pain-killers. But unfortunately they muddle her mind and so into the lavatory pan they go, more often than not.

Vera and I have telephone calls in which more is understood than can be said: Maudie must be kept out of hospital as long as possible. She must not be worried with Home Helps if she doesn't want, or with nurses coming in to wash her. We must make sure her landlord takes no notice of threats from the Council that he will be taken to court for the condition of her flat, and meantime Vera will have a word with the relevant official.

And how long can all this last? I find myself suddenly desperately wanting it all to be over. In short, I want Maudie dead.

But Maudie does not want to be dead. On the contrary. She is raging with a fierce need to live. It is Vera who has forced her up to the hospital, who made her doctor come, who has caused this diagnosis of stomach ulcer to be forced on her. It is Vera who is the enemy: but, as Vera says, this is a good thing, because the old have to have an enemy (only the old?), so she can have me as a friend and Vera as an enemy. Vera is used to it.

Maudie says to me, "Stomach ulcer?" She sits with her two large knotted hands on her stomach, gently feeling. There is sweat on her forehead.

Vera says that the cells of the old reproduce themselves slowly, and therefore the cancer may take a long time to become fatal, and Maudie may live three years, four—who could know?

Vera and I have tea in the café on the corner and eat baked beans on toast. We are both fitting a meal in, somewhere, before we fly apart to our different spheres of labour.

Vera says to me that yes, probably Maudie knows, but she also does not know: and we have to take our cue from her.

Vera tells me about an old man she is watching over who has

cancer of the bowel and has been keeping himself upright and viable (her word!) for two years. He knows. She knows. He knows she knows. His anguish, his contrivings, his slow deterioration—the squalor—they both of them ignore it. But yesterday he said to her, Well, it won't be long now, and I'll not be sorry to die. I've had enough.

Maudie won't have a Home Help, she won't. As she talks, I see that for years this or that social worker has been trying to get Maudie to see reason. The stories Maudie tells about them, you'd think they were a race of sluts and thieves. But now I know a bit more, because I see Annie's Home Help. And Eliza Bates is ill, quite suddenly very ill, almost helpless, and Annie's Home Help is now hers too, though one of the things she had been so proud of all these years is that she has never, ever, asked anyone for anything, ever let her place go, ever been a burden.

A Day in the Life of a Home Help.

She may be Irish, West Indian, English—any nationality, but she is unqualified and has a dependant of some kind or children, so that she needs a job she can fit in around her family. She is young, or at least not elderly, for you need strength for this work. She has bad legs/a bad back/chronic indigestion/womb trouble. But nearly every woman has womb trouble these days. (Why?)

She almost certainly lives in a Council flat and is a Council employee, as a Home Help.

She wakes at half past six or seven, when her husband does. He is in the building trade and has to get off early. One or other of them puts the kettle on and sets out the cornflakes for the kids, and both parents jolly them out of bed and through the business of washing and dressing. While she keeps an eye on everybody's breakfast, state of health, the cat's meal, the weather, her voice competes with the elder child's cassette player, kept low because she nags at him. But she is simultaneously planning her day. It is raining . . . the kids must take their macs . . . Bennie needs his football gear . . . she must pick up her husband's prescription for the skin infection that announced itself last week and shows no signs of going. While she telephones for a dentist's appointment for her "baby", now five, she urges on the middle one, the girl, to be quick and get the five-year-old's coat and scarf on, for it is getting late. Her husband has shovelled down cornflakes and toast and jam, while he reads the *Mirror* and absently scratches his neck, which is flaming red. She doesn't like the look of that at all. He says to the boy, the twelve-year-old, Come along, then, and as he goes past his wife takes from her hand (the one not holding the telephone receiver) the packet of sandwiches she made for him while he was in the bathroom. See you later, he mumbles, for he is thinking about whether he should drop into the doctor for his rash. She yells after them, Bennie, your football things, and the two males are gone.

There are left the two girls. The sound of music is stilled. Silence. The "baby" croons as she picks up her toast, and the girl sits efficiently ingesting toast and jam.

The Home Help lets herself flop into a chair, bringing the telephone with her, and she hooks the receiver under her chin while she pours herself tea and reaches for her son's unfinished toast and jam because she can't bear waste.

She makes half a dozen calls, all to do with husband and children, and then rings the Home Help Office to find out if there is anything new. They want her to do old Mr Hodges today, for his Help has just rung to say she has to take her mother to hospital and won't be working. The Office sounds apologetic, as well they might, for Bridget is already doing four a day, and they are all difficult. She gets the difficult ones because she is so good with them.

As she sits there, watching how the "baby"—oh, look at that, over goes the milk, what a mess—she plans how to fit in Mr Hodges. Then she gets up, says, Come on now, school time. She acquires from all over the kitchen, handbag, shopping bags and baskets, money out of a drawer, a plastic scarf for her head, the packets of sandwiches for the children, a dozen small items they need for school: books, exercise books, crayons. Objects seem to dance about her, in and out of bags and drawers and off hooks, and then the three of them are ready, all done up inside plastic for the bad weather outside.

When they are out, though, it is not so bad, damp but not cold. The school is only five minutes' walk away, that's something; Bridget never ceases to give thanks that this part of her life, at least, is so convenient. Having seen the two little girls run off across the playground, she turns away, thinking, Oh, she's not a baby any more, little Mary isn't—is it too late for me to fit in another? She yearns for a fourth, part of the time; her husband tells her she is mad when she mentions it, and she agrees with him . . . As she whisks past another mother coming to leave a child at the school gates, Bridget smiles at a small baby in a pram, and thinks, now stop that, girl, stop that! You know where *that* will lead you.

She goes back home for the few minutes in every day when she enjoys perfect peace. Sits at the kitchen table, sees if there is any tea in the pot—there is, but it looks too black and she can't be bothered. Sits in a heap, breathing steadily, in and out, a young woman still, on the right side of forty, and you can see in her the wildly pretty Irish girl she was when she came to this country with her husband twelve years ago. Cornflower-blue eyes, pink skin, a mass of dark waves and curls. Nevertheless, she is tired, and looks it. What she is—is tired.

In her mind she is listing all the things she has to buy, for her four regular customers and her own family and—of course, she was nearly forgetting—for old Mr Hodges. Is he on the phone? Oh *no*, Mother Mary, help me! Does that mean she will have to go out again to buy in food and stuff for him? No, she'll drop in and do him first before the shopping. A nuisance.

She does not look forward to Mr Hodges, whom she knows of old.

Bridget takes another look at the sky, decides it is safe to leave off her plastic wrap, and again gathers together her bags and baskets. Mr Hodges is ten minutes' walk away. She does not have the key, so she stands banging and banging, till at last the head of a cross old man appears in the window above and he says, "What do you want? Go away."

"Oh, Mr Hodges," cries Bridget gaily, "you know me, I'm Bridget. Do you remember? Maureen can't come today, she's taking her mother to the hospital."

"Who?"

"Oh, do be a dear now and let me in. I haven't all day."

This threat makes him open the door, and she casts the rapid skilled glance of a doctor, nurse, psychiatrist—or Home Help—over him, and decides that—thank God!—he's not too bad today. Mr Hodges is eighty-five. His wife got past it and she's in a Home, much to the relief of Mr Hodges. For they were near to killing each other from exasperation. Mr Hodges is a little stick of a man, his clothes hanging on him. He has got very skinny recently. Bridget thinks, cancer? Diabetes ? I must mention it at the Office.

As he clambers up the stairs in front of her, he is grumbling, And she didn't get me the sugar, and I've no cheese, nothing to eat, no one does anything . . .

"Mr Hodges," cries Bridget as she reaches the two rooms he lives in—if that is the word for it—and examines everything at a glance, "I can see you are in a bad mood today. Now, what can I do for you?"

"Do for me? You're doing for me, the lot of you," he snaps, and he trembles all over, with age and with rage.

He has no one to talk to but the Home Help, and for hours of every day he engages in angry fantasies because of his helplessness. He was (only the other day, it seems) an energetic and independent man, the careful and tender support of his wife, who cracked up before he did. And now . . .

Bridget sees that she need not clean today, the place is not too bad. It is no part of her job, but what he *needs* is to talk and to scold, and so she sits herself down on a kitchen chair, and listens to the old man's complaints and accusations while she examines the kitchen for what he might be short of.

"And what shall I get you?" she asks, interrupting the tirade when she feels he has had his allowance.

"I need tea, can't you use your eyes?"

He says nothing about the cheese and the sugar, and Bridget thinks, I'll get him those and anything else I think best, and if he doesn't want them, then Mrs Coles might . . .

Soon she has left him, urging him to remember that she will be back later with his things and she needs to be let in. Now she knows everything she has to buy, and she takes a bus down to Sainsbury's.

She has no lists, not even a scribble on the back of an envelope, but she keeps in her mind the requirements of ten people, and after half an hour or so emerges on to the pavement with basket-on-wheels and four heavy baskets. She is thinking as she proceeds soberly up the street, and for God's sake now, Bridget Murphy, mind your back . . . you don't want *that* again. And so she walks, does not take the bus, which means so much lifting and managing. It takes her half an hour to walk back up to where her work is. She feels guilty about this, but tells herself, It's sensible, isn't it? What use would you be flat in bed? She passes Maudie Fowler's place, from which she has been ejected more than once; thinks, thank God I've not been given her again, that'd be the last straw, really it would.

First stop, Mrs Coles. She is an old Russian woman who was once a beauty, with photographs stuck everywhere around her rooms to prove it. Furs, saucy little hats, naked shoulders, gauze—this great mass of a woman sits torpid in a big chair most of the day, gazing at her past. She is a complainer, and drives Bridget mad with it.

Bridget switches off as she goes in, always; and lets the heavy greasy voice sag on and on about this and that, while she puts away bread, butter, tins of soup, detergent—but then she realizes she ought to be listening, for Mrs Coles is saying, "And it was bright red . . ."

Bridget asks sharply, "What was bright red? What have you been eating, then?"

"What could I have been eating? What can you eat that makes your water red?"

"Did you keep it for me?"

"How? What in?"

Bridget whirls about and goes into the bathroom.

Mrs Coles has been rehoused, and this is the middle floor of a house, done up. Done up very nicely, but Mrs Coles doesn't like it because she never wanted to move at all. And she brought everything she owned with her. The two rooms are crammed with old heavy furniture, two wardrobes, three chests of drawers, a table the weight of a rock. You can hardly move. But there is a proper bathroom and a good toilet. Bridget peers in. It has been flushed. But there is a smell to the place. What? Something chemical?

She goes back to the other room, and Mrs Coles is sitting where she was left, still talking as if Bridget has not been out of the room at all.

"I think I might have strained myself, that's what it might be. I lifted that chair yesterday, when I shouldn't."

But Bridget is on the track of something.

"Have you been taking those tonic pills again?" she suddenly inquires, and darts off to the bedroom, and there she finds a bottle of enormous pills, good enough for a cart-horse, and they are virulent scarlet.

"Oh, my God," she says, "oh, Holy Mother, give me patience." She marches back and says, "I told you to throw that rubbish away. It's nothing that will do you good. I'm going to throw them right away, it's them that are giving you the red water."

"Ohhhhh," wails Mrs Coles, "you are throwing them away, you have no right . . ."

"Oh, keep them and take them, but don't complain to me about your water. I told you when I saw them, remember? I told you, they bring on red water. Because another of my cases did the very same thing."

Mrs Coles is holding out a fat dirty hand for the bottle of pills. Bridget puts them into it. Then Mrs Coles herself throws the pills into a pail and murmurs, "Good riddance, then."

Bridget has been here for fifteen minutes. She is supposed to be here an hour and a half. But included in that time is the time for shopping. Yet she shops for everyone together. She includes that shopping time as half an hour, separately, in the mental account she makes for each of her charges. And then she walked up the street for half an hour. That means she has fifteen minutes to go. Bridget's conscience troubles her daily over these calculations of hers. But she always makes it come out like this: and in the end she spends half an hour with Mrs Coles, if that. But then, what about those times when she has run around and about getting medicine, fetching the doctor, coming specially to let in electricity men, gas men, the man who mended the leak in the ceiling—and for these times she does not seem to charge. No, it probably all balances out. Yet she knows that, like Mr Hodges, Mrs Coles relies on her for company, and so she sits down again, fidgeting with impatience to be gone, and listens while Mrs Coles grumbles.

At twelve o'clock she hears the Meals on Wheels in the street, throws up the window, checks that she is right, and says, "Well, your dinner is here, and I'll see you tomorrow."

And she runs down the stairs, her mind already on Annie Reeves, who is next.

Oh, dear God, let her be in a good mood, she prays. For sometimes, after Mrs Coles's incessant grumbling, to walk in to Annie and yet another dose of the same is more than she can stand. She is thinking, if she's in one of her moods, I swear I might kill her.

She finds Annie sitting in a heap by the radiator and notices how the old woman looks up blinking, vague, a miserable, strained old face.

Annie starts at once, "I feel so bad, my legs, my stomach, my head . . ."

"Wait a minute, love," says Bridget, and goes into the kitchen, where she fumbles for the kettle and puts it on. It is all too much, too much . . . Perhaps I could do some other kind of work, thinks Bridget, her eyes shut . . . what, cleaning? No, wait a minute . . . "*coming*," she shrieks as Annie shouts, "Where are you? Are you here or aren't you?"

She goes into the other room and tidies this and that. While Annie complains. Bridget empties the commode. She sees the cat has made a mess and it has to be cleaned up. She sees that Annie's cardigan is grey with dirt and really ought to be changed.

But first . . .

She puts the Meals on Wheels food on to plates, helps Annie to the table, sits her down, puts the food in front of her, fetches cups of tea for both of them. And sits down, with a cigarette and her own sandwiches.

Annie eats heartily, and when she has finished, pushes away her plates saying she has no appetite. She complains the tea is cold, but Bridget does not budge and she drinks it, grumbling. Whining, she allows herself to be taken back to her chair. She says she doesn't see anyone, she doesn't get out, she never . . .

At this, Bridget, as she does every day, lists all the things Annie could be doing: she could go down and sit outside on a fine day and watch the people passing, she could walk up and down on her frame, like old Mrs This and That and the Other One, she could go on a Council holiday, she could go on coach trips, like Eliza used to do, she could say yes when Janna asks her to go for a drive instead of, always, no.

"Perhaps, when the weather is fine," says Annie, looking triumphantly at the rain, which has started to fall. "And I suppose you haven't brought me in the things I asked for?"

Bridget heaves herself up and brings in the things she has brought so that Annie may see them.

"I asked you for a bit of haddock," says Annie at the end.

"No, you didn't, love, but I'll get you some tomorrow."

"And where are my oranges?"

"Here, three lovely oranges. Would you like one?"

"No, my stomach isn't too good. I don't feel like eating."

Bridget fetches the work sheet, and sees to it that Annie signs in the right places.

As she goes down to Eliza Bates, she hears, "An hour and a half, I *don't* think. The Irish. Scum. They send all the scum to us."

Bridget finds herself muttering, "Scum yourself!" Annie's parents were both of them Irish, and in better moods she may say, "I'm Irish, like yourself, although I was born in the hearing of Bow Bells." And she will tell stories of her mother, who picked cockles and mussels off the rocks in Dublin Bay, who went to the races dressed in sprigged muslin—Annie has a photograph of her—in a jaunting car; of her father, who was six foot four inches tall and fought in the British Army in India, in China, and in Egypt, before he became a labourer, but always said to his family, I'm an Irishman, and I don't forget it; of how on St Patrick's Day he and her mother always drank to Ireland together, though they never had the money to visit it after they left it.

Bridget knocks on Eliza Bates's door, and there is no reply.

Her heart begins pounding. She lives in dread of walking in and finding one of them dead. It hasn't happened to her, but it has to other Home Helps. One of these days, it will. Bridget rang Vera yesterday to say that Eliza was not well, she was going downhill fast, they ought to be thinking of getting her into a Home. This was Bridget's tactful way of saying that she was not going to put up with it for long: Eliza's staying out of a Home was because of what she, Bridget, did for Eliza, beyond the demands of her job.

Eliza is sitting upright in her chair by her electric fire, asleep. It is very hot in the little room. Eliza is flushed with the heat, has sweat on her face. She is wrapped in shawls and blankets. Her legs are up on a pouffe, because she has suddenly developed a bad ulcer on one, and both of them are swollen.

Again Bridget sets out the food from Meals on Wheels, left outside the door in little flat foil containers, on plates. For Eliza she takes trouble finding pretty plates, for Eliza still cares and notices, not like that Annie, who wouldn't notice if she ate off a dog's plate. Bridget makes tea, remembering just how Eliza likes it, and then arouses Eliza, who comes awake staring and wild.

"Oh, Bridget," she says, in a trembling old voice, out of a bad dream, and then, hearing her own voice, changes it to her usual sprightly cheerfulness, "Oh, Bridget, Bridget dear . . ." But because of her dream, she puts up her arms to Bridget like a child.

Bridget, her heart at once melted, takes the old woman into her arms and kisses her and rocks her.

She could weep for Eliza, as she tells her husband, who has so suddenly found herself in a chair with her legs propped up, an invalid. It's not as if it was that Annie, who does everything to get herself waited on. No, Eliza is not like that, is independent, suffers. Bridget knows that twice recently Eliza has woken soaked in urine: Bridget has rinsed out the sheets for her. She knows that Eliza is afraid to go too far from the lavatory, for fear of worse. Eliza, who has spent the last fifteen years of her life in the company of the old, knows exactly what can happen at the end, the miserable humiliation that might be in store for her.

Bridget sits by Eliza, coaxing her to eat, chats about her children, her husband, says that the weather is not so good today as it was yesterday.

She establishes that Eliza has not been to bed all night but has sat up in the chair, sleeping. She has not had anything to eat yet, though the Good Neighbour made her a cup of tea. "Who is this Good Neighbour?" she asks Bridget, peevishly. "She comes in and out, I am sure she means well, but I don't know her."

"She lives next door," says Bridget. "Do let her in, she just drops in and out to make sure you are all right. We are worried about you, you see."

"Janna hasn't been in for days," says Eliza, but questioningly, for she knows she sometimes doesn't remember who comes in.

Bridget does not want to say that Janna has probably been busy, in what time she has, with Maudie Fowler, who is on her last legs—these old things are all so jealous, you've got to be careful what you say.

"Janna has got a lot to do," she says vaguely. She decides to leave a note addressed to Janna on the stairs, asking, if she does drop in, to make sure Eliza is all right.

Then she starts on the business of getting Eliza to take her pills. She herself is horrified at the number of pills Eliza is supposed to take, is sure that they must all quarrel together in the poor old thing's stomach, but the doctor says so, the nurse does what the doctor orders, and she, the Home Help, at the bottom of the heap, cannot disobey.

"Come on, love," she murmurs, beseeches, implores, handing Eliza pills and pills.

The nurse comes in to give her pills in the morning. The Good Neighbour gives her pills at night. But the midday pills (or some time in the day, for Bridget can never be sure of exactly when) are her job, for she has agreed to do it.

Eliza sits there, with tight lips, looking at the heap of pills, her face knotted up with resentment. But the habits of a lifetime's obedience keep her silent and she swallows them down, slowly, one, two, three, four, five.

Bridget has sworn that she would not be here more than an

hour at the most, but by the time she leaves it is nearly three hours, and she has the comfort of knowing that Eliza is almost her old self, alert and awake because of all that affectionate attention, a little tart perhaps in her comments, but smiling, even joking about her weakness, saying to Bridget that one of these days Bridget will come in here and find her gone.

Well, she's not so bad then, thinks Bridget to herself, if she can joke about it, but then, who can tell . . . ?

It is getting on for the time she should pick up her two girls. She never lets them go to school or come back by themselves, because of a big main road they have to cross.

She runs into a telephone booth, is lucky to find a friend at home, asks her to collect the two girls and take them to her place.

For it is nearly four, and she still has Mrs Brent and Mr Hodges.

The old man is easy, she has only to take in his food, having again banged and shouted and banged to be let in, and to say that either she or his own Help will be in tomorrow.

And now for Mrs Brent. Bridget does not have to pray that she will be in a good mood, for she always is, although she is part-paralysed. Not yet thirty, a beautiful young woman, she has a child of three, and it is Bridget's job to bring the child back from the nursery, where the young husband takes her every morning. At moments when Bridget thinks that she cannot endure this job one day more—though on the whole she does not mind it, it is only on a day like this, when there are the straws that *nearly* break her back, that she thinks she will give up—then she remembers Hilda Brent, who is always good for a laugh, even in such a sad situation.

Bridget runs as fast as she can along several streets to the nursery, finds the child ready, the teacher reproachful, for Bridget is late, and then goes to the little flat the Brents live in. She loves the little girl. She looks forward every day to this hour when she takes the child home to her mother, and gives her tea, for Hilda cannot do it, is dependent on her husband and Home Helps. But today she finds Hilda lying back in her chair, eyes closed, her pretty face all grey hollows.

Oh, Holy Mother, says Bridget to herself, oh no, *stop*, it's too much, *no*.

She knows what has happened, Hilda has these turns.

"Have you rung the hospital?" she shouts.

Hilda, without opening her eyes, shakes her head.

Bridget rings for an ambulance, and then rings the office where the young husband works. But, as she suspects, he will not be back until seven, he has to work late.

She gets the young woman's things ready for the ambulance, helps the ambulance men with her, sees her off, promises her she need not worry about the child, and then locks the flat, and puts little Rosie into her push-chair.

She wheels it to her friend's flat, collects her two children, and goes home with the three of them.

She is thinking that the last time there was an emergency, there had been a strike of the social workers for more money, and the Home Helps were supposed to be working to rule in sympathy. This struck her then and it strikes her now as the ultimate in stupidity. How can one work to rule in this job? How, tell me that! But she had been officially ticked off by some bright spark, who was organizing the pickets at the Office, for strike-breaking. But what was I supposed to do, then, let the baby fend for herself alone in that flat? What?

But the young hero had said to her, "If you ever do it again, you will be penalized."

Well, she was doing it again, but with a bit of luck there wasn't a strike on. She hoped.

At home she rushes about, getting her husband's tea. He needs it when he comes in, for he is working out on site this week and he is not well anyway, what with that nasty rash of his.

The boy comes in. "What shall I do with my football clothes?" he asks, and she says, "Throw them into the bath."

She has the table laid, tea made, the three children eating, and little Rosie on her lap drinking milk, when her husband comes in.

Again that rapid skilled expert glance. She knows at once he is ill and is not surprised when he says, "I'm going up to get into my bed, that's how I'm feeling."

"I'll bring you some tea, then."

"Don't trouble, love, I'm going to sleep it off."

And he goes upstairs.

Perhaps I can get Vera in her office now, sometimes she works late . . .

Bridget rings, and is lucky.

"Oh, thank God, Vera," she says, "thank God it's you."

"I'm just off," says Vera warningly.

"It's Eliza Bates. She can't go on. She can't."

And suddenly Bridget is weeping.

"Oh, it's like that, is it?" asks Vera. "Well, don't tell me, I know, I could howl my eyes out, what a day, and now they want me to go to a meeting on top of it."

"I'm going to ring off," says Bridget, doing so.

But by the time she turns to face the four children, she is smiling.

She cleans vegetables, puts them with a chicken into a pot, puts the pot into the oven, clears the tea things away, and says to the two older children, "And now get your homework done and you can watch television."

She sits down, cuddling the little girl, who, because of her father always being so desperate to catch up with himself, having a paralysed wife, and her mother not being able to hold her properly, is starved of proper comforting and cuddling.

The two needs are fed, together, for a blissful half an hour, the child crooning and snuggling, and Bridget sniffing at the deliciously smelling curls, which she washed herself yesterday (though it is not her job to do it), and stroking the soft plump little limbs.

Then she says to the older boy, "Keep an eye on them for me," and to the girl, "If you smell burning, then turn the oven down to three."

She ties a scarf over her head, pulls the plastic hood down over that and ties it fast, encloses little Rosie in plastic, and sets off along the dark streets to the Brents' flat, half a mile away. The young husband is back, grateful for her taking his child, wanting to know about tomorrow. For again he will have to work late, though he said his wife was ill, and he won't be home till later than today.

"Don't you worry about it," says Bridget, and she kisses little Rosie with all her heart, and goes home.

It is nearly eight. She will give her children supper, she will make herself take a bite, though she isn't hungry. She thinks that her husband had said something about their going to the Club for a drink tomorrow. Well, if he's up to it . . . And there's that wedding next week, of her husband's young sister, that's something to look forward to. She sits by herself, half watching television, listening that the children are not making too much noise and disturbing their father. There is a lot of cleaning she should be doing, but she seldom has time for her own place in the week. Bridget does not work at weekends. That is, she does not work as a Home Help.

Today, this happened. A telephone call from Jill, screaming, exultant. "Auntie, Auntie Jane, I've just done them, and I know I've done well."

"Done what?"

"Auntie! Oh *no*. It is too much." Tears. I thought, it must be that ghastly Kate, but no, it was Jill. What, then? I realized I'd been really stupid. "I'm sorry, it's your examinations, isn't it? They've gone well?"

Sniff. Sniff. "Yes, I am sure they have. I've worked so hard, Auntie, I've *worked*."

"Come up and tell me about it." I didn't mean that moment, but that is what I was inviting, and she shouted, "Oh, thank you, I'll be there this afternoon, but not till late, it's my turn to feed the neighbour's cats, she's away, and Mother is visiting Jasper in hospital, he's broken his ankle playing football."

I made myself sit down and think. Jill has never been renowned for her schoolwork, I remembered. She hated examinations, tended to fail. Now she's done well. She's been working: for Auntie Jane. She's been determined to pass well: for Auntie Jane. The whole family have been involved. Cheers and jeers, happy families. But Auntie Jane says, "Done what?"

She arrived, exuberant, shining all over.

She kissed me, spontaneously. Then seemed embarrassed.

"Tell me all about it."

"I know I've done well. The results won't be in for *weeks* but I know it."

She chatted on, giving me such a picture of what it must have been, Jill getting up at five to work, working all evening, and at the end of it the prize, a job in *Lilith* with Auntie Jane.

"When do you think I'll be able to start?" she inquired, and I realized she expected me to say, perhaps, "Next Monday." I was startled into silence. A long one. I was realizing a very great deal. She was waiting to move in here, with me, and to start work in *Lilith*—waiting for her adult life to begin. And I sat there looking at—myself, at her age. All pleasure, confidence, relish. She's not ambitious, Jill. She's being eaten up with excitement at the idea of being part of it all, *being able to do things well*. Emerging from loving family life, which grinds people down so, "Poor Jill, she's bad at examinations, poor Jill, she's not an academic". She is full of confidence at her abilities, which are bubbling in her; she doesn't know herself yet that she can do things; she knows only that she can't wait to start.

And suddenly as I realized that I had not *really* taken in that Jill, Sister Georgie's child, was going to come into my life, and take it over—I knew suddenly, beautifully, absolutely, how right it was, how apt, how fit, and I burst into laughter and sat laughing, unable to stop, while poor Jill sat there, all her joy ebbing away, tears coming into her eyes.

"Why do you hate us all so much?" she gasped. "Why, what have we done? You think we are all awful, that I'm no good, oh I know!"

"No, you don't know," I said. "I'm laughing at me. It is you lot down there who think *I* am no good, that I'm awful, and do you know what, Jill, at this moment I agree with them."

I watched her face, that had shrunk and gone white and pinched, absorb colour and confidence; and soon she smiled.

She said coaxingly, "You know, Aunt Jane, you've got me wrong. I never make scenes, slam doors, pout, leave things about, expect to be waited on . . ."

Teasing her: "A likely story, from your mother's daughter."

"I am *not* Kate. And I've been telling Mother, Why have you always let us do as we liked? Why are you a doormat?"

"And did she have a sensible reply?"

She laughed. I laughed.

"You could begin ingratiating yourself with me by not insisting on calling me Aunt Jane, or Auntie."

"Right, Janna, you're on."

"If my sister's daughter will allow herself to call me Janna, then . . ."

"Oh, Auntie, oh, Janna, what you don't realize is, you see, we were discussing it . . ."

"You *were*? A nice family discussion?"

"Of course. You can't believe, surely, you wouldn't be discussed? Why, you've been a sort of *focus* for—well, everything. There are splits and schisms in the family over you."

"There are?"

"Yes, and the way I see it is, it must go back to when you and Mother were children. Because it is quite clear to *us* that in let's say ten years we'll all have conflicts because of how we are *now*. Particularly Kate and me. If we ever want to see each other at all. She's such a *drag*."

"And it would help your mother and I to remember what we quarrelled about in our teens?"

"What did you quarrel about? Mother says you never quarrelled."

"What rubbish. She made my life a misery. It was the war, you see. Everything in short supply. She filched my rations. I had to wear her cast-offs."

"Ah," said the young psychologist.

I told Jill that of course she could not start at once. She will have to wait until there's a vacancy, and she won't get the job if there's an applicant who's better equipped than she.

"I don't believe in nepotism," I said.

"I hope you do, to a certain extent," said she, in the humorous voice that I know will be used to "handle" me.

When she went, I collapsed. I had taken it in, as a fact, as something that will happen. When Jill moves in here, my life will become shared. It is the end of lovely solitude. Oh, oh, oh, I can't bear it, I can't. Oh, how I do love being alone, the pleasures of solitariness . . .

*　　　*　　　*

I told them in the office I was going to take another two weeks' leave. Phyllis's look. She murmured, "Aren't you going to be here when the new editor comes in?"

"I shall take two weeks now. I'll be back by the time he comes."

Her look was meant to say, I don't understand you. My look at her, I understand myself, and that's enough.

Pleasure.

I woke early, the sun wasn't up, gold and pink cloudlets in a grey sky waiting to fill with sunlight. Early summer, a real summer's day. I lay in bed, looking, listening, the birds, the milk bottles clinking. I was inside my strong body, jam-packed with health and energy, and it stretched and yawned itself into being awake, and I jumped out of bed, with my mind on *Gracious Lady*. I wrote and wrote, Joyce rang, just off to bed. Amiable insults. I said, Niece Jill was going to take over my life, and she said, "Wonderful, now you'll really have a burden. A blossoming young soul and if she goes wrong it will be your fault."

"Your thoughts, not mine."

"Oh, yours, too, but they are unconscious, you can't win at this game. No, no, your portion is guilt, Janna."

"Not yours?"

"I'm liberated from it. By the way, how do you feel about taking on my two guilt-makers? The sooner the better as far as I am concerned."

"No, I don't know anything about *love*, you see. I'll leave your love-reared offspring to you, Joyce."

"I must say it's the neatest alibi you could imagine."

"What are you talking about?"

"If you have Niece Jill with you, you can't have your own life, you'll have no personal life, and as for a lover, out of the question."

"You assume I want one."

"Of course you want one. At least unconsciously. It is your right to have one. It is our right to have *good* sex. Surely you know that?"

"But I had good sex."

"No, it's your *right* to have good sex all the time. Until you are ninety."

"If you say so, Joyce. How's your good sex?"

"I'm working at it."

Then I had a bath, a quick one. What has happened to my long lovely baths, my scents and my oils and essences? I haven't time, that's what.

By nine I was down in the streets, sauntering along, enjoying myself in the way I do. Oh, the good humour of this city, the pleasantness, the friendliness! The sun was shining fitfully, in and out of rapid white clouds. Mild. I went into the boutique cum coffee room cum health food shop, and since there was no one in it, Mary Parkin left her counter and sat with me and told me the latest instalment in that long serial, her war with her neighbour over that wicked woman's insensitive treatment of her cat. I ate healthy, rich, delicious whole-grain cake. Then I walked on down the High Street, and in the newspaper shop stood on one side while a tall, rakish, handsome young labourer teased the two middle-aged and respectable women behind the counter because of a magazine they sell, which advised a young wife trying to reattract her husband to cut her pubic hair into a heart shape.

He had bought this mag yesterday for his wife, they had had a good laugh over it, and now he couldn't resist, he said, dropping in to share the joke with Madge and Joan.

"Well, you never know," says he, "we thought we should point it out, after all, you might not have noticed it, and you wouldn't want to let your pubic hair go ungroomed, would you?"

"I don't think I've had much occasion to notice mine recently," says Madge, and asks Joan, "How about you, dear?"

"My pubic hair is not what it was," says Joan, handing the *Sun* and the *Mirror* to an old woman (as it might be Maudie, or Eliza Bates) who is listening to this unable to believe her ears.

"If I wasn't married," says the young man, "I'd see what I could do, but as it is . . . well, ta, then, keep *Homes and Gardens* for us then, Lily says if she can't afford a new decor, then she likes to read about it at least."

And off he goes. The two women look at each other and share that laugh which means, Those were the days, and turn their attention to the old woman, who is scrabbling about in her handbag for change. They wait patiently, realizing she is upset by what she has heard, and then ask after her husband.

She and I arrive on the pavement together. She looks straight at me with shocked eyes and whispers, "Did you hear?"

I switch roles and say, "Disgraceful," thinking of the real pain of Eliza when she reports of the radio, the telly, the papers, But what is happening to everyone, why are young people like this now?

But Joan and Madge are not young, that is why she is miserable. We walk along the pavement, while she gently grumbles herself back into balance.

And now the bus. By now the office workers have ebbed from this area, and the bus is full of women. The freemasonry of women, who sit at their ease, shopping baskets and bags all over them, enjoying a nice sit-down and the pleasant day. A bus at half past ten in the morning is a different world: nothing in common with the rush-hour buses.

These women who keep things together, who underpin our important engagements with big events by multifarious activities so humble that, asked at the end of the day what they did, they might, and often do, reply, Oh, nothing much.

They are off to a shop three stages away to buy knitting wool for a jersey for a grandchild, buttons for a dress or a shirt, or a reel of white cotton, for one should always have some about. They are going to the supermarket, or to pay the electricity bill, or to get their pensions. The Home Helps are on their way to get prescriptions made up for Eliza Bates, Annie Reeves, Mrs Coles, Mrs Brent, Mr Hodges. Someone is off to the stationer's to buy birthday cards for all the family separately to send to Uncle Bertie, aged sixty-four. A parcel is being sent to Cape Town to an emigrated niece and her family, for she has asked for a certain make of vests you cannot, it seems, get in South Africa. Or a parcel containing homemade biscuits to Wales, for a cousin. Some are off down to Oxford Street, on a weekly or monthly jaunt, regarded as a holiday, a rest, and will spend hours trying on dresses and keeping a sharp eye open for clothes that might be suitable for mothers, daughters, husbands, sons. They come home from several hours' hard labour around the shops with a petticoat, two pairs of nylons, and a little purse. All of which they could have bought in the High Street, but it's not so much fun. They will later go to visit housebound relatives, taking with them all kinds of specially needed commodities, like tooth powder, or a certain brand of throat lozenges; they will go to the hospital and sit for hours with a granny; they drop in to have a cup of tea with a daughter or take a grandchild to the park. They are at it all day, these women, and the good nature that is the result of their competence at what they do overflows and splashes about the inside of the bus, so that smiles get exchanged, people remark on the weather—in other words, offer each other consolation or encouragement—and comment humorously on life through events glimpsed on the pavement.

The Victoria and Albert, all the time in the world, I looked at a little chair, early eighteenth century, of wood like silk, and its life and times seemed so enormous, all-encompassing, like listening to Maudie talk, or Eliza, such a statement it was, sitting demurely there, *Look at me!*—it was enough and I went off to the restaurant, and there was a gentleman, that's the word, courtly and humorous, ready like me for a few amiable words over a meal, and we sat together and did not say more than we had to about our lives and times. Enjoyable. On the steps he went his way, and I mine to the top of a bus this time, for it was afternoon, and it was no longer women's time, and I listened to the conductor's back-chat with a passenger, the London style, sardonic, dry, with its flavour of the surreal.

In the High Street, the café where I sometimes manage to find time for half an hour's lunch with Vera, but now I sit for an hour or so, listening to a couple of out-of-work youngsters at the next table. One black, one white. Youths. Passing the time away, like me. I said to myself, This is a tragedy, you should be feeling bad, but their faces were not tragic, but good-natured; yes, I would say sad, but far from hopeless about it all. They were making jokes and planning to go to the cinema. I was determined not to be sad, not today, not this perfect day. I talked to them a little, but I was this thing outside their experience, at their age probably the "old woman"; they were nice but not going to open up and share anything. They went off saying to me, "Ta, then, see you. Take care."

I went off to Maudie, and no, that was the bad part of the day. Maudie is so ill—but enough, I left her to walk up past the deer and the peacocks and the goats in Golders Park, to drink good coffee on the little terrace with all the shrewd comfortable elderly Jews who sit through the summer there, getting brown and shining, and with the mothers and the little children. On the long acres of green grass, the deck chairs were like sails, like coloured sails, miles of blue sky, with not a cloud anywhere, and people scattered about soaking in the sunlight.

I came back home in the dusk, late, after nine, and here I sit, at my desk, Diary Time, and I am trying to capture this day, this lovely day, so that it doesn't vanish away for ever. Because it is precious, it is rare. Oh, I know how to value it, such a day, time for the spending, all the time in the world—but only for one day, nothing I *have* to do, no one I *have* to see, except Maudie, oh, poor Maudie, but I'll not think about her until tomorrow. A day in London, the great theatre, lovely London whose quality is sardonic good humour, and kindness, a day to myself, in solitude. Perfect enjoyment.

The two weeks are over. That was the best day, because of the sun, but I enjoyed all the days, fifteen of them, long and lazy. Except for Maudie. I am doing all kinds of things for her again.

It is late summer. I have been working, working, how I do work, how I do like being able to—and how much I will enjoy not working so hard, when I go on part-time. Soon.

Jill is in my flat, my home, she is in my "study", a decent room, not too large, but she's hardly ever here. She's taken to the office—as I did, all those years ago. She's taken to Phyllis, and Phyllis to her. They work together, Jill soaking it all up. She does not see Phyllis as I do—as I *did*; Phyllis has changed, she's lost her cutting edge. She is kind to Jill, sensitive, generous.

The new editor. He was not the one I voted for, he's the

Board's choice. At first glance it was evident to me and to Phyllis, in fact to everyone, that he'd be a passenger. Phyllis was wild with the injustice of it: she's too young to be editor, the question did not arise of course, but she was fit for it. Now she has to work *through* him. I cannot say, My dear girl, take no notice, don't waste time being upset, nothing much will change.

Indirect instruction. What I did was to talk a great deal about when Joyce and I worked together in the old days, ran everything, while the so-called editor danced to our tune. Phyllis, with a small nice smile, listens, her eyes full of ironical enjoyment. Jill doesn't yet understand what I am saying, but she watches Phyllis with such concentration that she soon will. I have never once denigrated poor Charlie.

I'm engaged in "working in" Charlie, who will take my place at the end of that time. He's a nice man, I'm fond of him. Product of the sixties. What a sloppy lot, no discipline, they had everything too easy. Agreeable, greying, bit too fat, you almost expect to see food stains on his roll-neck. *He doesn't pay attention.*

I've been wondering for years what makes the difference between the ten per cent who really work and the rest who float along appearing to work, perhaps even believing they do. Poor Charlie arrived in the office, and waited to be told. I had given thought, of course, to *where* he should be. I wasn't going to turn the photographers out, they need the space. I didn't see why our room should be given up, and it has never been one of the best. No, the room used for board meetings, officious and rather upholstered and apart. I moved into this, with Charlie, and left the two girls where Joyce and I had been. Now I sit opposite Charlie, as I did with Joyce. We get on like anything.

Charlie has been running a trade mag, a clean, bright, good-looking production. (But who *really* ran it?) He sits there, sliding papers about all over the large desk, while I tell him the history of our mag, the changes, how it should be now "in my opinion"—God forbid that I think my opinion should matter now, I'm on my way out. Oh but Janna, of course we must take your ideas into account . . .

He never ever initiates anything . . . Well, does that matter?

Passivity is a great virtue, sometimes. To be able to let things happen: oh yes, one must know how to do that. But then to take control, at the right moment, make the machinery start, use inertia, *make* things happen.

Joyce was good at waiting, listening, then moving in and controlling. Perhaps, I thought, Charlie is such a one. But no, I am pretty sure not. *He does no work*—well, very few ever do. It is interesting, watching people not working. The mail comes in, he hands it over to me, I go through it with him. He says, How about this or that? I say, Don't you think if we . . .? He says, Well, perhaps . . . I find myself making the telephone calls, and then I have my secretary in, and Charlie is busy with papers as I dictate. He has a business lunch every day, with someone. He is back late in the office, and by then everything is under way. He sits around, we talk, he dictates a letter or two, and the day is over. *He has done no work at all.* He has even said to me, smiling, but the smile did have the faintest tinge of anxiety, A good organizer knows how to delegate.

Well, fair enough: all our departments would go along quite well under their own momentum for a long time, without intervention.

Meanwhile, there is Phyllis, there is Jill, and they have already got the idea. It is to them that he is—Charlie thinks—delegating responsibility. I watch Phyllis as she comes in to take instructions, to make suggestions. She does *not* allow her eyes to engage with mine, never is there the faintest suggestion of complicity. Oh, full marks, Phyllis! She sits there, competent, quiet, of course dressed in her soft silky reassuring clothes, and says, "Charlie, I was wondering what you'd think if we . . ."

"Well, I was rather thinking along those lines myself," he will say, half an hour later. And when I go into their office, to have a chat, we talk as if in fact it is Charlie who has initiated this and that, Charlie who is in control.

The wonderful autumn continues, day after day, and this afternoon I had cleaned out my flat (Jill's room is kept very nice indeed), and actually got my clothes, hands, nails, etc., up to the mark, and I was looking at the sky, and suddenly I was running down the stairs, into my car and to Maudie.

"Maudie," I said, "come to the park."

It could have gone either way, I saw that, and I said, "Come on, Maudie, do . . . Just for once, say yes."

And she smiled her sprightly amenable smile, the one I see with such relief, and she says, "But there's my sandwiches cut and the cups out . . ." I fly in, fetch her coat, her hat, her bag, and she lets me take over. In ten minutes, Regent's Park. I drive around and around the Inner Circle, looking at the gold and bronze and green under the blue blue sky, and Maudie has her face averted and her hand shading it. I think, she's crying, yes, but no, I *won't* notice it. So I keep my eyes well away.

"Can you walk a little?" I ask.

Luckily, a free space only twenty yards from the entrance to the café. It is a long twenty yards, and I see how she has deteriorated since we were here last summer. I hated that word when I first heard that snide little pretty-boots Hermione use it, and now I hate it when Vera uses it, and yet I use it myself. Maudie is deteriorating fast . . . like groceries.

At last we got into the place where the tables are. There are roses still, blobs of colour and scent, in their proper places, and the well-fed sparrows hopping everywhere. I settle Maudie and fetch cakes and coffee. Maudie eats, eats, in her slow methodical enjoying way, and in between cakes she sits smiling at the sparrows. *The darlings, the darlings . . .*

I cannot believe how much she can eat, when I think of that little yellow belly. And Maudie says, You must feed an ulcer, they say . . . not apologetic, but wondering, for she too is amazed at how she has to eat and eat, sometimes cutting bread and butter after she has polished off the Meals on Wheels or eating a whole packet of biscuits.

And then I drive her around and around and around the Inner Circle while she shields her face and gazes at the yellow trees and the shadows coming under them.

Maudie. She seems to be better: if you can say that of a woman with cancer. Her dreadful rages infrequent, her mood often friendly, even gay. This, paradoxically, because she feels that I have let her down. Just after I took her to the park, I again woke with my back in a knot. Nothing like as bad as last time, and it was gone by next day. But I knew what I had to do.

I rang Vera Rogers, we had a long talk, and I went in to Maudie, sat myself down, and said, "Look, Maudie, I have got to explain something and please listen, without getting cross with me."

This "getting cross" was already a note I had decided not to use: for I had spent hours the night before telling myself, she is an intelligent woman, she is sensible, I only have to explain . . . Oh, what nonsense; for almost at once she had turned her face away, and was staring with her hard trembling forlorn look at the fire.

I was telling her she had to have a Home Help, even if only twice a week, to do shopping; she had to have a nurse in to wash her. Or I would be permanently on my back in bed and she wouldn't see me at all.

She did not say one word. When I had finished, she said, "I have no alternative, have I?" Later she made it clear she blamed Vera Rogers, that villain.

I realized then that I must no longer expect sense from her.

The Home Help is a nice Irish girl, who was told Mrs Fowler was difficult and who stood patiently knocking until Maudie let her in, grinding her teeth and glaring and muttering.

Molly said politely, "And what can I fetch you in?"

Maudie said, "I've got everything."

"Oh dear," said Molly, trying something that works with another difficult old woman, "I am so tired, can I sit down and have a cigarette?" She looked at the dreadful armchair, and sat on the hard chair by the table.

Maudie did not miss that repugnance, although it showed itself for no more than a moment, and she decided she hated this girl. "I can't stop you sitting," she said.

And Molly knew that in this place she must not sit and be chatty. Soon she put out her cigarette and said, "If you've got nothing for me to fetch in, I'll be off."

At which Maudie was silent, and then said in a hurried offhand angry way: "There's biscuits . . . and you could get in something for the cat . . . don't want you to put yourself out."

On this basis poor Molly manages to get some of the things Maudie needs: but when she tried to see into the kitchen, where she might be able to use her intelligence to find out what

was missing, Maudie said, "I don't remember asking you in."
And so when Maudie forgets, which she so often does, she goes
without. And when I get in, I go out again for her. I feel
ridiculous; after all, it only takes a few minutes. She thinks it is
ridiculous, that she has to put up with that Home Help, and all
because I have gone cold and unforgiving.

But the worst, of course, was her being washed by a nurse
who is black, too young, too old, white, and with hard hands
or cold hands—who is not Janna. She would not let the nurses
in; then found I was being unkind and would not respond to
her silent appeals. Then she did let them in, but they could not
find washing things, could not find clean clothes, and their at
first gentle and patient, then increasingly irritated and peremp-
tory queries received only muttered replies. The first nurse was
black, reported that she thought Mrs Fowler would not stand
for a black nurse; the second, white, tried twice and gave up;
the third actually managed to wash Maudie, who found it so
shameful and painful a business that next time a nurse came,
she was screamed at: "Go away, I don't want any of you, I can
manage by myself."

Then there was a ridiculous time when, as I arrived in the
evening, I was confronted by Maudie, smelling horrible, looking desperate and ashamed. We sat there as usual, on either
side of the fire, and she entertained me with the same stories,
for she has run out of memories, and between us was this
knowledge that I would not wash her, that I her friend was no
longer her friend.

"When you were still my friend," she began once, not
meaning it as pressure, but because it is what she is thinking.

And soon I was thinking, this is an old woman dying of
cancer, and I won't even give up half an hour of my time to
wash her.

I rang up Vera, told her to cancel the nurses, but keep on the
Home Help, and I have been washing Maudie since. But not
every day, I simply cannot. I am afraid of that silent enemy, my
back.

When I arrive, Maudie is wondering, sometimes in real
misery and horror at her condition of dirtiness and smell, is she
going to be in a good mood today? And I sense this, and say,

"Do you feel like a wash, Maudie?" And her face! The relief on her poor old face . . . How she does hate being dirty, being repulsive to herself. And in a way my coming into her life was a bad thing for her, because before she had been able to forget it a little, had not been noticing her filthy clothes, her grimy wrists, the dirt in her fingernails.

And so, every third day or so, I wash her all over. And she has not been dirtying herself at all, though she is sometimes wet.

I partly understand the vigilance and effort that goes into keeping herself unsoiled: how often she drags herself out to the cold lavatory; how she studies to outwit her bowels. And besides, there is something else: she does not want Janna—the spy for Vera Rogers—to know what she is making; so she will do anything, even sit up all night, so as not to use the commode. But once she had to use it, she could not get out in time, and I came in before she could empty it. She did not stop me from taking out the pot, but she stood looking into my face in a way that told me this was a moment she had dreaded, and now it was here. I thought she had been drinking real coffee: then I remembered something about coffee-ground stools. And I did ring up Vera next day; and she said, Oh, I should call the doctor in, I *should*. Don't, I said, please don't. Leave her for as long as you can.

And so, now, instead of Janna the real friend, the *one person* (who is your other self) who can be relied upon, who will always say yes and do what is needed, she has this other Janna, who sets limits and sometimes she will and sometimes she won't.

I took Maudie to visit her sister. She chose a Sunday when she believed she would be well enough not to disgrace herself. She rang her sister, dragging up the steps to the telephone box at the corner, and told me afterwards it was arranged, and she would take herself by bus, she had done it often enough, I needn't put myself out.

It was a warm November day. Maudie had on a best dress of dark blue silk with grey and pink roses on it. It was given to her by her actress friend from Hammersmith soon after the Second World War. She wore a black coat with it, and a black straw hat with black satin ribbon and a little bunch of roses: she bought it forty years ago, for a wedding. When I went in to pick her up, I thought she could be Liza's mother in *My Fair Lady*: a shabby poverty, but gallant. But there was, too, something sprightly, even rakish about her, and thus it was that Maudie, visiting her relatives, whom she had not seen for years, presented herself to them as they think of her, an eccentric, gone-to-nothing poor relation whom they wish they could forget.

It was a nice little house, old, with a garden, one of several dotted about among the great new tower blocks, the massive shops, the garages, the roaring roads. We drove around for a while, looking for the place, and there it was: almost a village, or the fragment of one. A painted garden gate, a path up between autumn-dimmed roses, and there was the clan, waiting to receive Aunt Maude and her new friend. Curiosity. They are an awful lot, hard, bright, *common*—a word that should never have been allowed to go out of use.

The sister, older than Maudie, is a matriarch, still active and in command. She cooked the dinner, ordered daughters and granddaughters how to lay the table, instructed sons and grandsons that she needed the rubbish taken out, a jammed window opened, the lavatory chain lengthened.

Twelve of them, all in smart nasty clothes, talking about their cars, their lawn mowers, their holidays. They are all a good step up from Maudie and her sister Polly, but then, how would you assess them in relation to their wicked grandfather, Goodtime Charlie? I sat there brooding about our class system, not always easy to sort out; while I answered questions about what I did—I certainly did not tell them, for they would think I was lying, said I was a secretary; questions about Maudie. But I knew what was coming, and it came: "So you are Maudie's Good Neighbour?"

I was determined not to let Maudie be cheated out of a real friend of her own; and I said, "No, I am not. I am Maudie's friend. We have known each other for some time now."

They did not accept this, exchanged knowing glances. They

addressed loud patronizing questions and remarks to Maudie, as if she were a half-wit; and she sat there among them in her best clothes, her head trembling a little, defiant and guilty, and obviously unwell, and tried to stand up against this truly awful pressure that made her ridiculous and stupid. A timid question to her formidable old sister: "Polly, do you remember how I used to make fruit roll for Paul?" "Did you, Maudie? You were always busy with ideas of your own, weren't you?" And: "Polly, do I see that old sauce boat still? I remember it from home." Polly, then, with a large, angry sniff: "Well don't think you're going to get it now, because you aren't. You've had what you are entitled to!"

"Oh Mother!" "Oh Mum!" "Oh dear!" From the "children", elderly themselves now; and from the grandchildren, in their twenties and thirties, exchanging merry glances because here is a family tradition bought to life: how Auntie Maudie was always trying to make off with Granny's things, she was always scrounging and begging, and now she's at it again.

Maudie, realizing what is happening, goes silent, and stays silent, except for Yes and No, through the meal.

The fourteen of us around the long table that has a leaf put into it cram the dining room, which is the room everyone uses; there is a front room, like the old-fashioned "parlour", which is unnaturally clean and shiny. We pass around old-fashioned vegetable dishes full of greasy roast potatoes, watery cabbage, soggy parsnips. There is rather good roast beef. We pass around bottled horseradish sauce and ketchup and a silver cruet large enough for a hotel—or for this family gathering. We eat stewed plums, bottled from the garden, and marvellous suet pudding, light and crusty, with jam sauce. We drink cups of strong milky tea. The middle-aged ones talk of their vegetable gardens and bottling and freezing what they grow; the young ones talk of pizzas and foreign foods they eat on their travels. Apparently there are plenty of young children; but they have not been brought to this gathering, it would be too much for Auntie Maudie, they say; and the thrust goes home, for there are tears in her eyes; but I did not find out what it referred to. These people do not see each other except at Christmas, when they gather together here, all of them. They joke *at* each other all the time, a hard, cruel game, keeping alive moments of weakness, failure, treachery. Their faces are glistening with strength and confidence and this careless cruelty. And the matriarch sits calmly there, smiling. I easily see her father in her: I have never been able to catch a whisker of him in Maudie. She has a broad red face, under fluffy white curls that show the red shiny scalp. She has a massive body, in a crimplene brown and white figured dress, very tight and awful. She has heavy reddish hands, with shiny swollen knuckles. She walks with a stick. Ninety-six, she is: and good for another ten years. They eat, they eat, they eat; we all eat. And Maudie eats most of all, sitting silent there, her eyes kept down, thorough and methodical, she keeps us all waiting while she demolishes every last crumb.

And they all sit nicely around the loaded table, with their superior smiles, their false good humour, and they tease her with Auntie Maudie did this, Auntie Maudie did that.

And she answers not a word.

When the meal was over she said to me, "And now it is time for us to go." She looked straight at her sister, raised her voice, and said, "Now that I've eaten you out of house and home."

Uneasy titters from the children; amusement from the grandchildren. The absent great-grandchildren may never have heard of Auntie Maudie.

The matriarch merely smiled, queenly and hard. Said she, "I've made you a nice little Christmas pudding as usual, to take away home with you."

"I don't remember seeing one last year, or the year before."

"Oh, Auntie," said a niece.

The matriarch gave a directing nod at a young man, who took a little white bowl to Maudie. At first she was going to leave it, and then gave it to me: "Take it."

I took up the little pudding that might perhaps have fed a few sparrows, and we all went together slowly to my car, Maudie setting the pace. Oh, how yellow and awful she did look in the late-autumn sunlight. And the family saw it, and understood. Suddenly a chill on them, these large well-off fresh-faced people, as they stared at the family's little black scapegoat. They exchanged frightened looks and raised their voices and cried, "Goodbye, Auntie, come and see us again soon!"

"That's right," ordered her sister, "you must get your Good Neighbour to bring you another Sunday. But give me enough warning next time." For she had decided not to understand that Maudie would not come again. She said to me, "It is so nice for Maudie to have a Good Neighbour. If I've told her once I've told her a hundred times, you need a Home Help, I've said."

And in this way was Maudie finally robbed by her family of this achievement of hers, a real friend of her own, someone who loves her.

For I do love Maudie, and I couldn't bear it when she sat there beside me, trembling, whimpering.

I said to her, "Maudie, you're worth a hundred of that lot, and I am sure you always were."

And so we drove home, in silence. I stayed with her all afternoon, making her tea, making her supper, cosseting her. But she was listless and distressed. And next day there was a real change in her. That was three weeks ago. And it's been downhill ever since.

A week ago she began talking of how once, when she was a child, she was taken to Christmas Eve service, and she had never forgotten the Child in the manger, and the angels. I asked my secretary to find out where there would be an easily accessible service, but at last settled for the church down the street from Maudie, so she would not have to manage a long journey.

She has talked for the whole week, and for the first time, about the church services she was taken to as a small girl, but clearly Burlington Bertie and his fancy-woman and the poor wife didn't go in much for religion. What she talks about is the singing, the prettiness of the church, the coloured-glass windows, "the nice smell of the wood", the flowers.

I drove her last night very slowly the hundred yards or so to the church: and could see how much—again—she had deteriorated, for only five weeks ago I took her to her sister's; but now the gentle movement of the car was distressing her. I helped her out of the car and walked with her into the church. Outside it was the usual quite pleasant little building, nothing remarkable, but as soon as we reached the entrance, I saw through Maudie's eyes. She stood quite still gazing, lifting her eyes up to the dark spaces of the roof, and then to the blaze of candles on the altar. On one side, a pretty baby in the crib, and the angels, in blue and scarlet robes and gold crowns, knelt behind Mary, who was a shining young girl with pink cheeks and a lovely smile. The three kings stood near, their hands full of gifts wrapped in gold and silver, tied with scarlet. And all around, on soft glinting straw, were lambs. And a real dog, the vicar's, a white woolly terrier, lay among the lambs.

Oh the pretties, cried Maudie, so that people turned to see the old, bent, black-clothed crone smiling and trembling there. And they smiled too, for there was only the blurring gentle light of the candles, and no one could see how ill and yellow she was.

We went very slowly up the aisle, because she was not looking how she walked but at the beautiful scene there by the altar, and we sat right at the front, where we could see the obedient dog panting a little, and yawning because of the heat from the candles. Oh the lovelies, oh the pretties, oh my petty, my little petties, wept Maudie, stretching out her hands; and the dog, responding to her, came halfway towards her, and then, at a low command from someone out of sight behind a pillar, went back to lie among the lambs. The service was ordinary enough; and I am sure the scene was tawdry.

Afterwards she was worn out with it all, and I put her to bed, with some hot milk, and her cat beside her.

Lovely, lovely, my lovely petties, she was murmuring, and smiling at me, the cat, her memories, as I left.

But . . . she has to go into hospital. The doctor came last week, and not because the wicked Vera asked him to. He was expecting, he told her, that Maudie was "about ripe" for hospital, and what he found made him say that if it wasn't for Christmas she would have to go in at once. But she has a

week's grace. We know she will not come out again.
Does *she*?

Oh no, that's another two weeks gone . . .
   A nightmare. Maudie boiling and raging. Vera Rogers is
away on a training course, and since there has to be an enemy,
I'm it. "Maudie," I said, when she'd slammed the door in my
face one night, and admitted me next day, white-faced, eyes
blazing, "why are you treating me so badly?"
   We were sitting opposite each other, the fire out, the room
cold, her unfed cat restless and yowling. I was expecting her
capitulation, the sharp turn of her head, the prideful lift of her
chin—then the sigh, the hand up to shield her face, and, soon,
the small reasonable voice in an explanation. But no, she sat
sullenly there, her lower lip thrust out, eyes staring. I coaxed
and cajoled, but no; and I am wondering if perhaps I shall not
see *my* Maudie again. For there is no doubt of it, she is a little
mad. I have been thinking about this, what we tolerate in
people without ever calling them mad. What is madness, then?
Surely, losing contact with reality? For Maudie to scream and
rage at her only friend, to treat me as an enemy, is not rational.
   Nothing that is happening touches reality, it is all a horrible
farce, because I cannot say to her, Maudie, you have cancer. I
think of my mother, I think of Freddie. I lie awake at night and
wonder, what has made that difference, that those two people
could say, I have cancer, but Maudie cannot? Education?
Nonsense! But at no point before my mother, my husband,
died were they out of touch with what was going on. It was I
who was out of touch!
   And Vera is not here, and so I cannot ask her . . . what? All
kinds of things I need to know. I cannot handle Maudie. In
hospital or not.

Vera has come back, we have taken Maudie to hospital.

               *   *   *

I had to arrange for Maudie's cat to be fed by the woman next door, who said I mustn't expect that she would give it a home, so why not take it to the RSPCA? I went through the place, to make sure there was nothing that would smell—the commode, the kitchen. I found horrible caches of soiled knickers and underclothes and was able at last to dispose of them into the dustbins. And, as I did so, said to myself that it was as if I was disposing of Maudie.

It is true that I am thinking, why does she have to go through with this, the long sordid process of dying? If she could only just die in her sleep. But what right have I to feel like that, if she doesn't?

She is in our newest large hospital, in a ward that takes four, getting the best of modern medicine, modern nursing. She is surrounded by solicitude, tact, charm. And there she is, that poor Maudie, a little yellow angry old woman, propped up in bed, held up on cushions in a chair, brought food, brought medicines, and she does nothing but rage and rebel and mutter and curse . . . and yet they all of them love her. It is true. At first I thought it was just their marvellous training, but no. There's something about her, each one of the nurses has said to me; and the junior doctor said, "How did you get to be a friend of hers?" Really wanting to know, and it was because he, too, feels it in her. "She's very lovable," says the male nurse, who has just spent twenty minutes persuading her to take her medicine. It is a pain-killer. Not the ferocious potion she will be getting when the pain gets bad enough to make it essential: this is an intermediate brew. But Maudie says, It takes away my mind, my mind feels full of cotton wool, and she puts off taking it until, with an angry whimper, she jerks her head at the glass that is standing on her table, indicating to me that she will take it.

I go up every day after work, for a couple of hours.

"Oh, there you are at last," says Maudie.

And, when I leave: "Going, are you?" And she turns her face away from me.

The relief of it, not having to wash her and keep her clothes more or less clean; not having to sit opposite her, keeping down anger, depression, spite while she spits venom at me.

The family have already been, the tribe, admitted to her presence in twos and threes.

"Are you coming to see if there's anything for you when I'm dead?" she inquires. "You should know better than that, you've had everything off me years ago."

"Oh, Auntie!" say nieces, nephews, and, "What sort of talk is that, Maudie?" inquires the matriarch.

"You know what kind of talk," says Maudie, and turns her face to stare away from them; and she does not reply to their Goodbye, Auntie, Goodbye, Maudie.

I asked to start part-time earlier; I now go in two full days, flexibly according to need; one half-day on the Think Session morning; and I've agreed to another full day and a half in the few days before the mag goes to the printers.

Phyllis asked me to have lunch with her. A formal invitation. This is because she and Jill are inseparable now, Jill has attached herself to Phyllis, and it is not easy to find even a few minutes for private talk.

I thought she wanted some advice about the office, Jill perhaps, but she took my self-possession away by saying that Charles wants to marry her.

The possibility had not crossed my mind, and as I sat there, dabbing my mouth with a napkin, and taking some wine, to gain time, I was thinking it had not come into my mind because it was preposterous. That was my first reaction, and as I sit here writing (midnight) I think it was the right one.

Almost at once I recovered myself and sat there all sympathetic attention, and trying to make myself feel less critical of it all, by repeating silently that, as is well known, I am not equipped to make judgements in this area, due to my never having been really married, there is "something missing".

But how can she marry Charles, or rather, how can she stay married? He is getting a divorce, has three children, so there is so much to pay out for their education. Phyllis will have to support their life-style. What about children? All this was running through my head; while she sat there, leaning forward in her anxiety, such a pretty thing in her soft clothes. I would never before have thought to call her pretty, but she is these days. Hair shining, eyes shining, she seemed to gleam and glow against the dark wood walls of the restaurant.

She wanted advice. Well, I know better by now than to give people advice.

I wanted to find out how clear she is in her mind about what she is taking on; for that is the essence of it, surely? What she was talking about was how she and Charles worked together so well on the mag, how easy everything is: she talked on and on restlessly about work, and her eyes were expectantly on mine, for I had not said, Oh, Phyllis, you are crazy, or, What marvellous news. And I let her talk, and talk, saying not very much, but supplying the occasional worldly-wise remarks that one needs such a large supply of to cope with the moments when people expect you to tell them what to do.

And by the time our meal was finished, she was mentioning for the first time that they would not be able to afford to have a child, for she would have to work, and that she did not know what she felt about children. She kept giving me small hopeful looks, as if even now at this late stage, I might say, But of course, you must marry him!

But what I did ask was, in the hurried embarrassed way one uses when a topic you want to introduce is foreign to the texture of a conversation, "But what about your Women's Meetings, that sort of thing?"

She averted her eyes, smiling, and said, carelessly, "Oh, he doesn't mind what I do, he's quite interested, really."

That struck me as so off the point that I heard myself laughing nervously, as if at a joke that had fallen flat.

Charlie invited me to lunch too. He wanted to tell me about his problem. He feels it is unfair to marry Phyllis and burden her with his past. He is having second thoughts about marrying her? I had polished up an extra supply of remarks like, You must think it over seriously and do what you think best! And, I do see that you must feel like that! I used them while listening to what amounted to a two-hour monologue. When we parted outside the restaurant, he thanked me for good advice. Phyllis is too clever: when we parted (outside the same restaurant) a few days earlier, she gave me a cheeky grin and said, "Why won't you tell me what to do, and then I can put all the blame on you!"

It seems at least possible that these two might get married out of inertia; if then, after all, the marriage turns out well . . . ?

I had looked forward, now I have more time, to getting my clothes up to the mark. What hard work it is, my style. I stood in front of the glass in my best suit. Honey-beige wild silk. My bag. My gloves. My shoes. There is a roughness over the seat, and no way of curing it. The edges of the revers have a slightly dulled look. Two buttons are working loose. A thread showing from the dove-grey satin lining. My shoes have creases along the fronts. My gloves are less than ideal. All my silk stockings have ladders. What is to be done? Throw the whole lot out and start again! But no, the problem is, if I have the time now for my style, I do not have the inclination. I have been remembering how Colette's, or Chéri's, Leah greeted her old lover with the information of how she put on a suit and a good lace jabot and there she was, ready for anything and in full fig. And what hurt him (hurt Colette?) was that she no longer cared about these careful time-consuming luxuries. But I am not going to be slovenly, I will not. The trap of old age—after all, I am in my fifties, hardly time to abdicate—is a tired slovenliness. If I no longer can care about my style, which depends on time, trouble, detail, then I shall think out something intelligent, a compromise. Meanwhile, I have taken a load of stuff to the charity shop, and have asked my dressmaker to repeat certain items. I have never done that before; we have spent hours in consultation over materials, buttons, linings. She was surprised, rang me up on getting my letter, and what she was really asking was, Have you lost interest that you simply tell me please make the pale grey woollen suit again, and the material is in Bond Street?—Yes, my dear, it is so, I have lost interest; but after all, I did introduce Phyllis to you. And I shall ask you to make again for me the brown trouser suit, the black *crêpe de Chine* shirt, the cream silk dress.

*   *   *

How long has it been? Two weeks, I think.

Every day, in to Maudie. Hello, I say, how are you, in the same smiling friendly way that everyone uses, and which—putting myself in her position—I know seems to her a nightmare of dissimulation, of deceit. Here she is, trapped, our prisoner; and she is surrounded by our lying smiles. *Which she herself imposes.* I long for her to come out from her yellow sullen hostility, I long to communicate, if even for a few moments, with Maudie herself. But she is shut inside her rage, her suspicion; and from that prison, looks out at that *awful* charming smile which I can feel my face organizing itself into as I go in.

What an ordeal, what a horror! I am talking about my ordeal, not Maudie's now. Selfish still, obviously, though I believe that this Janna who goes in every day to sit with Maudie one hour, two hours, three (though never long enough, she always feels rejected when I leave), is not at all that Janna who refused to participate when her husband, her mother, were dying. I sit for hours near Maudie, ready to give what my mother, my husband, needed from me: my consciousness of what was happening, my participation in it. But what Maudie wants is—not to be dying!

She mutters at me, in a new hurried breathless way, "*I* know who to thank for this, *I* know who ordered me here!" And does not look at me, for she so much hates what she sees.

She means me, and she means Vera Rogers, whom she told not to come near her again, when she visited. "Don't want you," she said to poor Vera, "don't show your face to me again." And turned hers away.

I sit quietly there, in a chair that is rather too high, for she is propped in the low one. The big chair, the expertly set pillows, the blanket over her knees, seem to be trying to swallow little Maudie, who, whatever position she is put in, stares ahead of her. "How are you, Mrs Fowler, would you like some tea—some hot milk—some chocolate, some soup?" No queen, or rich Arab's wife, would get better nursing than she does. But what she wants is—not to be dying!

I sit by her thinking, ninety-two years old, and Maudie seems to believe that an injustice is being done to her! One of

the night nurses, witnessing Maudie's dismissal of me—
"Going, are you?"—ran after me down the corridor and said,
Mrs Somers, Mrs Somers . . . and took me by the arm, looking
into my face with the same gentle friendly smiling persuasive-
ness that Maudie experiences as a prison, a lie . . .

"You mustn't let yourself mind," said she, "it is a stage they
go through. You'll see, there are stages. First, patients, when
they begin to understand, think it is unfair. They are sorry for
themselves."

"Unfair? Unfair that one has to die?"

"Sick people aren't always the most rational folk in the
world. And then, next, they get angry."

"Yes, you could say she is angry!"

"Well," she said whimsically, while her expert eyes searched
my face for signs of over-stress, "it isn't nice to die, for anyone,
I expect."

"Is it possible that these stages get a bit mixed up?"

She laughed, but really, enjoying being able to laugh at "the
book". She said, "The books says, three stages. I would agree
that in life things are not so clear-cut!"

"And the third stage?"

"That is when they accept it, come to terms . . ."

A nurse came running up, Nurse Connolly, Nurse Connolly,
and with a quick, Excuse me, off she ran, back to some minor,
or major, crisis. And I went home.

It isn't fair . . . anger . . . acceptance.

An over-ninety-year-old woman finds it *unjust* that she is
dying?

And next day Maudie, allowing her sombre yellow gaze
actually to reach my face instead of—mostly deliberately, or so
it seems—avoiding it, said in a clear contemptuous voice, "It's
a tragedy, a tragedy!"

"What is, Maudie?"

She looked at me—contempt! "A tragedy," she said loudly
and clearly, and then averted her eyes, before saying in a soft
distressed mumble, a tone I do not hear from her these days,
"Now that we were so happy, you coming in every evening and
me telling you my stories. A tragedy this has happened . . ."

I hold Maudie's hand while I sit there, though she always lets hers fall, inert, from mine, once, twice, sometimes three or four times, before clutching at me. Turned from me, her eyes never looking at me, her mouth falling open, because the drugs make her lose control of herself, a sullen sulking furious old woman, her hand nevertheless speaks the language of our friendship.

Maudie feels it is unfair that she is dying.

Yesterday, she said again, a soft hurrying mutter, "A tragedy, a tragedy, a tragedy," and I hear myself saying, not in the "charming" winning concerned way that is, so to speak, the house style of the hospital, "Maudie, you are ninety-two years old."

Her head moved slowly around, and then the blaze of her blue eyes. *Furious.*

What I am thinking about is, who, or what, in Maudie believes herself to be immortal, unjustly sentenced? It seems to me there are several Maudies inside that tiny yellow cage of bones, dying at different rates, and one of them has no intention of dying!

Another of the nurses asked me, "Are you religious, perhaps?" I know why she did. It is because my general air, manner, behaviour belongs to those who are not upset by dying, death, instead of to those—whom I can easily pick out, as I look at other visitors, relatives and friends—who are.

She meant, I suppose *you* think there is an afterlife! The little sniff, due to the backward, was implicit.

I said, "No, I'm not religious," not answering her real question.

Again I brood about what I do, or might, think about a possible afterlife—for my mother, my husband, Maudie. I think one thing one day, and another the next. Have "believed" one thing one decade, its opposite the next.

Another week gone.

As I leave her, about nine or ten, Maudie's hand tightens around mine and she leans forward, with amazing energy, and says, Take me home with you, take me out of here! Her eyes, which have been avoiding mine for two, three hours, are suddenly all there, a furious demand.

How can I take you home with me, Maudie? You know I can't, I say, every evening, sounding distressed, and *guilty*.

To involve oneself with the infinitely deprived means you take on a weight of guilt. They need so much: you can give so little.

I have been going home every evening, thinking, Perhaps I could take Maudie home? She could have a bed in my living room. I could get in day and night nurses . . . Jill would help. This is stupid, but her need forces me into it. And it isn't even what she wants, which is that I, her friend, Janna, should nurse her, day and night, always be there, and there would be no smiling skilled nurses.

It is impossible; yet, every evening, I wonder how it could be managed.

Why not, why not, why not? she wants to know.

I would not be able to look after you, I say.

Why would it be any more absurd than my becoming Maudie's friend to the extent that I did, or visiting Eliza and Annie as I have done for months now? All that is judged, by Joyce for instance, as worse than eccentric. Looking at my behaviour from outside, as I would have judged it before my husband and my mother died, it has something about it obsessive and even unhealthy. (Of course, this view does not take into account that my lunacy might add something to the lives of these unfortunate old women.) And yet why? What has happened that, for someone like me, well off, middle class, and in possession of my faculties, to undertake such tasks without any necessity for it means that I am wrong-headed? Sometimes I look at the thing one way, and sometimes another: first, that I am mad, and then, that the society we live in is. But I do take on this responsibility, and I am a friend of Eliza's and of Annie's, and I am a friend (more than that, I think) of Maudie's only because it was something I decided to do. I did it. Therefore it works. If you undertake to do something, then it is not absurd, at least to you.

To Joyce I say, "What is the difference between your 'counselling', whatever that may mean, and my being a friend to people who need it?" I say this because I want her to say, "The difference is, I am paid for it!"

But once said, it is exposed as ridiculous.

"Are you saying, Joyce, that none of us should ever do anything we aren't paid for?"

"Well, all right, Janna, if you want to be *logical*, but all I know is, there's something neurotic about your doing it."

"I wouldn't argue about that."

So we wrangle, across all that water, but nearly always it sounds as if we are in houses half a mile away, so clear are our voices to each other.

For me to take Maudie into my flat for the weeks or months or even years before she dies, would be absurd, because I couldn't do it.

And yesterday she leaned forward and announced, as if regretfully, "You are a fair-weather friend."

I had to accept this.

And this afternoon she said, "Why can't I go home, why can't I?"

"You know you can't, Maudie! You can't look after yourself any longer."

"But I look after myself perfectly well, I always have," she says, amazed.

Maudie ought to be, she knows, in her sister's house, where she has given so much time, amounting to years, of her love and service to the family; she should be in bed there, and her relatives should be around her, with hot broth and hot milk, handing her medicines.

Something from *War and Peace* teases my memory, it is about the old Countess, who is in her second childhood. She needed to be allowed to cry a little, laugh a little, sleep a little, quarrel a little ... In that household, many servants and hangers-on and dependants and family; and an old woman, sitting in a corner in a chair, or propped in bed, would be assimilated.

I cannot think of any household I know where Maudie could be accommodated now, we all work too hard, have too much responsibility as it is; our lives are all pared down to what we can fit in, we can all just cope and no more.

What I think when I sit there, holding Maudie's hand, that she ought to be in a large loving family like a rubber net that could stretch a little here and there to fit her in, is of course nonsense. I am saying, as well, that she should have been an intelligently loved child of sensible parents, and that her mother should not have died when she was fifteen, and that she ought, *by right*, to have been happy healthy wealthy and wise her whole long life through. When I say what she, what an old woman, *ought* to have by *right* as she dies, forbids hardship, suffering, injustice, pain—denies, in short, the human condition.

Take me home with you, Janna, take me home with you.

I can't, Maudie, you can see that for yourself! And I have to run off home now, it's getting late and the night staff have just come on. I'll see you tomorrow, Maudie.

Today I went to the wedding. As always, relatives one had never heard of: one sees people known (in Phyllis's case), for years, in their matrix of work. Phyllis's family like mine. But—surprise! Charles turns out to be an exotic with wildly elegant mother from Paris and two fathers, real and step, both worldly, witty and charming. Phyllis looking marvellous, a credit to us and the mag. I enjoyed it.

Two weeks.

Maudie's pain is getting bad now. She has carefully adjusted doses of pain-killer, three times a day, but they watch her, with those skilled, careful, smiling eyes, question her gently, and according to what they see, what she says, gradually increase the dose.

At six in the evening, when I come in, the medicine glass is sitting on the table by her. They know that for her to take the stuff is a defeat, the worst—*the end*. So therefore they do not force her, or jolly her into taking it. "In your own good time," they say. "Take it when you need it."

Maudie sits there, and I feel her bony grasp tightening. She swings her head to look at her enemy, the glass with its contents. Then she makes her eyes turn away again. In a moment, her gaze returns to it. I can hear her gasping, as the pain burns in her stomach.

I have learned not to say, too soon, "Would you like the medicine, Maudie?" When I do, she nods, in a quick abstracted way, as if thinking of something else much more important; and I hold the glass to her lips, which reach forward in her eagerness, as if they were creatures independent of her, and curl around the glass's lip so as to suck the deadening stuff into her.

"They are taking my mind away from me, they are deadening my thoughts," she has whispered to me, reproachful, sorrowful, angry. At least she did not say, "*You* are . . ."

The last two nights, a night nurse has sauntered in, smiling around the room, checking her kingdom, one, two, three, four; has gone to one bed after another, eyes casually, but so efficiently, at work on each sick old face—they are all old women in this room—and then, having stood for a while by Maudie, "And how are you tonight, Mrs Fowler? Good evening, Mrs Somers"—has said to Maudie, "If you feel you'd like a little something to make you sleep, you have only to ring."

This means, "If the pain gets too bad . . ."

And both nights, before I have left, Maudie has grabbed at my skirt as I stood up, and whispered, "Tell them, tell them, don't forget—I'll take a bit of hot milk or something."

I go to the duty desk and translate this, "I think Mrs Fowler will be needing a bit more pain-killer."

"Don't worry about her, we'll be along to her in a moment."

And indeed they are.

And I can positively hear Maudie's thought, as I hurry away to get home, to reach my bath, which is *my* medicine and my oblivion: if I had had some of this offered me when I needed it, when I had nothing to give my Johnnie, and so he was stolen from me . . .

A month.

Oh, it goes on, and on, and on, and on . . . I am so *tired*. I am so absolutely *done*. I say to myself, What are you feeling tired for? This is nothing to how it was when you were in to Maudie sometimes twice a day, shopping and cleaning and doing her washing, and washing her. This is a picnic, going in to that lovely new clean ward, gentle smiling nurses, and Maudie looked after, and all you have to do is to sit there and hold her hand. And, of course, trying not to react when she blazes her eyes at you and says, "Why, why, *why*?" or "It is a tragedy, that's what it is!", for she is likely to say these things still. The truth is, it wears me out and there seems no end to it. I know the nurses expected her to be worse than she is by now: you can pick up what they are thinking, usually because they want you to! There has never been any place like a hospital for the unsaid, the unspoken, people understanding everything on a look. I was called to the duty desk and told that Maudie would probably be transferred to the old hospital, for old people, up the road. This appalled me. Because it will appal Maudie. Because, quite simply, I want her to die. It is all *awful*. And yet I cannot allow myself to think like this. She does not want to die, and that's all there is to it! It seems to me legitimate to want someone dead if they want to be dead, but certainly not when they are not ready.

I have been looking for signs of the beginning of "the third stage". Maudie seems as angry as she ever was. Perhaps there are only two stages, It's not fair!, which is anger surely; and acceptance. Oh please, let Maudie accept, and let her accept soon! There is something terrible about seeing this ancient woman die in this way, as if something were being stolen from her. If she feels her life has been stolen from her—by her own mother's early death, by bully-boy Papa, by the feathered fancy-woman, by her nasty sister—fair enough, I suppose, but where does that end? The point is, what does she *still* feel was owed to her that was taken from her? What does she feel is owed to her *now* that is being taken away?

If only I could get her to talk to me. But we sit in that large clean light room, at the top of the big hospital, with sky and air all around us, the birds going past, the pigeons cooing outside, and there are three other people in that room, and the nurses in and out, and the visitors and the doctors . . .

The doctor who is on duty most of the time is nice, and she

likes him—I can see she does, though he could be pardoned for believing she hated him. But the big doctor comes around with his chorus once or twice a week, and Maudie is still angry, more than angry, incandescent with fury, when I arrive at night.

"*He* was here again today," says she, her little yellow face working, lips trembling.

"And how was it?" I ask, though of course I know.

"They stand in the doorway, *he* and all those boys and girls. Doctors, are they? They look like children to me. And they have black ones too." Maudie, who is scrupulous, when herself, always remembers to say, if she has criticized a black person, "They are human just like us," has lost this now, and knows only that they are different and alien. In a churn and a tumult of contradictions, she is; for two of the nurses are black, and she likes them very much. But still, they are black, and a focus for her angers. She likes, particularly, the way one of them lifts her up and settles her in a chair, without hurting; I can see the softness on her face, just for a moment, before it is swept away—but she *is* black, and reminds Maudie that she has not chosen to be here, in this hospital, with no decisions she can make on her own account.

"Well," I say, "there have to be black nurses and black doctors trained, and this is a teaching hospital."

"Why should I have to be the guinea pig? They never asked me. And they are so young, how can children like that know anything? And he came over, Lord Muck, and stood over me, and he was talking to them the whole time about me. Oh, they think I am stupid! And then when they were all standing around me . . ." she went on; and I could see the scene, tiny yellow Maudie against her white pillows, and the forest of tall young men and women, and—not among them, but opposite them—the big doctor . . . "After he had finished talking, he said, And how are we today, Mrs Fowler? And then he started talking to those children again, about me. Does he think I am an idiot?" (This is a gasping shriek, she is so furious and so distressed.) "He said to me, Please pull up your gown, Mrs Fowler. I wasn't going to, why should I? And the nurse stepped forward, all ready to oblige, and up came my nightie, in front of them all, everything on view. And then *he* began his prodding and his pushing, I could have been a bit of pastry on a board, and he said to *them*, See that swelling there? Feel it. And not a word to me. They felt my stomach, one after the other. Thank you, Mrs Fowler, he said, but he hadn't ever asked me my permission, had he? See that swelling, he said, feel it—as if I can't see it and feel it! I'm not a fool, I'm not stupid, I'm not an idiot—" And Maudie is beside herself with anger, with helplessness. "*He didn't look at me, not once.* I might just as well have been a stick or stone. He looked at *them*, they are what is important to him. I was just here for their convenience."

They are going to tell Maudie that she is being moved to the other hospital. And indeed she is not stupid, and—I dread it.

They have told her. When I went in tonight, she was sitting turned away from me, from everything. After I had been there half an hour, not a word said, she began muttering, "I am not going, I'm not going into the workhouse."

"What workhouse? What are you talking about, Maudie?"

She persisted, "I'm not ending up in the workhouse!"

I found out the hospital she is going to was once, a long time ago, the workhouse. I rang up Vera Rogers. She sounds tired, distrait. "And what did you ring me for?"

"I want to know what Maudie means when she goes on and on about being put away into the workhouse."

A sigh. "Oh God," says Vera, "not again. All these old dears say it, We won't be put away into the workhouse, they say. There haven't been workhouses—for, well, I don't know. But you see, when they were young, a workhouse was what they dreaded. The idea was, if you were sent there, no matter how old you were, you had to work. They scrubbed floors and washed linen and cooked. And don't quote me, but let me tell you, I don't see what was so terrible about it. Because what happens now? We shovel them off into Homes where they aren't allowed to lift a finger, and they die or go mad of boredom. If I had any say, I'd have them all working from dawn to dusk, keep their minds off themselves. Oh, don't take any notice of me, Janna, I'm letting off steam."

I ought to be visiting Annie Reeves and Eliza Bates, just

occasionally, but I have no energy over from Maudie.

Today I went with Maudie to "the workhouse". A pleasant indifferent girl called Rosemary came with us. Her function was, she said, so that Maudie could see a familiar face and not feel abandoned. But Maudie asked her, "Who are you?" And Rosemary said, "Oh, Mrs Fowler, you know me. I've been in to see you." "I don't know you," said Maudie. "But I've been in nearly every day, Mrs Fowler."

"Janna?" asked Maudie, in a small weeping voice, "Janna, are you there?"

"Yes, I'm here."

In the ambulance, the three of us, Rosemary holding Maudie's possessions, a carrier bag with a comb, a washcloth, soap and her handbag. In her handbag are her marriage lines, and a photograph of "her man", a sulking handsome hero of about forty, in jaunty clothes, and another of a small boy, tidily dressed, smiling unhappily at the cameraman.

At the entrance to the hospital, the wheelchair was lifted up the steps by the matey reassuring ambulance men, and Maudie was holding on tight, and did not realize, until she was inside, that here it was, the dreaded workhouse.

"Is this it? Is this it?" she whispered to me, as we went along the passages, that had on them an exhibition of art done by the inmates, staff and patients. And, on the landing, a poster of Beardsley's *Salome with the Head of St John the Baptist*, put there by some joker (I suppose). But Maudie's astonishment at this took us up to the first floor. "Is this it?" she was asking, clutching on tight to the chair, sliding this way and that, despite all the care of the men, for she is so light she could blow away.

"This is the Old Hospital," said Rosemary cheerfully.

"They've changed it, then," said Maudie.

"Have they?" said Rosemary. "I know it's been painted recently."

But Maudie was here round about the time of the First World War, to visit an aunt, and she could not make these memories match with what she saw.

The wards we got glimpses of are the traditional hospital wards, with twenty or so beds, and the great windows all along. But when we reached Maudie's room, she had a room with one bed in it.

There sat Maudie, upright in bed, full in the bright light from the window, which showed her yellow against the massed white pillows. Through the window, a church spire, a grey sky, the tops of trees. Maudie was silent, looking bitterly round the room—as far as I was concerned, a hospital room, that's all—and then out of the window.

"Then this is the Old Hospital," she confirmed, staring at me, at the nurse who had settled her in, at Rosemary, who was on the point of leaving, her arms cradling a heap of files.

"Yes, love, this is the Old Hospital."

And Maudie bared her teeth at us, in a hissing gasp, and said, "Then that's it, then, isn't it? I'm here, then? And that's the end, then?"

"Oh, Mrs Fowler," said Rosemary, benevolently, "don't be like that. Well, I'm off, see you when I drop in next time."

And off went Rosemary, back to the new hospital.

I stayed with Maudie all afternoon. I wanted to find out who among the staff was the one I needed to talk to, establish relations with. This hospital is different in atmosphere from the other, something relaxed, amiable, slack about it. Of course, the other is one of the world's great hospitals, and the nurses there are the cream, and the doctors too. Nearly all the old men and women in this place will not leave it till they die. It is not exactly a hospital; it is not a Home—it is a compromise. The big doctor from the other hospital comes over with his retinue to teach Geriatric Medicine. Some of the nurses are the ambitious ones from the other hospital, here for a few weeks to learn what they can learn only in a place like this, full of old men and women who will never leave here, and who have the kinds of lengthy lingering diseases appropriate to their condition.

I was thinking, how lucky for Maudie to be in a room by herself; but Maudie, I knew (and I know now rightly), was interpreting it as her death warrant. And the place was abominably noisy. As so often with us all, beaten into submission as we all are by the noise and clatter and din, it was not until I saw that Maudie was suffering from noise that I opened

my ears, which I had shut, to the swing and the bang of the
doors, the crash and clang of food containers from the little
kitchen just opposite Maudie's room, the grinding of the food
trolleys.

Noise! I said to Maudie, "Let's shut the door," but she said,
"No, no, no," breathlessly shaking her head. She is afraid of
being shut in.

They had given her no medicaments when she arrived; and
she was in pain. I went to find the sister, and asked if Maudie
could have something.

She is an elderly woman, with the look of an old inhabitant,
for this place is probably her home as much as her own home
is. She looked at me in the shrewd skilled way they use to assess
you, Sensible, Silly, to be Relied On, to be Told the Truth, to be
Shielded . . .

She said, "You do know that we try to give as little as we
possibly can, so that when we have to use strong doses they
will have some effect?"

"Yes, I know," I said. "But she's had that move, and she's
frightened, because this is the Old Hospital—and she's in
pain."

"Oh dear," said the sister, sighing. "You know she might
live for weeks, even months. And it's a question of the pain at
the end, you see?"

"Yes, I do see."

But Maudie got something "to tide her along", and it wasn't
enough to send her under, though it was to stun the pain, for
when I left she was awake, alert, listening to everything, and
grimly silent. Is this, then, the "stage" of acceptance? Oh God,
I do hope it is.

Do not go gentle into that good night! Indeed. What wet,
slobbery, self-pitying rubbish! What self-indulgence! And how
like *us*, spoiled brats, with our demands, and our "it isn't fair",
and our *I haven't been given enough.*

Jill and I were both early this evening. I came in from the
hospital so tired I didn't know where to put myself.

Jill saw how I felt, made me tea, a sandwich.

She sat down opposite me, waiting for me to recover. Underneath her good nature, her need to please, her new confidence—for, as I did, she is learning with every day how much she can do, that she is clever and flexible—was something sullen and critical. I knew what was coming.

"Why do you do it, Janna?" And this had behind it all the explosive protest of the young: No, no, I won't, I can't, keep it all far away from me. Above all: *If you, who are so close to me, are prepared to accept this frightful, appalling ugliness as part of your life, then what is to prevent it all coming into my life too?*

"I suppose it is all discussed in the office, on its merits," I said.

She looked embarrassed, because the niece of Janna, living in Janna's flat, cannot resist: Janna says, Janna does, Janna is—this and that.

"Well, I suppose so."

"Typical upper-class behaviour," I said, "the tradition of visiting the poor, useless benevolence, but the revolution will do away with all that nonsense."

She was red and angry. Jill has become a revolutionary. When I teased her about it, she said angrily, "Well, what do you expect? You never have anyone here, there's no social life, what do you expect?"

"I expect," I said, "that, just like all the other revolutionaries, you make a social life for yourself—and call it something else." She did laugh, after a bit. But today she was too threatened to laugh.

"Never mind," I said. "She'll die soon. It will soon be over."

"I think it is ridiculous, ridiculous," she said, furious, aggressive. "Hours and hours, every day. Who *is* she, who *is* Maudie?—I mean, of course, she's just a substitute for Granny, you weren't nice to her, so you are making it up with Maudie Fowler."

"What subtlety, what insight, what penetration!"

"Well, Janna, it's obvious, isn't it?"

"And if so, what of it?"

"Well, it's so peculiar of you, you must see it."

"Listen to me, my dear, when you came to live here, I made

no promises about adjusting my life according to the prescriptions of my sister, you—or anyone else."

Silence. A proper full-blown sulky silence, adolescent pouting lips, imminent tears, lowering looks.

But it has been the first, and I give her full marks, seeing that in her mother's house this kind of thing is *de rigueur*. And this was our first quarrel, too.

"If you like," I said, "when Maudie's dead, we can have nice little dinner parties. I'm very good at them. You can ask your comrades, and we can talk about class warfare."

She *almost* laughed.

Maudie has been in the Old Hospital a week now. She is no less angry than she was, but she is more silent. Grim. She is holding on. She has so little energy, because of the pain, which is much worse. The sister, without words, showed me the glass she took in to her last night, with a gesture that said, You see? I did. It's the potion they use when the pain is really bad, though it is a killer, a mixture of morphine and alcohol.

Maudie sits straight up, staring, her lower lip pendulous, a drop of saliva gathering there and falling, gathering and falling, her eyes sullen. As soon as I arrive, it starts: "Lift me up, lift me up." I stand by her, lifting her so she is sitting straight up. But no sooner have I done it and I have sat down, she whispers, "Lift me up, lift me."

I lift her, sit down. Lift her, sit down. Then I stand by her, lifting her so that she is leaning forward, unable to stop herself.

"Maudie, you are already sitting straight up!" I protest.

But: *"Lift me up, lift me up!"*

I do it because at least she feels she is able to exert some influence on this world she is now in, where things are done to her, and she cannot combat them; and because I can hold her and touch her. Though she never says, Hold me, I want to be held: she says, Lift me up, lift me up.

The last two days I've stood by her, lifting and settling her, lifting and holding her, an hour at a time. I've said, "Maudie, I'm tired and I've got to rest." She acknowledges this with a little jerk of her head, but in a moment it begins, "Lift me up, lift me up."

I think perhaps this is a way of keeping herself awake, because the potions are now so very strong.

She is drowsy for a good part of the time. They say she is asleep most of the night. But she is conscious, knows what goes on, suffers, badly, from the clang, the clash, the loud feet on the uncarpeted corridor, the grinding wheels of the food carts. Crash, go the doors, every few minutes. I find myself sitting there, nerves alert, waiting for it.

Yet still the door must be open, for Maudie fears the silence and indifference of the grave, where she will be shut in.

Maudie is not ready to die.

I do not now have long periods of sitting by her *thinking*, for I am too busy lifting her up, settling her pillows, cosseting her, but here at home, in the bath, I think. What about these euthanasia societies? I do not believe my mother, or Freddie, wanted to go before they had to; they were resigned, they were *grown up*, but I am sure I would have known if they had been longing for one of us to slip them a deadly draught. (Would I, though? I must ask Sister Georgie, when I see her next. If I ever do.) *Why* is it so hard to die? Is it legitimate to wonder that? Useful? Oh, it is hard, hard, hard to die, the body doesn't want to let go. There's a struggle going on, it's a battlefield.

But suppose Maudie's will and mind wanted her to go, would that mean her body would fight less? If it *is* her body that is fighting.

Maudie is sitting there, willing not to die. I simply do not understand it; and that's all there is to it!

Contrasting myself with Maudie, I know that sometimes it is not possible to put oneself into the place of another. Though I know that what I am doing is to contrast my present state of mind, that of the woman of fifty who is physically not near death, with that of a woman of over ninety who is near death. One's frame of mind changes as death comes near? For of course there is some absolute barrier, or wall, between my mind and knowing I shall die. I mean, I know I shall die, but not as a vivid violent fact. Perhaps we are programmed, as animals, not to know it; because knowing it would prevent us from living. For whatever else Nature is interested in, she wants us to live, breed, populate the earth, perpetuate—anything beyond that, Nature can't care about. And therefore do I, Janna, or Jane Somers, sit by a dying woman, fighting to make my mind change gear, lose a layer or become more raw and exposed, so as *really* to know that I shall die. But Nature won't let me.

I imagine, deliberately, all kinds of panic, of dread: I make myself visualize me, Janna, sitting up on high pillows, very old, being destroyed from within. I reduce my outer boundaries back, back, first from my carapace of clothes, how I present myself; and then to my healthy body, which does not—yet—suddenly let loose dirt and urine against my will, but is still comely and fresh; and back inside, to me, the knowledge of I, and imagine how it is a carcass I am sitting in, that's all, a slovenly mess of meat and bones. But it is no good. I do not fear death. I do not.

And, paradoxically, watching Maudie die, I fear it even less. For those who are concerned with dying, these professionals, have a brisk intelligence about it all that is exactly what I would like for myself. And even an honesty, for I know now that if Maudie is not told "the truth"—as if she didn't know it already—she would be told it, for the asking, by the nurses. And if they didn't say in so many words, Maudie Fowler, you are dying, they would allow her to know it. Which now, because of her attitude, they are not doing: no, they understand that she is "not ready to know"—the sister's phrase, to me. And so the atmosphere in her room continues friendly, casual, almost indifferent, as if she had no more than a cold or a broken leg.

And as for living afterwards: the fact is, I cannot make myself believe that this furious bundle of energy which is Maudie is going to disappear altogether. It is more than I can make myself believe. Good God, Maudie makes such a claim on one, well or sick; such a statement does she make about herself, about life, the nature of what she has experienced; so strongly does Maudie come over that I cannot believe she could dissolve like vapour when the air warms up. No.

I am so involved with the *now* of Maudie that what might

survive of her impresses itself on me not as a question at all, such as, what will she look like, will she be young or old, would "her man" recognize her, or her son as a baby or as a middle-aged man, all this is irrelevant.

"Lift me up, lift me up," says Maudie, and I pick up this little bag of bones and set it upright, and smooth back her wispy hair, and say, "Enough for a minute, Maudie, I must sit down."

For, a little bag of weightlessness she might be, but with enough repetitions, my back starts complaining. My back is very vocal, in short, and I find myself apostrophizing it, Just hold on there, wait a little, you've got to hold out, you can't give in yet.

For the first time, I find being in the office a strain, I am too tired to do more than go through the motions, and Phyllis covers up for me, and Jill too as much as she knows how.

When I come home with Jill from work, I let her drive, climb the stairs like a zombie, fall into my big chair and sit there, absolutely done, hardly moving, getting up energy to drive to the hospital. Jill says, "Don't go, Janna, don't, you'll be ill."

"Of course I have to go."

Coming back at ten, or later, I fall into a bath for an hour or so, or lie on the floor in the living room with a cushion under my head. Jill brings me tea, soup. Like Eliza Bates, I have more than once not bothered to go to bed, but have sat through the night contemplating Maudie's drama as if it is being played out somewhere inside me, on my stage, while life goes on, noises off, elsewhere. Jill has come in, two, three in the morning, and I've said, "Never mind, leave me." But if she had not been here, I would not have seen anything untoward in all this. Of course I'm likely to be "upset", as Jill puts it, and it's only a question of living it out. It is Jill who is upset, she is frightened when I don't go to bed, or fall asleep on the floor. But she is being sweet, considerate; her mother's daughter.

This has not stopped her, more than once, from saying, "Living with you, Janna, I'm going to become a real chip off the old block." Meaning me. This with hard, amused looks, and an expression of well, if so, it's because I have to look after myself!

"You mean, I'm such a hard taskmaster?"

"Not that, exactly, but I have to give as good as I get, don't I?"

"I didn't realize I was as bad as that."

"I don't mind really. I told Mother it's good for me. Bracing."

"Like cold baths."

There's also the problem of Mrs Penny.

"Why do you hate her so much?" asks Jill, quite amazed, so I have to ask myself why I do. "She's quite nice really, she's quite interesting, she has all those stories about India, and she's so lonely, she's such a poor old thing."

"I've been doing great damage to my character by being unkind to Mrs Penny, for she's one that if you give an inch to, she'll take a mile."

"You go and visit those other old women, you put up with them. When Mrs Fowler's dead, are you going to visit the other two?"

"I can't drop them just like that, can I?"

"You really are very stubborn, Janna, you must see that."

What I must see, have seen in fact, is that having admitted Jill into my life, so that my gates are down, the defences breached, my territory invaded, no place I can call my own, Mrs Penny is irrelevant. I find Jill and Mrs Penny enjoying a nice cup of tea in the kitchen, and I nod with a calculatedly stern absent-mindedness, a busy woman with important things on my mind, and retreat to my bedroom, the door firmly shut.

From where, very soon, I go up to sit with poor Maudie. I am thinking of her, at home, when "resting" as Jill recommends, so I might just as well be with her, which I am all the time in thought. And the nurses and the doctors are used to me, I go in at all times, without their minding.

I have been seeing something of the life of the big ward. Maudie has been going off to sleep after her midday potion, and I was sitting there for an hour or more, waiting for her to wake up.

The ward sister came to stand at the bottom of Maudie's bed and began chatting in that apparently vague way in which so much information is given in hospitals. And directives, too. She said that some of her patients never got a visitor at all. "They might just as well not be in the land of the living as far as their relatives are concerned."

So, keeping an eye on Maudie to make sure I am there when she comes fully awake, I go into the ward and talk to whoever seems to welcome it.

Once I was so afraid of old age, of death, that I refused to let myself see old people in the streets—they did not exist for me. Now, I sit for hours in that ward and watch and marvel and wonder and admire.

The nurses . . . what patience, what good sense, what good humour! How do they do it? For there are eighteen or so old people here who are difficult in one way or another, incontinent, or lame, or witless, or ill, or—like Maudie—dying. Here they are, these aged creatures, together in this intimacy, in a ward with beds all along both sides, and what they have in common is their need, their weakness. And that is all. For they were not friends before they came in. At the other end from Maudie's room is a ninety-six-year-old woman, a grinning clown who is totally deaf and quite mad, who does not know where she is. She is put to sit in her chair, and remains there, perhaps for an hour, two hours, and then up she jumps, and takes herself for a walk between the rows of beds. But at once she is lost, and everyone is watching her, perhaps smiling, perhaps irritable, for now she cannot find her way back. She will stop arbitrarily at this bed or that, and try to get into it, regardless that there is someone in it already. "Maggie," shouts the occupant, "can't you see I'm here?" "What are you doing in my bed?" shrieks old Maggie, and at once the call goes up, "Nurse, Nurse, it's Maggie!" And the nurses come running, laughing usually, and say, "Maggie, what are you doing?" and take the opportunity to lead her off to the lavatory, since once she's up they might as well . . .

In the bed next to Maggie is the "difficult" one.

Oh, you are so difficult, sigh the nurses, as she asserts herself yet again. She is a massive woman, with a strong face always on the watch for threats to her sense of what is due to her. She has bad legs, which are propped in front of her. She sits with her arms folded, watching. Or she reads. Romantic novels, usually, or sometimes sea stories, of which she is fond—*The Cruel Sea*, *Hornblower*.

She has been in for three months. Some of these people have been in for years. When she came in, she said, My name is Mrs Medway. I am not going to be called Flora. And I'm not going to be treated like a baby.

When a new nurse comes into the ward and calls her love, dear, darling, or Flora, she is told, "Don't baby me, I'm old enough to be your great-grandmother." "Oh," says the poor nurse, who has been trained, by watching the other nurses, to coax a difficult eater to "take another spoon for me", as one does for a child, or "eat up your pudding for me, lovie", "Oh, Mrs Medway, just as you like, but you call me Dorothy, I don't mind."

"*I* mind," says this formidable one, and while she listens to the nurses discussing their tasks, Maggie needs this or that, and Flora needs . . . "Mrs Medway," she corrects them, calmly and loudly.

"Oh, Mrs Medway love, why are you so difficult, darling?"

"I am not a darling."

"No, sometimes you aren't . . . Can we take you down to Physio now, please?"

"No."

"Why not?"

"I don't like it."

"But it's good for you."

"I don't want to be done good to."

"Oh, Mrs Medway, don't you want to get your legs right?"

"Don't be silly, Nurse, you know they won't get right for a few kicks and bends."

"No, but it will stop them getting any worse."

"Well, I keep them moving all the time up here."

And she does. Every half-hour or so she removes the light plastic boots she has on, I suppose to stop sores from pressure, and moves her legs and feet about, and rubs them with her hands. Then the loud flat voice: "Nurse, I want you to put my boots back on. And I want to be walked to the door and back."

In the bed opposite her is a woman of over ninety who was,

so the sister told me, "a lady". The sister is that person in this cast of people, all of whom seem to be admirable, who represents "the one" that Joyce and I used to talk about. It is she who sets the tone of the ward. She is middle-aged, rather tired, has thick legs that seem to ache, and a broad sensible pleasant face that gives confidence. She is always on the watch for the slightest sign of unkindness or impatience by her nurses. She does not mind that they are slapdash, casual, and—apparently—sometimes inefficient, forgetting to do this or that, recovering the situation with a laugh and an apology. On the contrary, I have understood she encourages this atmosphere. But when I saw one of the more brisk quick nurses using a sharp edge on her voice to old Maggie, Sister White called her over and said to her, "This place is her home. It's all the home she's got. She's entitled to be silly if she wants. Don't hurry her and harry her. I won't have it, Nurse!"

Sister White said to me that the woman who is a lady was a countrywoman in Essex. She used to breed dogs. She rode to hounds. And she had a large garden. How did she come to be here, in a London hospital? But Sister does not know, for Ellen has been here seven years now and does not like to talk about her past.

Ellen is completely deaf, and she has bad legs, so that when she goes to the lavatory it might take her ten or more minutes to get there, and as long back again. She has to be helped to sit. She has a thin sweet keen face, and her eyes are full of life. For she sits watching everything that goes on, misses nothing, smiles to herself when something charming or funny happens, sighs at the bad things . . . She will smile at me as I come in, and indicate with a gesture that she has been reading the magazines I take in for her: *Country Life, The Lady, Horse and Hound.* She cannot hold a conversation, because she is so deaf.

Sometimes I talk to Mrs Medway, who was not so long ago the proprietor of a newspaper and sweet shop in Willesden, and whose husband died last year. She has one daughter, in the West Country, who comes up sometimes to visit her. Mrs Medway does not have visitors much. Ellen never has visitors, she has been forgotten. Except, of course, for the ministers of various churches and for the young people who volunteer to visit the old and whose visits charm them. Mrs Medway, the terror of Tennyson Ward, entertains her visitors with reminiscences of her young self, at their age—back in World War One. When they go off, shaking their heads and laughing, exchanging glances because of the nearness—to her—of that impossibly distant world, she looks at me, and we, too, laugh because of time, and the tricks it plays. "Well," she might say, as she imperiously waves a hand towards the nurse, for she wants her glasses brought to her (they are to be reached by leaning over four inches, but she doesn't see why she should), "well, I tell you something. I could have danced any one of that lot into the ground, any night! A poor lot, compared to us, I'd say." And she picks up her novel, probably called *Passion at Twilight*.

What I am thinking about, as I sit in that ward, watching; as I sit with Maudie, watching; is a possible new novel; but this time not a romantic one.

I want to write about these ward maids, the Spanish or the Portuguese or Jamaican or Vietnamese girls who work for such long hours, and who earn so very little, and who keep families, bring up children, and send money home to relatives in Southeast Asia or some little village in the Algarve or the heart of Spain. These women are taken for granted. The porters are paid well in comparison; they go about the hospital with the confidence that goes with, I would say, not being tired. I know one thing, these women are tired. They are tired. They are so tired they dream of being allowed to get into bed and to stay there sleeping for weeks. They all have the same look, of a generalized anxiety, that I recognize; it comes from just keeping on top of things, from a fear of something happening, an illness, a broken bone, that may make them fall behind. How do I recognize this look? For I cannot remember seeing it before. I have read about it? No, I think it comes from Maudie: probably, when Maudie talked, dredging up from her past some tale that now I have forgotten, there was on her face, because it was in her mind, this look. These women are frightened. Because their poverty allows them no margin, and because they support others. In the wards it is they who slip purses out from handbags, help themselves to a pound here, a few pence there; nick a bit of jewellery, transfer an orange to a pocket. Nothing is safe from these needy fingers, and it is because of them that the great hospitals of London, the exemplars for hospitals all over the world, hospitals with names that inspire doctors and nurses in poor countries from North India to Southern Africa, are unable to protect their charges from the theft of everything that is thievable. I watch these women work, putting a hand briefly to the small of their back and letting out a sigh that is a half-groan; slipping off their shoes, while they stand for a stolen few moments behind a half-shut door to ease their feet; drawing in a couple of breaths of smoke from a half-smoked cigarette squeezed out and replaced in a pocket. They are kind, too, bringing cups of tea to such as me, or putting into the hands of some crazed old one a bright red flower which she may sit and stare at, seeing it perhaps as she has never done in her life, or popping into the mouth of another who never has visitors a chocolate which has been filched from the box of one who does have visitors. They observe everything, know everything that happens, are every-where—and, as far as I can see, no one notices them. They are taken for granted. And why aren't the bully boys and girls of the barricades, or our busybody unions, doing anything about them?

Well, that is what I would like to write, but a novel of this kind is hardly the same task as one about those gallant milliners or the sentimental lady.

Today, the big doctor and his neophytes.

I was sitting with Maudie, with a sound as of a herd of goats, clatter, click click, on the bare cement stairs. Voices, and above them, the firm loud voice of *him*.

Maudie's door is open. Outside the flock comes to a stand-still.

The big doctor, the expert on the aged, a world expert at that, so I am told, is holding forth.

This is the stomach cancer, they have their notes. They have seen the slides. It is typical in that . . . I do not understand the next few sentences. It is atypical in that . . . again, I lose the thread. And now if you ladies and gentlemen will kindly . . . The flock appears, all at once, crowding into the doorway. Maudie is sitting straight up, bent forward a little, her head hanging, awake, staring at the bedcover.

She looks uncomfortable. The nurse who is with the doctors sees Maudie through their eyes and comes forward to say, "Mrs Fowler, lie back dear, yes, lie back . . ." Yet she knows how Maudie says, Sit me up, sit me up, and how I do this, over and over again, and how Maudie sits exactly like she is now for minutes, for hours at a time.

We play the charade through: Maudie is laid back on her pillows, silent, and the mass of doctors watch.

Maudie has her eyes shut.

The big doctor is in two minds about whether to examine her, for the benefit of the student doctors, but decides not: let us hope humanity is making up his mind for him.

They all retreat a few steps, to outside the door.

The big doctor explains that Maudie is now in a coma and will slip away in her sleep.

This astounds me. It shocks the nurse, who lets out, involuntarily, an irritated sigh.

For Maudie is awake most of the time, fighting pain. She sleeps heavily for an hour or two after she has had the potion, and then fights herself awake again.

The big doctor is saying, to a respectful silence, that Mrs Fowler is a woman of great independence, self-respect, who has never wanted to be drugged at all, and in such cases, of course, it will be necessary for them to monitor very carefully—and etc., and so on—but luckily she is in a coma now, and she will die without coming to herself.

The nurse is angry. Her discipline makes it impossible for her to exchange a glance with me, but we vibrate with understanding. Because, of course, it is the nurses who monitor, the changes of need, of mood, of the patients, and the doctors appear from time to time, issuing commands. For that is the most striking thing that is to be seen while I sit there, observing, listening, the utter and absolute gap between doctors and nurses. It is the nurses who know what is happening, the nurses who adjust, temper, and very often simply ignore the doctor's instructions. How did this extraordinary system grow up, where those who issue the orders don't know what is really going on?

The noise of the doctors diminishes as they all disappear into the main wards.

The nurse gives me an apologetic smile, as Maudie whispers, "Lift me up, lift me up," and I get up to put her back as she was, where, for some reason, she is more comfortable.

"I'll just shut the door a minute," mutters the nurse, meaning, The doctors won't know you've sat her up.

She does so. Maudie: "Open the door, open it, open it."

"Wait a minute, Maudie, till they have gone."

In a few moments, they all come clattering and chattering back and off down the stairs.

I open the door again. The food trolleys are approaching, crash, bang.

"Mrs Fowler, soup? A sandwich? Jelly? Ice cream?"

I say for her, "Some soup, please, and jelly," though she doesn't eat anything at all these days.

I hold the soup to her lips, she shakes her head; I offer a spoon of jelly, "No, no," she whispers, "lift me up, lift me up."

I do so, on and on, through the evening.

And then, it is nine, the night staff are on. I wait to establish contact with the night nurses and tell them myself what sort of a day she has had—the same as yesterday and the day before—and the night nurses smile and bend over Maudie and say, "Hello, love, hello, dear, how are you?"

There are three brown night nurses and one white one, and Maudie feels herself surrounded by the alien.

"I'm off, Maudie, and I'll be in tomorrow."

"You're off already, are you? Good night then."

Milliners came out today. They reprinted twice before publication. I've been too busy with Maudie to enjoy it all as I would otherwise have done. It is going to be a wild success. My secret moments of terror that I was mad to jettison my lovely well-paid job were for nothing.

I read it very early this morning, a dark winter's morning,

dreary and cold, but the jacket of *The Milliners of Marylebone* bright and pretty. How I did enjoy making Maudie's relentless life something gallantly light-hearted, full of pleasant surprises. In my version Maudie has her child stolen from her, but knows where he is, visits him secretly, they support each other against her wicked lover, whom she loves, heigh-ho! But then a long mutually respectful relationship with an older man, a rich publican, who cherishes her, and helps her get back her son. She is the valued head assistant in the milliner's workrooms, and with the aid of this disinterested gentleman buys her own business, which flourishes, enjoying the patronage of the nobility, even minor royalty. Maudie would love her life, as reconstructed by me.

Maudie has been in the Old Hospital three weeks now. I see no difference in her except that she is steadily more restless. She asks to be put flat, and then, when down, asks to be put up. She begs incessantly, Lift me up, and when she is lolling forward, for she can't help but do that, hisses, Lay me back.

The nurses come in and out, watching, "monitoring". Maudie gets these terribly strong doses, Maudie is not really sane at all, but the one thing she is not is in a coma. Maudie is not resigned, not accepting, not anywhere near resignation or acceptance.

Maudie is still saying to me, or muttering rather, "Take me home with you—yes, take me with you when you go home."

Maudie knows and does not know that she has cancer of the stomach and is dying.

Rather, there is a Maudie who knows this, and another who does not.

I suspect that it is the Maudie who does not who will still be there when Maudie actually dies.

Oh God, if only Maudie would die, if only she would. But of course I *know* that is quite wrong. What I think now is, it is possible that what sets the pace of dying is not the body, not that great lump inside her stomach, getting bigger with every breath, but the need of the Maudie who is not dying to adjust—to what? Who can know what enormous processes are going on there, behind Maudie's hanging head, her sullen eyes? I think she will die when *those* processes are accomplished. And that is why I would never advocate euthanasia, or not at least without a thousand safeguards. The need of the watchers, the next of kin, the nearest and dearest, is that the poor sufferer should die as soon as possible, because the strain of it all is so awful. But is it possible that it is not nearly so bad for the dying as for those who watch? Maudie is in pain—intermittently, in between those ferocious doses she is getting—but is pain the worst thing in the world? It certainly never has been for me. It wasn't for Maudie when she was herself. Why is it, as soon as the dying move away beyond a certain point, that the decent, human criteria are no longer used, or are not so easily used, for them? Maudie would never in her life have judged what happened to her by the physical pain she felt. So why should we assume she is different now? She is still afraid of dying, I know, because of her need to keep open the door, that terrible door which admits so much noise (admits *life*)—the banging feet, the voices, the wheels, the clatter of crockery. But what she is really thinking is probably nothing to do with pain at all. The pain is something she has to cope with; it is there, she feels it come and go, lessen and become sharp, she has to shift her position—Lift me up, lift me up!—but we don't know the first thing about what is really happening.

Maudie died last night.

The last few days there has been a pretty little dark nurse, I mean a white girl with dark hair, dark eyes, not a black nurse. She is vague and good-natured and careless. She drifted in and out of Maudie's room, helped me lift Maudie, helped me lay her down, brought me cups of tea. I knew that Maudie was deemed worse, because I was offered tea several times yesterday. But I couldn't see much difference, except for her truly incredible restlessness. In that high smooth tailored hospital bed, that jet of energy, Maudie, wearing me out, tiring the little dark nurse too, who said, "Goodness, Mrs Somers, but you must be a strong one." Last night this happened. The nurse brought in Maudie's potion, which nearly filled the glass, there was so much of it. As it was not quite time for it, she put it down on the table, went out. She came back in a hurry about something, said, "Oh, I forgot Mrs Fowler's medicine," and, in picking it up, knocked it over. All the wicked liquid lying splashed about.

The old dramatic gestures are quite true, accurately observed: she gasped, her eyes widened in terror, her two hands flew to her mouth, and she stood biting her nails, staring at the spilt concoction. Then those eyes were on me, in the most abject appeal: Was I going to give her away? she was demanding.

I was astounded, not being able to see that nice, rather vague ward sister in the light of a tyrant, but I assured the poor girl silently that I would not.

She fetched cloths and pads and mopped it all up, and meanwhile Maudie was sitting silently there, head hanging, needing her potion.

It happened that last night I had to go off half an hour before I usually do, at nine or after. I had said I would take at home a telephone call from Rome about next week's shows.

So I said to the nurse, "You'll see that Mrs Fowler does get her medicine?" Though now I see quite well that she was likely not to report her crime, seeing the state she was in. But anyway, if Maudie has been bad in the night, I know she has been given extra pain-killers, the sister told me so.

But I wonder now if the nurse did not get the spilt dose replaced, and if perhaps Maudie was wanting something in the night and did not get it—whether, in short, she died of an excess of pain? I don't know, and I won't know.

I took the telephone call, worked for a while on files I had brought home from the office, had a bath, got very late to bed, and was woken about four by the telephone: Mrs Fowler has just died, would I like to come?

I was at the hospital in ten minutes.

At that hour, the place had a dimmed humming quality, a soft vitality to it, that was pleasing. I raced up the cold stone stairs and into the ward. Caught a glimpse of two minute brown girls, they are Vietnamese I think, wrestling an enormous mass of aged woman out of bed. They saw me. I saw their harassed faces: Oh God, one more thing to cope with. But their faces had all the harassment wiped off by the time they reached me and they were smiling nicely, and they said that Maudie had died about an hour before, they thought; but they had had a difficult night, with a sick old woman, and when they went in to check, Maudie was gone.

The last thing she had said was, "Wait a minute, wait a minute," as they left her, because they had to leave her, with so many others to deal with.

"Wait a minute," she had muttered, or cursed, or cried, as life went surging on, leaving her behind, but life had taken no notice and had gone on past her.

I would not be at all surprised if Maudie hadn't died of —well, yes, rage. Janna not there, but then she never was!— and the black nurses, look at them, in and out, no time for me . . . In this way, probably, Maudie had died. But I don't believe that that was what really went on behind her scenes.

One of the girls brought me a cup of tea. The ritual. There I sat beside dead Maudie, who looked exactly as if she were asleep, and who was warm and pleasant to the touch, and I held her dead hand, and in my other hand a cup of tea. The decencies must be preserved.

When a patient dies, the nearest and dearest should be offered a cup of tea. And quite right too.

In came the sister, another one, the night sister; or perhaps she was the matron. At any rate, she stood there, chatting away, restoring normality. It was necessary for me to say certain things, and I said them: such as that Maudie was a wonderful woman, and that she had a hard life, and she had faced all her troubles with such resource and courage.

And the matron stood there smiling and sympathetic, listening.

And then there was nothing more for me to do.

The trouble was, I could not feel that Maudie was dead at all, although this was the first time I'd seen her still for months; I was even worrying that she was not dead, not really. But her hand was stiffening and cold when I put it down. The moment I stood up and was collecting my things, in ran one of the little brown nurses, laid Maudie's hands together on her breast, and whisked the covers up over her face. She had the look of a housewife: That's done! And what's next? Yes, now I must . . .

As I drove along the front of the hospital, homewards, I saw the pretty nurse of yesterday evening. She looked like a soft ripe raspberry, in a reddish jumpsuit, with a vast pink scarf wound around her neck and shoulders. She was smiling, flushed, indolent, assuaged: every atom, every movement shouted that she had been making love all night, and that she was still in imagination back in the warm bed she had left with such reluctance a few minutes before. She had her uniform in the carrier bag in her hand, and she was swinging the bag around and back and forth, and she smiled . . . She was early for her shift, and planned to creep into the hospital, find a bathroom, and use it, hoping that the matron or sister would not see her. Though it was easy to imagine how this older woman, ready to reprimand, would find herself saying, "Well, never mind, but don't do it again"; and then, feeling the total, reckless, unfair claim, find herself examining the sleepy happy face, and understand her own capitulation. And she would think, well, she won't be with us for long . . .

The bath over, this lucky one would go from ward to ward, where everyone was frantically busy getting things done before the day shift began, but find a friend who'd say, "Of course, use our kettle, what's it like outside? Warm, is it?"

Coming on duty, the girl would yawn, think, well, the day will soon pass, and then . . . Oh, Mrs Fowler's dead, is she? Has she been prepared? She has, oh super! For she of course loathes the task of laying out the dead, and always tries to get out of it.

Going into Maudie's room, and seeing the white tidy bed hardly disturbed by the slim mound that is Maudie, she remembers, and again her hands fly towards her mouth in that ancient gesture, *Oh, what have I done?*—but thinks, well, if she did die a day or two earlier than she needed, what of it? Thinks that she will go and look at the chart and see if Maudie was given extra potion in the night, she would like to have the reassurance that it was not pain that killed the old woman, but she forgets.

I rang Vera as soon as the office was open. She burst into tears, surprising me and herself. "Oh God," said she, "I'm sorry, it's the last straw, it's too much—how silly, she was due to go, but . . . Are you all right? I hope so. Oh, I don't know why, there was something about her, what was it?" Vera chattered on; it was a nervous reaction. She wept again. She said again, "How silly . . . take no notice. You say you met the relatives? Will they pay for the funeral, do you think?"

"They can certainly afford it."

"I'll ring them . . . Oh dear, I do feel low. No, it's not just Maudie, I've such problems. No, I don't want you to ask. When I got this job, I said to myself, my job is going to be one thing and my home life another, and I'm not going to mix them. So far, I've done it. I got the job because if I hadn't I'd have gone mad. Though you could say, frying pan out of the fire, I do the same kind of thing at home as I do at work—and let's leave it like that, if you don't mind."

She rang up later to say that Maudie's sister had said that Maudie had paid for years to get herself buried decently, and she couldn't afford to put anything to it.

"God," said Vera, "doesn't it make you sick? Funny thing, I had a feeling she'd say just that. Right, it will have to be the Council, then. And now I have a favour to ask—will you do something about the cat? It's the one thing I can't bring myself to do, when these poor old things die, taking their cats to be put down."

Frightful rushings about and commotions in the office because of Phyllis getting to the spring shows in Rome—said I wouldn't go. Said I had "problems"; the problem being Maudie's death. Crazy, and I know it. Except that it makes sense, to me. Late snow, airports tricky—well, we got that over and she's off, and I went to Maudie's. Oh, the smell of the place, the dark nastiness! Without that blazing fire there, there was no life. I spent half an hour sweeping all the old food into carriers and dumping them into the bins. Including perfectly good tins and jars, unopened. But I was in the grip of a need to be done with it. And that is why, Vera says, when old people die, the second-hand dealers get windfalls: everyone feels the same, including the Council people who come in to sort and assess: Oh, let's be done with it, let's get it over. Maudie's bookcases, I think, would fetch a bit in an antique shop; she has some engravings that aren't too bad; there's a fine chest of drawers. But who will get the benefit of it, if I say to Vera, Make sure whoever it is who goes in gets the value of those good things? That sister of Maudie's that's who . . .

The cat. I went out the back and found the poor beast sitting outside the door, waiting, I suppose, for Maudie to come back. About fifteen years ago, this cat arrived on Maudie's back step, crying for help. She was pregnant. Maudie took her in, found homes for the kittens, had the cat operated on. Love and kisses ever since and now, suddenly, again, a homeless beast crouched on a back doorstep. I went to the woman who had been feeding her, hoping for a bit of luck. But she was angry and said, "If I'd known it was going to be so long! I didn't bargain for weeks of it . . . I've got a cat of my own . . ." Then, she softened and said, "I'd have her if I could, but . . ."

I got the cat into Maudie's cat basket and put the animal, crying, into my car and drove down to the RSPCA. Just in time before it closed.

Maudie's funeral today.

Maudie paid weekly for many years into a Funeral Benefit. In hard times she went without food to keep up the payments. When she had finished, there was fifteen pounds. Enough, then, to bury her properly. She wanted to lie near her mother, in Paddington, but those graves had been emptied and built over long ago. She did not know that cemetery has gone, nor that her fifteen pounds would hardly pay for the hire of a spade.

The funeral the Council lays on for those who die without means is adequate: I wouldn't mind it for myself, but then I don't care about all that.

I realized today that I switched off for my mother's funeral and for Freddie's: I was there, I suppose, but that's all. I was certainly *there* for Maudie's . . .

A nice spring day, pale blue sky, busy white clouds, some snowdrops and crocuses in the grass around the graves. An old cemetery full of birds.

The clan turned out, but not the great-grandchildren whom Maudie longed to know. And besides, these days *of course* children are not supposed to put up with anything as basic as death and funerals.

There were thirty-three people, all well off, well dressed and complacent.

I was *furious*, through the whole thing. And there was the matriarch, predictably blubbering away, being supported on either side by her elderly sons.

Afterwards, up came the son of a nephew and began to talk about Maudie. I could see us standing there, near the great mound of fresh-smelling yellow earth, me impeccably dressed for a funeral, dark grey suit, black gloves, my black hat (that Maudie adored so much, she said it was a wonder!), black shoes with heels about a foot high, black silk stockings. I had taken all the trouble I could, to signal to that lot that I valued Maudie. And there he was, a grey, paltry, diminished man, and I began to wonder *who* I was being so angry with. He was smiling, doing his best.

He offered, "Auntie Maudie had her sense of humour all right, oh she liked her little joke . . ."

And he told me a story I had heard often from Maudie. People she cleaned house for had a fruit and vegetable shop, and the woman said to her, "Would you like to taste this season's new strawberries?" And set in front of the expectant Maudie a single strawberry on a good plate, with the sugar bowl and the cream. Maudie ate the strawberry, and then said to the woman, "Perhaps you'd like to sample the cherries on the tree in my back garden?" Brought the woman a single luscious cherry in a large brown-paper bag, and gave her notice there and then.

By then several of them had crowded up. Some I had seen at the famous lunch, and others were new. They were curious about Maudie's fine friend.

I said, "There was another story she used to tell, it was this. She was out of work, because she had flu and had lost her cleaning job. She was walking home with no money at all in her purse and she was praying, God help me, God please help me . . . And she looked down and saw a half-crown on the pavement. And she said, Thank you, God. She went into the first shop and bought a currant bun, and ate it standing there, she was so hungry. Then she bought bread, butter, jam, and some milk. There was sixpence over. On her way home she went into the church and put the sixpence in the box, and said to God, You've helped me, and now I'll help You."

Around me faces that said they did not know whether to laugh or not? A joke? For Maudie was always such a joker! Very doubtful they looked, they glanced at each other, they wondered whether to offer more reminiscences. And I was thinking, what is the point? They had simply written Maudie off years ago. The sister (still weeping noisily as the earth thudded down), unable to come to terms with how she used Maudie, and then dismissed her, used her and dismissed her, had said she was *impossible*—for one reason or another; and therefore had the family been able to forget her. I stood there looking at the uneasy *stupid* faces, and decided not to bother.

And they had the last word, after all, for, as I reached my car, one of the elderly sons came after me and said in a kindly patronizing way, "And now I suppose you'll get yourself another little job, will you?"

And so that's that.

I got home raging, went around the flat slamming and banging and muttering to myself. Like Maudie.

When Jill came in from the office she stood looking at me for a while, then she deliberately came over, took me by the hand, and led me to my big chair.

As I stood by it, she reached to take my hat, and I pulled it off, and gave it to her.

"Lovely hat, Janna," she said.

She looked at my gloves and I peeled them off and handed them to her.

"Lovely gloves."

She gently sat me down in the chair, fetched a stool and lifted my legs on to it.

"Lovely shoes," said she.

"I'm so angry," I said, "I'm so angry I could die of it."

"So I can see."

"If I let myself stop being angry, I'm going to howl and scream."

"Jolly good idea, that."

"Meanwhile, I am angry."

"Provided you know *who* you are being angry with," said Niece Jill, and she went off to make me a nice cup of tea.

A NOTE ON THE TYPE

The text of this book was set in Sabon, a typeface created by
Jan Tschichold, the well-known German typographer.
Introduced in 1967, Sabon was loosely patterned on the
original designs of Claude Garamond (1510-1561).

Photoset in Great Britain by Rowland Phototypesetting Ltd.,
Bury St. Edmunds, Suffolk.
Printed and bound by The Haddon Craftsmen, Inc.,
Scranton, Pennsylvania.